A GIFT

FOR THE

MAGUS

By the same author:

A TABERNACLE FOR THE SUN
(first part of The Botticelli Trilogy)

PALLAS AND THE CENTAUR
(second part of The Botticelli Trilogy)

THE REBIRTH OF VENUS
(third part of The Botticelli Trilogy)

KNIGHTS OF THE GRAIL

CONSIDER ENGLAND

CHRISTIANITY – 2000 YEARS

ICONS – A SACRED ART

ANGELS

A GIFT
FOR THE
MAGUS

the story of Filippo Lippi and Cosimo de' Medici

LINDA PROUD

GODSTOW PRESS

First published 2012 by
Godstow Press
60 Godstow Road, Oxford OX2 8NY
www.godstowpress.co.uk

978-1-907651-03-8

Typeset in Aldine by Jean Desebrock
Cover design by David Smith

Printed and bound in Great Britain by
Hobbs the Printers, Totton, Hants.

In memory of my mother, Sybil Grace Proud, 1915-2009, whose life showed that goodness does not depend on abiding by the rules.

To be a good painter you must be a good man.

Leon Battista Alberti

God is willing to bear the brunt of sins and often winks at them, mostly sending them to those whom he has destined for great things... And still today one seldom finds that people come to great things unless they first go somewhat astray.

Meister Eckhart

Note

There is a more extensive set of notes at the end of the book but it's worth mentioning three things in advance. English readers would expect monks to live in monasteries, friars in friaries and nuns in either convents or nunneries. In Italian, however, there are no words for 'friary' or 'nunnery'. 'Monastero' refers to male enclosures, 'convento' to either male or female enclosures. Although the Carmine would be called 'a convent', to avoid confusion I've chosen to demark male and female enclosures with the words 'monastery' and 'convent' respectively.

The character of Fra Giovanni is known to us today as Fra Angelico. Vasari, writing about him in *The Lives of the Artists* a century after the painter's death, referred to him as 'Fra Giovanni Angelico' (Brother John, the angelic one), denoting his saintly nature. In his lifetime, and since, Giovanni was called 'il Beato' (the blessed one), referring to his skills as a religious painter. The title was made official by Pope John Paul II in 1982 when Giovanni was formally beatified, the third of four steps to sainthood. His official name today is 'Blessed Giovanni of Fiesole, nicknamed Angelico'.

When it came to saints' names, it was difficult to decide whether to use the Italian or the English forms. Finally I decided to use English when referring to the saint and Italian when referring to something named after a saint, such as a church. So, for instance, in the church of *Santo Stefano* the life of *Saint Stephen* has been painted on the walls. As the masters of the Early Renaissance demonstrated, to appear natural one often has to employ the artificial.

Contents

Padua 1434   1

Two Years Later   25

Prato 1455–56   95

Florence 1457   269

The Adoration 1458   323

The Chapel of the Magi 1459   375

A Portrait of the Virgin 1461–67   431

Hereafter   461

Author's Notes   467

Padua
1434

THE FRIAR ARRIVED EARLY IN THE CRYPT. ABOVE, IN THE church, Mass was in progress and the notes of the Kyrie chant rose and dipped like birdsong in a place elsewhere, hidden and beyond view. *Lord have mercy.* Here in the stone crypt, lit by a few stinking tallow candles that marked the vaulted ceiling with rings of soot, it was damp and chilly. Fra Filippo sniffed and huddled deeply within his black Carmelite habit and white mantle.

The habit was paint-spattered and long overdue a laundering. He had been told many times that, having left the monastery to become a painter, he should not wear the habit, and certainly he should not wear it as a work apron, but one of the joys of living outside the Carmine was that he did not have to do what he was told. Not that he ever had. He liked wearing the habit. It gave a useful impression of holiness, even when it was caked with dribbles of raw egg.

As his eyes grew accustomed to the dark, he explored more deeply into the crypt. The group had several meeting places in churches of the city, but it was his first time in Santa Sofia. Old. Old beyond time. Certainly beyond the last century that, with its plague, war and famine, had reduced all cities to a third of their size so that they sat shrunken within their ancient walls like dried kernels in their shells.

Some said it was time for renewal and that the way to regenerate was to return to the past, not the harsh, recent past, but the long-ago golden age of ancient Greece and Rome. The crypt followed the shape of the circular apse above and was supported by squat, sturdy pillars capped with grotesque animal carvings. He wondered what people meant when they said 'ancient Rome'. Was this crypt ancient Roman? It looked old enough and good enough, but he thought it was not that old. This church's past

3

was the exotic one of converted pagans, of goths and franks and langobards: the invasions of the barbarians, bearded chieftains with names like Dagobert and Rothari and Pandulf Ironhead. He wondered who had ruled here in Padua at the time this holy church was built. The crypt and its many passages and chapels seemed haunted by the ghosts of long-haired and recently converted warriors speaking in strange tongues.

The walls, damp and peeling, were painted with the arms of the city of Padua and its great families, most of whom were no more, for the fortunes of Padua were more transient than most. Now it was ruled by Venice and people acted as if it would be so for ever more, but one reading of these walls would remind them how fickle fortune can be. The dagged sleeves, tourney helmets and eagle crests of dead families on lime-encrusted walls proved it.

Filippo liked the lettering of the names and mottoes and held his candle up to study it. Masaccio would have disapproved, of course, but he was dead and Filippo was free to enjoy what his betters considered to be barbaric and long out of fashion, these curious letter forms with their curlicues and adornments that hung off the capitals like earrings. These days they wanted Roman letters, smooth, round and rational, written letters based on forms made by the chisel.

Above in the church the deacon was intoning from the Gospel the story of the prodigal son. Filippo returned to the centre of the crypt and its altar which seemed very ancient indeed. And that stone chest over there. He went to examine it and found it carved most wonderfully with the figures of Roman gods. A sarcophagus, surely, which had once contained the corpse of someone impor-tant. Ah! Ancient Rome – he had found it! Was the church built on an old pagan temple? He studied the images carved on the sarcophagus and tried to learn from them. Masaccio used to say that we can find all the instruction we need in ancient Rome, but try as he might, Filippo could never discover in sculpture the lessons he needed in paint. He traced the muscled figures with his finger. Perhaps he would return on the morrow and make some studies. But of what use would the figure of Apollo be to the painting he was making of Saint Anthony of Padua?

'*Look not on our sins,*' intoned a distant voice, filtered by the tiled floor above Filippo's vaulted ceiling, '*but on the faith of your Church, and grant us the peace and unity of your kingdom where you live for ever and ever.*'

The chant of the Agnus Dei soared up into the rafters of Santa Sofia and rained down even into the crypt. Filippo looked upwards, his eyes moist, his face wistful, an expression that those who knew him called 'his orphan face'. It was the expression of one who always found himself outside, cut off from life by a door for which he had no key. He listened to the faithful making their way to the Eucharistic bread, to be blessed and made new.

At the rough-hewn altar in the crypt three benches had been put out. With not much time left now, he sat on one and, taking a ball of mastic from his draw-string purse, warmed it by rolling it between his palms. He stretched it and stuck it beneath the bench and into it he pressed three dice. Tonight he had to win by whatever means he had at his disposal or he would be sleeping on the banks of the Bacchiglione with the star-strewn sky for a blanket, at that time of the year when the nights were getting cold.

On the altar was a wood carving of the Madonna, old and worm-eaten but sweet in her modest demeanour. Someone had placed a small vase of cornflowers before it many months ago, the blooms now mere ghostly forms, grey and brittle with none of the colour. Cobweb flowers.

He heard the steps of men approaching and rose to make it seem that he had himself arrived only moments earlier.

The game had lasted a week so far with a pot getting ever-fatter. Each night they met in a different location and on this night their host was the deacon who had just presided over the Mass above. An elderly man, he had two broad front teeth separated by a gap that made him look as if he had the cloven foot of the devil

5

in his mouth; whenever he spoke or laughed he threw back his head and gave everyone a far greater view of his ugly teeth than was necessary. He welcomed the group of players to Santa Sofia, 'The first church built in Padua, on the site of an ancient Roman temple.'

The painter, Francesco Squarcione, was already on his knees before the sarcophagus, imprinting his memory with the figures of Apollo and those he immediately identified as the Muses. Squarcione, who was the first choice of painter in Padua, had far more confidence than either his skill or his original trade as a tailor should have allowed. 'I know this well, of course,' he was saying, 'but I have not studied it enough. I go to Verona, to Rome, all over Italy, to draw ruins and add to my collections of coins and statues, and I neglect what is at home. When I win this pot, I'm going to Greece.'

'Is there much of ancient Rome in Greece?' Filippo asked, making a show of inspecting the dice that the deacon had placed on the altar table, blowing on them and weighing them in his hands as if he had the sensitivity of a gold scale.

Squarcione looked at him as if unsure whether Lippi was joking or merely stupid. You never could tell with Florentines. 'If we are rediscovering the beauties of our ancient Roman past,' he said carefully, 'imagine how much there is to discover of ancient Greece, which inspired Rome. Inspired her, yes, in the imitation of nature and beauties of proportion. Greece! Oh, Mother Greece! Matrix of all the Arts!'

Two students of the university who had just arrived were imitating Squarcione behind his back, strutting with toes turned out, capturing the swagger of the painter whose opinion of himself outstripped his opinion of anyone else – although it had to be said that his opinion of others tended to be high. He was the first to admire those worthy of admiration – Filippo Lippi included – but he admired no one so much as he admired himself.

The sixth and last man of the group to arrive was the sacristan from the Scrovegni Chapel. Part of Filippo's aim in winning this game was to get this particular man in his debt, for he desired to gain admittance to the chapel when there was no one else there, to be alone for hours with the paintings of Giotto. Given his inability to afford the necessary backhander, he must encourage the sacristan to play on beyond his means and then offer to cover his debts.

'Come my friends,' said the deacon, 'let us recommence our game, here upon this sacrificial altar of the pagans.' So saying, he covered the statue of the Virgin with a bag, whether to protect her purity or hide their impurity, Filippo could not tell, but he was grateful for it.

'Those flowers need changing,' he said, sitting down on the bench where he had hidden his dice. 'Is this really a sacrificial altar?'

'It is indeed,' said the deacon. 'Those godless pagans would strap a living virgin to the table, plunge a knife in here,' he pointed to his breast, 'and slit her down to the navel to pull out the living heart.'

'That's not true!' Squarcione protested. 'The Romans did not practice human sacrifice!'

'What did they do to Jesus, then?'

One of the students had become bug-eyed and green-tinged but Filippo was rather enjoying the image of a writhing, naked virgin strapped to the slab. He liked that picture and had to wake himself out of it. Business was afoot, serious business. The pot had swelled to ten ducats and he meant to have every one of them, plus whatever was added this evening.

'Thanks be to God that we are Christians,' said the sacristan.

The deacon crossed himself and, taking up the dice and praying for all the help in heaven, blew on his fist and threw. The first to throw a six would start the game. It was Filippo. And it was luck. His special dice were still under the bench and yet to be deployed.

✢

'Cosimo de' Medici is back in Padua,' said the deacon an hour later when they had paused to relieve the tension in their shoulders and necks. The pot was now twelve and a half Venetian ducats, two hundred Florentine soldini and the promise of a ham from the sacristan of the Scrovegni chapel. The rule of playing with gold ducats only – which had kept the group small – was becoming strained. One of the students and the sacristan were now playing on promissory notes.

'He arrived yesterday,' said Squarcione, who knew everything about everybody. 'He's waiting for a message from Florence and this is as close as he can get without breaking the terms of his exile.'

'What message?' Filippo asked, locking his fingers and stretching his arms towards the ceiling. He stood to relieve his back.

'Florence is bankrupt. There is no other banking family who will lend the government so much as a pistachio nut. When the Medici were exiled, the money drained out of the city and followed them to Venice. They are to gold coin what lodestone is to iron. The latest news is that the Albizzi are losing their grip on power and Cosimo is expecting to be recalled.'

Filippo blew through his lips. 'Exiled for ten years and back in one?' He smiled. If he were a party man, which he wasn't, he would have supported the Medici. There was something wily and fox-like in Cosimo that appealed to him. 'Takes a rogue to recognize one,' he thought as, sitting down again, he delicately felt beneath the bench for the die he was about to play.

Apart from the rattle of dice in clenched fists and the occasional expletive, there was nothing to be heard from the players other than whispered curses when they lost. Filippo Lippi was down to his last half ducat when suddenly he won two Dogs. He already had a Coin; all he needed were five sixes for a Venus. The student who had confidently put the last of his ducats on the sacrificial altar began to sweat. The friar, wearing his orphan face, rolled the dice between his palms, blew on them for good luck and made the throw. The dice tumbled and rolled, one six after another. '*Jactus Veneris!*' he cried.

His opponents stared at the table like men who have been knifed but can't quite comprehend it. The deacon jumped to his feet in fury while the sacristan made the sign against the evil eye, for this friar's luck was unholy. 'Well!' said Squarcione, magnanimously, 'I must leave my trip to Greece for another year.'

Pink with pleasure and gloating merrily, Fra Filippo Lippi swept fifteen ducats, four hundred soldini and three promissory notes into his purse.

'What does a friar want with so much money?' growled the deacon.

'Whores,' said one of the students.

'I am a painter,' said Filippo, his eyes large and doleful with compassion for the losers. 'The expenses of life far outweigh my income and I am threatened with eviction by my landlord. I thought as I grew up in the Carmine that the free life was just that – free – but it's proving a costly business, as you all know. I shall not press you for your debts,' he said, looking at the sacristan. 'Pay me in your own good time.'

'Very generous of you,' said the sacristan sourly.

Filippo ran up the stone stair and out into the arcaded streets of Padua. The sun was setting and he made his way straight to his lodgings to beat the curfew but sheep being driven down from summer pastures filled the streets and obstructed his way. Passing a square near the castle he saw a great many Venetian soldiers loitering in groups. On enquiry, he learned that they were Cosimo de' Medici's armed escort. The clink of armour and clonk of sheep bells that had filled the air were suddenly drowned by the curfew bell.

Filippo hurried on and was on the very threshold of his lodgings when a hand clamped down on his shoulder. 'Hold, there!'

He froze. His pounding heart added to the din of the city.

'Turn!'

9

He turned to face four scarred, pock-marked, broken-toothed pike-bearers of the city guard with their short swords drawn.

'Take your hands off me! This is holy cloth! Is it past curfew? Very well but only just. And here I am, here at my lodgings!'

'Empty your purse!' The captain of the guard held out his hands. The friar, swaying with nausea at the loss, poured out fifteen gold ducats, four hundred soldini and three promissory notes, knowing he would never see them again.

'Where are the dice?'

'What dice?'

'The dice you were playing with.'

'They belonged to the deacon of Santa Sofia.'

'No, not those, *your* dice. The ones you palmed on the table. The ones you drilled and filled with lead. Where are they?'

The friar said he knew nothing about any loaded dice, except that he'd suspected that Squarcione had been using them. 'Terrible, isn't it? You would expect better from such a fine painter.'

'They're on your person somewhere. We'll strip you down in the gaol and find them. And then we'll leave you naked. Cold last night, wasn't it?'

Filippo gulped. He'd been so cold he'd had to rise from his bed to get a fur hide from the floor.

'Comes down from the mountains, that cold Alpine air, full of snow and ice. First sign of winter, my wife says, is when the air bites you.'

They marched him to the palace of the city captain hard by the castle. Once he was in the cell he was stripped and searched. They found the dice in a pocket he'd sewn into his Carmelite mantle and left him naked to face the night and its biting Alpine air.

'Oh, Madonna,' he prayed, down on his knees. 'Help me, help your poor son. A cheat, yes, but better that than a thief. What choice have I?' His prayer came to a chattering close as his teeth began to rattle in his head. His hands and feet had turned to marble, marble that was starting to burn in a fire without heat. He would rattle himself to pieces before the dawn and must surely die of chilblains. He howled in grief and self-pity, shook the bars of his cell door and called for any scrap of mercy his gaolers might offer. They offered none.

By dawn he had prayed to the Holy Trinity, the Virgin Mary, all the saints he could think of and was crying – sobbing – for his mother; a mother so long dead he had no face for her but pictured her looking like his aunt, who had taken him and his brother in before dumping them in the Carmine, saying they were more trouble than they were worth. His mother would never have dumped them in a monastery, even though she was a widow. Not at the age of seven. To take a child from its home and lock him up for no sin at all! To put a coarse, hairy habit on him and tell him to spend his days in endless prayer. What had he done to deserve it? 'Love God!' they told him. How? Why?

His boyhood and novitiate had been one long storm of resentment until that bright day when Masaccio had arrived, sweeping into the cloisters like a prince among painters with assistants and apprentices in his wake. Filippo had spent hours each day watching the walls being prepared for fresco, rolls of designs being fastened up, images transferred to the plaster. Then the ultimate magic, when colour and form began to emerge.

Ambition was seeded in his soul, then, though he was told it was hopeless. Painters required long apprenticeships; novice friars could not be apprenticed. It was not possible to teach yourself. And no, Masaccio would not let him help as a special favour. Then it got into his soul, the twin vices of envy and anger creeping through his bowels. He would show them, yes, he would show them that a painter is born, not made, that talent – his talent – was natural, that he was quite possibly a genius. He'd just been unlucky. This commission here in Padua had been his first of any importance and now he was freezing to death in a stone cell where if he were to survive the torture of the blains he must piss on his feet for warmth. No mother, no father, his brother still in the Carmine and he, all alone here in cruel, vindictive Padua where the blood of the longbeards was as cold as the air of the Alps. Who had accused him? At first he suspected the deacon, for he had been on the point of winning the pot, but he decided it was Squarcione who, obviously, was beginning to feel threatened by Filippo's skill. Painters were like that: back-stabbers and cup poisoners. You couldn't trust any of them.

✝

Cosimo de' Medici was dictating letters by candlelight to his secretary, waiting to receive a messenger who had ridden at speed from Florence. The main city gate was on alert to admit such a man but no one came.

'It's cold,' he said, noticing his secretary shiver. 'Move closer to the fire.'

'Can I fetch you a rug?'

'Please.'

The two men sat by the fire and dozed in the heat of its flames, all letter-writing abandoned. 'There will be a messenger soon,' said Cosimo.

'Yes, indeed, and we must be ready when he arrives.'

Cosimo awoke when the rising sun shone in through thick glass windows. Its beam of gold brought the colour back into the hangings of his guest chamber in the royal palace. The room was fine and beautifully furnished with his own tapestries hanging on the panelled walls, his own chairs and clothes chests. The Medici arms decorated the velvet hangings around the bed. But nothing could obscure the painful vacancy of the palace, as empty as a shell since the ruling Carrara family had been winkled out thirty years earlier. Now the Venetians were in charge of Padua, and the royal palace was but an administrative centre and a fine accommodation for important visitors. It was not his house and Padua was not his city. He had lived as an honoured guest in Venice for much of this past year and had nothing to complain of but now he was gasping for his own element, for Florence.

Since his ignominious exile he had awoken early each morning with such an aching sense of severance, of bereavement that he could never get back to sleep again. When he had looked out of Venetian windows, it was on to water. At least here in Padua he had streets and walls to look upon. But he craved the pine woods and forested mountains, the little hills with villas or castles on top, the blue skies and the circling eagles, those Tuscan hangings which were the backdrop to his city life. In Florence there wasn't a street which didn't have some prospect of the beautiful at the end of it. His own Via Larga contained a vision of Paradise at the end, the conical, terraced hill of Fiesole which had inspired Dante. He had only to be walking north along the Via Larga to feel soul and spirit yearn towards the divine.

For the past year he had arisen early, filled his days with work and befriended every Florentine he came across, as though he would rebuild his patria abroad, just as the Jews out of Israel had done. He had his furniture, his family, most of his fortune, but it was not enough. He needed Florence in the pit of him, and now he was going home. Exiled for ten years, returning in one: that thought alone brought a smile to his severe face.

A servant knocked and entered.

'Yes, what is it?' he snapped, jumping to his feet.

'There's a friar in Padua, a Carmelite from Florence. He was thrown into gaol last night. Fra Filippo Lippi is his name. We thought you should know.'

'Lippi, yes, I know of him. A friar as fit for his sacred vocation as a donkey. Well, it's common enough. What's he done?'

'He's accused of cheating at dice.'

'By whom?'

'By the deacon of Santa Sofia.'

'And how does the good deacon know about this, hmmm?' Cosimo let the question reverberate in the air a little like an harmonic note on the lute, then said, 'Who doesn't cheat at dice? Amongst the clergy, that is.'

His secretary and servant both laughed.

13

Cosimo peered at his secretary as if the man were selling wool bales at a cloth fair. 'How much?' The secretary held up four fingers. Cosimo held up two. The secretary held up three. Cosimo held up two again and gave him a steely look. The secretary counted two silver ducats into his own hand and left with the servant to get the friar freed from the gaol.

'Don't be long,' Cosimo said. 'The messenger will be here soon.'

✝

The sun rising at the high open window scraped across Filippo's consciousness like a file on rough metal. He was neither awake nor asleep but in some place between where his feet were burning in the fires of hell and devils were pulling his teeth out. But he must have been asleep since a foot jabbing his ribs and a hoarse voice now woke him.

'You're free.'

'What?'

'Free to go.'

'How can that be?'

Big hands hauled him to his feet. 'You are protected by your cloth, Brother.'

'What cloth?'

The gaoler spat on to the floor, to show what he thought of holy men. 'And by other things. Florentine, ain't yer? And who have we got in the city right now but Cosimo de' Medici, lodged like a king? We can't keep you however much you want to stay. Pity.'

'How does he know I'm in here?'

The gaoler shrugged and pushed the friar's habit and mantle at him. Coarse and hairy it might be, but Filippo put on his habit as a flayed man would put on his skin. Tears of relief and gratitude welled in his eyes as he fastened his sandals over his throbbing toes.

Outside the bitter cell a secretary with a servant in Medici livery were waiting for him. 'We've come to collect and escort you to Cosimo,' he said in that sweet dialect of Tuscany that suddenly

14

was like honey to Fra Filippo's ears: his mother tongue. 'I hope they haven't treated you too badly.'

'Robbed me of fifteen gold ducats!'

'But you're alive and have all your limbs and digits?'

'Not sure about the digits. Do my toes look black to you? How did Cosimo know I was here?'

The secretary went down on one knee. 'My master knows everything. At least, everything Florentine. Someone will have informed him. Your toes are fine – a little purple at the ends. Chilblains, that's all.'

When they came to the royal palace hard by the castle Filippo looked at stuccoed walls covered in the most intricate designs and patterning. Cosimo – king amongst bankers and still the richest man in Christendom despite his 'ruin' – was a great and honoured guest of the city.

'I'm filthy,' Filippo muttered to his companions as they entered through the high double gates into a courtyard made serene by potted palms. 'Look at me.'

'He will understand,' said the secretary. 'Cosimo is not interested in superficial appearances.'

'But what about superficial smells?'

The secretary laughed and ushered the friar up the marble stairs and straight into a chamber in which sat the most powerful man in Florence, even in his banishment.

Cosimo, tall, angular and intense was reading at a desk. He turned at the opening of the door, rose and came to meet the Carmelite. He was not smiling.

'You bring disgrace on your order, your mother house and your mother city,' he said without preamble.

Fra Filippo could not but agree. 'I'm ashamed,' he said, 'but it is so hard to make a living!'

'Friars do not make livings, they beg for alms. Why are you outside the Carmine? And outside, it seems, of all convention?'

'I was born a painter, not a friar. The wise prior of the Carmine saw and understood that my talent is the gift of God.

15

He relieved me of all duties and bade me go out into the world and spread the Word with my pictures.'

'Tell me the truth.'

Filippo screwed up his face and scratched his head. 'The prior found me difficult.'

'Recalcitrant is the word.'

'Is it?'

'A heel-kicker.'

'Oh, well, yes, that's true enough. I've been thrashing my heels since they took me in as an orphan. I try to be good, believe me, but the more manacled I become by duties and disciplines, the faster the vision fades.'

Cosimo bade him sit and take some refreshment. 'Vision?'

Filippo found it hard to say. It was more a feeling than a picture. Indeed, his work was largely a quest to find an image to portray that feeling. And what was the feeling? This was not something he discussed with any man, least of all a banker. He said nothing but eyed the refreshments greedily. Not having eaten for nearly a full day, his tongue was like cowhide; he took a glass of wine, poured it down his throat and wiped his hand across his mouth. Cosimo de' Medici grimaced as he handed him a plate of figs and cold meats.

'What are you working on in Padua?' he asked.

'I have a small commission for a tabernacle at il Santo,' said Filippo. 'It's to house a relic of Saint Anthony – nothing important, just a thumb or a rib or something, but still, it's an honour.'

'What have you done previously?'

'I did a good fresco at the Carmine of the history of the Order, but since then, since I've been outside, I've done nothing but Madonnas on panels. That's all anyone wants, Madonnas.'

Cosimo smiled. 'Are you speaking of Our Lady?'

'No disrespect meant! No, none, but it's repetitive work. How many possibilities have we? Madonna and Child, enthroned, not enthroned, Annunciation, Assumption. There's Pietà, but I won't do that, no, I've never painted a crucifixion or anything sad.

16

Haven't the stomach for it.' He took another slice of mortadella sausage, folded it in four and pushed it into his mouth. He chewed and sucked for a while then continued.

'I work from pattern books and when I have no commissions I work on stock that I sell to agents, that every humble dwelling should have its humble image. But to live, Cosimo, to have shelter and to eat, by my reckoning I have to do two small panels a day, and that's impossible.' Resentment oozed out of the pores of his skin. Bankers made fortunes while he, a holy man doing holy images, was close to starving and reduced to loading some dice. He realized that a more suave, professional painter such as Squarcione would now be buttering up Cosimo in hope of patronage but high among Filippo Lippi's paltry virtues was the inability to be sycophantic. His peers did not consider that a virtue, just stupidity; no doubt they would be richer, but he would have better chance of heaven.

Cosimo leaned forward in his chair. 'Do you ever make studies from life?'

'Of the Madonna?' Filippo laughed so suddenly that he sprayed the banker with flecks of ham. Cosimo could not help smiling even as he brushed the stuff off his sleeve.

'Do you use a model for her?'

'No, of course not! It's forbidden. No, I work from the archetypes of tradition.'

'Masaccio had no such concerns with tradition.'

'That's true but he still didn't use live models for the Trinity or the Madonna.'

On reflection, Cosimo decided that Filippo was right, that even the great Masaccio could be wooden when it came to the set pieces. His greatest virtuosity had been reserved for acts of the apostles. 'Hmmm,' he said, rising to his feet. 'Let us go and see what Giotto did.' He called to his secretary that, should a message from Florence arrive, he could be found at Scrovegni's Chapel.

✢

17

Filippo, much impressed by Cosimo, ran to keep up with his long strides as they made their way across the city to the Roman arena, discussing as they went the cyclical fate of painting over the centuries, forever declining and reviving. His words tripped over themselves like the sheep in the streets, crowding in their eagerness to get out. He told Cosimo that Florence had been in a period of decline since the death of Giotto a hundred years before.

'Masaccio,' said Cosimo.

'Yes, Masaccio! The new Giotto! But the course of his star was so brief, extinguished so early by death. Now, well, if you wish to work, it's best to leave Florence.'

'I don't agree. Many excellent things are happening there amongst the artisans, especially those who are seeking to be free of tradition and to find new forms in ancient works.'

'But they are not painters. Sculptors, architects, yes, but not painters.'

'That's what painters need to do, then, the same as the sculptors. You must forget the modern Greeks and their icons and return to natural forms as the ancients did. Copy from nature. That's the way. If our faith is true, it's not only true in some rarified place but true here, true now. Nature is the face of God. That's my belief.'

'It's a good thought! But we need enlightened patrons like yourself and they are not to be found in Florence. Do you know how many painters left the city in your wake? We were like crabs pulled out by the tide.'

Cosimo laughed. 'Well, the tide is turning, so you can all wash back in again. Do you know the story of how Giotto was discovered by Cimabue?'

'Of course.' Giotto had been a shepherd boy. One day he was amusing himself drawing a goat on the face of a rock when who should come along but the greatest painter of the day, Cimabue. Cimabue was so impressed by the boy's skill that he said, 'You must be a painter, not a shepherd!' and took him at once into his workshop. Filippo sighed. It was his favourite story.

18

'Ever thought about that story, about what it tells us?'

'It tells us that Giotto would have painted on rocks all his life if it hadn't been for Cimabue. Yes, it tells us that you are born with genius, not trained into it, but you still need that training. That's what the story tells us: good painters are born but still need to be made.'

Cosimo, smiling, shook his head. 'No. What it tells us is the importance of drawing from nature. Giotto was painting a goat from nature, not copying someone else's painting of a goat. That's what it tells us.'

Filippo looked up. The sky which had been pure ultramarine since dawn was now the colour of beaten pewter. He could feel the first drops of rain on his upturned face. They hurried on, impeded by bleating, clonking sheep at every turn.

✝

Since coming to Padua, Filippo had contrived several times to be alone in Scrovegni's Chapel but had only succeeded in being present during one of the many masses held there for the salvation of the old rogue's soul. The wall-eyed sacristan squinted at the friar who, the previous night, had been arrested for cheating and now was here with the great Cosimo de' Medici, who himself was pushing a silver grosso into the sacristan's palm and folding his fingers over it, saying, 'For the church, for the church.'

'Where are my ducats?' the sacristan hissed at Filippo.

'With the authorities. But I have your promissory note. You owe me!' Filippo hissed back.

The sacristan gave a mean and spiteful bow to the banker, ushered the Florentines into the chapel and closed the door behind them, saying that they would find a ladder in the sacristy should they need one.

The single-nave chapel was vaulted with a deep blue and star-pocked sky, belying the sky beyond which was now tipping rain heavily upon the roof. Blue. Blue. Not only in the vaulting, but in every scene that ran in three bands across the walls; each had

19

its blue-sky background. True to life? No. This blue was purely symbolic. No expense had been spared by that old usurer, Scrovegni. The chapel was a treasure box of ultramarine and gold leaf, with all the banker's illicit profits given back to God in paint. Filippo fetched the ladder and climbed to the top tier, there to gaze upon the work as only Giotto and his assistants would have seen it, face to face. The large figures, mostly in profile, were almond-eyed and static.

'Not from life this lot,' he called down. 'All idealised.' And yet, and yet... The stillness of the silent forms calmed his beating heart. They were alive and not alive. In such stillness were the stories of Joachim and Mary told at the top register. Parades of silent figures passing in and out of temples. Giotto had been ignorant of perspective, of course, but he had made valiant efforts to paint what he saw in the buildings of the streets of his time.

'Look up there at that donkey that Christ rides into Jerusalem,' said Cosimo. 'Drawn from life, wouldn't you say? That's what the boy grew up to do.'

With a somewhat critical air, as if he were here to judge Giotto, Filippo moved up and down the ladder, pausing to dwell on each scene in detail. But when he came to the Annunciation at the chancel arch, and when he looked at Gabriel, tears began to roll down his face, and once they had begun, they would not stop.

Why was he crying? He was crying because Giotto made him cry; that was Giotto's power. He cried for want of Giotto's talent, for want of Giotto's heart. Yes, that's what it came down to, Giotto's love of Christ. His devotion. This was what Fra Filippo lacked: outwardly, Giotto's talent; inwardly, his devotion.

Below, Cosimo was looking up with the very same emotion on his face. A banker he might be, thought Filippo, but this man has a good soul. Cosimo turned and walked down the nave then came back, looking now at one wall, now at another. 'What better way to spend one's fortune,' he said meditatively, half to himself. 'I'm on my way back to Florence, you know.'

'So I hear! Banished for ten years, back in one.'

20

'It took them that long to realize they can't live without me, or, more accurately, without my money. The city is bankrupt, you know. So I am on my way home. And when I get there I'm going to make things right with God by giving my fortune to a project such as this. Or some of it at least.'

Filippo itched to say that what Cosimo would need, then, was a good painter, but decided not to. This was the best conversation he'd had with anyone. Why spoil it by touting for business? It was enough to be here, now, pretending that Cosimo was his friend. For what finer friend can a man have than one who shares your knowledge and even, perhaps, your inexpressible vision?

Together they explored the chapel, studying every detail from floor to ceiling. Beneath the three registers of scenes was a parade of allegorical figures, the Virtues on the right and the Vices on the left. Filippo gazed at the grotesque figure of Envy disgorging a fat snake that twisted back on itself to bite her nose. 'The vices and virtues are matched in pairs,' Cosimo observed. Filippo looked to the other wall to learn what the opposite of Envy was. He found it was Charity. The truth of this burrowed into his soul. As his old spiritual confessor had once said, 'If you feel inclined to take, then start to give.'

Cosimo, who had cast off his mantle on entry, now picked it up and swept it round his shoulders. 'Stay as long as you like – I've bought the entire day – but I need to attend a meeting. When you're back in Florence, come and see me.' He looked Filippo straight in the eye to show he meant what he said.

'How can you value any man's work once you've seen this?' Filippo said hopelessly, suddenly feeling squashed by Giotto.

Cosimo stopped on his way to the door and said over his shoulder, one eyebrow cocked. 'Giotto is no longer accepting any commissions. Besides,' he pointed up to the Last Supper, 'he was good but he made mistakes.'

Cosimo left by the heavy wooden door. The rain was cascading in sheets as though the chapel were behind a waterfall. Cosimo had to raise his voice above its din. 'Come and see me when you're back in Florence,' he repeated. 'And don't be tempted to make copies of these. Go and draw from life.'

Alone suddenly, Filippo drew a shuddering breath, set the ladder to the wall and went up to look at the Last Supper. 'Mistakes, eh? Where? Oh!'

Now the Last Supper presented a difficulty in composition. People at supper usually sit all round the table, but if you compose your picture that way, you will have half the disciples with their backs to the viewer; worse, what to do with their halos? Many painters side-stepped the problem by having all the disciples and the Lord on one side of the table. It was an artificial arrangement that somehow looked natural: it worked. But Giotto, in his quest for realism, had placed his disciples all round the table, and those with their backs to the viewer faced into their own golden halos. Filippo agreed with Cosimo: it was a mistake. It looked ridiculous.

He came slowly down the ladder and looked around him. A great work by a great master, yes, but what Cosimo had shown him was that even great masters are flawed – and may be improved upon.

✝

Cosimo's servant, who had been waiting for him outside the chapel, offered to hold his mantle over his master's head. Cosimo declined. 'No message yet?'

'Alas, no.'

They set off for the university where Cosimo had a meeting. He walked upright and proud through the rain, as stoic as any philosopher of ancient Rome, wondering what he could give to the city in return for its generous hospitality. Should he found a hospital or fund a chair at the university? He closed his eyes momentarily to commune with God. He had so much he needed to give back in gratitude. 'Forgive me, Lord,' he prayed, 'if I give to learning. I know, the poor, yes the poor and the sick, I know – I will – But the University of Padua! Is this not the city that recognised the greatness of our Tuscan son, Petrarca? Forgive me, Lord, and grant me the time to make all good in my account with You.'

But the Lord frowned upon him and Cosimo changed direction. The Basilica of Saint Anthony of Padua, known affectionately as 'il Santo', was on the far side of the city; the sky had spent itself of rain by the time they got there. Cosimo stood sodden and dripping on the threshold of the basilica.

'Come in, come in,' said the verger, recognising a rich man even when he looked half-drowned.

Cosimo entered reluctantly. Churches, especially pilgrim churches, made him tense; made him, indeed, mean and selfish. Anthony of Padua had been a holy man, but now his sacred memory and the power of his relics were being used to exploit the gullible. Cursed with a penetrating vision into other men's hearts, Cosimo often found entering a church was like entering a den of vicious thieves. He knew that light in the verger's eyes. He saw it daily in the men who sought audience with him, a glittery light of self-interest that said, 'You are rich. Give to me.' He was becoming increasingly reclusive as a result. The only men he could trust and be relaxed with were scholars and artisans – skilled artisans who loved their work more than money.

Cosimo was concerned about Friar Lippi. The fellow was one of those hand-wringing poor-me types, full of stories of how the world had done him wrong, though it was always possible of course that the world had indeed done him wrong. The verger was circling like a dog.

'Where is Fra Filippo working?' Cosimo asked him sharply.

'Fra Filippo?'

'The Carmelite painter.'

'Oh, in the workshops in the back cloister. But he's not there at the moment.'

'I know. I just want to see his work.'

The verger walked off, beckoning Cosimo and his companion to follow.

'I won't pay you for this service,' Cosimo said.

The verger shrugged. 'There's no one meaner than a Florentine.'

They ducked through a side door into a cloister, around the arcaded walls and through into another cloister lined with store-rooms and workshops. They were directed into one that had several men working in it, one of whom when asked pointed to the corner where Fra Filippo worked. Cosimo stood and looked at the image of Saint Anthony that Filippo was painting in tempera on panel. He stooped close to look at the brushstrokes, he stood back to view the entire design. The pots and utensils on the table were surprisingly clean, all the brushes washed. The friar was more careful with his work than with his own person.

Cosimo went in close again. There was something here. He raised his face as if catching some subtle scent like a truffle.

'Yes,' he muttered.

'Yes?' said his servant, used to his master's connoisseurship.

'Yes, an Alba Madonna if I am not mistaken.'

The servant raised his eyebrows. White truffles were rare enough, but the Alba Madonna of Piedmont was the rarest of all and Cosimo valued it above exotic spices, pepper and cinnamon, nutmeg and mace. The truffle to Cosimo was the edible soul of Italy.

'An Alba Madonna...' he breathed.

The servant was growing agitated about being late for the meeting at the university. Cosimo allowed himself to be drawn away from the scent of genius. The brush with the verger and the sanctimonious stink of the basilica had made his mind up: he would be giving his money to learning. And that young friar-painter, well, he would find him work less pedestrian and closer to home. Florence was in need of good painters.

On their arrival at the university, they found Cosimo's secretary awaiting them in a fever of impatience, saying that a letter had come from Florence. He thrust it at Cosimo who broke the seal and read the formal invitation for his return.

Two Years Later

1

TURNING HIS SPLENDID WHITE HORSE, COSIMO LOOKED
down the long procession of King Melchior which had come to a
halt at the Baptistry. Holy banners snapped and filled like sails on
a ship. At the steps of the Duomo the boy who bore the six-
pointed star of Bethlehem struggled to hold the long pole upright
in the fierce wind. Men rushed to help him and get him back to
where he was supposed to be, at the head of the procession.

Cosimo held on to his hat of gold brocade. He longed to play
the part of the king, to lead this mighty procession in a trail of
crimson silk with a gilded crown on his head. Of course he
longed for that. Had he not been a boy once? But now he was
a man, a wily man who knew that the Florentines would not
appreciate seeing him riding about like a monarch, albeit a
festival monarch and one of the Magi. No, what they appreciated
him for was paying for all this splendour and glory, and they
appreciated him for playing a minor role himself. Just as he did
with the government of the city, Cosimo led from behind. But at
least he had some golden spurs. He stuck out his legs and admired
his yellow boots and golden spurs. His wife had put them out for
him herself this morning, all polished by her own faithful hand.
Silly dumpling.

Still, for all her bovine intelligence, she had accepted Carlo
as her son, and Cosimo loved her for that. He looked down
on the six-year-old, his processional page, who was holding
the bridle of Cosimo's splendid white stallion. With his dark
skin and shock of springy black hair, Carlo looked the child of
a Moor although his mother, Cosimo's slave girl, had been
Circassian. Cosimo dwelt on her for a moment with a pang
of grief that he had sold her on to save the family from further

27

disgrace. He wondered where she was now, and which master she served.

Carlo looked up at him with a grin. Dressed in a parti-coloured tabard, he was just a boy thrilled by pageantry.

Carlo's older half-brothers, Giovanni, aged fifteen, and Piero, aged twenty, were in the processions of Caspar and Balthasar respectively. Cosimo was blessed with his boys. They might not be proving to be the sons of a banker – he'd had to whip them into attending lessons in arithmetic and abacus – but in their love of art, poetry and music, they were the sons of his soul.

He looked up at the balconies adorned with flags and hangings and peopled by the great families, the Strozzi, the Albizzi, the Tornabuoni, familiar heads staring down at him benignly, all friends now. He nodded to those he wished to acknowledge.

A blare of trumpets set the procession off again from the Baptistry to San Marco, up the Via Larga, past his house – too small, that house, the family needed something bigger and more appropriate – where he saluted his womenfolk and servants standing at the top floor windows.

The star led the way. The cathedral square behind them, they had left the vortex of wind that had made everything so difficult and the star-bearer now walked with a proud and steady tread between the men in white who lined the Via Larga. With their tall, pointed hoods with eyeholes, and their mantles of white wool each emblazoned with a six-pointed star in golden thread, the Company of the Magi bore silent and solemn witness to the procession.

Wild men swayed past on stilts, tumblers tumbled, a cacophony of various strolling musicians clashed with one another, but the steady thump of drums set the pace for the procession, and King Melchior and his train went nobly up the Via Larga, thrilling the Florentines with the re-enactment of Epiphany.

Cosimo was now looking ahead with a level gaze, trained as he was in ceremonial dignity. He was home. It had been two years now, but he never failed to remind himself that the air he breathed was cool and pine-scented from the Apennines. At the end of the Via Larga was the city wall; beyond the wall the hills; beyond the hills, the mountains. He was home, and he was not going to take it for granted.

'Father! What's that man doing?' Carlo pointed ahead to a trundling cart drawn by decorated oxen. On the back of the cart David was slaying Goliath. Each time the giant fell, he rose to be slain again. An angel at a portable organ on the float played the tune of a psalm, to remind everyone that this boy David was also the psalmist and the King of Israel. With trumpets ahead and bagpipes behind, the organ's sweet notes were hard to hear but they had drawn from the crowd a man dressed as an Arab, wearing a turban and pointed slippers that turned up at the toes, skipping after the cart and trying to pinch a contadina's bottom.

Cosimo's eyes narrowed. The man was deeply tanned and dressed as a Moor, but it was undoubtedly Fra Filippo Lippi.

'He's abusing that maiden,' said Cosimo tartly. 'That's what he's doing. Go and tell him to stop, on my orders.'

But before Carlo had taken a step, Filippo had turned and his ever-ready smile froze on his face as he saw Cosimo staring at him.

He dropped his eyes and backed away from the cart and the exceptionally pretty contadina guiding the decorated oxen with a switch. He stood still, waiting for Cosimo to come up beside him.

'Where have you been?' Cosimo demanded from the saddle. 'I told you to come to me as soon as you returned to Florence!'

'I've been in Barbary.'

'*What?*'

'I was captured by pirates. At Ancona. On my way back to Florence.'

'Ancona does not lie between Padua and Florence.'

A strolling choir shouting rather than singing lauds in startling harmonies drowned their conversation for a while.

'*What?*' cried Cosimo.

'I said I went via the COAST.'

29

'Why?'

'I wanted to see the mosaics of Ravenna.'

'Do you never walk a straight path?'

The white stallion was becoming restless and Cosimo had to turn it twice to keep it still.

'I've only just got back!' Filippo shouted. 'Look at me – this is no costume for the pageant! This is the authentic garb of a slave!'

Although slaves rarely returned from Barbary, Cosimo had seen one or two, and it was true, this was the garb of a slave: a small turban, a simple djellaba, cheap slippers. 'Show me your throat.'

Filippo pulled the djellaba away so Cosimo could see the brown line that had been left by the bruising neck iron. He also showed him his wrists, still bearing the marks of manacles.

Cosimo shook his head and, in doing so, marked the transition from anger to compassion. 'You have a story to tell.'

'I do indeed!'

'Come to my house tomorrow evening,' he commanded. 'I'm having a symposium.'

Filippo looked blank.

'It's Greek for drinking together.' Cosimo smiled. 'Yes, I thought that would appeal to you. Come to my house – I've invited all the leading artificers of the city, and Leon Battista Alberti. Have you read his book on painting?'

'I told you, I've been in Barbary...'

'It is the most extraordinary book and needs to be discussed. For instance, at the beginning he lists five men of *virtù*, of surpassing excellence, but only one of them is a painter, and he dead many years ago.'

'Masaccio.'

'Yes, but the other four still live and have accepted the invitation: Brunelleschi, Donatello, Ghiberti and Luca della Robbia. All architects and sculptors, so I've invited a few painters, as well, to discover what we must do to revive painting. Tomorrow evening then, at sunset. Filippo?'

30

Cosimo had been softening in his manner and now Filippo felt as if he were being addressed by a friend. 'Yes?' he said, affectionately.

'If you're not there I'll have the city guard seek you out and flay you alive – skinned and salted – understood?'

'Oh!'

'But if you are there, well, I have some commissions.'

'Oh!'

Cosimo rejoined the procession, which Filippo followed up the Via Larga to San Marco.

The piazza San Marco had become a small town of tents huddled in front of the monastery. People pressed around the elevated stage, eager to see the rude stable and the Holy Family and to hold up their children to stroke the noses of the ox and ass. The stable had a thatched roof behind which, draped over poles, was a blue canopy appliquéd with stars. The boy at the head of the procession brought the Star of Bethlehem to rest just above the canopy. Within this 'sky', boys dressed in flowing chitons and bearing garlands of evergreens descended slowly and then rose again, rising and falling on invisible ropes.

'Filippo Brunelleschi made it!' whispered those who like to destroy magic with an explanation. Fra Filippo Lippi was annoyed with them for spoiling the illusion. Now he couldn't help but look for the ropes and pulleys. They were hard to find, though. Brunelleschi was a master of sacred theatre. He remembered the Ascension he had staged at the Carmine once, where Jesus rose so slowly to heaven that he seemed to take the entire day.

At each corner of the stage were shepherds dressed in skins and bearing crooks, with small children covered in sheepskins crawling on their hands and knees. A narrator was explaining to the crowd the story everyone already knew so well, but for Filippo it was a story he had been violently snatched from two years previously and, in those two years, had never thought to experience again, the story of his faith, his beloved faith. A man of thirty years, he stood with his mouth open like a boy as he watched this sacred representation of Epiphany and the Holy Family receiving a visit from wise men from afar.

Filippo, ever cynical, could barely comprehend the swelling fullness of his heart to be back in Florence and seeing this enactment of the Gospel. He gazed on the Virgin Mary and, though she was a local girl swathed in a blue mantle, kneeling over the baby's cradle, her hands pressed together in prayer, for him at that moment she was the Virgin and he pressed his own hands together, brought them to his lips and thanked her for his salvation.

'I will be good,' he promised her. 'From now on, I am a new man.' He became breathless, as if the reality of his life was losing its edge and definition while he looked upon the Virgin and saw her as a living, breathing woman, mother of a son, a real baby crying lustily. It was like waking from a dream feeling, for the briefest moment, that you possessed the secret of the universe. Tears of wonder pricked his eyes.

As the three processions arrived, each from a different quarter of the city, Filippo watched the kings dismount and approach the stable bearing elaborate urns and chalices. One by one they went up the steps to the stage and knelt before the cradle, bowing their heads low and proffering their gifts.

The narrator explained what they were doing, and what happened next – how the three kings laid down to sleep, and an angel whispered in their ears – how in a dream they were told not to return to Herod. When this little dumb show had finished, the three kings rose up, mounted their horses and departed for their lands in the East.

Filippo's interest turned to the monastery of San Marco, its new stone and scaffolding glowing in the sun. 'Tell me, friend,' he said to a man standing next to him. 'What is happening here?'

The man looked at him askance. 'Haven't you heard?'

'I've been away for two years.'

'Two years? Well, that's how long the Medici have been back. Had you heard that? Or,' and here the man stared pointedly at

Filippo's costume, 'have you been in Barbary?' He laughed at his joke. Filippo laughed with him.

'I'm in King Melchior's procession and, yes, I did know they'd been recalled.'

'Well, the first thing Cosimo did when he got back was to ask the pope what he should do to make amends with God. The pope instructed him to spend ten thousand gold florins on restoring San Marco. Ten thousand! Gold! So the first thing he did was to get rid of the Silvestrines, and good riddance, I say.'

The Silvestrines were a dissolute order much akin in some people's minds to the Carmelites.

'I agree! Lazy dogs. I'm surprised the place didn't fall down round their ears.'

'It nearly did.'

'So who is taking over?'

'The Dominicans of Fiesole. They will be moving in once the work is completed. The place has been gutted and completely renovated on the inside.'

'Freshly plastered walls everywhere, eh?' Filippo asked.

'What kind of question is that?'

'I'm an itinerant painter.'

'Oh, well, yes, that explains it. Yes, freshly plastered walls, ripe for fresco.'

Filippo licked his lips. He was looking forward to painting of any kind, as a man needs food, drink and air to breathe, but he was hoping for a change. Before his captivity he had become known for his panel paintings of the Virgin and Child, but now that he was home he longed to do fresco and itched for a good wall. A whole monastery of walls, perhaps. Those commissions Cosimo had mentioned: what else could they be for but the walls of San Marco monastery?

2

CROSSING THE RIVER ARNO, FILIPPO WALKED TO SANTA Maria del Carmine. He looked up at the bland, undecorated face of the church then stepped forward and ran his hand lovingly over the rough, sandy stone. How long he had dreamt of this moment, of hurrying back as if to the arms of his mother, a free man again. As soon as he stepped inside the monastery, however, and his nose was assaulted by incense, and he saw Carmelite friars gliding through the cloisters like hypocrites on wheels, he remembered that he had never been a free man here.

Things had changed in his absence, however. There was a new effort in the place to live by the Rule. The prior greeted him as if he were the prodigal son. No hypocritical remonstrance; no curious questions; just a purely Christian welcome and the offer of a bath, a meal and a bed. And a habit.

Filippo joined the brethren for the office of Compline in the church, standing where he had a good view of Brancacci's chapel, but it was in darkness, with no candles on the altar. He snuggled into the office of Compline, the scents of wood and wax, the pools of candlelight, the voices of his brethren singing psalms and the rising and falling cadences of the chant.

Hear me when I call, O god of my righteousness: thou hast enlarged me when I was in distress; have mercy upon me, and hear my prayer.

When he had set foot once more on Italian shores he had expected to feel a rush of relief. Yes, he had felt the comfort of language and familiar food, but it was only now, being back in the Carmine at Compline, that he reached the heart, the inner sanctum of home. The changes were disquieting, however. He had walked around the place in the afternoon and discovered that the priest in the confessional no longer smelled of wine, the gap in the monastery wall on the brothel side had been plugged, and that the friars were keeping to their duties rather than to their beds. In his youth, Filippo could spend all day watching Masaccio at work on the walls of Brancacci's chapel with but the mildest rebuff from a passing elder; now, like a creeping fog, a holy fervour was arising in the cloisters.

O ye sons of men, how long will ye turn my glory into shame? How long will ye love vanity, and seek after lies? Selah.

If only he could see Masaccio's frescoes, then his sense of having returned home would be complete.

Stand in awe and sin not: commune with your own heart upon your bed, and be still. Selah.

He looked about at the familiar and unfamiliar faces. There were new novices in the Order, and some of the older friars had passed on. One aged face that he looked on fondly, a long face etched by time, was that of his old master. On the eve of his novitiate, he had been screaming, he remembered, and running round the dormitory squealing like a wild pig, but the master had caught him and taken him to a chapel where they had sat alone together and talked. The master told him what would happen when he took his vows.

'When you become a friar of the Carmelite Order, such is the pleasure of heaven that something very special is granted to you. For every friar of the Order is assured a place in paradise and, on the Saturday following the day of your death, the Virgin Mary herself will come to collect your soul.'

Filippo had stared at his master open-mouthed, for there were implications in this immediately apparent to him. What he wanted to ask was, 'No matter what you've done?' but he restrained himself. The meaning was clear – how could it be clearer? – that just being a Carmelite would absolve him of sin. He had been trying to be good, but then all his intentions began a slow unravelling, for he did not have to struggle any longer. All he had to do, after a year of being a novice, was to take his vows.

Now his old master was gazing at him queerly, as if to see what was written on his soul. Filippo flinched and looked away.

Lord, now lettest thou thy servant depart in peace, according to thy word.

With the closing of the Nunc Dimittis, the friars began to leave the church for their beds. Filippo lingered. He had bathed, had his tonsure renewed and was wearing the dark tunic of the Order with its white mantle and copious hood. This he kept over his head, not wishing to be recognised and caught up by questions about his prolonged absence. Nor did he wish to hear anything further on the cause of all these changes, a new preacher exhorting the brethren to renew their observance of the Rule. Filippo had an innate distrust of such men, especially when he was told that roses poured from his mouth when he preached and angels had been seen holding up his copy of the Gospels.

When the friars had all departed, he took a candle from the altar and went into Brancacci's chapel.

It was all so fresh in his memory, the scenes of Saint Peter and the Tribute Money, Saint Peter Preaching, Saint Peter Healing the Sick with his Shadow, Saint Peter raising the son of Theophilius. But, holding up the candle, his jaw dropped. This last scene was of a miracle witnessed by many onlookers, several of whom had been portraits of Brancacci and his friends, but rough-edged holes in the plaster now stood where faces once had been.

At first it looked like an act of vandalism, as if a passing horde of barbarians had come into the chapel to destroy one of the greatest paintings ever made by man, but Filippo understood at once that the barbarians were not a passing horde: they were resident in the city. The fresco had been defaced by someone with a grudge against Brancacci who, as Filippo remembered it, had been instrumental in Cosimo's exile. This had been a savage act of revenge. Therefore, Cosimo was the vandal. Could that be true? Certainly it was true that Cosimo had arranged for Brancacci himself to be exiled, but had he ordered the erasure of his image? Filippo could understand Cosimo's anger, but he could not sanction this act of destruction. Nor could he sanction the complicity of his Order.

36

Suddenly he felt trapped within the Carmine and its hypocrisies. He needed to leave now, at once. The cloisters were silent; all the friars were abed; he went to the stores and helped himself to another habit and two shirts – one should always have a clean change of clothes. Then he went to see whether a hole he had made himself in the western wall when he was a boy was still there. He pulled aside a shrub that had grown up and found that it was.

The last time he had gone through this hole was to see Brunelleschi's dome being built on the Duomo. He'd heard about the gigantic hoist and needed to see for himself the enormous winding drum and the vertical shaft driven by oxen, lifting huge loads of stone up to the double-shelled dome. He remembered the excitement so well: Brunelleschi's ingenuity and self-confidence had solved a problem that had seemed insoluble: how to build a large octagonal dome without internal supports or external buttresses. Now he was going through that hole in the wall that would lead him to supper with the great Brunelleschi at the Medici house tomorrow. Blowing a kiss to the Carmine, he squeezed through and hurried to the house of a relative to beg for lodging for the night.

✝

On the morning after the procession of the Magi came the dissolution. The palace of Herod was reduced to a pile of kindling, as was the stable at Bethlehem. Costumes were put into store, along with beards, wigs and outlandish hats. Floats became farmers' carts again and it was on one such, leaving the city through the Porta San Frediano on the road to Soffiano, that Filippo saw his peachy girl again, sitting in the driver's seat and switching the rumps of the two oxen.

He ran to catch up with the cart. 'Are you going to Soffiano?' he asked. 'Could you spare a holy friar the trouble of walking?'

She looked at him undecided. He told her that the saints and angels were waiting on her answer. She nodded and he climbed up on the driver's seat beside her, telling her that the saints and angels took account of all good deeds. 'They are always watching.'

She had long, curly brown hair of the kind that gets bleached by the sun in the summer, a sweet child's face that was at odds with the heaviness of her breasts: she was mature and young both at once. But definitely lamb, not mutton. Lovely, lovely lamb. Just before they reached the village, he got her to stop the cart and dismount. He took her standing up. She protested prettily, squirming in his grasp, but she knew what he was about – when he put his hand up her skirt, he found her damp in anticipation. He pressed his hand over her mouth to stop those little love-screams all women make, took her hard and kept going until she crumpled, moaning and half unconscious, to the ground. She'd clearly enjoyed herself but he left her some money anyway: he was not a bad man.

He returned to the city, pleased with himself. The arts of love he had learned in Ifriqiya had made him a bold, confident lover, he thought, but how much easier it was when the wench didn't affect reluctance. It was cold and few people were abroad, yet after a while came the sound of a cart on its way from Soffiano to the city. He stopped to hail it but to his surprise he found it was the same cart, with the same driver, that he had just abandoned. For a moment he presumed that she had come back for more – who could blame her? – but the cart did not stop; it kept going, the two beasts lumbering with their great horned heads down. As the cart passed him, the young woman rose up like Boudicca in her chariot, balled her fist and rammed it hard into his cheerfully expectant, upturned face.

'I trust the Virgin herself was watching that one,' she said, flinging down his coins and leaving him for dead.

It was the bitter cold that roused him. He touched his face gingerly and found to his relief that his nose was not broken.

3

FROM THE WINDOW OF HIS CHAMBER, COSIMO WATCHED his guests coming towards his house along the Via Larga from the Duomo. Shops were closing with the bang of shutters, and early-rising bats squeaked in the air among the diving swifts. The bells of San Lorenzo were tolling gently for Vespers and the street-lighters were out with their tapers, lighting the lamps and the torches set in sconces on the walls of grand palazzi. He loved this time of day, this transition from the public life governed by the sun to the private life under the moon. Somewhere in the house his wife would be reading from the psalter to the younger members of the family; they would have supper and then retire to bed. This was the hour of peace.

He glanced sideways at Leon Battista Alberti who had arrived early.

'Well, Battista, here they come, your men of *virtù*.' Cosimo smiled at the approaching architects and sculptors whom Alberti had immortalized in his book. Donatello, straight from work and looking like a miller in his dusty white cap and rough tunic, Ghiberti, bald and dapper, dressed in a pleated gown as smart as a notary, Luca della Robbia in simple hose and jacket, walking beside Donatello and watching his feet as if he would match his step. And leading them, Brunelleschi, thin-lipped, jug-eared and indifferent to his appearance as he flung his arms about to make a point so loud it would drown any opposition, he who had created the dome under whose shadow they walked. They all swam behind a goose, this motley of fowl.

'I'm not sure I've understood what you mean by *virtù*,' said Cosimo.

'It is excellence, of course.'

'Then why not call it excellence?'

Cosimo's son, Giovanni, standing on the far side of Alberti, laughed, but immediately checked himself so that Alberti would not be insulted. Alberti smiled like a courtier. 'It is more than excellence and combines several qualities: daring, courage, innovation. Think of it as putting the work before yourself. Anyone can make a living in the crafts by following tradition and giving people what they want. The man of *virtù* goes further and gives the people what they never dreamt of. Like that dome.'

Together they stared at the view from the window to the cathedral capped by a feat of engineering everyone had claimed could never be accomplished; everyone that is except Brunelleschi himself. He often said it had been easier to build the dome than to get the permission to try.

'That man's belief in himself is towering,' said Cosimo, looking down on the architect who, having arrived below, was pulling on the bell and awaiting admittance into the palazzo. 'And you will find that I am right,' he was telling his companions loudly. 'That man Alberti is a bigot.'

Cosimo cleared his throat loudly to cover what Brunelleschi was saying, but Alberti had caught it. Again he smiled as only a secretary to the pope can smile, easily, as fluid as ink on smooth vellum. 'Brunelleschi hates me,' he explained. 'He says that the discovery of perspective was his, while I write of it as if it were my own. He overlooks that I dedicated my book to him. He has great faith in himself, but none at all in what others think of him. Truth to tell, he has protected himself with a double-walled shell built of herringbone brick but inside he quivers like a snail.'

Again Cosimo's son Giovanni laughed, this time more freely. His brother Piero entered and announced that their guests had arrived. Cosimo turned to welcome them and introduced them to his guest of honour, Leon Battista Alberti, the papal secretary and author of *On Painting*. 'Which I trust you've all read?' he asked.

To his horror Cosimo was greeted by shaken heads and lame excuses, even though almost every man here had been included in the list of 'men of *virtù*'. Brunelleschi, to whom the book had been dedicated, said he was far too busy to find time for reading; Donatello claimed he could not read; Luca della Robbia said he could not afford a book. Lorenzo Ghiberti alone had read *On Painting*. He had graciously had a copy made, had read it carefully and had brought it with him for Alberti to comment on the notes he had made in its margins, for unfortunately, as he said with a sweet smile, he could not agree with everything Alberti had written.

Making a mental note never to write a book himself, Cosimo ushered his guests to the polished table, including the lately-arrived painters, Fra Giovanni and Paolo Uccello. He had chosen the intimacy of a small, panelled chamber without ostentatious hangings. Its only furniture were two ancient cassone used to store linens, a credenza, his grandfather's chandelier: there was nothing else in the room to excite curiosity or, worse, envy. For all their brilliance, these were, except for Alberti, simple men and he did not wish to intimidate them by vaunting his wealth. The meal was simple for the same reason, but did he detect disappointment as the first course of dried figs stewed in wine was served? These artisans were not as jaded by banquets as he was. Perhaps he should have served them something more unusual.

'Where is Fra Filippo?' he asked.

Most of the company knew neither the friar nor his where-abouts, but Ghiberti said that he had heard a rumour that he was in prison in Rome.

'No, indeed, I saw him just yesterday,' said Cosimo. 'He claims to have been a slave in Barbary for the past two years.'

'Barbary! Did you believe him?'

Cosimo nodded. 'Yes, I have reason to believe he's telling the truth and I invited him to join us here this evening.' He looked at Alberti sitting at the opposite end of the table, flanked by Cosimo's sons. 'You call your book *On Painting*, Battista, yet you mention only one painter: Masaccio. I thought you might wish to meet those competing to be his successor. Fra Giovanni,' he indicated the friar in a white tunic, 'is of the order of Dominicans, about to take up residence at San Marco. Few will have seen his work, but I have, and I see in him a painter of sublime quality.'

'Oh, no, please…' Fra Giovanni raised his hands as if offering the compliment up to God. When he smiled, his cheeks dimpled like a girl's.

'Then there is our Paolo Uccello.' Cosimo nodded towards the man sitting between Brunelleschi and Luca della Robbia. A consummate diplomat, Cosimo neglected to say, 'whom you must already know' since that would reveal that Alberti had deliberately left Uccello out of his list of excellent men – which he had.

A tall, thin painter with beetle brows and startling eyes, Uccello gazed at Cosimo with a bright and open smile. If ever he felt insulted, he never showed it, because his mind was always on a problem of the science of optics or the laws of perspective. *He spends so much time wondering how we see,* thought Cosimo, *that he can't hear a thing. Or he would not smile so…*

'Then there is Fra Filippo Lippi,' he continued, 'who is perhaps not known to any of us. I met him in Padua two years ago and detected talent in him; even, perhaps, genius.'

'Ah,' said Alberti, 'genius. Now that is a quality hard to define.'

'I have no idea what I mean by the word, but it's a good enough name for that indefinable numinous something I detected in the man. I only saw a little of his work, but among his sketches were studies of things he had seen in the people around him, a face, an eye, a mouth, a leg, and they were magnificent. I am disappointed that he has not come tonight.'

Brunelleschi, who did not enjoy any conversation that was not about architecture, interrupted to ask Paolo Uccello what he was working on, hoping it would afford an excuse to tell the company what he was working on himself.

Uccello, glancing shyly at Cosimo, said he had a new commission, to paint a portrait of Sir John Hawkwood on a wall of the Duomo. The company exploded at this, claiming that it

42

was the time of the apocalypse if sacred walls were to be used to glorify mercenary soldiers.

Cosimo, who had made the commission, called for more wine and tried to change the subject.

'Really!' Lorenzo Ghiberti was exclaiming for the benefit of Fra Giovanni. 'Whatever are the canons thinking of? No doubt some rich man has paid for this!'

'No doubt,' said Cosimo, clearing his throat. Embarrassed and ashamed, he forbade Uccello with a look ever to mention the name of his patron. The head of the Medici family, the lover of wisdom and would-be philosopher had a private and very boyish passion for military heroes. When he wasn't carving sculptures in his dreams, he was leading armies into battle. There was not a condottiere of recent history whose life, exploits, victories and defeats Cosimo did not know and remember in exquisite detail. His favourite was Niccolò Tolentino, who a few years earlier had led Florence to victory against Siena in the Battle of San Romano, but the canons of the cathedral had thought it more appropriate to recognize the aid that Hawkwood and his army had brought to the city.

Alberti had quite a lot to say on the value of history, and was saying it when Brunelleschi interrupted, asking for the plate of cheese and pigeon breast to be passed to him. 'All these fancy ideas of yours,' he said to Alberti, 'would not build a beehive.'

Alberti, who had withstood everything he had received so far, now crumpled. 'Are you calling me a mere theorist? I paint, as you well know, and I design buildings.'

'Which buildings?' Brunelleschi demanded. 'Do any of them stand? Can I walk in any of them?'

'What I enjoyed most in your book,' Cosimo said quickly, 'is your call to the artificer to imitate nature. What is your meaning?'

Alberti found the power to smile again. 'Well, I hardly mean that we should go out and copy the forms of trees and flowers.'

'No?'

'No! Of course not! What I mean is that we should imitate nature in that nature is beautiful.' Alberti began to discourse on beauty, saying how it was a certain harmony of the parts to the whole; that proportion was the secret of harmony; number the secret of proportion; and as he spoke he tracked back through Plato to Pythagoras and Hermes Trismegistus before him.

'The works of Hermes, like most of those of Plato, are lost to us, but I have seen many quotations, most of which I have by heart, and one of them speaks of how Nature, seeing the beautiful form of Man, fell in love with God, the source of that beauty. And God loved her and wished to dwell with her.'

Fra Giovanni began to frown at Alberti. Cosimo noticed it and grumbled in his throat but Alberti rushed on like a river in spate. 'Thus God and Nature embraced and were united, for they burned in love.'

Brunelleschi, seeing the Dominican's reddening face and mistaking it for embarrassment, laughed and pointed his knife at him.

Heedlessly, Alberti went on: 'This is the precise quote. *Man, having taken on a mortal body in order to live with Nature, is alone of all beings of a double nature, mortal through his body, immortal through his soul.* This is where beauty enters life, through the soul, the place where we are joined to God. And this is what I mean by imitating nature: that we should do as she does, and derive beauty from God.'

Cosimo apologized to Fra Giovanni for his friend. 'Battista has read every book ever written.'

'There is only one book and that is the Bible,' said Fra Giovanni. 'That is the only book I require, except perhaps the works of the Early Fathers and the Lives of the Saints.'

Alberti looked on him pityingly.

'I hope we're not offending you with all this talk of philosophy,' said Cosimo to the Dominican.

'No, of course not. We owe so much to the ancients, not least the trick of perspective. But sometimes I worry. With too much

44

reading of ancient philosophy it's easy to cross the invisible line and become pagan in your thinking.'

Cosimo had been building a library since he was a young man and he wished to endow the monastery of San Marco with it. His aim was to have a copy of every book ever written available to all, to enlarge the minds of Florentines. It would not suit his purpose if there was too much zeal amongst the Dominicans. He made a mental note to argue with Fra Giovanni later about invisible lines. Wisdom, to his mind, had no boundaries.

'*Virtù*,' he said to Alberti. 'What I think it means is this, the ability in a man to go beyond his limitations. God is limitless.' He glanced at Fra Giovanni and to his relief saw the Dominican nodding in agreement. 'So,' he continued with caution, 'when a man steps beyond his own limits, he is stepping into a higher realm. He is, for that moment, partaking of divinity.' Again he glanced at Fra Giovanni and again – to his surprise – he received a nod of assent. 'That is *virtù*, and though it contains all the moral virtues it is not in itself moral. It's not a question of being good but of being bold.'

'Bravo!' said Brunelleschi. 'That is exactly what it is.'

Cosimo looked around and realized in a flash of insight that there was not a man at the table who was not as vulnerable as Alberti's snail: each was unsure of himself, each determined enough to ignore this and push on, striving always to exceed and excel, excel even the ancient Romans who were their models. The greatest praise of the age was, 'You've exceeded the Romans!' That was their aim and, like warriors, they were prepared to die for it. 'I understand now,' he said, 'what *virtù* is. And I believe we look for it in vain in the ancient Romans.'

The air in the chamber thrilled with this statement: he had the attention of everyone. Their dreams and visions were so filled with ruined arches, buried buildings, noble, broken statues and exquisite letter carving that they could not comprehend his meaning. Fra Giovanni looked momentarily hopeful that Cosimo was undergoing some Damascene vision but his face fell when

45

Cosimo declared, 'Ancient Greece! That's the real source.'
The Dominican shook his head in sorrow.

'I agree with you,' said Alberti. 'Not only ancient Greece but, more precisely, ancient Greek philosophy.'

Cosimo and Alberti began to talk to each other along the length of the table, over the glazed platters made by Luca della Robbia to bear pyramids of fruit, over the silver salt cellar in the form of a boat that came from Ghiberti's workshop, over Venetian glasses sparkling in the candlelight, over the empty dishes being cleared by servants, talking as if there were nothing between them, as if they were the only men in the room who understood each other.

'Do you think Plato's works are irreparably lost?' Cosimo asked.

'No, I don't. Somewhere in the pit of me I believe they still exist. Almighty God would not have allowed their extinction, surely. Somewhere, by some miracle, they survive. I think a copy of the *Dialogues* may be found in an Arab library one day, or even in a Christian one, for many books are mouldering from neglect in our monasteries, and the monks rarely know what they have.'

Cosimo's eyes glittered. 'I have agents from London to Peking, dealing in many goods. If I asked them to search for Plato's works...'

Now Alberti's eyes were as bright as Cosimo's. 'That would be a monument to your memory greater than any dome or church.'

Filippo Brunelleschi, who considered the dome to be his own monument and not the Medici's, scowled at this remark.

'And this Trismegistus you keep mentioning,' Cosimo continued.

'An Egyptian sage and author of two books: the *Poimandres* and the *Asclepius*. Both are lost to us but extant in the world somewhere, I'm certain. I think we could find them in Greece.'

'What are they about?'

'The divinity in man, and man's ability to become a god. I believe there is an excellent passage on the birth of the soul, how it picks up the vices and virtues on its descent through the planetary spheres, and leaves them behind again when it re-ascends after the death of the body.'

Fra Giovanni slapped his hands together in prayer.

'But they will be in Greek,' Alberti went on, unmoved by the Dominican's call to Christian orthodoxy, 'and in that respect they are lost to us, for who in Florence can read Greek? Both Plato and Hermes are lost to us until we raise ourselves to receive them. We must learn Greek!'

Cosimo nodded energetically. 'You're right. I'm getting too old for the task myself, but I see it as my duty to find teachers for the young.'

He looked pointedly at his sons, who both professed willingness to learn. 'To be as fluent in Greek as we are in Latin,' said the eldest, 'would give us unequalled insight into the philosophy and culture of Athens.'

Alberti agreed. 'We need to go beyond what others tell us of these things and experience them ourselves. But we need the books.'

'If they exist, I shall find them,' Cosimo promised.

'And teachers.'

'Ah, that could be harder. They are a proud race, the Greeks, and unlikely to share their wisdom with us, perfidious Latins that we are in their eyes.'

'To explore Plato would be an excavation,' offered Donatello with his mouth full of cold pigeon and bread, 'as great as anything going on in Rome.'

Ghiberti winced at the stonecutter's lack of table manners. Uccello was staring at the ceiling, his fingers tapping out a rhythm on his chin. Luca della Robbia was trying to have a private conversation with Fra Giovanni. Brunelleschi kept his head low over his dish.

Cosimo was cursed with insight: it was as if his guests were sitting naked at table. Each of them brilliant, each of them insecure, each of them so vain he could not speak without

47

mentioning himself. 'As I said in my book;' 'As you will see in my dome;' 'As you will have noticed on my doors;' 'As I was thinking last night whilst I was trying to draw a cloud in perspective…'.

He glanced at his two sons again, suddenly very proud of their decorum in that they only ever spoke about others, preferred questions to statements, had been raised so well! Apart from them, only Fra Giovanni knew what humility was and how it may be practised.

'What do you think, Pippo?' Cosimo asked Brunelleschi, who had withdrawn from this conversation that did not have himself as its subject.

'About what?'

'About the need to learn Greek and read Plato.'

'I didn't need the Greeks to show me how to build the dome.'

Ghiberti turned and smiled graciously at Cosimo. 'Pippo, we must remember, has achieved the highest aim of his life, reached the pinnacle some years ago.'

'That is not true,' said Brunelleschi, stabbing his finger at Ghiberti. 'There's a good deal more in me yet!'

Donatello raised his eyebrows at Cosimo, as if to say, 'Did I not warn you not to have these two at table together?' Over thirty years had passed since Brunelleschi had lost to Ghiberti in the competition to win the commission for the bronze doors of the Baptistry – thirty years and not a day when Brunelleschi hadn't brooded on it.

'Well?' asked Cosimo.

'I don't see how all this learning and book-reading helps a man with his craft. Except that if he writes it down it makes him famous. It was I, if you remember, I who worked out the laws of perspective and demonstrated them so that all could see. But it was he,' now the finger jabbed at Alberti, 'who wrote them in his book, and how long will it be before men are speaking of *Alberti*'s laws of perspective, not *Brunelleschi*'s? Eh? How long?' He became so angry he gave himself indigestion. He stopped eating, rubbed his chest and belched loudly.

'Oh!' said Ghiberti in distaste.

'That was never my intention,' Alberti protested in dismay. 'It was because I worried about that that I dedicated my book to you, Pippo!'

'Oh, that was the reason, was it? Not because you admired me, but because you feared me!'

Cosimo had once tried making a clay pot on a wheel. His dinner party was quickly becoming like that lump of clay, spinning into unplanned and chaotic shape and about to fly off across the room. None of these men would keep to the point. He was no longer quite sure what the point was. What was the point? Why had he gathered them together? Oh, yes, to find a painter, but Fra Giovanni was a friar before he was a painter, Uccello had made himself insane with his calculations, and Filippo Lippi had not come. He turned smartly to the sulking Luca della Robbia to tell him that his relief panels for the organ loft in the Duomo were sublime, his men and angels more lifelike than anything achieved in ancient Rome.

Donatello snorted at this. 'That may be so,' he said, 'but you need a pair of ladders to discover it. The work is fine, all right, but too fine given its height from the ground. No one can see it.'

His own solution for a companion organ loft had been to use impassioned carving on fewer and larger figures.

Although Luca was ten years younger than Cosimo, and twenty years younger than Brunelleschi and Ghiberti, he had as much pride as any man in the room and looked like a cornered wolf.

'I accept I made a mistake,' he struggled to admit, 'and Donatello has shown me the solution, but try as I might, I don't seem to be able to impose it on my piece.'

'You must find your own solution,' said Cosimo.

'Lowering the organ loft to a braccia off the ground should do it,' said Donatello, picking up a handful of shelled nuts and throwing them into his mouth one by one.

'Don't listen to him,' said Cosimo, smiling. 'Luca, if you try and be anyone other than yourself, you risk losing your genius. You must stay true to your inner guide. We already have a Donatello – we don't need another. We want our Luca.'

'Our invisible Luca,' Donatello agreed cheerfully, crunching hazelnuts, 'who distracts no one from my work.'

Luca, who had been stung by what Cosimo had said and infuriated by Donatello, got up and, with a lame excuse of feeling tired, left early.

The grand ideas Cosimo had had in arranging this symposium were becoming food for the dogs under the table. These men of *virtù*, as Alberti had described them, were proud, arrogant and intractable. He was tiring and, catching his eldest son's eye, gave the slightest nod of his head.

Giovanni raised his hand to catch the attention of a servant and told the man to fetch his lute. When the instrument came, he tuned it up.

4

COSIMO SAT WITH HIS CHIN ON HIS CHEST, HIS ARMS folded on his stomach and his legs extended. He was frustrated. Yes, he was happy to pay for as many projects as he could afford, but really he wanted to be involved. He wanted to wield the chisel, pour the bronze, file the stone, get his hands muddy with clay; but he was condemned to reading ledgers and making a fortune. These surly, grumbling bears had no idea how fortunate they were.

Giovanni played a setting he had composed of a poem of by his brother, Piero, who now stood to sing. Cosimo gazed on his sons – half of him, more than half of him – swelling with emotion at the beauty of their music and words; the other half moping about their lack of commercial acumen and interest in the bank.

He closed his eyes to listen but was transported back to his own youth and to a quarrel he had had with his father, who told him, No, No, No! He could not go to Jerusalem with his friend Niccolò to hunt for ancient manuscripts! Scholarship: that was Cosimo's true love. He could not sculpt, build, paint, play the lute or write poetry, but he knew a good book just by the touch and smell of it. Books were his soul and his soul was a book. Wisdom! That was his heart's desire. But, on that day, his father had spoken as fathers should speak, with the power of Abraham and the law of Moses. He had propounded an argument of filial duty so compelling that from that day on Cosimo had dedicated himself to the bank. In duty to his father and his family, Cosimo had sacrificed his desire to be a scholar – had slit its throat and bled it dry on the altar of necessity – but he had not given up his love of wisdom. That he could indulge, even if only by patronising the scholarship and creativity of others. But still he itched.

He did not regret his sacrifice. What he regretted was his inability to be equally strict with his own sons, but half of him, more than half of him – and here he half-opened one eye – wished to grant them their heart's desire.

At the end of the third song by the brothers, Cosimo called for the servants to clear the table. He felt low, now, and wished to retire. He walked with Fra Giovanni to the door of the chamber.

'Your brethren are moving into San Marco very soon. The monastery, as you know, is being beautifully renovated by Michelozzo.'

Brunelleschi, just behind them, snorted with derision.

'You were busy, Pippo,' Cosimo reminded him. 'Michelozzo did the work and it's very fine, even you will admit. But the walls are bare. Fra Giovanni, I've seen your work at Fiesole and much admired it. If you will dedicate your life as Lorenzo Ghiberti has done, to a single project…'

'My life is my Lord's,' said Fra Giovanni quietly.

'And your Lord has given you an incredible talent. I have spoken to your prior and he is content that you divide your time between painting and prayer.'

Fra Giovanni coloured with pleasure, a response he immediately tried to damp down by freezing his expression into solemnity.

'I want a fresco in the chapter house and in the refectory, an altarpiece for the church, and I thought each cell on the dormitory floor could have a devotional image for private reflection.'

'A lifetime's work indeed!' said Fra Giovanni. 'And I am forty years old!'

'That's why I invited Fra Filippo to join us. He's a Carmelite, I know, and not a Dominican, but you are both friar-painters and I thought perhaps you could work together.'

Fra Giovanni blinked at this. For all his piety, he was suddenly as jealous as the next man, who happened to be Brunelleschi.

'I wonder where Lippi is?' said Cosimo. 'He seemed eager to come but he slips through your fingers like water.'

'I'll make enquiries at the Carmine,' said Fra Giovanni, overcoming his momentary lapse into the vice of envy.

✝

Down in the kitchen of the Medici house Fra Filippo was waiting for the symposium to end so he could see Cosimo alone and apologise for his absence, telling him that he could not face such a company of great men with two black eyes and blood clots in his nostrils. What had he done? Why, he had trodden on a rake in the dark. Or so he told the cook who was applying raw meat to his purpled, swollen eyes.

Before long came the sound of voices on the stairs, growing louder and amplified by the inner courtyard, where the men lingered to continue debating genius and whether it comes by grace or if one can work for it. Brunelleschi thought that if you waited for grace your only gain would be the virtue of patience. Donatello was inclined to agree with Alberti that a man should have talent and practice in equal measure. Those who had trained with Ghiberti were careful to emphasise the value of such training.

Standing slightly apart and close to the kitchen door, quietly listening to these ambitious men, stood someone whom Filippo recognised. 'Psst! Fra Giovanni!' he hissed.

Fra Giovanni turned in surprise.

'Has the simporium finished?'

'The symposium, yes, it has. Are you Fra Filippo?' asked the Dominican.

'Yes. And you are Fra Giovanni.' Filippo would have recognised those dimples anywhere. Despite the passage of years, Fra Giovanni remained the handsome youth that Filippo had hero-worshipped when he was a novice.

'How do you know that?'

'You were at the Carmine about twenty years ago.'

'So I was, before I became a Dominican.' Fra Giovanni peered at him but failed to recognise the man with two soaked prunes for eyes. 'What happened to you?'

'I trod on a rake in the dark. That's why I didn't attend – too embarrassed.'

'Cosimo missed you. He has a high opinion of your work.'

'In a city of no painters, is it any wonder? I'm sorry – I didn't mean to offend you. I haven't seen your work. But I've seen Uccello's and it's mad.'

Fra Giovanni blinked as if to get the grit of this criticism out of his eyes. 'Were you in the Carmine when Masaccio was working there? That must have been – well, shall we say – if you were there when Masaccio was working, and you learnt from him, that was grace. Yes, that's the point I've been struggling with all evening. It's not a question of grace *or* work: it's a question of grace *and* work.'

'Eh?'

'That's what we've been discussing over dinner, that and other matters of philosophy – some of them suspect, I have to say.'

'Then I'm glad I didn't come or I'd have been snoring with my head on my trencher. All this philosophical thinking – just pale goings-on in the mind if you ask me. It turns the imagination into a veal calf, bloodless and blind.'

Fra Giovanni smiled. 'Alberti would say you are ignorant.'

'He's probably right. But as a painter what need do I have for philosophy? What I need to know is how heads join to necks and necks to shoulders, how muscles work, how to create the illusion of space, how to depict emotion. What does philosophy have to do with that?'

'When I move to San Marco in a month's time, we should meet.'

'San Marco?' Filippo's voice rose to a squeak.

'The Dominicans are moving into the new monastery in a month's time.'

'Yes, I know,' Filippo cleared his throat. 'I expect you will be called upon to do some paintings?'

Fra Giovanni laughed. 'Cosimo has asked me to paint *all* of it. We shall have to see if God agrees and grants me a long enough life. But come and see me. I'd be grateful for your advice.' He neglected to mention Cosimo's idea that they work together. 'We have much to discuss out of earshot of architects and engineers.'

'Such as?'

'Alberti says painters must copy sculptors, that if we copy one another we shall end up with shadows. Now is that true?'

'Tell me,' said Filippo, not listening. 'Who defaced Masaccio's frescoes? Was it the Medici?'

'I've heard it from Cosimo himself, who was in tears when he told me about it, that it was nothing to do with him. It was some over-zealous friends, trying to gain his favour. He feels guilty that he hasn't reprimanded them, but that's all he is guilty of.' Fra Giovanni walked off to join the others who were now leaving. 'Mind out for the rakes, Brother,' he said as he left.

Fra Filippo sent word upstairs to Cosimo, asking if he could see him briefly. The servant returned to say that his master had retired. He handed a slim manuscript to Filippo, a copy of Alberti's book on painting. 'Cosimo says you are to read this then come and see him.'

Filippo read the first page where he stood under the light of a flickering candle in a sconce and found it mentioned every man he had failed to meet on this fateful night. He wondered at what he had missed. He wondered at why he had missed it.

✛

Filippo read the book and, following its advice, began to copy sculpture, particularly that of Donatello. When he eventually met Cosimo again, he had a sheaf of drawings that he laid out proudly, but the banker showed no sign of being impressed.

'I thought we had agreed that a painter should imitate nature,' said Cosimo.

'But Alberti...' spluttered Filippo.

'Forget Alberti. Go to Mother Nature and learn.' Cosimo leaned forward in his chair. 'I hear you walked out of the Carmine the day you returned there.'

Filippo shrugged. 'It's restrictive. A painter needs to be free. You know, they tell me to keep the hours and use my time of work for painting. It sounds simple. But it's not just the hours, is it? With the curative duties, the masses, divine offices and all the feast days, it's most of each week! Then there is the question of working space. They give me a little hole somewhere but expect me to clear out of it at a moment's notice. I need space, I need time, I need peace to paint. I am better living on the outside.'

'You're living with relatives? That can't be any easier.'

'It's only until I can earn enough to rent a workshop.'

Cosimo took up a large iron key on a ring and held it out to him. 'It's nothing grand but it will serve your purpose; a workshop two steps from the Carmine.'

Filippo put out his hand gratefully but Cosimo held the key out of reach. 'It's a workshop, not a house. I've arranged it with the prior that you will sleep in your cell each night, but that you will have dispensation from attending offices.'

Filippo was taken aback at having his life arranged for him without his knowledge but he agreed nonetheless and took the key.

'After all,' said Cosimo. 'You need somewhere to do the commission I have for you.'

'A commission?' asked Filippo eagerly.

'I'd like a panel of the Virgin and Child.'

5

IT WAS TO BE A GIFT FOR MONSIGNOR VITELLESCHI, the archbishop of Florence, and it was to be 'innovative'. Well, of course, any painting done in Florence must be innovative. But what did the word mean? New? Original? Shocking? Filippo had had a question lurking in his mind for some years, as to why the simple, innocent Virgin was usually shown enthroned. How, he wondered, would she have looked in life? It was a question, he knew, which haunted the Flemish painters, and it was a good question. So, in masterly perspective, he showed the Madonna seated with her Child in a bedroom. *A bedroom!* said one shocked friar to his brothers when they visited Filippo's workshop for a game of dice. *A bedroom!*

When the panel was finished, the archbishop found it 'enchantingly novel'. He told his friends and neighbours that painting was at last catching up with sculpture and architecture, 'and will soon overtake them'. The one person not convinced was Fra Filippo himself, who fretted about his difficulties in painting the human form. The Virgin had been oddly stiff and the Child seemed to be throttling her.

'I must go back to Ifriqiya, convert to Islam and content myself with geometry,' he thought. 'The Moors are right: no human hand may paint God. It's not a prohibition, it's a fact.'

But Monsignor Vitelleschi was delighted with his panel and showed it off to all his friends, who sought out Lippi to paint something like it for themselves. For two years, Filippo painted Madonnas.

With Cosimo's advice in mind, he often sat in city squares, drawing the forms of living mothers and children. When asked what he was drawing, he would answer, 'Giotto's goat'. He did studies of a child standing by his mother's knee, or half-falling from her lap, laughing, or reaching out with pudgy hands. This was not the infant Jesus, the tiny Emmanuel old before his time. These were infants and infant gestures the friar saw for himself in city squares and marketplaces. His dice-playing brethren, sitting at his table and eating his food, said he was pulling heaven down to earth, which was profanity. He should be painting holy things, they said, as Fra Giovanni was doing at San Marco. He prayed for hours, they said, before he began work each day. Fra Giovanni would not pick up his brush, they said as they quaffed Lippi's wine, until tears were running down his cheeks.

At such times, Filippo rolled his eyes and was pleased he was too busy to visit Fra Giovanni.

✝

The arrangement regarding his workshop had been explicit: Cosimo required rent, which Filippo was to pay on quarter days. It was not much, but it still had to be found. He was not to sleep in the workshop but he soon discovered that, if he sat down to rest at the end of a long day, he fell asleep at once and did not wake until dawn. It seemed reasonable to install a truckle bed. Who would know? As for the rent, it tended to fall into arrears, but what possible difference could a few overdue soldini make to Cosimo de' Medici?

Occasionally Filippo went into the Carmine for divine office, just to show his face. The Masaccio frescoes were becoming veiled by shadows and cobwebs. Current opinion within the monastery was that the ability to draw lifelike figures was the trick of an illusionist and not the kind of imagery to inspire devotion. A miracle-working image of the Madonna had been put into Brancacci's chapel and the candles on the Madonna's altar threw the chapel walls further into shadow.

Although some friars remained impervious to the new mood of piety, and drank and gambled as before, others were adopting severe spiritual practices. Filippo's friends said that the zealous walked about the cloisters during the night calling on God. One had been seen accompanied by a floating ball of light and, when questioned, had said it was the Archangel Raphael. Filippo began to shrink from the company of the Carmelites, whether fervent or hypocritical. He worked alone for days in his workshop, his door barred to all comers.

When people bothered him, as people were wont to do, he would immerse himself in his work. He neglected to eat, to wash, to go to the barber, wanting only the tranquillity of feeling the brush on the panel. This time his hermit phase endured. He lost his appetite for everything and would not leave the workshop. He began to sicken and grow feverish. Feeling the dampness of his brow, he took himself off to the Carmine infirmary where he was put to bed.

During that night and the day following he wrestled with angels and roses in his delirium. Then came one to lay a cool hand on his brow and talk him down from the heights of delusion. 'Fra Filippo, come back to us, come back. You are needed here.'

Filippo's eyes tracked left and right, trying to be still and to take in the Dominican bending over him. When he saw who it was, he smiled like a baby.

'Come back, there is work to do. Beautiful images to see, paintings to paint. Come back now.'

'There are too many saints.'

'Yes, I agree, far too many. One for each day of the year. Listen. Are you listening? I need to talk to you.'

Fra Giovanni... The handsome face close to his, those kind eyes and dimpled cheeks of the man who, through faith and work, was becoming unworldly even in life: Fra Giovanni of San Marco, Filippo's rival for Masaccio's crown – the one he should hate, only he could not, for there was nothing about him either false or vain. To hate Fra Giovanni – Filippo did his best, but it was like trying to hate Jesus.

'Talk about what?' he asked hoarsely through dry lips.

'Cosimo de' Medici wants a panel, a circular panel, and he wants us to do it together. Impossible, I know. We shall kill each other before a month is out.' Fra Giovanni lifted Filippo's head and gave him some watered wine. Filippo drank until he ran out of breath.

'What is the subject?'

'The Adoration of the Magi.'

'Why does he want us both?'

'He says it will cure you and help me.'

'In what way help you?'

Fra Giovanni laughed suddenly, a magical, musical sound that echoed in the spacious infirmary. 'He said that keeping your company will make me even more ready to shun the world and fly to heaven.' He laughed again. 'In truth he wants to see if we can work together, because he thinks that I'll take too long doing the walls of San Marco alone. So will you take the challenge? And it is a challenge.'

Filippo looked up at the vaulted ceiling and the restful arches of the aisled infirmary. This news was a tincture for health that even now was running through his body, performing the magic of healing. 'Of course I will,' he said.

6

FILIPPO WAITED FOR FRA GIOVANNI IN THE CHURCH attached to the monastery of San Marco. On the main altar stood a great painting depicting the Virgin and Child enthroned in a garden, attended by many saints in conversation, including the two Medici saints – Cosmas and Damian. Filippo was awestruck. The figures had all the reality and solidity of any created by Masaccio but their features were so fine they were ethereal. These were divine figures, truly divine.

Desperately, Filippo searched for faults and soon found one. Saint Damian, with his back to the viewer, was facing into his halo. Why do it like that? Why follow Giotto when Masaccio had shown them a new way? Filippo's sense of superiority was momentary, however; he soon noticed the Turkish carpet that covered the dais of the throne – a marvellous innovation by Fra Giovanni. Since the invention of perspective, all painters tiled their floors to give an illusion of space, but Fra Giovanni had covered his with a soft rug, still divided into squares but with nothing plain about them.

Instead of Fra Giovanni, a young apprentice came to fetch Filippo and guide him to the workshop. They passed through two cloisters, most finely arcaded, and inhabited now by the grave Dominicans in their white habits and black mantles. Walking amongst them in his black habit and white mantle, he felt in strange contrast to them, as if the Carmelites were inverted Dominicans.

The workshop overlooked a newly established, peaceful garden at the rear of the monastery. Filippo squirmed under the nicks of envy. This was how he should be working as a friar-painter, with an enclosed workshop filled with fine, thoughtful assistants who never swore or played practical jokes; a workshop warm and cosy in the winter bleakness; a workshop where painter and assistants prayed at the start of a day's work. Here he could concentrate; here he could thrive.

Having welcomed him, Fra Giovanni deferred to him in every particular – where they should sit and how they should work and for how many hours. 'I never work,' he said, 'without praying first, because I consider work a form of prayer.'

'As do I,' said Fra Filippo. He knelt with the rest of the painter's assistants and apprentices. Fra Giovanni's hands were long, slender and mobile; as he prayed, he looked up at the vaulting and held his hands out, palms up, or cast his eyes down and crossed his hands over his chest, or pointed to the heavy wooden crucifix on the wall – all the time his restless hands were at work, praying in a form of aerial calligraphy. Fra Filippo became transfixed by Fra Giovanni's hands in their devotions.

He waited to see Fra Giovanni weeping, as they said he did, but was disappointed. Perhaps that only happened when he was doing a devotional fresco in one of the cells. In the busy workshop perhaps he felt intimidated. He was certainly dry-eyed as they began work together. They discussed the design at length and the difficulties thrown up by the panel's shape. Domenico Veneziano had recently done a circular panel for the Medici, which both painters had seen and admired for its clever innovations and solutions.

'What I have in mind is this,' said Fra Giovanni, and he inscribed a curlicue in the air. 'Two processions meeting at the stable. Cosimo said he wanted many figures. I think before we go any farther ...'

'We're going to pray again!' thought Filippo.

'... we should establish what we know about the Magi.'

Fra Giovanni's chief assistant was an eighteen-year-old called Benozzo, whom he now sent to get the Bible from the shelf. 'It's in Matthew,' Giovanni said, taking the big, paint-spattered book from the youth. Filippo noticed that Giovanni opened the book precisely at the beginning of St Matthew's Gospel. He remarked on it.

61

'Oh, well,' said Giovanni, 'your thumbs get used to where all the books of the Bible begin, especially the Gospels. Don't you find that?' He read aloud the short passage about the Magi coming from the East, saying that little information was in the story. 'What we know has been supplied mostly by the Early Fathers. The word magus for instance in Latin means wise man but in Greek means philosopher and in Hebrew it means doctor. In origin the word is Persian and refers to a member of the priestly caste of the Zoroastrians. The word is the root of magic – which means "the art of a magus" – so we can assume that the Magi had powers perhaps of a supernatural kind. Certainly they were astrologers and seers, or they would not have recognised the star as a sign of an ancient prophecy being fulfilled. Nor could they have received and correctly interpreted the dream that God sent them, warning them not to return to Herod. So they were very great men indeed.'

'But were they kings?'

'According to tradition, yes. With vast entourages growing ever smaller the closer they are to the vanishing point.' Fra Giovanni smiled.

'Is that why Cosimo wants so many figures, to test our skills?'

'I believe so. To test them and to display them to guests. We are about to get vast entourages of visiting foreigners ourselves. Have you not heard? The Great Council of Churches is moving from Ferrara to Florence at Cosimo's private expense. Cosimo wants the panel quickly and he thinks that two of us working together will do it in half the time.'

Filippo laughed, then he asked Giovanni why the Medici were particularly associated with the Magi. 'The Company of the Magi seems to consist of the richest and most powerful men of the city, with the Medici at the head of them.'

'The Magi were philosopher kings who ruled their lands with wisdom. That's one thing. The other is that these great men fell down and worshipped Truth in the form of an innocent baby, born in a stable! It means that however rich and powerful a man may be, he should kneel before the Lord. Surrender himself. I think this is what appeals to Cosimo: the reminder that he needs to prostrate himself before the Lord.'

'That's the meaning of the word Islam: to yield.'

'Is it? How do you know that?'

'Oh, I was a slave in Barbary for two years.'

While Fra Giovanni looked at him doubtfully, Filippo closed his eyes and for a moment he felt the sand sharp in his nose and smelt the scent of jasmine. Here he was, home where he had dreamed of being whilst in Ifriqiya: here he was, in Florence, in lush Tuscany, working with Fra Giovanni – no less – on a large circular panel filled with representations of human and animal forms. Oh bliss! So why, for this moment, did he ache for the desert?

'I want to hear all about it, but later,' said Fra Giovanni, as if he were pacifying a lunatic. He told Filippo that on the dormitory floor of the monastery, Cosimo had a cell of his own. 'He comes here regularly – at least once a week, sometimes more often – and he spends hours in his cell in prayer and reflection. He's asked me to decorate it. In each cell I'm doing a scene from the Life and Passion of Christ but for Cosimo I'm doing an Adoration of the Magi. Or, that is, my assistant Benozzo will be. Whenever Cosimo wants something, he has to have it at once. Have you noticed? I told him I can't do it at once, not when he also wants me to do this tondo at once. He looked at me as if I had failed him utterly. But I don't hold it against him: it's a mere foible. If the Magi represent those who seek wisdom, Cosimo is one of them.'

'What are you saying? That he is a magus?'

'Not a magician so much as a seeker of wisdom. He can build libraries and commission books much more easily than he can succour the poor or found hospitals. It's just the way he is.'

'Wisdom is for pagans and Jews. What wisdom do we need when we have the faith?'

'Can we have faith without wisdom? Yes, but it is a dangerous thing, where men kill one another for what they believe. Faith and wisdom are like two wings, and a bird needs both to fly. What the story of the magi represents is that seekers of wisdom, or philosophers, can get close to the goal of their quest, but the last step is surrender to faith. There are plenty in this town who, with their images of the Virgin and Child, are men of faith; there are few who are men of wisdom, and we can recognise them by the image of the magus. Cosimo is chief amongst them. Do you think he's offered to host the Great Council because he wants unity between the Latin and Greek churches? Or because he wants immortal fame? Or to assure himself a place in heaven? No. He'd like all those things, of course, but the real reason is that he's fascinated by the theologians and philosophers in the entourage of the emperor, particularly those who have studied Plato and Aristotle. And chief among the Greek philosophers is one they call "Plethon" – the new Plato.'

'I've heard of him. A queer fish by all accounts. A pagan, they say. A heretic. Worships the sun and writes hymns to Zeus.'

'The cost of bringing the Council here is beyond counting, and Cosimo is paying for it all simply to bring Plethon here. Plethon, to Cosimo, is a magus, a magus of the line of the Magi, which runs back to the beginning of time.'

Filippo looked questioningly at Giovanni.

'What is it?'

'Suddenly you don't sound like a Dominican.'

'Why, because I speak of ancient philosophy? Does that make me a pagan heretic? Not so far as I'm concerned, nor Cosimo. That's the point of the Magi, that's what they represent: the union of wisdom and faith. I've heard that Plato prayed to a trinity of Truth, Goodness and Beauty. What kind of Christian would denounce such a philosophy? Remember what Ghiberti said at the symposium: a painter should ennoble his mind with philosophy. I've been trying to do that.'

'I don't know what Ghiberti said, I wasn't there.' Filippo, roughing out a design in charcoal, sniffed. 'My genius,' he said, 'is native.'

'As is your pride.' Fra Giovanni nudged him and Filippo's charcoal line slipped. They grinned at each other and went back to work.

7

THE TURKS WERE PRESSING ON CONSTANTINOPLE; IF the ancient city were to fall, it would be the end of Greece and the Greek Church. The emperor had applied to the pope for help but the pope had said that, before such aid could be granted, the Greek and Latin churches, which had been separate for centuries, must reunite under the papacy. So Greece had a choice: submit to the pope or die. A Great Council of Churches had been convened in Ferrara but, in playing host to the extravagant Greek emperor, the city had soon run out of money and patience. Everyone believed that the Council was doomed until Cosimo de' Medici offered to host it in Florence at his own expense.

The Greeks had been arriving in the city since early February – men in exotic dress speaking an unintelligible language who filled the piazzas of the great churches, Santa Maria Novella, Santa Croce, the Duomo itself. Now, a fortnight later, Emperor John Palaeologus was due. In the streets and squares of Florence there were crowds of men dressed in the glittering court costumes of Byzantium – dark Greeks, swarthy Greeks, bearded Greeks, Greeks with long plaits down their backs, or plaits in their beards, golden earrings and thumb rings; Greeks with bushy eyebrows and faces eroded by the sun; Greeks in tall hats, conical hats, squashy hats, hats like crooked drainpipes. Accompanied by the Patriarch of Constantinople, Emperor John rode into the city at the head of a vast entourage. Cosimo, mounted on a humble mule, awaited him at the Duomo.

The brim of the emperor's hat was in the shape of a boat, with a great dome for a crown, topped with a glowing ruby. He wore a robe of crimson over a doublet of green damask; the low winter sun glanced off this small man with sloping shoulders in a thousand particles of dancing light. Beside him rode the patriarch, robed in black, his hat holding his hood above his head by half a braccia's length. As bearded as Byzantium, both men rode as the representatives not just of a country but of an ancient culture of labyrinthine complexity, a Christian culture that had been sorely tried by its Latin brother, that had been the victim of the Fourth Crusade and would never have countenanced reunification of the churches had not a greater enemy presented itself in the form of the Turks. And so they rode into Florence, their pride and hurt as hard as jewels, determined to make negotiations difficult though without failing in the end to reach an agreement.

Cosimo tried not to appear nervous. Why should he be nervous? He was richer than emperor and patriarch put together; probably richer than the whole court. He presumed that, with so much wealth displayed upon their persons, they'd left nothing at home. Yes, that was the way of the wise man: portable treasure. He straightened his spine, summoned his ingrained Tuscan republicanism, reminded himself how many kings and princes he had on his ledgers, raised his chin and waited. When, led by a procession of chanting priests, the emperor and patriarch appeared, Cosimo was overcome by sticky heat despite the chill winds of January. The Emperor of Constantinople! The last emperor of the Roman Empire! Suddenly he was a child again and in Ravenna with his father telling him the history of Byzantium through the mosaics of Sant' Apollinare, with all those large-eyed figures in togas wearing crowns like chandeliers.

When the emperor finally came into view, the ground seemed to tilt and Cosimo realized he was close to fainting. He grasped the pommel of his saddle and held on to the present moment. This was just a man in fantastic garb with a hat as big as a ship. He must not be swayed! *Remember, remember*, he told himself, *I am the host here, and he is the guest. Be gracious. Be patronising. Put him in his place.* That's what the mule was for, to disarm the Greeks.

Ferrara had warned Florence that the Greeks had wagons laden with their own herbs and oils, for they could not tolerate food cooked in the Italian way. The Ferrarese also said that, for all their carts of books and codices, the Greeks would frequently be sending back home for more, for delay in Byzantium was all but a sacred rite. They had found the Greeks an impossible strain, but Cosimo would endure it, and not entirely for the sake of church unity either.

Cosimo's mule was good – wouldn't move if the ground shook under her. Accompanied by his sons and the leading citizens of Florence, he sat watching the approach of these wise men from the East, who came with their secretaries and scribes, their tyros and their neophytes, carrying impressive loads of books and scrolls that would win for them the age-old argument that had riven the Church in two.

The Greeks claimed, with pride that towered higher than Babel, that they were the true inheritors of the original church. When they used a prefix meaning 'through' then 'through' was what they meant. 'From' was just a loose and erroneous Latin translation of the *original Greek*, for the New Testament had been written in their own language, and who could say better what it meant than they? So the Son came *through* the Father and not *from* him. And on this they were going to debate daily from dawn to sunset with such self-assurance as to make the Latins quiver with doubt.

Cosimo had in his party Ambrogio Traversari, prior of Camaldoli, who had the wit and knowledge to convince the Greeks that essentially they were all saying the same thing. These subtleties of language would not be easily conveyed in translation, but happily Traversari was fluent in Greek, while his chief opponent, Bishop Bessarion, was just as fluent in Latin.

67

Cosimo sat with his peers and companions, a group David as a group Goliath approached. Gold-glittering and cymbal-playing Byzantium twinkled and crashed along the streets and finally emerged into the piazza San Giovanni. Cosimo did not quail. Back straight, head held high, he rode out to meet Emperor John Palaeologus. 'Just a man,' he told himself, 'the same as I, except that I am not deluded into thinking anything else of myself.'

He welcomed the Greeks to Florence. The Emperor Palaeologus, he thought, was rather short.

✝

They worked together cheek to cheek, Fra Giovanni on the right side of the design, Fra Filippo on the left, drawing a crowded Nativity with all characters arriving at once, the beasts and the shepherds, the neophytes, the Three Magi followed by a vast entourage that receded into the distance, and a train of onlookers coming down from Jerusalem. Fitting a design into a circle was difficult enough working alone: working as some monstrously fused twin it became more and more impossible the closer they approached the centre. Sometimes Filippo was so absorbed by his work that he forgot Giovanni's presence, but more often he was distracted by Giovanni's hands, their trimmed nails so thoroughly clean, the skin unstained by pigment. Then he felt jangled by his proximity to one so pure and began to worry if he had bad breath or nits.

In the entourage of the emperor came the philosopher called George Gemistos Plethon who, people said, was not a Christian. He had been born a Christian but with all his philosophising had become pagan. Such were the exotic sights to be seen in the city that sometimes Filippo spent all day trying to reach San Marco and never arriving. One day, having heard about Plethon, he became obsessed with the need to see him and toured the city looking for the Apollo-worshipping heretic. Plethon, he thought, must surely have a stubby horn on his head, long, curling finger-nails and a plaited beard, but he met no one of that description.

At the Baptistry he saw Brunelleschi and Donatello standing with Ghiberti, watching the exotic passers-by. He realized with a pang that, had he attended Cosimo's symposium three years earlier, he could have joined them as a friend if not an equal. Now he was condemned to walk by with a mere nod of acknowledgement. As he passed, he overheard Ghiberti saying that he had dined with Plethon the previous evening.

On the Via Larga, Filippo saw Bishop Bessarion strolling with Ambrogio Traversari and was struck by how the Greek gazed upon the prior of the Camaldolese Order with an expression of respect bordering on adoration. He followed them to see if they would lead him to Plethon but they led him only to the house of the Medici.

He turned back, remembering having seen the shop of a cloth merchant near San Lorenzo. Fra Giovanni was adamant that the way to achieve unity in the picture was to dress all characters alike and he was allowing only four colours, with no fancy brocades or velvets. Filippo loved fabrics and liked to treat himself to one or two lengths of something luxurious at the beginning of each project – less a prop than a self-indulgence – although he always used it as a prop.

He went into the shop of Francesco Buti under the sign of the weaving shuttle and breathed in the warmth of his pleasure. He ran his hand over griccia velvets and damasks, his senses quivering at the softness, smoothness, roughness, woodiness and silkiness of whatever he touched. What must it be like to wear such stuff, to have it next to your skin? The merchant, occupied with a customer, kept looking at the friar suspiciously.

'I intend to buy,' Filippo assured him. He went to the silks. His kings and their entourages might be reduced in colour and ostentation, nevertheless, what they wore should still be the best and nothing flowed into folds like silk. He picked up a roll, unravelled it, bunched the length with his left hand and shook it so that its fineness shimmered in front of his eyes, catching the light like dragonfly wings. He imagined it made into a blue gown adorning a kneeling figure, the yoke perhaps embroidered in golden thread...

'Can I help you, Brother?' Francesco Buti demanded.

'How much is this?'

'Three florins a braccia length.'

Filippo felt the colour drain from his face. 'Do you have any samples or remnants?'

Francesco Buti sniffed and pointed to a large basket. 'You can search in there if you like and see what you can find.'

'It's for the church, you understand.'

'Is it?'

'I'm painting an altarpiece for San Marco.'

Francesco looked at the Carmelite's habit doubtfully but said, in that case, he could take one remnant of his choice without payment.

Fra Filippo knelt by the basket and began to rummage, his hands tickled, stroked and brushed by the fabrics he sifted through, feeling for silk. As he searched, a child of about five crawled silently out from under the merchant's bench and came up to the basket. She gripped its rim and, with her chin resting on her hands, watched the friar with wide, serious eyes.

'What are you looking for?' she whispered.

'Blue silk, like that up there on the roll.'

'Yes, we have it.' She up-ended like a pearl diver, going head first into the basket to emerge in a moment with her treasure. 'Here you are. Chinese blue. It's our most expensive.'

'It's for one of the Three Kings.'

The child pouted. 'He should be in brocade,' she said.

✝

By the time Filippo arrived at the San Marco workshop everyone was cleaning tools and equipment after a long day's work. 'Sorry – I got distracted,' he said, thumbing through his notebook.

Fra Giovanni looked at him mildly. 'As painters it behoves us to observe nature at first hand,' he said. 'But as friars, we must

70

learn to withdraw from the world and its sensations. It's difficult for us, but it's what makes us special.'

Fra Giovanni's speaking of 'we' and 'us' seeped into Fra Filippo's soul as water to the roots of a plant. He resolved to be on time the following day, but the next morning his path was crossed by a party of mule-mounted, astrolabe- and quadrant-carrying astrologers, one of whom had a pet leopard. He saw the grave, unsmiling apprentice, Benozzo, in the crowd of staring onlookers, drawing the leopard in his notebook. 'Fra Giovanni is not well today,' Benozzo told Filippo. 'So I thought I would do as you do.'

✝

The following day, they were ready to begin painting. Fra Giovanni swilled his brush in a pot of terra verte and, throwing back his sleeve, took the brush to the panel and let it alight there with all the delicacy of a butterfly landing on a flower. 'Each time we put the brush to the surface,' he said, 'it is an act done in love of God.' Fra Filippo suddenly discovered that it was he who was crying as Fra Giovanni began work.

A question neither had asked aloud began to throb in the air between them: which of them would paint the Virgin? Both knew better than to claim the honour for himself, so it became a competition in generosity. 'I think you should paint the Virgin.' 'No, no, your skills are so superior to mine. It has to be you.' So it went on day after day, to the growing irritation of the assistants and apprentices, the brushes of Filippo and Giovanni edging ever closer to the centre as they painted their multitude of figures, each thinking always of that one figure at the heart of the painting.

When they argued, it was about other things, and they argued most spectacularly about halos. Filippo told Giovanni that he should not paint halos like golden platters behind – or, worse, in front of – the heads of saints. 'How then should I paint them?' asked Fra Giovanni, aggrieved.

'Foreshortened and transparent, as Masaccio did. So if, as with Saint Joseph here, you have a three-quarter profile, the halo should match.'

'That's ridiculous!'

'Golden platters are ridiculous! Have you ever seen one on a saint?'

'I've never seen a saint.'

'Then come to the Carmine. We have many.'

'Light,' said Fra Giovanni, suddenly authoritative and much more a painter than a friar, 'light flows in all directions at once. If you paint halos in perspective, then what you are saying is that halos are physical objects like golden platters, that can turn this way and that. But radiance is uniform, however a head turns.' As an illustration, he took a lighted candle and, though he held it in a variety of ways, the flame always remained upright and leaf-shaped.

Filippo, on behalf of Masaccio, was mortified. He flew out of the workshop and refused to return for days. 'Sometimes,' he said, when he did return – to find that in his absence Fra Giovanni had painted the figure of the Virgin – 'we must show reality by creating illusion. You are right about radiance, but I am right that halos should obey the laws of perspective. For what reason? None except that it *looks* more real. It's the same at the edges of a painting: if you carry perspective right to the edges, you lose the illusion of reality.' He wanted to say that, by this law of the illusion of reality, you must never have a saint facing into his halo, but he had no wish to further hurt or dismay Fra Giovanni. 'You must always trust the judgement of your eyes and stay true to the laws of perception. She's beautiful,' he said, seating himself in front of the panel and gazing on the delicate Virgin.

'You're not angry? She was on my side, you see, more to the right than in the centre.'

'So she was.'

Fra Giovanni hung his head. 'I have done wrong. I told myself that you might not return, but it was a lie. I knew you would.'

'What were we supposed to do? Rope our brushes together and paint as if running in a three-legged race? No, I'm glad you've done her. She's beautiful.' *In a completely remote, transcendent kind of way,* Filippo thought, but he did not want another argument about reality.

8

WHEN FRA GIOVANNI WAS SUDDENLY CALLED TO ROME to work on a commission for the pope, Fra Filippo completed the panel by himself. He drew a dog in the foreground – a Domini Cane, hound of the Lord – to show who deserved the credit for the painting.

Before leaving the workshop at San Marco for the last time, he contrived to lose his way in the cloisters and find himself mounting the stairs to the dormitory cells. He was discovered there, peering through low doors, by a diminutive friar with a thin-lipped smile on a kindly face.

'Are you lost, Brother-Painter?'

'No,' said Filippo. 'I wanted to see the paintings in the cells.'

'Access to this floor is closed to all but the friars of San Marco.'

'And Cosimo de' Medici,' Filippo added, so quickly that the Dominican flushed.

The friar, who introduced himself as Antonino, Little Anthony, recovered, smiled and took his Carmelite brother by the arm. 'You are right. Why shouldn't you see them? Although there is nothing in the cells yet, apart from some sinopia drawings. The fresco in Cosimo's own cell, down there at the end, is nearly complete – an Adoration of the Magi – but Cosimo is in occupation at the moment.' A slight narrowing of the eyes – so slight perhaps no one else would notice, but Filippo was alive to such nuances: the Dominican did not approve of a layman having a cell, however exalted he was. A slight flinch that said, 'discipline is what is required, not a room to pray in.'

Antonino led Filippo to the new library, a vaulted room of three aisles of considerable length, supported by a graceful arcade of slender, Ionic columns. Benches had been installed, filling the air with the fragrance of cypress wood, but there were no books yet.

'It will be a library open to all, not just the friars, and men will be able to study theology, law, Greek and Roman literature, devotional works and poetry in the vernacular. It's Cosimo's wish that it be a public library, and not what he calls "confined" to theology.' Again that spit in the tone that left Filippo in no doubt as to what Fra Antonino thought of this. 'Pagan and Christian knowledge will be what he calls "equally available and without censure".' The friar sighed. 'What are your views, Brother, about all this eager study of the Romans? Have they forgotten who persecuted Our Lord? Now we are encouraged to extol the virtues of that oppressive empire. Fine buildings and sculptures! What are they compared with the Gospels? What truth do they convey? These men kneel before Trajan's column, that spiralling sculpture depicting slavery, as if it were an altar. Indeed, say "altar" to them and they think immediately of the Ara Pacis of Augustus. That's where they say their prayers. They treat their faith not as a belief but as something to *think* about, even *question*. It is not real for them. Not real. When they say they are going to Rome, is it to see the shrine of Saint Peter? No, it is to study pagan images. What would Our Lord say to that?'

Filippo knew who 'they' were: Cosimo and his favoured scholars and artisans – Alberti, Donatello, Ghiberti, Brunelleschi. The short friar, becoming increasingly splenetic the longer they stayed in the library, led them back to the corridor and took Filippo to a window to look down on the graceful cloisters that, despite being inspired by the architecture of pre-Christian civilisation, met with the Dominican's approval.

'Michelozzo bows to the new style, but he's no slavish copier of the past. Some say Cosimo appointed him architect instead of Brunelleschi because he is more tractable,' said the Dominican.

'What do you mean?'

'More open to Cosimo's ideas and willing to do what he's told. But in my opinion he is indeed the better architect and that's why Cosimo commissioned him.'

Filippo reeled.

'Have I shocked you? Then I'm sorry. Ignore me. I'm a philistine. But you know, to me a man's style is a man's nature. A bad man cannot produce good architecture, and Brunelleschi is a brute.'

'Vain, perhaps, and self-important. But a brute?' Filippo grinned.

'Use your eyes.'

Filippo looked around him. Whatever the truth was, Fra Antonino was right about the quality of this work of Michelozzo's. The rebuilt monastery had become a place of sweetness and simplicity – the extraordinary simplicity of obedience to the Rule. Filippo suffered an attack of envy, so sudden and severe that it gave him a pain; he had to sit down on a bench below the window and rub his burning gullet, thinking unhappily of that image of Giotto's in Padua, of the snake coming out of Envy's mouth to twist back and bite her. How ridiculous, to envy obedient men.

Fra Antonino sat down close to him. He had high bones over cheeks sucked in by hunger, a living head impatient to be a skull. 'If you don't mind me saying so, if you were in this order you would not suffer from indigestion.' His eyes rested on Filippo's belly. 'The Carmelites have become lax.'

'On the contrary, all our disciplines are being renewed. I am the one who has become lax, living as I do outside the Carmine.'

Fra Antonino raised one eyebrow almost imperceptibly. 'Outside? What do you mean?'

'I am not a friar by choice, as Fra Giovanni is. I was dumped in the Carmine as a child. My prior recognised my difficulties and gave me permission to live the life of a painter.'

'The life of a hypocrite more like! Renounce your vows, Brother, if they mean nothing to you.'

'Oh, but they do mean something to me. I love the monastic life, I aspire to the Rule, but I fail daily and I cannot live with that. If I wore a hair shirt it would torment me less than my conscience. If I were to put some cakes on a table and lock you in a room with them, they would still be there in the morning. Lock me up with them, and they wouldn't be. They wouldn't last the hour. Indeed, I would eat them straight away to avoid all that struggle with failure as the only certain outcome.'

'So you suffer from weakness of will, that's all. The troubles of our bodies often have their roots in the soul. Do you garden? Have you ever struggled to draw out a long tap root without breaking it? Fennel, say, or dandelion?'

'I've never gardened.'

'Oh, you should. Weeding is a lesson in the life of the spirit. There's nothing worse than a broken tap root for your efforts, for what is left, seated so deep within the unyielding soil, will sprout again with renewed vigour. So it is with our vices. Having identified them, we need to uproot them. We do not always succeed but we must try and, if we fail, then we must do some strenuous work with a sharp spade.'

The friar said this with such relish that Filippo drew back.

From along the corridor came the sound of intoned prayer – or was it an incantation? The two friars glanced at each other, puzzled. Then Antonino arose, brushed himself down as if steeling himself for war, and walked off purposefully towards the end of the corridor. He looked in at the last cell on the right. 'What is happening here?' he demanded.

'What is happening, Brother,' came Cosimo's gravelly voice, 'is that you are interrupting our prayers.'

'Prayers in *Greek*? This is a Dominican house!'

An old man left the cell, one of the Greek philosophers, saying in broken Italian that he had no wish to be the cause of strife. He came along the corridor, remarkably upright for one in his eighties, and Filippo found himself in the green-eyed stare of a man whom he knew in his gut to be Plethon. As he had hoped, Plethon had a long grey beard forked and plaited but, in the face of that stare, it seemed a petty detail. It was the eyes that struck him. It was like being studied by an angel and found wanting.

In the cell, Cosimo and Antonino were arguing. 'I will not be spoken to like this! Fetch the prior!'

'The prior does not have the courage to speak the truth to you!'

'And you do, do you?'

'My faith gives me strength, my Lord supports me.'

'How dare you invade my private cell? Do you know how much money I've spent on this place?'

'You may rule the prior through dependency, but not me. I embrace poverty.'

'Of course you do, fed and clothed as you are by my money!'

'Your profits from usury you mean,' Antonino flung behind him as he came out of the cell. When he rejoined Filippo he was wearing that sweet, imperturbable smile again. 'Oh,' he said, 'I wish the Lord would not test me so.' He took Filippo by the arm and led him away. 'Stay pure, Brother. It is by far the easiest course. Do not let your humours become muddled. What happens when you mix too many pigments? – they go brown. They lose their purity. To reach God, we must not sully the colours. Innocence and purity – they are our armour against the Evil One.'

✝

When Fra Filippo went to the casa de' Medici to see the Adoration of the Magi hung upon the wall of the main sala he was a calmer, quieter man with clean fingernails and a tendency to pray before he began work each day. His choice of colours had changed and he no longer painted strongly like Masaccio, but gently, like Fra Giovanni. Cosimo stood gazing at the tondo.

'I did the left side,' said Filippo.

'I know. I can tell. Your figures have died,' said Cosimo. 'Where's the life? In Padua I told you to paint from life. Giotto's goat, remember?'

It was true: Filippo had forgotten. Although he had been out in the streets sketching, he had not let these studies inform his work. What madness! Was it for that reason that no one had said anything about him assisting Fra Giovanni with the walls of San Marco?

After several days of such ill humour that he did not even speak, much less pray, Filippo went out into the marketplace and renewed his practice of observation, of seeing how this man sat and that one stood; how a mother held her baby; how light modelled an elderly face. He had spent nearly a year with Fra Giovanni, fretting that he could not draw hands (he hid them up sleeves whenever he could), when even in his miniature paintings Fra Giovanni could display the full range of human emotion through gesture. Now Filippo forgot hands as he returned to his practice of seeing souls betrayed by their bodies. 'Be yourself,' Cosimo had counselled sternly, and Fra Filippo's figures sprang back to life.

When the prior of San Marco died suddenly the pope asked Fra Giovanni to take the position but he refused, saying that Little Anthony was a better man by far. Fra Giovanni came back to Florence with his reputation much enhanced by his humility. Filippo went to San Marco to see him. Fra Giovanni looked, if anything, sweeter and said how content he was to serve Prior Antonino, 'who is so much better fitted for the job than I.' He said he desired but one thing these days: simplicity. 'I've been offered a fresco cycle in a chapel of Santo Stefano at Prato but I've refused it.'

Filippo cleared his throat. 'Are they still looking for someone?' he asked, nonchalantly.

'No, the commission has gone to Paolo Uccello.'

Filippo let fly with a quiverful of abusive and destructive criticism of Uccello's skills and the commissioning panel's ability to see. Fra Giovanni staggered backwards in shock.

'I had no idea you wanted the job, or how much.'

'Why should you? You are removed from the need to earn,' said Filippo, bitter with resentment.

'My friend,' Giovanni advised him, 'always be content with what you are given and never long for anything else. Believe me, God knows what is best for you.'

'And that's how Brunelleschi came to design and build the dome, is it?' Filippo stormed from the workshop, relishing the sound of a slammed door in the otherwise silent cloisters.

9

THE GREEKS FINALLY LEFT FLORENCE, A UNITY BETWEEN the churches achieved, though one that did not survive their journey back to Greece. By the time they were home, all was as it had been before they set out, but Cosimo was not disappointed. The Greeks must take the fate that awaited them, but he had achieved what he'd desired: the university was now well stocked with Greek scholars, some of whom were teaching the ancient form of Greek to the Italians. Plethon remained behind to lecture on Plato. Everything that Cosimo had hoped for when he offered to host the ruinously expensive council had been achieved. Florence, often called 'The New Rome' was on her way to becoming 'The New Athens'.

From many conversations with Plethon and with Leon Battista Alberti, Cosimo now knew what he wished to create, but he also knew it inwardly – as if it had been written into him, into his marrow – the idea of the new Platonic Academy. This was his life's work – the bank, merely a means to that end. Plethon confirmed it. Plethon, with Traversari as interpreter, had taught Cosimo what he knew of Platonic wisdom that could not be spoken of from university lecterns: the secret wisdom of the ages, taught by a line of wise men going back so far that Plato seemed a recent addition.

It was in Cosimo's cell in San Marco that Plethon had initiated him into the Mysteries in a secret rite, of which the Dominicans were oblivious.

When Plethon left to return to Greece he took Cosimo's hand, turned it palm upward and placed his own palm upon it. His green eyes held Cosimo's steadily. 'I pass to you the wisdom,' he said. 'I pass to you the crown and sceptre. Greece is destroyed. Let her be reborn here in Florence.'

Plethon was old. No matter that he seemed to be drinking the elixir of youth: Cosimo knew they would never meet again – not in this realm under the moon.

✠

Filippo had not intended to slam the door on friendship, but it was to be many years before he saw Giovanni again. For six of those years Giovanni worked single-mindedly on the frescoes in the cells of San Marco, received no visitors and was rarely seen on the streets. Filippo meant to write to him but was always busy with work himself, commissions for panels and altarpieces coming to him steadily now that he had dropped his clumsy imitations of Masaccio. One, an altarpiece for the church of Sant' Ambrogio, was an important commission and at the start of it he resolved to live a clean and orderly life, but he found that the more he drew back the bow of restraint, the faster flew the arrow of desire.

Taverns and brothels surrounding the Carmine too often prevented Filippo reaching his mother church. The more he thought about the visionary ecstasies of his brethren, the more he sought his own in his own way. Each time he set out to attend Mass, he failed to arrive. One tavern, the Lion Rampant, he visited under the pretence that it was a necessary part of business: frame-makers of the Santo Spirito district met there and if he could get one drunk he could get a good price, better than the one he'd quoted to the patron. Given the iniquity of frames costing more than paintings, he saw no reason why he should not make a margin of profit on the transaction. Next door to the Lion Rampant was the Lion Supine, that house of pleasure where women could make a man forget himself. If Filippo could ever pass the Lion Rampant, he rarely succeeded in passing the Lion Supine. And this, too, he justified as work, for a very pretty whore called Dianora was acting as a model for him.

In the great altarpiece he was doing for Sant' Ambrogio, she played the part of Saint Theopista, an obscure early Christian, wife of a Roman cavalry officer, a minor figure, but with her ringlets of fair hair and cherubic face done very carefully from life, she drew every devout eye away from the coronation of the Virgin by God. Men who came to see the work in progress winked at one another and whispered *Dianora*.

As the whispers made their way around the city, the Sant' Ambrogio altarpiece, which in all other respects was a master-work, became equated by the pious with scandal. Filippo ended each modelling session by ravishing the girl on her mucky bed, pounding at her until she screamed for him to stop, which in his view was most unprofessional of her. But it was an ecstatic release for him after work and for her a cure for any false identification with sainthood.

Whenever Fra Filippo tried to get from his house to his church and failed, he told himself he suffered from weakness of will. One day he tried going in a different direction and found himself at San Marco's. He asked at the gate for Fra Giovanni but was told that he was in Rome, working on frescoes in Saint Peter's. Filippo sniffed: there was nothing quite like the odour of sanctity to get up his nose and make him sneeze.

·'Is that Fra Filippo?' asked Prior Antonino, straightening from his work on the border of the cloister garden.

When he approached his fellow friar, Filippo found that Antonino reeked of the peppery smell of marigolds and then he did sneeze.

'Uh!' he said. 'What's good for the bees is not good for me.'

Prior Antonino smiled. 'Will you join me in some refreshment?'

Filippo entered the garden cautiously. Whatever Antonino meant by 'refreshment', it would not come out of a jug pulled dripping from a barrel. 'When did Giovanni go to Rome?'

'A few years ago.'

'How long before he returns?'

'A few years yet, I believe.'

They sat together on the low cloister wall and, as Filippo had feared, shared some dandelion cordial.

'It's excellent for the liver,' said Antonino. 'A purifier and a diuretic.'

'I have no need for a diuretic. If anything I need its opposite.'

'But from what I hear you could do with some purification, eh? Filippo, is it true you are using whores to model for holy figures?'

'Who else can I use? No decent woman would model for a painter.'

'Why do you need a model? Sacred art uses divine archetypes.'

'Cosimo insists on it. It is my direction in life, to imitate nature.'

'Nature? That wanton! You imitate her far too well! I shall give you a new direction: praise God and respect his holy saints.'

Filippo inhaled sharply, jumped to his feet and declared he was sitting in the path of ants. 'They're biting me!'

'That's your conscience.'

'What, biting my arse?'

'Filippo, God speaks through me, I know it. How long is His patience, I wonder?'

'Infinite, I trust, like His mercy and forgiveness.'

Prior Antonino looked at him with a steely gaze – that bright, metallic light of ascetic righteousness. 'Reform, Brother, before you are reformed.'

'What do you mean?'

'If a man takes control of himself, it is far less painful than God's punishment for sin. Reflect on that.'

Incensed, Filippo said that he would not be spoken to that way by one who was his equal.

'*Equal?*' Now Antonino was outraged. 'There is no equality between us. We could not even be weighed with the same set of weights.'

Filippo grinned, believing he had revealed hubris in the holy prior, but two days later, when he heard that Antonino had just been appointed the new archbishop of Florence, he blanched with embarrassment.

✝

Fra Giovanni returned from Rome to take up the position of prior of the Dominican mother house on the slopes of Fiesole. He had resisted the appointment, made by the archbishop, but was eventually persuaded that it was God's will.

Filippo was called to visit him. It was hot and he toiled on foot up the hill, though glad to be out of the city and on his way to see Giovanni again. He arrived weary but smiling and rang the monastery bell. The place was silent except for bird-cheep and the bell sounded very loud. Admitted by a shy novice, Filippo was shown to the prior's cell.

As usual, in giving up everything to do the work of the Lord, Giovanni had been given much in return: a clean cell sweet-smelling of wax polish that overlooked a garden watered by hidden springs and lush even in the height of summer. Dark cypresses and laurels stood out against the sky, lemon trees grew in large terracotta pots and lilies bloomed in stone urns. The spicy scents of the bee-tickled herbs – rosemary, thyme and oregano – wafted into the room on waves of birdsong through an open door.

Fra Filippo looked on it all in dismay. His workshop in Florence was dark and grubby and had become festooned with cobwebs. His life was dedicated to painting: what need did he have of thrushes and squirrels and lilies that smelt like paradise? Somehow, dimly, he had expected Fra Giovanni to look the same and be the same as he had known him at the time of the Great Council, instead he found in him a prior conscious of his role and authority. The dimples had been displaced by the severe and prominent features of the ascetic, his cheekbones pushing like rock through the soft undulations of youth.

'I have seen your *Coronation of the Virgin*, Brother,' Giovanni said. 'Colour confined to pink, blue and gold, halos like golden platters. I could have painted it myself.'

Filippo shifted uncomfortably. Cosimo had stormed at him when he'd seen it, had told him to stop pretending he was Fra Giovanni.

'Truly it is your masterwork. Very fine, indeed. A mystery.'

'What is a mystery, Giovanni?'

'That a scoundrel can paint so divinely. I have heard the gossip about your night life yet you still live as a friar and even enjoy a benefice. You're the rector of San Quirico. Is that true?'

'Gossip is gossip, Giovanni. I live outside the Carmine and rarely go there, even as an occasional visitor. The friars are all become mad. Did you not hear of the apparition of Fra Andrea Corsini?'

Giovanni smiled. 'Of course, I was still in Florence when that happened. Directly after the Council, was it not?'

'Those half-starved holy men with their brains addled by prayer claimed to see the saintly Andrea, come amongst us once again as a prophet.'

'Prophesying that the Florentines were going to win a great battle against the Milanese at Anghiari.' Giovanni nodded soberly.

'The spectre even gave the date – June 29th.'

'And it turned out to be true.'

'Meh! It was a self-fulfilling prophecy that gave our army the impetus it needed. And, now that the pope has sanctioned an official cult of Fra Andrea Corsini, the Carmine attracts pilgrims. You can sit there smiling, Giovanni, in that supercilious fashion, as if I am the fool who must surely come to his senses one day, but I know stagecraft when I see it. I became so distressed – I cannot abide spiritual hypocrisy – that Cosimo arranged for me to detach from the Carmine, to be rector at San Quirico and, lately, chaplain at San Niccolò de' Freri.'

'A convent?' Fra Giovanni's eyebrows dipped.

'The young ladies are safe with me.'

'If you are as a frequent a visitor at San Niccolò as you are at San Quirico, they are very safe indeed.'

'As a friar-painter, I cannot beg for alms. I'm not provided for by the Carmine, as you are by San Marco. How am I supposed to live?'

'Honestly. As a friar, you are supposed to live honestly.'

Fra Filippo shifted uncomfortably; he had no wish for a fellow painter to start giving him spiritual advice, even if he were a prior; he needed to move the conversation away from himself, and quickly. 'What are you working on?' he asked.

'I have renounced painting. My duties here do not allow time for it. The pope asked me to give my talent back to God. I did so – and He kept it.' Fra Giovanni smiled wanly. 'My work at San Marco is finished. I've done an altarpiece for the church here. There is nothing left for me to do, at least, not here. So be it.'

Fra Filippo leaned forward on the wooden slatted seat. 'Do not give up!'

'I am not giving up! I have neither the need nor the desire to put myself up for sale in the marketplace, so I wait. If God needs my skill, he will tell me. If not…'

'This is the sound of a man giving up.'

'And you? What commissions do you have?'

'None at the moment. But I cannot rest on my laurels as you do. I live outside the Carmine, must pay the rent on my workshop, and pay my assistant. I have one now, you know, a young Carmelite called Diamante. By the time I've paid someone else to do my duties at San Quirico and San Niccolò, there is precious little left. So I knock on doors. I have to.'

Fra Giovanni looked on him with compassion. 'If you would allow God to rule your life rather than trying to govern it yourself, then –'

'Giovanni, do not preach.'

'Archbishop Antonino asked me to speak to you. He is indignant that you are making no effort to do your duties. He says it is the sin of hypocrisy. "Spiritual hypocrisy" were his precise words.' Giovanni smiled. 'He says it is not right that a friar should be so publicly sinful. He wants to know if you would agree to surrendering your benefices.'

'That's impossible. I would starve.'

'I was called to Prato two days ago to discuss another commission there. Once again I had to decline because of my duties here, which must come first, but this time I told them that I knew of another friar-painter, just as skilled.'

Filippo grew thoughtful. 'What is it? Is it lucrative?'

'It's the main chapel, in the choir of Santo Stefano. A fresco sequence is required.'

Filippo had not worked in fresco since his youth, when he made his first attempts to paint on the walls of the Carmine. 'How big is the chapel?'

'Large. Large enough to keep you out of trouble for years. I believe the commission is very lucrative indeed.'

'Do you think they would consider me?'

Fra Giovanni grinned suddenly, awakening the dimples. 'If I have any talent, it's in persuading others I am not the one they want. They wanted me to be archbishop, you know. Me! Archbishop! I had to apply all my skills to persuade the pope that Antonino was the better man.'

Filippo looked at Giovanni in admiration. Only he could speak so candidly without tainting his soul with the pitch of vanity. Antonino himself could not do it. There had been real pride behind his slapping down of Filippo as one who could not be weighed against him with the same set of weights. This was real humility – not a pretence of being less than others, but an ability to speak of oneself truly and with detachment.

'But I was not allowed to slip the hook completely. So here I am, prior.'

'It is God's will. Well, in truth, God wished you to be archbishop, but when you insisted on being only prior, he willed that instead.'

'You are incorrigible. Could you imagine me as an archbishop?' Giovanni threw back his head and laughed. 'Filippo, leave it to me – and to God – to arrange things at Prato but, if you take the commission, it is on condition that you resign that living at San Quirico. Agreed?'

'Agreed!'

10

THE GREEK COUNCIL HAD FAILED IN ITS OBJECTIVE, WHICH was to get the help of Rome in its battles with the infidel, and, fourteen years later, in the spring of 1453, all that Greece had dreaded came to pass when the Turks laid seige to Constantinople; in May they breached the city walls and swarmed in. For three days they slaughtered the Christians until finally the sultan commanded his men to stop. Amongst the dead in the streets, in the churches and the palaces were the Emperor Paleologus and many of his court. With the fall of Constantinople, the civilisation of Byzantium had come to an end.

When Cosimo received the news, he slumped in his chair. Tears welled in his eyes that Christendom should be so reduced. 'Do you realize,' he asked his sons, now grown men and fathers themselves, 'that this is not just the end of Greece but of the Roman Empire? We think that ended with the barbarian invasions, but the Empire was divided, and the Greek part survived until this week. This week! In my own lifetime the Roman Empire has come to its end. *Ohimè!*'

But through his tears he could not help wondering at the mystery of life. Like spring flowers in the rain were the thoughts of his collection of Greek manuscripts that he kept at San Marco. It even included a copy of the *Dialogues* of Plato, which Plethon had presented to him, although it may as well have been written in hieroglyphs for all that Cosimo could read it. Greece was dead – and born again in Florence.

Cosimo had found, in the son of Ficino, his physician, a young man capable of learning Greek and willing to devote his life to the task of translation. It would be long work and Cosimo was not going to rush anything: the Platonic Academy would be founded when the time was right, when the influence of the stars was more propitious. Right now the astrologers were warning of impending catastrophe, saying that the events in Byzantium were only the beginning. Christendom, they said, was under threat and needed to be renewed, strengthened from within, if it was to withstand the onslaught of the Turks.

Renewed from within: the very work the Platonic Academy had been conceived to do. According to Plethon Christianity had lost its way and needed to return to its original principles. So, Cosimo thought, we must begin the work now and not wait for better times. When things become very dark, that is the time to light a new candle. But it must not be rushed. He must bide his time. That was what astrologers were for, to find the propitious hour, not to scaremonger with prophecies of doom. He sighed. Sometimes it was difficult to distinguish between patience and procrastination, but young Ficino, he could read the heavens, he would know the best time. Cosimo must leave it to him.

✝

In the house of Francesco Buti, the wealthy silk merchant, his daughter of eighteen years was pulling a comb through the long, wavy hair of her thirteen-year-old sister. Together they were singing, as quietly as they could, a love sonnet that had been sung to them by a street poet beneath their window. Lucrezia had remembered the words and Spinetta the tune: now they were rehearsing what they had remembered, *sottovoce* so no one should overhear them.

> *But now I see full well how long I earned*
> *All men's reproof; and oftentime my soul*
> *Lies crushed by its own grief.*

They were together in the chamber recently appointed to Lucrezia. The two sisters, who had always shared a chamber, were on the threshold of a future that was going to separate them, for Lucrezia had recently been betrothed and would be moving to the house of her husband in due course. Her removal into a room of her own was the first act of severance in the coming separation. This thought made every moment exquisite for the sisters.

'I think –' Spinetta began but did not finish. A wave went through the floor as if the tiles had turned to water. There was a moment, a long moment, in which both of them thought many things before they knew for certain what was happening. Every ornament and object clattered and danced about on shelves. Glazed vases and Venetian glass fell from the credenza; a terracotta image of the Virgin and Child done in blue and white slid down the wall and exploded into dust; their bed trundled towards them. And then the screaming began, inside the house and out in the city, followed by a slow, continuous thunder of falling buildings.

✝

Cosimo was in the library at San Marco with Johannes Argyropulous, the scholar who was teaching Greek to Cosimo's young protégé, Marsilio Ficino. They were discussing what books could go out to Ficino on loan, and whether the Plato was too precious to be one of them. Cosimo had just decided that, in this instance, it could go out – indeed, he could present it as a gift to Ficino – when the monastery lurched like a ship. Spontaneously he grabbed the Plato and wrapped his mantle about it. The vaulted ceiling fell in great chunks knocking books from their shelves and buried Cosimo and Argyropulous under what was, since the fall of Constantinople, the largest collection of Greek manuscripts in the world. The bookcase that fell on them did them no harm and indeed protected them from the falling plaster and masonry as they huddled together in a pocket of space. When they were rescued by the friars, Cosimo embarrassed himself by weeping like a woman over the fate of his books, even though almost all of them were unharmed.

✝

In Prato, Fra Filippo Lippi was overseeing the erection of scaffolding in the chapel he was about to decorate. As the earth-wave from Florence rushed down the Arno valley, he was climbing the ladders to inspect the plaster of the vault, for it was looking crumbly and in need of repair. He was on the third and last ladder when the scaffolding wobbled like a drunk, its firm, straight poles becoming as limp as boiled pasta. He was simultaneously wondering what was wrong with him and grasping at anything to hold on to. By the time he'd realized it was an earthquake, he was dangling from a pole high in space with the plaster of the vaulting snowing down in flakes of pigment.

✝

Francesco Buti first made sure his family was safe, shepherding them all into a basement room that had suffered little damage. Then, telling his eldest son to take charge and keep the women calm, he went out to see if he could be of help to his neighbour. He never came back. A strong aftershock turned the neighbour's house into a pile of rubble, killing all inside.

Francesco's sons went out to find their father. His wife and daughters stayed indoors. They stayed there all night and into the following morning, then they, too, went out, to find their menfolk. They came upon the brothers digging in the rubble in vain hope of finding their father alive. With them, working with his bare hands, was a diminutive Dominican wearing his white gown with the sleeves rolled up, pulling building stone and great timber joists away as if he were three times his own weight and size. Lucrezia did not believe her brother when he told her it was the Archbishop of Florence.

☩

Filippo Lippi was finally persuaded to jump into a blanket held out by several men far below him.

☩

Cosimo de' Medici turned to the stoic philosophers for help in coping with the loss of two rare books in his wrecked library. After a short reading of Marcus Aurelius, he was back at San Marco and ordering an inventory to be made and plasterers to be hired to repair the vaulting in the library. Lucrezia Buti attended first the funeral of her father and then that of her betrothed who had also died in the quake, thrown into the river by a collapsing bridge. She returned to live in the house now belonging to the new head of the family, her brother, Antonio Buti.

☩

And in the Ognissanti district of Florence, the son of a tanner used the earthquake as an excuse not to attend school. It was a week before his father learnt that the schoolroom had been unaffected by the quake. The truant was beaten for his lies and made to tread hides in a trough of dog dung. 'If you don't go to school because you'd rather be a tanner, you may as well start now!' shouted his father.

11

THE CITY WAS BUSY WITH THE CLEARING OF DEBRIS AND the burial of the dead. Some houses were pulled down, others propped up by beams. It took over a week for the dust to settle and in that time the survivors went around either wearing linen masks or just choking and spluttering. Fires were built and lit in fields by the walls for the burning of ruined stuffs and the corpses of animals. Much had fallen, but one thing remained that gave them all hope. That the dome on the cathedral had withstood the quake convinced the Florentines at last of its permanence. It sat there now like a brood hen, giving the people comfort and restoring their faith. All would be well. Brunelleschi had gone to his grave six years previously without knowing the full depth of appreciation and gratitude felt by his fellow citizens for his achievement.

In the Buti household, what damage there had been was quickly cleared up and repaired. After the funeral of their father, Antonio Buti at once set about finding another husband for his sister, Lucrezia, because she would soon be nineteen, he said, almost too old and there could be no further delay. He was eager to get the expense of her out of his ledgers, even at the cost of a dowry. He had a wife and two children, with another on the way. There was no room in the Buti house for spinster sisters.

Antonio found amongst his friends a handsome young man and Lucrezia made no objection. With his long, lustrous hair, slim waist and slender legs, he was so handsome, and what is beautiful outside must surely be beautiful inside – how could it be otherwise? He had the eyes of a deer, soft, large, non-judgemental. He was kind to all things, especially to her. She loved to watch from the window as he walked down the street, mingling with the people yet isolated by his perfection. He owned the world. He owned her. They were betrothed.

On those frequent occasions when he joined the family for dinner, her body trembled under his gaze. Sensations ran through her, as if candles had been brought to corners never lit before. One night, however, he returned and climbed a ladder to her balcony, into her room and her bed. She had accepted him before she was fully awake. She awoke to his body, the warmth and naturalness of it. How could God-given love be wrong? They were betrothed. The worst they could be accused of, he said as she made a feeble protest, was impatience.

He came into her and she felt no pain, only rightness. The very rightness of him inside her. But when she awoke at dawn he had gone. She stretched and luxuriated in her bed, wishing to stay there all day, awaiting his return.

She was oblivious of everything but her dreams of love. There were distant howls in the house – there often were, faraway noises echoing in the courtyard. The clatter of a dropped cooking pan, the wail of a frustrated nephew, an argument between the brothers. The house was a world in itself and she lived in her part of it, not wishing to be disturbed.

A pitiful wailing and someone, a man, shouting. Spinetta was in trouble? Lucrezia pricked at the sound as one cat listens to the distress of another; listens then curls up again and returns to sleep. But Spinetta burst into her room, followed by their brother, Antonio.

'Tell her, you whore!' he shouted. 'Tell your sister what you've done with her betrothed!'

Spinetta fell sobbing to her knees at Lucrezia's feet, her hands together in prayer, imploring her as if she were a plaster saint. 'He forced me!' She was retching. 'He hurt me, Lucrezia! It was not my will!'

Lucrezia could not hear what she was saying. Their ruckus was bringing down the towers of her dreams, everything crashing and collapsing in explosions of dust. Her lover, her husband-to-be, had been found in her sister's bed that very morning.

Lucrezia thought she would never forgive her.

'And you,' Antonio thundered. 'Have you slept with him?'

'No!' Lucrezia shouted. 'How dare you suggest it?'

The physician was summoned. After an intrusive examination of the sisters, he pronounced them both spoiled.

'The man I once called friend,' shouted Antonio, 'has brought ruin to this house. The marriage contract is broken!'

'No, Antonio, no!' Lucrezia had no argument in her lover's defence, nor did she wish for one, but she wanted, somehow, for things to return to how they had been only the day before. When she was not spoiled. Marriage to a monster would be preferable to what was now unfolding before her.

Her betrothed was found later, in one of those alleys where night soil is thrown. His head had been held down in brown stench until he had drowned. No one knew who did it – it was just one of those revenge murders in Florence that people shrugged at. He had not been a popular man among men: too easy with the ladies, they said.

Antonio made immediate arrangements. His sisters were penitent Magdalens. They had been deceived, true, but they had fallen through their weakness and ruined the family and its reputation. No one would have them now except God in his mercy. To avoid gossip, he was sending them to a nunnery outside the city. There was a good one, he'd heard, in Prato.

Prato
1455–56

12

of frustration and delay. Before he could begin on the vault of the chapel of Santo Stefano it had to be repaired, and it was for him to organize the scaffolding. The first summer had been lost on that. Although he had paid for the scaffolding himself in cash, the commissioning body, the so-called *buonomini*, or 'good men', of the Ceppo, repaid him in grain and wine. He spent the following winter doing panels, tabernacles and wall decorations just to fill his purse, for the games of dice and the local wenches were not to be paid for in grain.

In the summer of 1453, when the rest of the world was concerned with the fall of Constantinople to the Turks and the earthquake in Florence, Filippo was fighting for justice in the courts against a merchant who claimed the Saint Jerome he had commissioned had never been finished. Whenever Filippo could get free of lawyers, he continued his work on the vault portraying the four evangelists against the background of sky. Sky. Ultramarine. If you were to cover a wall with the blood of dragons it could not be more expensive. The Ceppo's funds were soon drained by the cost of pigments and the next payment to Filippo was in wool. He had lawyers's fees to meet, and they would not take wool.

The next year, all the Ceppo's funds drained away on one thousand four hundred sheets of gold leaf. When Filippo was not up the scaffolding gilding the ceiling, or in the courts defending himself, he was at the offices of the Ceppo pleading for payment in money.

'I have a house full of fleeces and yarn! What am I supposed to do?'

'Sell it!'

'I am a painter and a friar, not a textile merchant!'

This was evident to everybody, especially to the crafty fellow who made him an offer for the wool that proved to be only half its worth.

Sometimes Filippo Lippi ached for the cloisters and for peace: life in the world was wearying and there was no place for rest. But while he was up the scaffolding, breaking his neck painting and gilding the vault, there came a painter called Gianello di Francesco with a wild and extravagant claim that Filippo owed him eighteen florins and had done so for the last fifteen years.

'Preposterous!' said Filippo.

'You are commanded to attend the court of the archbishop of Florence,' said Gianello's lawyer.

'I am under the jurisdiction here of the Bishop of Pistoia,' said Filippo, and refused to go to Florence.

✝

While waiting for the spring and the new fresco season, Filippo was working in the Palazzo Datini, busy on a tabernacle for the Ceppo. He was vaguely aware of the fuss at the town hall that attends the coming of the herald from Florence, bringing all the news from the great city and beyond. Now the criers were out and amidst the news of wars and treaties they shouted on street corners there was an item of little interest to the Pratese. But Filippo heard it as he worked in the palazzo's courtyard. 'On the eighteenth day of February in the year of Our Lord, 1455, Giovanni, Prior of the Dominican monastery at Fiesole, died in Rome. God rest his soul.' Filippo's spine melted like a candle and he went down on the ground, boneless with grief. Boneless and silent. His good memories were spoiled by memories of a door slammed in anger. 'He was my only true friend,' he told himself, plunging into agonies of remorse.

He staggered up the lane to Santo Stefano where he knocked upon the door of the provost and insisted that he be confessed, at once. They went into the church and, in the confessional, where Filippo blubbered incoherently about slammed doors and San

Quirico and everything burdening his conscience, the provost sat patiently listening. When the storm at last began to abate and the friar was reduced to hiccupping and heaving for breath, Provost Inghirami told him he must go to Florence.

'What? I cannot!'

'This is your penance. Go to Florence, see the archbishop and surrender that benefice. This is the way to say farewell to your friend. Put things right, Filippo.'

Filippo could not. The archbishop had a warrant out for his arrest. In Prato, where he was under the jurisdiction of the Bishop of Pistoia, he was safe.

'I owe a man some money,' he muttered. 'I dare not go.'

'Make things well, Filippo. Pay all your debts.'

And what about what is owed to me? Filippo thought, but kept quiet. 'Yes,' he said, 'you are right. I will go.'

✠

He came to the city early in the morning, slipping through the gate, an anonymous Carmelite, and made his way to San Marco. Arriving at the workshop in the monastery cloisters, he met other painters and sculptors who had gathered to mourn their friend: Domenico Veneziano, Piero della Francesca, Lorenzo Ghiberti, Luca della Robbia, Donatello. The funeral had been held in Rome before they'd even received the news and, thwarted of ceremony, they now gathered to reminisce. Donatello's tears made runnels in the fine dust that covered his skin. 'In Giovanni we had sweetness,' he said. 'Now the sweetness has gone from our lives.'

Luca della Robbia wrung his hands. 'Who will remind us now of the sacredness of our calling?'

Fra Filippo sat cradling his head, dry-eyed and hollow. It was the first time he had ever felt part of the group around Ghiberti and Donatello, but it was no cause for celebration, only grief.

Giovanni's assistant, Benozzo, challenged them. 'Why do you cry? Of all men, we can be assured that Brother Giovanni is in heaven. The Virgin herself came for his soul.'

Filippo found himself envying Giovanni even in death.

Successfully evading the notice of the archbishop, he returned to Prato as soon as he could. In Florence they were an earnest, pious lot, those sculptors and painters, devoid of humour; he would never fit in. No, he was better off in Prato and vague thoughts he had had about buying himself a house there took form and became a decision. He chose a solid, stone-built house of three storeys on the bank of the canal separating the district of the weavers from the environs of Santo Stefano. The house was on the weavers' side. From the windows at the front he looked out to the great piazza in front of Santo Stefano. From those at the back he looked out to a huddle of houses, workshops and mills. It suited him, for he straddled both worlds as the little bridge leading to his house straddled the canal. The house was not cheap but the San Quirico benefice would pay for it in instalments. And that was why he must keep the benefice. It was God's gift to him, to help him live in this mean world.

San Quirico – the very name bit his conscience like a flea. He scratched himself. Had he not promised Giovanni he would surrender the benefice? He had meant to but had never quite summoned the courage. Had he not promised the provost he would surrender it? Well, he would! – but not before he had been paid in cash for his work. He had received the benefice on his solemn promise that he would attend his duties there as rector. That had been ten years ago. How often had he been since? Twice? Three times? It was a sleepy hamlet east of Florence – no one knew whether he was there or not, particularly the parishioners – a straggle of contadini so stooped from tending vines that they never looked up.

'I must go,' he thought. 'I must visit San Quirico.' But the words became as sawdust on his tongue – dry, fragile, turning to mush in his saliva. He had said them so often they had lost their meaning. His intention had no force of will.

✝

Made bold by having evaded capture in Florence, he returned to the city to attend a memorial Mass that had been arranged for Giovanni at San Marco. He was dismayed by his stupidity when he saw that the archbishop himself was presiding – of course Antonino would do that for Giovanni – and it seemed dreamlike when he noticed Gianello di Francesco looking his way whilst speaking to the archbishop's secretary. He was hardly surprised when he found the officers of the archbishop waiting for him as he left the church.

He somehow endured one night in the piss-stinking dungeon before the trial on the following day. He was dragged, manacled, to the archbishop's palace and its great hall where Antonino sat on a high throne, his legs dangling, and called on both Gianello and Filippo to give their versions of the story. Gianello claimed that Filippo owed him eighteen florins and had done so for fifteen years.

'If I had had notice of this arrest,' said Filippo angrily, 'I could have produced the contract that, signed by a witness, states that Gianello was paid for his work as an assistant.'

'You added that passage later!'

'No!' Filippo shouted. 'It was witnessed by Ventura di Moro himself!'

'Who is this man? Produce him!'

'What, out of thin air?' Filippo lifted up his palms in supplication, to appeal to Little Anthony, that kind friar whom he had first met on the stairs of San Marco who must be somewhere still within the archbishop's stiff cope. That man who, in a recent outbreak of plague, had been out in the streets doing what he could to help the sick and dying. Little Anthony! – a fellow friar. 'All this may easily be settled by my paying another eighteen florins. Let me pay it and be done.'

'What do you mean "another"?' cried Gianello.

'I paid you!'

'Prove it!'

'You will have to take my word for it! What more do you want from me?'

101

'The truth!' squealed Gianello. 'You never paid me the eighteen florins.'

'As I've said, I did, but I will pay them again now.'

Archbishop Antonino banged his staff on the floor. 'For the sake of your soul I would prefer to have the truth than any easy resolution. Fra Filippo Lippi, swear on the soul of our dead friend, Fra Giovanni, that you paid the eighteen florins.'

Filippo gulped.

'Swear on his soul that you've given up your living at San Quirico as you promised him you would.'

Filippo could not speak.

'If you will not speak willingly, you will be induced.'

Still Filippo could say nothing.

The archbishop commanded that he be taken away and put to the rack.

'Why me?' shouted the friar, finding his voice suddenly. 'Why not torture him? He's the false accuser! I'm just the victim!'

'Because I want the *truth*,' said the archbishop, signing the warrant.

'I've told you the *truth!*'

'I want to be certain of it.' But the archbishop was not deaf to the pleas for justice and agreed that Gianello should also be tortured.

Filippo was dragged back to the dungeons, a dead weight between his captors. He was half-fainting even when they were only manacling his wrists and ankles to the rollers at each end of the frame of the rack. He had had nightmares about this punishment since he was a child – who had not? He had heard the screams of prisoners coming up through ground-level grilles. This could not be happening to him. Not for eighteen paltry florins! The leather-clad gaolers began to turn the rollers, one at each end.

'Not my right arm!' Filippo wailed. 'Please, *please*, not my painting arm!' The machine ground with a screeching noise, wood against wood, as the handles were turned. One step at a time. Stretch. Stop. Stretch. Stop. And soon the stops became the terror, because the relaxation only intensified the pain to come.

Fra Filippo screamed in his agony. He told the truth, the untruth, whatever they wanted to hear. 'Yes, very well, I falsified the contract, signed it myself, and there is no Ventura di Moro! I was only trying to avoid unnecessary expense. Do you know what notaries charge to act as witness? I admit it! I confess!'

He heard a crack as one arm dislocated – his left. He screamed all the way to heaven. He called for his mother. He called for the Virgin Mary. He felt something tearing inside him and his mouth filled with blood.

Stop! The voice was human, not divine.

On whose authority? the gaolers demanded.

That of Cosimo de' Medici.

Filippo Lippi slid into unconsciousness.

13

IN A TAVERN NEAR THE SANTA TRINITÀ BRIDGE IN Florence, a tanner was telling his friends that he had been cursed in his youngest son. His eldest, as they knew all too well, was a very successful notary; his second son was a gifted goldsmith; but his third was a dreamer who kept getting expelled from school.

Just that day he had been thrown out by the priest at the school of Santo Spirito, who said he was a waste of time. 'Your son is good for nothing but tanning. Take him into your trade. He's old enough now.'

Having been stung by the priest's words, Mariano dei Filipepi was complaining to his friends about priests being above their station. 'Good for nothing but tanning! Tanning is a hard-won skill requiring hours of dedicated work. I'd like to see any priest sully his soft hands with it. What that priest doesn't know is that

Filipepi leather is the softest in Florence and that men pay good money for it. Am I not famous in the Santa Croce market?'

His friends, all tanners and leatherworkers themselves, thought that, though Mariano was good, he was not as good as that and said so.

'Meh! I get no sympathy!' Mariano complained. 'What am I going to do with Alessandro? He's an oaf. I'd no more have him in my tanning shop than a ham-fisted, brainless cretin. Besides, he wouldn't stay but would disappear as soon as I turned my back.'

'Where does he go?'

'I don't know,' grumbled Mariano. 'Around the city's churches, his brother says. He likes to look at paintings. He can draw as it happens. I've seen his sketches. But how could I afford an apprenticeship for him? No, the best we can do is apprentice him to my goldsmith son. Yes, that's the best. I've spent so much on his schooling and I'm not spending a soldo more. He's bright, you see, brightest one of them all, but can't pay attention to this world. His head is up with the angels.'

✝

The object of this paternal concern was, at that moment, spending his stolen day working with his goldsmith brother. He enjoyed the work; it was so much more interesting than anything he learnt at school. Antonio engaged him in sweeping the floor, or brushing bits of gold from the workbench and putting them in the crucible to be melted later. He tidied the tools and learnt their names and functions as he hung them on the long rows of nails on the wall. He put the bellows to the fire when they were smelting and watched his brother stir the molten gold. In a cupboard were the pattern books. Sometimes Antonio let him spend time tracing designs – swags of vine leaves, faces of saints, forms of goddesses – but soon he would wag his finger and say, 'This is work for an apprentice in his second year. Go and catch a rat, Alessandro.'

'Catch a rat' was Antonio's phrase for menial tasks in the workshop, since he himself had spent his first year in the craft doing just that: catching rats.

Alessandro preferred even catching rats to sitting in school listening to lists of Roman Emperors, doing Latin grammar or reciting his catechism. It wasn't that he didn't like the lessons, just that they were so slow. Because of the other children, so slow. He only had to hear something once to know it; in school he heard everything over and over until an unstoppable power suddenly sprang through his body and he was leaping like a hare for the door.

Out in the sunshine and the city he was free to roam. He was on a quest like a knight of old, like Roland or Arthur, for a Lady who lived in the air and the sunshine, who breathed on him at dawn and smoothed his brow at dusk. He could never quite see her, but felt her presence, often in a church, hovering near a painting.

Most of the new works did not invite his Lady: the Donatellos and Brunelleschis and Masaccios. He could see their worth, but he could not see his Lady. Then he would glimpse her in the work of an uncelebrated painter, someone who loved colour and form above fame. Suddenly she would be there, shimmering invisibly in the air: Beauty.

He found her in the works of Piero della Francesca, Fra Filippo Lippi and, most of all, Fra Giovanni. In the church of Santa Trinità, next to his father's tannery, was the painting of *The Descent of the Cross*, the large single scene with its triple-spired frame, the sweetness of the figures even in their grief as the body of Christ was taken down, the deep landscape of Tuscany in the background, stretching away into infinity but, most of all, the colour, the richness of the earth pigments, the peculiarity of the dominant red, a colour that ran through his soul like a hand through water. He fed on that red, and went often to the church to do so. It was there that he had first met his Lady, had felt her hand laid upon his heart, the breath of her sweet

105

lips close to his ear as she whispered, 'This is why you were born.'

He had often wondered, what if he became a Dominican, could he be Fra Giovanni's rat catcher? But he did not relish the strict celibacy enforced at San Marco; while his body was celibate through lack of opportunity, his mind was a bacchanalian orgy.

He was saved from the question by the death of Fra Giovanni. Alessandro stood in the goldsmith's workshop, going both hot and cold at the news. Tears ran out of the sides of his eyes, because he had lived so close yet had never so much as met Fra Giovanni. He wiped his sleeve across his face and went back to work, reconciling himself to an apprenticeship to a goldsmith. Once the dust settled after this, his latest expulsion from a school, he must speak to his father.

He itched to chase a design on to metal. He could draw most of them freehand, without recourse to the pattern books, but he wanted to feel what his brother felt when he tapped his punches into the soft metal, the soft, incorruptible metal that was gold.

'The price has gone up again,' Antonio muttered. 'When the Turks captured Constantinople, it went up like a lark.'

'Mmmm,' said Alessandro. In his simplicity he thought that, if the price of materials went up, then so did the cost of the finished product.

'It's serious, Alessandro.'

Alessandro tossed his head. 'We'll just charge more.'

'We are at the limit of what people either can or choose to afford. We haven't had a private commission in months, not even from the Medici. All we do now is for the Church.' He was working on a piece of church plate as he spoke. 'Only the Church can afford it.'

Alessandro looked at him blankly. What did it matter who they worked for?

'And now even the Church is saying the cost is too high,' Antonio explained. He had been looking for a moment to tell his brother this. If you're going to kick a fellow, you might as well kick him when he's already down. 'Alessandro, I'm going out of business. I shall struggle on as long as I can, but one more rise in the price and it will be the end. We need to find you another craft.'

Stricken, Alessandro stared at his brother. Then he bolted for the door.

14

IN HIS BLACK TUNIC AND WHITE MANTLE, FRA FILIPPO Lippi stood at the threshold to the little church, not wishing to enter in the middle of the abbess's sermon and cause a disturbance. Beneath his feet, the world met the convent in a sharp line separating light from dark. Outside, the noisy marketplace, bright in the sunshine of early spring, inside all dark apart from the weak illumination of tallow candles. The sun on the floor seemed to know where to stop, to know where it was not welcome.

As his eyes grew used to the gloom, he could see a few bowed heads. 'Some of you have told me you are hungry,' said the abbess, her pudgy hands clasped over her voluminous bosom. 'My dear Sisters in Christ, we are nearly at the end of Lent – of course you are hungry. But you would not feel it so keenly if you had not been spoiled by doting parents in your childhood and brought up in a sinful life of pleasure. Now that you are in a convent and keeping the fast properly, you feel deprived. But to experience the desire of the soul and its thirst for God, we have to overcome the desires of the body. So rejoice – hunger is progress in faith!' She twitched her snubbed nose.

Filippo tried to guess what the nuns looked like. How can you tell from the back of a veiled head whether a woman is young or old, pretty or ugly? The abbess was now telling them about the famous relic of Santo Stefano. 'The Virgin's Girdle, right here in

Prato! On her ascension she gave it to the apostle Thomas, as if to say, "Here Thomas, something tangible for you." And it was brought here to Prato, all the way from Jerusalem, as a blessing upon our fair town.'

The Holy Girdle! That piece of bare-faced fakery: a green woollen belt that some Pratese had bought for three denari in a souk in Jerusalem during the crusades. Filippo looked about for somewhere he could sit but there was not a seat in the church apart from that of the abbess. The nuns were kneeling on the hard floor. He hoped the convent was a reasonable place and not a temple of asceticism. His gaze fell on the confessional and he wondered how many hours of boredom he must endure in that box, then his ear cocked to that rising tone that signals a sermon's conclusion.

'I have touched that belt that circled the Virgin's hips with these hands. You may touch it, too, when you prove to me your sincerity. So speak no more of hunger. Be grateful for the pangs, for they remind us of the sorrows of our Lord and keep us steady in our way.' The abbess crossed to her nuns and allowed them to kiss her hands, which they did, with varying degrees of fervour.

Despite the stink of tallow and the mustiness of stale incense, the friar was content and gave thanks to Cosimo de' Medici for snatching him from hell and putting him here. From the rack to a convent of nuns! Paradise! After all, what did a chaplain have to do other than take confession? In a convent this small, any inconvenience would be made up for by his charges being pretty young women (which he had, in his imagination, decided they were). With his finances settled, he could concentrate at last on the frescoes.

Once the service was over, the nuns filed past, heads lowered, going towards the door that led to the cloisters. He appraised each woman. Alas, not all were buxom – two were like spindles – but three out of five was a decent proportion to have decent proportions. There was something disturbing about those bowed heads, however. Although the truly humble keep their heads down, so, too, do beaten animals. Anger rose off these women like a heat haze.

The abbess approached him, accompanied by a nun much her own age and of similarly generous build. 'Fra Filippo? At last! I've been expecting you for two months! I am Abbess Bartolommea Bovacchiesi, and this is my sister, Jacopa.'

'I'm sorry, Mother. I've been busy.'

'Busy?' The face of the abbess was isolated by the fine linen bands of a wimple under her black veil. She had high arching eyebrows like a double–spanned bridge, large nostrils and an expression of such superiority that he felt like a worm. Obviously he could have no idea of what being busy really meant.

'Yes, busy! You must have heard that, after I'd painted the vault in Santo Stefano, half of it fell down. And who paid for the bricks and mortar to make the repairs? I did.' He could have added how much time he had had to spend working on tabernacles and altarpieces just to pay the instalments on his house, how much time had been spent appealing against the sentence of the archbishop, who had stripped him of his benefice at San Quirico, even unto writing a letter to the pope to say that his confession, elicited by torture, was invalid. 'And then, just when I heard that I had been appointed chaplain here, the roof of the choir collapsed. That church is near derelict, and it seems to be my job to build it up again all alone and with my own hands. Yes, I have been busy.'

Then there were the days spent wandering in a tavern-fuelled stupor after the pope had upheld the archbishop's sentence and declared the friar to be 'the perpetrator of many wicked crimes.' The choice was simple: burst from rage or get drunk.

All this he had had to endure in his struggle to keep his house. The house that he had bought himself within steps of those of the archpriest and the provost, within steps of the cathedral itself. He was almost part of the cloister of Santo Stefano. He was its painter, Fra Filippo Lippi, a master painter of Florence, and he should not feel cowed by this woman; but Bartolommea Bovacchiesi took his arm as if he were under arrest and steered him towards her office, telling him on the way that, though small and poor, the convent enjoyed the riches of spiritual wealth. 'We are small, Fra Filippo, but this is the finest convent in Prato and we are strictly obedient to the Rule. We are renewing ourselves. All my nuns are from good families and are pious. Most of them are Florentines, sent here because of our reputation and our proximity to the Holy Girdle.'

'And because you are cheap,' thought Fra Filippo. Entry into a good convent in Florence could cost as much as a dowry. It would cost less in Prato.

'Your duties as chaplain will be light,' continued the abbess. 'There is no need to avoid us by pretending to be busy. If you do your simple duties, you will feel surprisingly refreshed and unburdened. I've heard about your last living, at San Quirico, where you paid others to do your duties for you.'

He wondered bleakly what else she might have heard.

'Now tell me,' the abbess clucked like a hen, 'how did it feel to take the fruit of that living without doing the work? Did you not feel burdened? Yes, I thought so. It is guilt, Frate, the weight of guilt. And the quickest way to be free of guilt is to do your duty! Taking confession, giving spiritual advice when required, little more will be asked of you. I conduct all the services myself, except Mass, of course, but the local priest does that. When your duties are done, your conscience will be clean and you will be free to paint.'

'But Mother,' he said, 'you make it sound as if my priorities lie here. They do not: they lie in the main chapel of Santo Stefano.' He had been working four long years in Prato's mother church. Four years crippling himself painting the chapel's high arched and crumbling vault, spending too many days overseeing the removal of the tall window that was to be replaced, years of scaffolding and precious little painting, years of preparation. 'Let us be frank,' he said stiffly. 'I am being paid to act as chaplain here,

110

my duties shall be light and it's for me to determine what they are. That is the sum of it. The Bishop of Pistoia told me so.' *More or less,* he thought.

Now the abbess flushed with anger. But worse than her anger was the sense that she was overcoming it in some triumph of Christian will. He watched her swell then subside. 'We must naturally do all we can,' she said, 'to keep the Medici happy. You are their darling, after all. Who am I to question that?'

Ushered into her office, which had a far door leading to the street, he found himself as if in the shop of a haberdasher with large bales of cotton and wool: simple, cheap, undyed stuffs to make gowns and wimples; then more expensive linens and silks for making undergarments. These fabrics the abbess bought in bulk from local weavers for her industrious nuns to make into useful garments that she then sold to an agent. Fardels of linen shirts were stacked one atop another, awaiting embroidery. A tall lectern held a large ledger recording the sales of all the items that the nuns stitched in those hours which the abbess had designated 'leisure'.

'My girls are hard-working,' she explained. 'As we know, the Devil makes work for idle hands, so we have no idleness here. Every moment God has given us we must use to give back to Him, either in prayer or good deeds and works. Don't you agree?'

Fra Filippo said nothing.

'So that is why I said that in your spare time you will be free to paint. Of course your work at Santo Stefano will continue, but I believe the fresco season does not start until after Easter. One such as you must never be idle. I want an altarpiece for our little church, which I would have you make for us.'

His eyebrows shot up again. How could such an impoverished little convent, where the nuns were half-starved, possibly afford his services as a painter?

'Altarpieces are expensive,' he said.

'Of course they are,' she replied, lifting her nose. 'But we make a good income from our sewing and I intend to spend it wisely. I want an altarpiece, showing the Virgin bestowing her girdle upon Saint Thomas.'

'It's only two weeks until Easter. I've been known to take up to a year on an altarpiece.'

The abbess inhaled so sharply it sounded like a hiss. 'Do you want my commission or not?'

'Of course, Mother.' He had taken a loan from the Ceppo to buy his house and the next instalment was due, while money owed to him by the Ceppo for the frescoes was, as usual, long overdue. That the charitable fund established by the famous merchant, Francesco Datini, was more active in chasing a debt than in paying one was one of those things that caused him heartburn. They were even saying he'd had all the money allocated to the project and that there would be no more. Fra Filippo rubbed his painful chest and nodded. 'Of course I do,' he said again.

'You may start on my altarpiece tomorrow.'

The abbess was clearly a woman used to having her own way: her eyes commanded him to bow his head in submission. But to hell with that! He was the chaplain and must establish his authority. He took a deep breath, straightened his spine and was about to say something about appealing to the provost when she continued, 'I know all about you, Brother, and your indiscretions. The provost warned me. You have been given to us specifically for you to practise your vows of poverty, chastity and *obedience*. You can begin my altarpiece tomorrow. Of course, the more quickly you complete it, the sooner you can continue your other work. But I don't want haste at the cost of quality. I shall be watching every stroke of your brush. Diligence, Brother, that is what is required of you. Diligence.'

'Thank you, Mother, I'm sure I can do your altarpiece,' he said, wishing to be gone.

15

'I'M INNOCENT!' HE SHOUTED, SITTING BOLT UPRIGHT in bed, prickling with sweat. Realising he was not on the rack and did not have blood spilling from his mouth, he fell back on his pillow and stared at the brick vaulting of his own house. It was Prato, middle of March, late afternoon. 'Oh, God!'

His assistant and companion, Fra Diamante, hurried into the room. *'Caro mio!* That nightmare again?'

'My bones being yanked out of their sockets and my innards tearing.' Fra Filippo rubbed his stomach, which still pained him, especially when it was empty. 'I did pay the bastard. You believe me, don't you?'

'Of course you did. It's just that no one saw you do it.'

'Apart from Gianello himself.' Fra Filippo threw back the sheet, moved his legs slowly to the floor and sat moping on the side of the bed, his chin on his chest. That you could work with someone, trust him, and be betrayed by him. Judas, he muttered.

'It's all in the past now, caro mio,' said Fra Diamante, fetching his master's black habit. He held it out at arm's length for it smelt like an old cheese cloth.

Being called 'my dear' by a man half his age irritated Fra Filippo. If it hadn't been for that sense of sincerity in his assistant, he would have dismissed him long ago.

'Soon we'll be back to work at Santo Stefano and you can forget all that's happened,' said Diamante, sniffing his own fingers.

'How can I ever forget it? Being put on the rack by the Archbishop of Florence, the saintly Antonino, just because of a stupid squabble over eighteen florins – it was like being tortured by God himself. I'm not going to forget that, Diamante. The one who is really blessed is Cosimo de' Medici. If it weren't for him, I'd be dead now. Then what?' Fra Filippo had had much to think about following his trial, torture and near death. Before he had been released, he'd had a private audience with the archbishop, who spoke to him gently as a spiritual advisor. It was time to reform, to become the better man he knew he was, in essence.

'You need to exert some self-control and discipline,' the archbishop had said. 'Follow the commandments: do not lie, cheat, covet. Be virtuous. If you find your mind drifting on to lascivious thoughts, turn it. How? Usually I recommend prayer but with you, turn it however you may. Hum if necessary. Give yourself something else to listen to, that's the trick of it.'

Filippo had resolved to try to be better. His encounter with death had been too close: he had felt the fires of hell licking his feet. Time to change, before it was too late. 'Mother Bartolommea has commissioned an altarpiece,' he told his assistant.

Fra Diamante looked shocked.

'Quite, that's what I thought,' said Fra Filippo, pulling the habit over his head. He wrinkled his nose in distaste. He tied the rope girdle round his girth, which had shrunk following his ordeals but was now recovering. 'The convent of Santa Margherita looks like a hovel for abandoned girls, yet they can afford an altarpiece by Fra Filippo Lippi.'

'We haven't got the time!' Diamante protested.

'She sees it as being in lieu of my other duties. All I have to do is paint an altarpiece and I won't have to do anything else.'

'Are you sure? Have you got that in writing? Make sure you get the contract right this time,' said Fra Diamante. 'No more cutting out of notaries and forging the signature of a witness to save the expense.'

Fra Filippo grimaced. 'Believe me, I'll not be making that mistake again. Now, what is there to eat?'

Finding only a loaf and some cheese in the larder, he sent Fra Diamante out to buy some dried fruit and cooked pigeon at the market. 'Go to that good stall at the west end.' He gave Diamante money from the leather purse that hung from his girdle. 'And we'll need some wine for later, and mortadella and eggs. Stock up, Brother, stock up. Our larder is empty.'

'It is Lent after all.'

The very word made Filippo's stomach rumble. He upturned his purse into his assistant's open hand. 'Not for much longer. Here, take some more. Get whatever you can.'

Although Fra Diamante lived in the Carmine house near the castle, he spent so many hours with Fra Filippo that he lived more like his servant than his apprentice. When he had left with the large basket, Filippo took a sheet of tinted paper and began a rough sketch in charcoal of what he had in mind for the altar-piece. A single, square panel – he did not wish to be too delayed by this project, so nothing fancy such as wing panels or a predella. Virgin enthroned in the middle, of course, Saint Thomas on his knees before her. He had a clear image of Thomas as a lean, bearded man with a grave expression, like the weaver whose workshop was opposite the convent. Who else? The convent was Augustinian, so Saint Augustine. He sketched a bearded bishop. Saint Margaret, of course, as the patron of the convent. Who else? No doubt Mother Bartolommea would have her own ideas, but Filippo had learnt to pre-empt patrons with strong ideas of his own. So he sketched and re-sketched before meeting the abbess again three days later.

He found her praying with a nun who modestly avoided his eyes.

'Mother? Do you have a moment?'

'We shall come back to this, Suor Brigida,' she said, placing her hand gently on the girl's bowed head.

'I want to stay in prayer. I must stay in prayer,' said the girl, muffled by her veil. 'He wants nothing less of me.'

'Of course. Go to the church and I will join you later.'

The nun rose, curtsied before the crucifix, and again before the chaplain, and left.

The abbess turned to Filippo wearing a smile of compassion. 'God has graced Suor Brigida with His special favours. Between you and me,' she came close to whisper, though there was no one else in earshot, 'we may have a saint in the making here. Have you heard what happened in December? No? The Archangel Gabriel appeared to her.'

Fra Filippo grinned. 'Last time that happened, the young lady was left with child.'

The abbess took a great intake of breath. 'Abominable!' she muttered. She was panting with moral effort but gradually calmed herself. 'This is a convent, not a tavern! Please keep such jokes outside the gate.' She leaned heavily on her table, her head hung low. 'It's not even theologically correct.'

'You mean it was the dove? The Holy Spirit was the impregnator? Well, yes, I suppose it was.'

'Fra Filippo! Are these the kind of thoughts you have in mind while you paint the Annunciation? Are they?'

'Of course not.' He spread his arms wide, palms up, beseechingly. 'It was just a joke. And it has come right back in my face like piss in the wind.'

'Oh, dear God.' The abbess had to sit down.

'I've been considering the altarpiece.'

She shuddered.

'I think it should include Saints Augustine, Margaret and Bartholomew.'

'Why Bartholomew?'

'To indicate you, of course.'

She flinched. 'In the tabernacle you did for the Ceppo, you included a portrait of the patron.'

'But not from life. The merchant Datini is long dead.'

'How much better it will be, then, to work from life. Is that not what you like to do? It's what I heard you like to do.'

Oh, Mother, Mother, don't spoil your painting with your own image. Have you never looked in a mirror?

'I shall be kneeling at the Virgin's feet beside Saint Thomas. I could be available this afternoon for a sitting. And I would like to be shown beside Saint Margaret.'

'Can you come to my workshop?'

'I cannot! You must work here.'

116

'I need equipment. I can't carry a porphyry slab with me once, let alone back and forth. It takes a cart to carry it. Then my easel: it can't be in two places at once.'

'Are you going to paint here?'

'No, just do drawings.'

The abbess took him to a desk where she kept ledgers. Once it had been used as a surface for the copying of manuscripts, its slant well-suited for the purpose and with a shelf for a scribe's equipment. 'Would this do?'

Filippo said it would and, taking his sketched composition, unrolled it on the desk and drew the abbess in rough outline between Saint Margaret and Saint Thomas.

'Who is that?' She pointed to the bearded saint.

'Saint Thomas.'

'Nonsense! That's the weaver across the way, who always overcharges me. That's not Saint Thomas. He should have golden hair, like the angels, and no beard. And we need an archangel – I thought Raphael, since he governs good health, and this convent was originally a hospital, you know. And we should have Tobias.'

'Why Tobias?'

'With his fish. Such a wonderful story of trust and guidance. Now, Saint Augustine needs to be matched for the sake of symmetry, so I think Saint Gregory should stand on the Virgin's right, just here.' Coming close to Fra Filippo, the abbess's nose wrinkled. 'When was that habit last washed? How many do you have?'

'Just the two – one on, one off. Last washed – this? I think it was probably before I was in gaol. And I think the other one isn't too clean either. My laundry system broke down during my incarceration.'

'That was a year ago!'

'Well, ten months – around Saint John's day it will be a year.'

'Dear God in heaven! Bring it tomorrow and put it in the wash. I cannot have my chaplain smelling like a dead dog.'

Angels, fish, a miscellany of ill-assorted saints, dead dogs – Fra Filippo went out into the vast marketplace where each September the great wool fair was held and stood grimacing in the fierce sunlight. People like Mother Bartolommea compel a man to break the fast. He thought he deserved cakes, but where can you find cakes in Holy Week? He knew where, and turned down some dank lanes to the Jewish quarter. He needed something sweet in his mouth to take his mind off things and, once he'd bought some cakes, he stopped off in a deserted alley to eat two. Wiping his mouth of marzipan and chopped nuts, he went back to the canal path that led to his house and made his way along wearing his reflective, Lenten look.

Fra Filippo went through the barrel-vaulted ground floor that was his workshop and up the narrow stairs to the kitchen, calling 'Diamante!' The young friar came from the hearth where he was making a stew.

'I have a job for you. It's about time you had a project of your own to win your spurs. It's a panel of the Virgin enthroned, bestowing her girdle on a most angelic-looking Saint Thomas. I'll do the design, of course, and paint one of the figures. The rest is all yours.'

Diamante clasped his hands together in pleasure. 'Which figure will you do?'

'A portrait of the patron that needs to be lifelike, so I'll do that, even if she does look like a stupid sow. What fish is in the stew?'

'Carp.'

'Wonderful! I'm starving.'

16

SUOR LUCREZIA AND SUOR SPINETTA WERE STRUGGLING to carry the cauldron from the fire and tip its contents into the vast washtub when the new chaplain walked into the laundry. With their habits pulled up through their girdles, their thin legs were bare right up to their thighs though, ludicrously, the women still wore their veils. Lucrezia did not care how she looked, such was the weight of the cauldron. She had noticed the chaplain in the church, thinking there was something familiar about him, but now she could barely spare him a glance. Only when she and her sister had tipped the hot water into the tub, creating clouds of steam, could they pause.

The chaplain was smiling as if he expected a smile in return. Well, let him wait! Lucrezia had not smiled since the betrayal. She gave him a cold-eyed stare and asked him what he wanted. Spinetta was wriggling her habit free to cover her legs but Lucrezia stared at the friar as if daring him to look at her thighs.

He had a broad and liquid smile that was oddly comforting and his large, innocent eyes reassured her that he had no lascivious thoughts. Lucrezia's face screwed up with the effort to remember where she knew him from. 'The abbess said to bring my washing,' he said. 'Please do not examine it before you put it in the tub. I lent my habit to a fellow brother who always dribbles food down his front.'

'Oh, yes?' Lucrezia glanced pointedly at the dried scabs of food on the habit the friar was still wearing. She took the bundle and threw it irritably into one of the many woven baskets filled with tablecloths, napkins, dishcloths, scapulars, foot warmers, aprons and patched sheets. Spinetta began to scrub with a rough brush on the washboard.

'No soap?' said Filippo, surprised.

'Martha and Mary had no soap,' said the younger woman. 'So the abbess says.'

'This task is difficult enough but without soap!'

'We are not here to wash clothes, Frate,' said Lucrezia. 'We are here to wash the sin of pride from our souls. We don't need soap. Lye will do the job better.'

'So the abbess says, eh?' He asked them if they were sisters. When they said they were, he asked the family name. 'The Buti? Is that Francesco Buti the silk merchant?'

'It was. He died.'

'I'm very sorry to hear it. He always dealt with me fairly.'

Lucrezia, too determined to be cross to listen to him, bustled past with armfuls of wet sheets, nearly knocking him over.

'The Buti are a good family,' Fra Filippo continued. 'Yet you are doing the work of some ham-armed peasant woman. How often do you have to do this?'

'Too often! We're in the laundry almost every day.'

'But this is a small convent of how many? Seven? Plus the priest, procurator and now, me. Once a month would be enough, surely?'

'The abbess puts much store by cleanliness. She even wants her dishcloths boiled. As for that lot!'

'No!' Mortified with embarrassment, Spinetta tried to stop the chaplain going to the soaking tub that Lucrezia had pointed out to him. The iron-tasting smell of blood told its tale; he needed only a glance at the towels therein staining the water red. His look of compassion, however, increased and he sighed.

'What a waste,' he muttered.

Lucrezia sensed that in Fra Filippo there might be someone who could share her thoughts and feelings. She flinched involuntarily when he took hold of her hands and studied their rawness.

'How old are you?' he asked.

'Twenty-one.'

'And you?' he turned to Spinetta.

'Sixteen.'

'Your father sent you here rather than find dowries for you?'

'Our brother did, after our father died,' Lucrezia said hurriedly, withdrawing her hands and not giving Spinetta the chance to speak first.

'My brother and I were dumped in the Carmine when I was just seven,' said Fra Filippo. 'It didn't make me any more pious.'

Lucrezia looked at him guardedly. He was portly and he was old. Why did she feel as if she wanted to embrace him and make him feel better? 'The abbess says that all we have to do is our duty with a good heart and God will favour us with His Love.'

'I was taught that God loves sinners and saints alike and shows no favours. I hope it's true.' Fra Filippo laughed, and his laughter was like the music of Orpheus drawing the animals. The sisters gazed at him as if their souls could hear faint music.

'It's a good drying day,' muttered Lucrezia, annoyed by the rising desire to reciprocate his kindness. 'Your habit will be ready by tomorrow. And then we can take the one you're wearing, since your slovenly friend has obviously been wearing that one, too.'

When Fra Filippo returned to the convent on the following day to make studies of the abbess, he took two bars of Genoa soap into the laundry.

'Where did you get these?' Lucrezia asked.

'In the market. I bought them as a gift. To thank you. Keep them hidden – no need for the abbess to know, is there?' When he winked like a conspirator, Lucrezia found herself smiling.

'No need at all,' she said, quickly lowering her eyes.

17

'IT IS MY IDEA THAT ALL FIGURES IN PAINTINGS, APART from the Virgin and the Lord Himself, should be realistic – portraits of real people,' said Fra Filippo as he drew the abbess in profile, on her knees, her hands clasped in prayer.

'Nonsense,' she said. 'All holy figures must be shown as divine archetypes and not be based on sinful mortals.'

'But Saint Augustine was a sinful mortal by his own confession, and in my opinion anyone deserving to be called a saint must be the first to admit to his or her own weaknesses, or else they are not being honest. If you would allow me to paint this altarpiece in the new style, pioneered by Masaccio,' he noted with gratification that she blinked at this – she knew her art, 'people will flock to the convent to see it and be amazed. As at Le Murate in Florence.'

The abbess blinked again. The Convent of Le Murate was famous for its piety: the most prestigious convent in Tuscany, brimming with nuns from good families. And it had been endowed with some fine altarpieces by rich men wishing to get closer to God.

'We can include some real figures, perhaps,' she said. 'But not for the Virgin, or the angels, or Raphael, or the apostle Thomas. I don't want that weaver in my painting. He works on Sundays – I've seen him. But the saints, well, I could consider it.'

'You have a beautiful profile,' said Fra Filippo, drawing her snub nose, high eyebrow and tiny, disdainful eye. 'Such a natural expression of devotion: we must set it off properly. I was thinking that one of your nuns might pose for Saint Margaret. If she were to have her hand resting gently on your shoulder, those who know you will recognize the love the nuns bear for you, their Mother.'

'Oh, ho, Fra Filippo!' She turned to him, that thin eyebrow cocked. 'Do you think I haven't been warned about you? You want to hide yourself away in your workshop with one of my young ladies? Over my dead body!'

He smiled the smile that erases doubt. 'My reputation is ill-deserved, Mother, although not without foundation, I admit. But I have done my penances and learnt my lessons.'

'It is my job to have you practise your vows: poverty, obedience and *chastity*.'

'I have had much spiritual instruction from the archbishop. I would be a fool not to want what is best for my soul. If only I could find a way to strengthen will. However, I hear what you say and am happy for you to select the model for me. Choose the thinnest, most miserable, most flat-chested of your girls – I will be content.'

'And that will be a model for Saint Margaret?'

'I can fill her out with paint and add the beauty. I just need the pose. And I'll do the work here, in the open cloister – April is nearly upon us, the trees are in leaf and the weather is warming now. What harm could she come to?'

Mollified, especially as the painter had not mentioned his work on the frescoes, the abbess agreed. 'I need you to sign the contract I've drawn up. Here's your copy for consideration.' She handed him a roll of parchment.

His eye glanced over it. *An altarpiece of single panel, with the Virgin enthroned… four saints… two angels… painted by his hand only…*

'There's no mention of a fee.'

'The notary says that in a standard contract, such as this, the fee is never mentioned. We will discuss it on completion of the work.'

Fra Filippo felt his back turn cold. The last time he had signed a contract like this, with a merchant of Perugia, the man had declined to pay him anything at all, on the grounds of 'dissatisfaction'. Fra Filippo had won that court case but nothing would erase the humiliation of receiving such a critical judgement from a man from god-forsaken Perugia. 'I'll study it more closely later,' he said.

'We'll have it signed in the presence of real witnesses,' said the abbess.

Sometimes Fra Filippo wanted to just walk away from the world, filled as it was with the righteous who sit in judgement over others every working day of the week. 'A fat man can have no place in heaven,' was what they said, in essence, as they pointed out his weaknesses to him, itemizing them like an inventory, as if they themselves had no weakness at all. 'Leanness is next to Godliness.'

He was tired of being criticized. He wanted to be left alone to paint. He walked home, head down, following the bank of the canal. Contracts, contracts, contracts: they went on at such length about what the painter should do, and never said anything about what the patron should do, such as pay the painter.

He was in such a bad mood he had to take to his bed. He was roused later by Fra Diamante, who had received a message from the convent.

'The abbess writes that she has chosen a model for the Saint Margaret and that you're to go there tomorrow afternoon to meet her.'

'I'm busy tomorrow afternoon! *La porca!* Who does she think she is?'

'You don't like her, do you?'

'She is convinced that pride is best driven out by hard work, so the nuns, these daughters of rich Florentines, wash clothes, clean latrines, cook and scrub. She thinks it is the practice of virtue. I say it is spite on her part, jealous as she is of their youth and beauty.'

Fra Diamante yawned. 'Are we busy tomorrow afternoon?'

'What day is tomorrow?'

'Palm Sunday.'

'Is it? So soon?'

'We shouldn't be working on Sunday, especially not Palm Sunday.'

'I've no intention of working on Sunday or any other day, not until they find more funds. I'm not working for nothing! They keep blaming me, saying how much I cost. *I* cost? It's the materials. Do you know how much lapis lazuli costs now? It's twice the price of gold. As for gold, the price is beyond belief. Of course my price will go up. But the doddery old men of the Ceppo live in the past, when merchants of Prato were so rich they could found hospitals and create funds for the deserving. Now they squint at their ledgers and say Fra Filippo has had too much already, not realising that for every five florins they pay me, I pay six in materials.'

'Well, not quite–'

'They're robbing me blind. Ow!' Filippo rubbed his stomach. 'Get me some oil of celery will you?'

'The apothecary recommended vinegar.'

'Let him drink vinegar. Get me some celery oil.'

Fra Diamante went to the larder.

'And who paid for the scaffolding?' Filippo shouted after his assistant. 'The scaffolding! And the roof repairs! They are bleeding me dry!'

Fra Diamante returned with a small bottle and a wooden spoon. Fra Filippo poured the oil into the spoon and sucked on it with an expression of supreme distaste, but it was better than vinegar.

'You mustn't get angry. That's what the apothecary said.'

'Yes, then he told me to drink vinegar and charged me ten soldi. If I were being paid what I am worth, I could afford a physician. Cosimo de' Medici has his own physician.'

'Caro mio, you are not Cosimo de' Medici. So you're not going to return to the frescoes after Easter?'

'No, I'm not. Let them sweat. I have this substantial commission from the convent, and a painter must go where the money is. It's a law of nature.'

'Of course it is, caro mio.'

As the oil made its way down his gullet, it soothed Fra Filippo's pain and anger. 'I've applied to the Commune for a charitable donation to the work. It is the main church of Prato, after all. If they cough up, then of course I shall return to the frescoes.'

Fra Diamante relaxed.

'But it will have to be enough!' warned Fra Filippo.

18

AFTER THE PALM SUNDAY PROCESSION THROUGH THE city, Lucrezia was summoned to see the abbess.

'The new chaplain is a painter and he has agreed to do an altarpiece for us,' the abbess said. 'He needs a model for the figure of Saint Margaret and I thought of you.'

Lucrezia turned a sullen stare on the abbess as if her words were making no impression.

'You're obviously surprised and wondering why I've chosen you. I have to punish you, Lucrezia, for the sake of your soul – you must understand that – but it doesn't mean I cannot treat you fairly in all other respects. I have chosen you because, despite your sin, you have a saintly look to you. Yes, preposterous, I know, but there it is – a certain modesty and grace. But Suor Lucrezia, my dear, I must warn you not to believe his stories. He once did a painting at Le Murate when I was a young nun there. He was very young and handsome – he could get anything he wanted from us. Within the bounds of decorum, of course. Such big eyes and that lovely smile. A little boy lost. And he told such stories! About how he was dumped in the Carmine by a cruel and heartless mother; how he trained in painting with the great Masaccio; how he had recently escaped from Barbary pirates. Yes! Barbary pirates! All lies of course. He just likes having women look at him with pity. Listen to him always with a sceptic's ears. Was he captured by Barbary pirates and enslaved? If so, how is it he's here? He just likes the sound of the words – 'Barbary pirates' – and it accounts for the years he spent sleeping under tavern benches in puddles of wine and vomit. Was he abandoned in the Carmine by a cold and loveless mother? Of course not. Don't listen to his stories, Lucrezia. You may not be aware of this, but the pope himself has condemned our chaplain as a "wicked, contumacious, shameless liar". Yes, I know, shocking isn't it? That's who they've appointed as our chaplain. I thought it best to warn you.'

19

FILIPPO WENT TO THE CONVENT IN THE AFTERNOON. He could not find the abbess but he came across two nuns who appeared to be waiting for him, along with his desk which had been moved into the cloister. One, in her thirties, sat on a chair outside her cell; the other, standing beside her, was the young nun from the laundry, still clasping the olive branch she had carried in the morning's procession. He smiled, delighted that the abbess had chosen the one he wanted. 'Are you my Saint Margaret?' he asked.

The young nun nodded without looking up.

'I am Suor Piera,' said the other, genially. 'Whenever you meet, I shall be present also.'

'You will find my activities so dull you will soon be asleep.'

'Nonsense. I have my sewing.' She held up a shirt she was embroidering, as if to prove it.

'*La mia bella donna!*' said the chaplain, chucking her under the chin and making a big fuss of her. 'What beautiful stitch work!'

Suor Piera shook him off irritably but a smile twitched at the corner of her mouth.

'*Santo cielo!* – you're an angry bunch,' he said. The sloped desk had been moved to the cloister at his request but left facing the wall. He manoeuvred it until he got the best light on its surface.

'We're a hungry bunch,' Suor Piera replied.

'Tomorrow I shall bring you cakes.'

'In Holy Week?'

'God will forgive. Well, my Saint Margaret,' he said turning to the young nun from the laundry. 'I know your family name but what were you christened?'

'Lucrezia,' she replied, fiddling with olive leaves.

Fra Filippo fastened a sheet of tinted paper to his desk and began to draw in chalk and charcoal a face that, out of the steam of the laundry and in the cool of the cloisters, had a beauty so fine it was transcendent. Her eyes were liquid, her skin was flawless and her cheeks dimpled when she spoke. It was a beauty that made him feel old and soiled, the kind that arouses worship, not lust: all he could do was what he was doing, which was to use his skill to capture its likeness and to sorrow inwardly at his age and advancing decrepitude.

'I…,' Suor Lucrezia began. 'I wasn't expecting to start today.'

'I haven't much time to spare.'

'But it's Sunday.'

He smiled. 'Busiest day of the week for the priesthood!' Then, when she didn't laugh, he assured her he wasn't working but merely making studies. Filippo needed to reassure the girl; it was like creeping up on a nervous doe.

He worked on in silence with strokes that were deft but occasionally required some erasing. Fifty years he had been on this earth. His work at Santo Stefano was to be the climax of his life. After that he would slide into the grave, forgotten except by those who thought of him as 'the man who would be the new Masaccio and failed'. That was how he supposed his life's course to run, falling somewhat short of his goal, whatever that might be. Fra Giovanni must surely lie incorrupt in his tomb and would be beatified in time; Fra Filippo would turn to dust.

Having made several sketches, all on one sheet of paper, he thanked her graciously and said he would see her the following day. 'I'll bring cakes. Certain occupations require more fuel, and modelling is one of them,' he said cheerfully. She looked so wan and brittle.

20

AFTER FRA FILIPPO HAD TAKEN THE DIMENSIONS OF THE altar in the chapel, he found Lucrezia in the cloister, once again bone-still and hidden by the tent of her habit, the tent of her veil and the virtue of her calling. This day, instead of an olive branch she carried a Jesus doll dangling from one hand. She was as remote as a dead saint but a little life showed in her face when he offered a cake to her and to Suor Piera. She took one and ate it slowly, despite her hunger. When she had finished, she took another. He left the basket of cakes next to Piera.

'Where do you find cakes in Holy Week?' she asked, helping herself.

'The Jewish quarter.'

He again worked in silence for an hour. Although it was cool in the cloisters of green and white banded marble, sweat beaded Lucrezia's face where it was edged by the wimple and the veil. Suor Piera had her chin on her chest and was fast asleep.

'Lucrezia,' Filippo whispered, 'Saint Margaret never wore a veil. Can you take it off?'

She glanced at him in shock but, held by his kind eye, she put down the doll, slowly released the veil and wimple and shook her hair free. It was as fine as spun gold, as fine as the beams of radiance that were the final layer of any painting he made. He wished he had not said anything, that she had remained wearing the veil and hidden by virtue. Now his appreciation of beauty was clouded by desire. All he wanted was to run his hands through those fine filaments of hair and bring his lips to hers and…

He coughed. An image of the archbishop loomed in his mind. It was time for his spiritual practice. He began to hum.

✝

The convent slumbered. The only sound apart from Suor Piera snoring was the skitter of lizards over the stone wall of the cloisters and through the fallen, dried leaves of the bay trees. Lucrezia sat on a stool facing the painter. For a long while she kept her eyes lowered and just listened to the rhythmic, unhurried sound of chalk on paper, plucking at the stuffed doll the abbess had given her in the mistaken belief it would make her happy. It would take more than a stuffed doll to fill the longing that ate away at her innards. She glanced up. As Fra Filippo was absorbed by his work, she began to study him as he studied her. She looked away abruptly when he caught her gaze. He was humming tunelessly.

'What are you humming?'

'Nothing. It is a trick taught to me by the archbishop. It helps me concentrate.'

'You've met the archbishop?' Lucrezia was impressed. 'Were you in Florence during the earthquake?'

'Not in the city, no. I was here in Prato.' Filippo shuddered at the memory of hanging from a pole in mid air. 'Were you in Florence?'

Suddenly Lucrezia was speaking, inspired at last by having something to say. 'I was combing my sister's hair when it happened. One moment everything was normal, the next it had all turned to pork jelly: the floor and the walls, everything wobbling. There were great rumbling and cracking sounds and everything kept shaking. Our house survived but I didn't think it was going to. I clung to the door handle, Spinetta to the window. Then the explosions started. We didn't know what it was at first, but soon we realized it was the sound of houses falling down. Dust billowed in through the window and made us choke. My father came and got us. He walked in leaning to one side.'

'As on a ship in a storm.'

'I suppose so. He got hold of us and helped us out and downstairs, saying it would be safer downstairs, and put us with the rest of the family in a small store-room full of bales of wool that would do us no harm. Then he went out, saying that it was his duty as a Christian to help his neighbours. We were in that store-room all night. All night the earth kept lurching and every now and again there were those great explosions as houses came down. The earth would be quiet for an hour or so, and then the shock came again, but never as much as the first time. My father did not return. The following morning we went out to find him and we came across the archbishop pulling at rubble with his bare hands, trying to find anyone still alive. That tiny little man. They say he had worked all night without stopping for any kind of rest. That's what I call goodness.'

She stared down at her hands. When she wasn't in the laundry, she was cleaning latrines or helping in the kitchen, but the laundry was the worst, because of the rope on the well-bucket, thick and coarse, and so many buckets to be drawn up to fill the cauldron and the huge tub. Her hands were permanently red, but the scars from blisters had turned white and were becoming calloused. She hid her hands under the gown of the baby doll on her lap.

'They found my father under the rubble of our neighbour's house, his skull crushed.'

'Madonna! You poor child. Is that when you were sent here?'

'My brother said there were too many mouths to feed in the house. There were no more mouths than when my father was alive, one fewer indeed, and my brother inherited everything, but suddenly there were too many.'

'A brother's love is not the same as a father's.'

'He brought us here and left us here. For ever. Until I die. I shall be scouring my hands and bruising my knees until I die.' Tears welled in her eyes but did not fall.

'Prayer alone will give you solace.' Fra Filippo was sitting back from his work, peering at it, biting his lip and clearly not attending to what he was saying.

'Does it give you solace?' she snapped.

His head jerked back. 'What?'

'Prayer. Doesn't it depend on who's praying, and the condition of her soul?' Lucrezia began to breathe heavily. 'She doesn't mean what she says, have you noticed?'

'Who doesn't?'

'The abbess. She's all gushing about Our Lord but she's mean with people. That's not living by His teaching, is it? Well, is it?' Lucrezia's beauty was now frosted by her anger.

'*Cara mia,*' he said. 'From my experience the hardest thing in the world is to live by His teaching. We each do what we can. And remember, part of His teaching was "Judge not that ye be not judged".'

Lucrezia had never heard of Scheherazade or any of the characters of ancient tales who postpone their fate by storytelling; it was an instinctive knowledge that told her that if she wanted to stay here as long as she could, modelling for the painter rather than scrubbing linen, she must keep him distracted.

21

'THEY'VE GIVEN ME ONE HUNDRED AND TEN FLORINS!'
Filippo told Diamante, coming home from his meeting with the
officials of the Commune at the town hall.

'How wonderful!'

'Wonderful? It barely clears the debts we've incurred, but they
are treating it like charity! They say the Ceppo has already
paid me one thousand florins; I say I spent it all on scaffolding
and materials; they say, in that case, we grant you, *grant* me, one
hundred and ten florins, but it has to last us until Michaelmas!
Those good men sitting in musty chambers, doling out funds to
the needy, they have no idea of the costs of painting. They lured
me here from Florence, promising me the moon.'

'Lured you?'

'Now I'm reduced to knocking on doors, always asking for
more money. And they look at me with distrust, as if I've spent it
all on myself. So I told them to keep their one hundred and ten
florins.'

'*What!*'

'And there will be no more work at Santo Stefano until they
accede to my demands.'

'Caro mio!'

'Diamante, arrange a meeting for me with the Ceppo.'

✣

Lucrezia was in the cloister when the chaplain arrived looking
cross and irritable. She allowed him to set up his equipment in
peace, waiting for the right moment to speak. He was jarred and
out of kilter and needed to be brought into tune; she gave him the
silence he required. Once he had the paper fastened and had
sharpened his charcoal with a knife, he looked at her for the first
time. His eyes were twinkling suddenly; whatever irked him had
been forgotten.

'Good afternoon, Suor Lucrezia.'

'Good afternoon, Fra Filippo.'

Both glanced at the chaperone who was dozing over her needlework. 'Good afternoon, Suor Piera,' Filippo whispered and Lucrezia smiled.

He began to sketch rapidly in chalk and charcoal, his eyes sliding repeatedly from his work to her face and back again. At these times, his eyes were professional and carried no emotion, but she bore it.

'They say you are very skilled,' she said.

'What do you say?'

'I haven't seen very much yet.'

He smiled. 'You'd see a lot more of my work if you didn't keep distracting me with conversation.'

Lucrezia was quiet for a while, then, 'How did you acquire your skills?'

She expected that oily glow that comes on the faces of those who love to speak of themselves, the sheen of self-satisfaction; she expected him to sit back and tell her he was a born genius and that the skills had come to him without effort. Instead, he flinched and concentrated on his drawing.

'Were you apprenticed?' she asked.

His wrist flicked down the paper in a series of hatchings.

'It is odd, to be a friar and a painter.'

'But not unique,' he said, smudging some lines with his thumb.

'What a blessing, to be born in Florence, in our time! Who was your teacher, Fra Filippo?'

He inhaled and sat back. 'Nature,' he said. 'Nature was my teacher. Yes, it would have been a blessing to have been taught by any of our great masters, but I did not deserve such a blessing. The son of a butcher, thrown into the Carmine when my mother died, an apprenticeship into painting was hardly written into my destiny. But sometimes you have to carve your own destiny. Sometimes, I think, fate makes a mistake and you have to take matters into your own hands.'

Lucrezia frowned. This was not the story the abbess had led her to expect. This was not boasting – it was a story of anger and resentment.

'Oh. I heard you trained with Masaccio.'

Fra Filippo closed his eyes momentarily as if in pain.

'I'm sorry. I shouldn't interrupt you.'

'No, you shouldn't. I have asked you to model for Saint Margaret; now I will ask you to let Saint Margaret model for you. I'm sure she was a very quiet, circumspect woman who knew her place.'

Lucrezia thought that any woman who had been swallowed by Satan in the shape of a dragon and had escaped by irritating the monster's guts with a crucifix was far from demure. As she began to wonder why the Virgin of Antioch was the patron saint of pregnant women, she gazed up at the vaulting.

'Lucrezia, please keep your eyes on me.'

She did as she was told, but with such an expression of sullenness that Fra Filippo looked taken aback. He began to sketch again rapidly.

She wondered how old he was. Old enough to be her father, that was sure, but in no other respect was he like her father. His eyes were large and, yes, he did sometimes use them to look appealing, but there was something else there, a look behind the eyes of distrust and caution, the look of a wounded animal.

'It must have been so sad, to lose your mother and be put in a monastery.'

'Sad, yes. I was so sad I ran up the walls like a monkey in a cage, roaring with pain.' He glanced up. The twinkle was back. 'I was so sad, they had to lock me in a room until I wearied of being sad and stopped biting people.'

Lucrezia laughed.

Filippo's face changed as he realized something. 'I suppose that was why I always got my own way. They were afraid of making me sad again.' He sat back from the desk, his arms folded. 'I'd wanted to be a painter from the first time I saw one. Lorenzo

Monaco it was, painting on the walls of our parish church. I had to do what he did, I knew it. It didn't matter that I was the son of the butcher. Painters are rarely born of painters. They spring from lowly loins. Carpenters, glassblowers, weavers. So I determined to grow up to be a painter, and Lorenzo the Monk said he would take me as an apprentice, but then the Fates decreed otherwise.' He sighed.

'So you screamed until the Fates changed their minds?'

Filippo smiled. 'My prior arranged for me to have a few lessons from Lorenzo the Monk and then gave me a wall to practise on in the Carmine. It wasn't altruism on his part; what he wanted was a cheap way of decorating the monastery, at least in those areas where no patron could be found to pay for the work. So I did things in dark corners and remote corridors. When it came to decorating the chapel funded by Filippo Brancacci, they sent for what they called "a real painter".'

He told her the story of how Masaccio had shrouded the chapel in oilskins so that his work could not be seen, but how Filippo had spied on him from the shadows, learning by looking; how he had gone to the walls when the painter and his assistants had left for the day and analysed and studied for himself what they had done; how he had filled with wonder as the scenes took shape, forms drawn on the walls first in charcoal, then in sinopia; how he had worked out for himself what the receding grids of lines drawn on the cartoons were for.

'Have you heard of perspective? No. Why should you? But have you noticed how these days paintings imitate nature, how buildings look right, how the proportion of people to buildings looks natural, how paintings now show us scenes as our eyes see them? Yes? Well, that's the trick of perspective. The sculptors had been practising it on their relief panels but Masaccio was the first to do it in painting, and I, at fifteen years old, tried to work out for myself what he was doing and how.'

He told her of trying in vain to draw in perspective, of writing down the recipes for perfect plaster, noting the details of

Masaccio's palette of pigments, and how he had cried when at last he saw the forms on the walls take on colour. She watched the nervous ticks run through his face, emotion flowing just beneath the skin, as he relived a boyhood divided equally between bitter envy and hard work. When he spoke of the finished scenes of the life of Saint Peter, tears spilled from his eyes to roll down his cheeks and plop on to his chest. She wanted to rise then and go to him, to hold his head against her breast and comfort him.

This was not the story the abbess had warned her about. Was it?

'He was the best painter we have known since Giotto,' Filippo said, and then began to choke on his sobs. 'Dead at twenty seven! Snatched from us by death!' He caught up his left sleeve and wiped his face with it. 'Forgive me,' he said, muffled from within the folds. His face appeared again.

Lucrezia was sitting on the edge of her seat, staring at him.

'Have you seen those paintings?' he asked, genuinely interested in her answer.

'No.'

'No? Oh, of course not, you wouldn't. You're too young. They are buried now by darkness and cobwebs. And some of the faces have been hacked out of the plaster.' He seemed to be having trouble breathing.

'I know them!' she said. 'Yes! My mother did take me once, to worship the Madonna of the People.'

'That blackened abomination? Yes, they put it into Brancacci's chapel to cleanse the place of association with an enemy of the Medici, and to cover those wonderful paintings with the soot of votive lamps.' Filippo sighed. 'Cosimo de' Medici is a great friend of mine, did you know? Yes. But I can't forgive him that act of vengeance when he came back from exile. He claims it was not him, that it was the work of friends wishing to obliterate his enemies, but he's never made any attempt at restoration. Here I am, the inheritor of Masaccio's skills, ready, always ready, to do the work, but he never asks.'

This was the boaster she'd been warned about. Friend of the Medici indeed! As she smiled to herself, Filippo took up his chalks and began sketching again.

'Those faces were hacked out because they were portraits of Cosimo's enemies, perhaps, but also because they were just that, portraits. It had never been seen before, after all, and sometimes people are not ready for the new.'

'Paintings of holy scenes shouldn't look real.'

'Why not? Even Our Lady was a real person once, wasn't she? Isn't it important to remember that? Otherwise holiness is something removed and inaccessible.'

Lucrezia looked shocked. 'But you wouldn't paint Our Lady as a real person, would you?' She was still recovering from his denunciation of the Madonna del Popolo as 'a blackened abomination'. Holy images were not real, must never be real, because they were sacred. Worthy only of respect. If someone had taken a chisel to Masaccio's portraits, it was because as portraits they did not merit any respect. No one would have dared to deface the Madonna. She bit her lip as she tried to understand her own questions and objections.

'Do you think I shouldn't imitate nature, then?' Filippo asked.

'Yes! I think you shouldn't. It's not right. We're not to make graven images, not of the holy figures.'

'Hmmm.' Filippo looked disappointed but sympathetic. 'You are right of course. But would you object to a graven image of yourself?'

Lucrezia leapt to her feet. 'What have you done?' She thought she had been posing for the form only, not for a likeness. She went and stood behind him and saw in white chalk on red paper two portraits of herself, one sullen, the other smug. Perhaps it was the shock, but her response was a bark of laughter.

'What is it?' he cried, stung. 'What amuses you?'

He looked like a snail whose shell has been crushed underfoot, writhing and dreadfully vulnerable.

'I'm sorry,' she said quickly to reassure him. 'I didn't expect a likeness, that's all. Do I really look that miserable?'

'You should see yourself in the laundry.'

She shuddered.

'We'll continue tomorrow. I hope you don't mind surrendering your hour of rest, because as you can see I'm quite slow. We shall have to meet day after day.'

They both glanced at Suor Piera and, seeing that she was asleep, smiled at each other like two little ones conspiring. He had the face of a friend – that was what she liked about him. She had only known men as thundering fathers, strident brothers, seductive lovers and dogmatic, self-righteous priests. She had never met one before who was friendly, not like this. 'Do not trust him,' the abbess had said.

Lucrezia straightened and decided that the one not to be trusted was the abbess.

✝

Fra Filippo put away his things for the day and, taking up a basket of fresh cakes, woke Suor Piera by waving under her nose one sodden with honey.

She stirred and looked alarmed at the cake before her eyes. 'No, I don't want your sticky cakes,' she complained, pushing his hand away. 'I can't sew with sticky fingers.' She snatched the cake before it disappeared. 'Sewing in the afternoon, I ask you! It's just impossible. I'm too tired.' She pushed the cake into her mouth before anyone could stop her. 'Thank you,' she said, spitting crumbs. 'I'm not usually this greedy, you must believe me.'

Fra Filippo squeezed her shoulder. 'I've seen what's on your plates in the refectory. It wouldn't feed a mouse. Here, have another.' Suor Piera nodded and, before she had swallowed the first cake, she was pushing in the second.

Suor Lucrezia declined when the chaplain held out a cake to her. 'I really can't bear sticky hands.'

Fra Filippo broke off a piece of cake and put it in her mouth for her. How white her teeth, how pink her tongue, how soft her lips. 'More?' he asked. She nodded. He broke off another piece and put it in her mouth.

Suor Piera averted her eyes, cleaning her hands on her habit and putting away her needlework.

22

FROM THE ROOF OF THE CONVENT, WHERE CLOTHES HUNG out in a rickety loggia could dry, Lucrezia looked down upon the Piazza Mercatale. Today was not a market day and the dyers, taking advantage of the breeze from the hills, had stretched their fabrics the length of the long piazza. Lucrezia looked wistfully at the scene below which, against the backdrop of blue hills and the battlemented walls of the city, was a waving sea of bright colour.

She wriggled in her chemise made of rough linen. Her sister Spinetta was often scratching, but Lucrezia would smack her hand and tell her to stop it or she would spoil her skin. Spinetta would laugh and say, 'Spoil it for what?' To which Lucrezia had no answer. She could not say, *I used to stroke you like silk.*

She had held Spinetta after she was born. Swaddled in fine linen bands, there was not much of her to see, but Lucrezia touched her sister's face with her lips and with her lips she felt the softness that no fabric could emulate. Then Spinetta had been taken away to be nursed in a nearby village and Lucrezia wailed in grief. It was a year before she was reunited with her little sister and the first thing that Lucrezia wanted to do was to touch her with her lips to see if she was still as soft; she was, almost, but she smelt differently. Spinetta smelt of a peasant woman's house, of animals and foul straw. Lucrezia took her sister from the nurse. Avoiding the hands held out by her mother and the servants, she took command of Spinetta and, in a voice that was loud for a six-year-old, demanded that the bathtub be filled. The adults

139

found it entertaining, this child insisting on bathing her infant sister, and they watched fondly as Lucrezia kissed Spinetta all over. When the infant's country smells had been soaped away, Lucrezia told a servant to lift her out and dry her, 'with the softest towels!' And then she oversaw the dressing of Spinetta in fine silks. The finest. Chinese silk.

Francesco Buti remonstrated with his wife, that she indulged their daughter this way, in the use of the most expensive fabrics. 'I shall be ruined!' 'Nonsense – she's just using scraps from your shop floor and sewing it all herself.'

Francesco Buti's shop was, for Lucrezia, heaven lacking only angels. She had hiding places under counters and tables where she could listen to customers discussing their needs with the assistants. She loved the thump of a bale as it hit the counter above her, and the lesser thumps as it was flipped over and over, the swish of the fabric lengths, the click of the measuring stick, the crunch of shears, but above all, the smell, the sweet smell of newness, of dyes and finishes.

She seemed to have grown up knowing that cotton and linen come from plants, wool from sheep and silk from Chinese worms. In her hiding places, she learnt the names of places and everywhere seemed exotic, even nearby Lucca and Prato. But she could tell from the intonation of the speaker, the respectful hush, how important and distant places could be, so she worked out for herself that Lucca and Prato – both mentioned matter-of-factly – were close-by whereas Venice was farther, and absolutely nowhere was as far away as China.

She learnt the names of fabrics as if they were a map of the world: damask from Damascus, rascia from Raska in Serbia, samite from Greece, fustian from Egypt, baldacchino from Baghdad. At the end of a bale there was often a remnant. Some-times an assistant, if her father were not present, would give it to the customer at no extra cost, but what they were supposed to do was put it in a basket for sale as off-cuts or, for those pieces that could not be sold, for sale in bulk to a local paper-maker.

If Messer Francesco Buti was feeling benevolent or was worried about the state of his soul, he would give off-cuts to the hospital of Santa Maria Nuova – linens for bandages and the rest for small clothes for orphans. What he had not known or approved was that his eldest daughter was helping herself from these baskets, pulling out short lengths like treasures.

She knew what she wanted. Half the shop, with its camlets of goat hair, its mattress-fustian and stuffs for horse trappings, shelf upon shelf of coarse fabric in brown or grey, was outside of her interest. The middle range of simple cottons and wools in single colours was better, but best was the top range, the stripes, the checks, the brocades, the wonderful Florentine fabrics painted or block-printed with flowers. Fabric so fine it could dress angels. Fabrics that, tossed in the air, floated slowly to the ground. Fabrics you could bury your face in as if in a cloud. Fine gossamers, as soft as a baby's skin. These she stole from the off-cut baskets and took away to make clothes for her little sister.

For Lucrezia, the world was a place of wonders, where babies can appear out of nowhere, and fabrics be made of the thread of worms.

Now, dressed in a rough linen chemise and a tunic of unbleached wool, her skin itched as if she were flea-bitten. She hung her head. It was punishment. God was making her pay for her sins. He had dressed her in rough cloth and put her in Prato, where the very streets were draped with fine fabrics that she would never be able to wear again. She had hoped, when she came to the convent, that she could at least sew and embroider linen shirts, if not altar frontals and vestments, but she had been put in the laundry as a rite of purification. Laundries, where prostitutes went when they desired reform. She, Lucrezia Buti of Florence, had become a washerwoman. She sighed, lifted her head, looked across to the mountains and inhaled their freshness and freedom. The unusual heat was over and the air was sharp and spring-like again, but the trees were coming into leaf now and soon it would be summer.

Her eyes sprang open suddenly as she realized why the chaplain seemed familiar. He was that friar, yes, the one who had come to the shop when she was a child and she had found for him a remnant of Chinese silk. She remembered the silk better than she remembered him, for she had regretted ever since being so soft and sentimental. She should have kept that piece for herself and given him something else. He would never have known. But she had learnt that one should give alms to friars and so she had given him the best piece of silk in the basket. It had puzzled her at six, why a friar should want remnants of fine fabric, but now she could work it out. They were for costumes in his paintings! She brushed the wistful smile from her face with her sleeve and turned back to collecting washing from the poles.

23

THE CEPPO HAD CALLED FRA FILIPPO TO A MEETING AND he made his way to the fine palazzo that had once been home to Francesco Datini, the famous merchant of Prato. A rich and ruthless businessman of the previous century, Datini had died childless and, for his salvation, had left his fortune to the poor of the city. The fund was administered by 'the best and most honest' men of the city – the *buonomini*.

The exterior walls of the palazzo were frescoed with scenes of the mean old merchant's life of generous benefaction. The pictures showed none of his cruelty to his wife and his business partners nor his sharp dealing with his clients; no, they showed his donations to charity and gifts to the poor. The greater the gift, the greater the guilt, Filippo always thought.

These second-rate frescoes and their subject spoiled a fine house, a house that Filippo liked to imagine himself living in. The courtyard had a garden with beds of spring flowers – violets, hyacinths and early roses – filling the arcaded loggia with fragrance. The back wall of the loggia was decorated with the seven vices and seven virtues, painted by Agnolo Gaddi. Frescoes from the distant past, from the days B.P., Before Perspective, yet Filippo was admiring them when he was called upstairs to the office of the Ceppo.

He mounted the stairs to the upper loggia and a studded oaken door leading to a vaulted room decorated with oak leaves and acanthus, chevron stripes and fleur-de-lis. He sat on a leathern chair and tried to listen to what the council had to say to him, but he was busy imagining decorating his own chamber in his own house with just such designs as these.

'Fra Lippi?'

'Eh?'

'We were saying how disappointed we are at your progress and want to know how much you have spent so far.'

'I'm not sure – perhaps a thousand florins.'

The grey men in crimson gowns and caps sitting round a big sturdy table of polished oak stared at him as if he were on trial for his life. Filippo snapped out of his pleasant dreams and began to explain to the *buonomini* as if to simpletons that they were not treating him justly or humanely. As his argument gathered momentum, his voice began to rise until he was all but preaching. They had no right to be parsimonious just because he was a man of the church. He had a living to make – they were the charitable body, not he. After a long time examining their souls and finding them wanting, Filippo wore the good men out and with an air of exhaustion they arrived at a new agreement, increasing the total expenditure on the frescoes to one thousand, seven hundred and twenty-five florins.

'And,' said their spokesman at the end, wagging his finger, 'the work will be completed within two years.'

'How long it takes is entirely up to you,' Filippo flung back. 'If you will only stop calling me to these unnecessary inquests – always at your convenience, never at mine – I shall finish with months to spare. Which is exactly what I want, given that the

Medici have a commission waiting for me.' He was making it up but he dropped the name on them like a lead weight and it brought forth a spray of bitter invective. They were not going to be threatened or challenged or intimidated this way. The argument flew back and forth until one of the Ceppo banged his fist on the polished table and denounced Filippo as a puffed-up, conceited troublemaker.

'I don't care what I am as long as you get your frescoes and I'm given my dues, food in my belly, a roof over my head and uninterrupted time in which to work!' And thus the new agreement was reached and concluded.

✝

He growled and grumbled to himself all the way home, going over and over the argument, saying ever more pertinent, crushing things about business and businessmen. He stumped across the canal bridge and into his house.

Diamante was with the carpenter they had hired to make the panel for the altarpiece, discussing woods and dimensions.

'Ah, caro mio, just the man. I've been telling our friend here that we want poplar, yes? White poplar?'

Filippo shrugged, going towards the stairs. 'Whatever is cheapest and easiest. I want to get started as soon as possible.'

'The meeting didn't go well?' Diamante asked his disappearing back.

'Well enough.'

'So it should cheer you up that you have a letter from Giovanni de' Medici.'

Fra Filippo jumped back down the stairs to snatch the letter from his assistant. If the carpenter was already impressed by the status of Fra Filippo's correspondent, he was even more impressed by the friar's reaction.

'So! Now the Medici want an altarpiece as well. Well, let them wait, let them wait. Santa Margherita asked first. My duty is here, in Prato.'

When he went back up the stairs, taking the letter with him, his step was lighter.

'Altarpiece for where?' Diamante called after him.

'For Naples,' Filippo replied flatly. 'A gift for the King of Naples.'

Now the carpenter's eyes were huge and he became impatient to leave. By that evening, word had gone round the district: they had a great painter in their midst. Not only a master of his art, but a man who championed the people and put Prato before the Medici. As this gossip swirled round the workshops, Fra Filippo was chewing his quill, wondering what to say to Giovanni de' Medici in reply. He tried the alternatives on Diamante.

I accept your commission and will come to Florence straightaway.

With great regret, I cannot accept your commission. My duty to Santo Stefano here in Prato forbids it.

I accept your commission and will come to Florence in a month's time.

'Caro mio, tell Giovanni de' Medici the truth. He will arrange everything.'

Fra Filippo pulled a face, reluctantly acknowledging that his assistant had come up with the right answer. *I long to accept your commission but I am contracted here to the Ceppo, am bound to finish my work at Santo Stefano by the feast of the Assumption next year, and I have hardly begun.*

He sat back and wondered why he had found it all so problematic. It was a risk, of course, because Giovanni could respond by finding another painter, but he knew that behind Giovanni was Cosimo, and Cosimo always got what he wanted. Filippo smiled to himself, imagining the response at the table of the *buonomini* when in due course they received a letter with the Medici wax seal.

'Meanwhile we'll be starting on the frescoes again?' Diamante asked.

'When the money is in the bank and not a day before.'

Diamante groaned in frustration.

'What's the matter with you?' Filippo demanded. 'Are we not busy enough with the convent's altarpiece? The frescoes can wait a while longer.' He rubbed his face wearily. 'When I was a boy I dreamed of becoming a painter. I thought I would paint holy pictures in peace and tranquillity, breaking off every few hours to attend to my devotions.'

'You did?'

'I believed I would begin a painting, paint it and finish it.'

'To great acclaim?'

'Of course. There would be queues round the church of those wishing to see it. But my dreams have not come true. I either have no work or too much. How I hate having two things occupying me at once. I wish to concentrate, to devote all my thoughts and attention to one project at a time. Surely Giotto worked that way? Masaccio? Fra Giovanni.' He thumped up the stairs to fetch his notebook, hoping that there would be a delay in the money reaching the bank, affording him a few more precious days at the convent. Because, alone in all the world, that was where he found peace. Remembering something suddenly, he called down to Diamante, 'Jesus! What day is it?'

'Holy Thursday.'

Fra Filippo thundered down the stairs and flew out of the door, his mantle flying behind him. He had agreed to say Mass at the convent.

He was late. The abbess had begun the service without him. They were finishing the Kyrie as he hurried into the chapel, breathless and sweating.

'I'm sorry, so sorry,' he panted, adjusting his habit and mantle. The abbess rose and, with a withering glance at the chaplain, invited the congregation to pray. Fra Filippo bowed his head and tried in his soul to exchange the world for the cloister. As the prayers concluded, he moved towards the Gospels but the abbess intercepted him. With a glance she told him to do his duty to the sacrament while she did the reading. Half listening to the story of the Lord's Supper, Fra Filippo prepared the sacrament at the altar.

Feeling Lucrezia's eyes on his back made him more reflective than usual and he performed the rite with care.

'Frate, Frate,' the abbess whispered sharply. 'The homily.'

The homily! He had forgotten and had prepared nothing. He turned to the small congregation, the nuns at the front, local residents behind, all staring at him, wishing him to fail. Perhaps not Lucrezia. No. Her eyes were soft and friendly.

'Love,' he said. 'The Lord gave us a new commandment. In the old dispensation, all the commandments tell us what we should *not* do, but in the new, the Lord tells us what we *should* do. We should love one another. "A new commandment I give you, that you love one another as I love you." If there is no love, then we are not Christians. It is as simple as that. Look into your hearts now, good people, and see if love is there, love of your family, your neighbours, your commune, your God. Is it there? Make sure it is, for the Lord commands it.' He fell quiet, wondering if the old commandments were indeed all prohibitive. 'Ermmm. This is the point, you see, this is the crux of the matter. We can keep all the commandments; we can even torture people to make sure they keep them; but what does it amount to if there is not love? This is what Saint Paul was talking about in Corinthians.'

He noticed everyone looking blank and reminded himself that they were simple folk without Latin. Bible references meant nothing to them. So he paraphrased Corinthians and filled out the rest of the homily using the poetic rhythms of St Paul's rhetorical masterpiece on love. *Though I speak with the tongues of angels and have not love, I am nothing.* He was pleased, pleased because he himself found what he had to say moving and so, therefore, must everyone else. Daring to look, he found it was so: he had their full attention. 'There's nothing you have to do but let love in – just open the door of the heart,' he concluded and stepped back.

'The feet,' hissed the abbess, looking pointedly at the large chair and the basin of water and towels before it.

'Me?'

'Yes.'

'Everyone?'

'No. Just the nuns.'

One by one they came to him and sat in the chair before which he was kneeling. He had watched this rite and had had his own feet washed often enough. He knew what it involved. A splash of water and a brief wipe across the foot with a towel. But his words, Saint Paul's words, were haunting his heart. Suor Brigida came first. Her feet were blue and cold. He took one and then the other and placed them both in the bowl where the water was warm. She inhaled sharply, surprised by relief. He took one foot and then the other out of the water and dried each carefully with a towel. 'Thanks be to God,' she whispered.

Next came Suor Piera, who watched him with her cheerful gaze. Suor Piera, he realized, really did have love in her heart. Her feet were blunt and beautiful in their way, and he washed and dried them with the same care he had shown Brigida.

Spinetta's feet were long and bony, tender and young. A plump, buxom nun called Simonna he had not properly met before had pointed feet, the big toe slanting inwards from an enlarged joint. They looked painful. The sister of the abbess, Suor Jacopa, had ageing feet with yellow, brittle toenails and hard skin. The abbess herself had the same. All these feet he washed with care and attention and love. But Lucrezia's feet, they aroused him and he nearly wept over them for his spiritual failure at this, a rare moment of spiritual victory. Lucrezia's feet with their sweet little toes he washed and dried in haste.

Fra Filippo spent the rest of the Mass in a mist of regret, eager to administer the sacrament and be gone, but the abbess caught his arm before he could hurry away.

'That was very good,' she said, as if astonished at her own generosity. 'We shall be stripping the altar this evening at sunset. Will you join us for that?'

'May I have Suor Lucrezia for the afternoon? I have done some studies of her and would now like her to strike a pose for the painting.'

The abbess looked uncertain because there was much cleaning to be done on this day, but her own heart had not been impervious to the homily. 'You may,' she said.

✝

Lucrezia could not understand the pose he wanted her in, so he demonstrated it for her. While she knelt in the position of the abbess, he stood next to her as Saint Margaret, his hand gently resting on her head. She knelt there with her hands held together at the fingertips, everything in her rushing to that place where he was touching her, the warmth and gentleness of his hand surprising, and she wanted to take hold of it, to kiss it, to place it on her breast.

'Yes, I understand,' she said, and used his arm to steady herself as she came to her feet. Such a warm, solid arm. She could feel the life and strength, the muscle and sinew of him. Now she struck the pose that Filippo had asked for and reached out her right arm to rest on the imaginary head of the abbess. Filippo put a chair there so her arm would not tire.

'I was thinking of a velvet brocade in green for Saint Margaret. What do you think?'

'The Virgin of Antioch? In velvet brocade? And you say you paint from life!'

'Well, I also use my imagination.'

'But not too well. I see her in a simple shift of Syrian wool.'

'Syrian wool?' His forehead puckered.

'It has a sheen to it, like goat's hair. My father used to sell Syrian wool.'

'Could I find some here in Prato?'

'Of course. Is this not the capital of fine fabrics? Find the leading cloth merchant and ask him.' She stood facing to the right, her head in profile. He came forward and took hold of her chin

149

to adjust her head slightly so he could just see the lid and lashes of her left eye beyond her nose. He felt her tremble involuntarily under his touch and he immediately started to hum tunelessly.

The humming grated on her. She asked him to tell her the story of Cosimo's exile.

'Fourteen thirty-four. Remember?'

'I wasn't born until the following year.'

He looked at her sharply, and she knew what he was thinking, about the difference in their ages and how he could be her father. Well, he was her father, her spiritual father, she knew that now, after the homily in the morning. This was a deeply spiritual man who knew the difference between the letter of the law and the spirit of it. *That you should love one another.* She had glanced sideways at her sister, Spinetta, at that, and caught Spinetta blinking and looking away.

'And there was a great hollering in the streets and people banging pots and pans and riding about shouting out the names of the great families.' Filippo grabbed her attention with his tale of the tumult which had led to the imprisonment of Cosimo de' Medici in the tower of the Palazzo della Signoria. 'Shops were boarded up. Armed men galloped through the streets shouting *Strozzi!* or *Albizzi!* or *Medici!* or *Viva Repubblica!* I hid in an alley as armed men spurred the flanks of their rearing horses and shouted their affiliations.' Florence was being called on to choose which family should govern its affairs.

'What had he done?'

'Upset his rivals, nothing more. The people still loved him.' Filippo tried to explain the politics of Florence but Lucrezia's eyelids soon grew heavy. 'Both the Strozzi and Albizzi families knew that, given a choice, the people would choose the Medici. The Medici had always been good to the people. So the Strozzi and Albizzi tricked Cosimo into visiting the Palazzo della Signoria and, when he arrived there, they locked him in a room in the bell tower. *Death to Cosimo! Kill the Medici!* Such cries echoed round the city. Am I boring you?'

'What happened to Cosimo?'

'They nearly killed him but then the sentence was commuted to ten years' exile in the Veneto. Many of the artists followed in the wake of the Medici family, and I persuaded my prior to let me live outside the monastery as a friar-painter, like Lorenzo the Monk.'

Lucrezia's eyes narrowed. 'Was it that easy?'

Fra Filippo cleared his throat and a patch of red spread up from his neck to his very hairline. 'I've never told anyone this before,' he said. 'Masaccio and his assistants liked to make a fool of me. Yes. They called me an idiot. So one night I painted some fools' caps on paper, cut them out and stuck them on the figures in the scene of the raising of the son of Theophilius, the very scene that was later hacked about. But I did it first, I was the first vandal.' He was starting to choke on his words. Lucrezia reached out and touched his hand comfortingly.

'Put away childish things,' she said, repeating the words of Saint Paul he had spoken that morning in the chapel.

'Was that a childish thing? Yes, I suppose it was. Anyway, the prior was only too glad to be rid of me and agreed to my petition without a quibble. I went north to Padua where I found a few small domestic commissions, enough to bring me to the attention of the authorities at il Santo, where soon I was given an important commission for a reliquary.'

He told her nothing of his gambling and drinking; he told her instead about his studies of Giotto and meeting Cosimo in the Scrovegni Chapel.

'You met him? What's he like?'

'Tall and thin, very thin. I'd expected him to be fat. Wouldn't you? There he is, richer than Croesus and thin while I, poor and starving, am almost portly. Would you say I'm almost portly?'

Lucrezia glanced at his waist, which he was pinching between thumb and forefinger and producing a roll the size of a loaf of bread, and tried not to laugh.

'Nhmph.' Filippo breathed in hard to shrink his stomach. All the weight he had lost during his ordeal seemed to have been regained. 'Everyone said I was a good painter, but Cosimo is far-sighted and saw my hidden talents, my potential. He told me to stop copying archetypes and begin to imitate nature. I was fired by the suggestion. It was as if some sleeping thing within me had come awake.'

They were interrupted by Simonna and Spinetta coming into the cloister with their brooms and making a resentful din with their brushing – irritable Marthas who wished to disturb these two peaceful Marys. Suor Piera awoke with a start.

'The whole convent to be cleaned by tomorrow?' said Spinetta loudly to Simonna.

'How will that be possible?'

'I should help,' said Piera, abashed.

Filippo continued with his work but with cobwebs being brushed out of the vaulting above his head and buckets of water being thrown on the paving slabs of the cloister and brushed away with stiff brooms, he found it difficult to concentrate.

'We shall meet tomorrow,' he told Lucrezia.

'Tomorrow?'

'Well, no. Good Friday, perhaps we can't. Saturday, then.'

✝

That evening, finding he could not wait until Saturday, he went back to the convent for Tenebrae. The abbess presided. He merely stood and watched as the darkness grew in the chapel and the altar was stripped of its plate and frontal. The solemnity of the moment affected his heart and he felt almost suffocated by sadness. All would be quiet now. No flowers, no bells, until Sunday. For they stood on the threshold of the Day of Death when the world held its breath. They worked by the light of candles which illuminated the faces of the nuns and made them soft and golden. Then one by one the candles were snuffed out, leaving only one alight at a side altar so that they could find their way back to the cells.

As they were leaving, he felt a hand brush his, Lucrezia's, as if to say, 'I am here, even in the dark.'

24

AT DAWN ON GOOD FRIDAY, FRA FILIPPO LIPPI WENT OUT of the city gate and over the river Bisenzio to the foothills of Monte Retaia. Mist from the river filled the valley leaving the mountain tops floating like islands, but he wished to be out, touching and smelling the world. He had a fancy to find some flowers as a gift for Lucrezia. In a pasture meadow a few docile bullocks were grazing in their somnambulant way, their beefy shapes instantly recognisable in the mist. Filippo, stooping to pick a posy of violets, heard the horses before he saw them, their hooves thudding the turf like someone beating a carpet. Then he saw them, their fine forms and manes flying, cantering in a line in the distance. They were on a path to a place they desired to be, a place designated by the spirit of the hour, and nothing was going to get in their way. The bullocks, realizing this as the horses thundered towards them, scattered. The horses plunged through where, seconds before, the bullocks had been.

Filippo stood and watched this drama in silhouette, impressing on his memory the sight of misty horses – but what was that? One form in the herd was different, shorter in the leg, blunter in the head. It was a bullock, running with the horses, and everything in Filippo exulted. The beast slowed, of course, after time, and went back to grazing. This Filippo ignored. He wanted to stay with the understanding that *nothing stopped* a bullock running with horses, except the bullock's desires and its expectations of itself. For once, just for once, he knew where the blame lay for his sense of entrapment: it was not with those who would bind him, not with his vows, not with his constant need for money, not with his humble beginnings and lack of training: it was with himself. He went back to his house, put his flowers in water and began to draw them, trying to capture their form, colour and quality as if party, suddenly, to the secrets of nature.

The city was quiet with all bells muffled until the Easter Vigil on Saturday night. People were going solemnly to bare chapels for private prayer and reflection but Filippo had no wish to dwell on the crucifixion and was not one to contemplate the wounds of Christ. He stayed painting his flowers but by the evening they had wilted.

25

ON ENTERING SANTO STEFANO THE NEXT MORNING, Fra Filippo paused to say a prayer at the Chapel of the Holy Girdle. The church was busy with preparations for the Easter Vigil that would begin at midnight but the chapel of the relic was quiet. It had been decorated a hundred years previously by Agnolo Gaddi. As he prayed, Filippo opened one eye to judge the frescoes critically. They were outmoded, of course, but fine, nonetheless. He craned his neck to see if the repair and restoration he had carried out on one wall had held good, then he turned and looked along the nave of the church towards the raised choir at the end. The nave was an avenue of marble pillars and rounded arches, all leading to the supreme place where his own work was being done. It was an old church and smelt of the centuries, its tall arches banded with serpentine and albarese stone in the style of yesteryear. The style of the twelfth century that permeated this town, the style of the convent of Santa Margherita, the style that, in Florence, Brunelleschi had swept away. But Fra Filippo liked Santo Stefano, its echoing height and narrowness. It made him feel secure. As he approached the choir, he was intercepted by Provost Inghirami coming out of the sacristy.

'Ah, Fra Filippo, has the fresco season begun at last?'

Gemignano Inghirami had, after a long and notable career in Rome, returned home to Prato at the age of eighty. Instead of spending his days in retirement, reading in his beloved library, he had taken on the role of provost and went about his duties with the alacrity of a man half his age. Filippo knew Inghirami had been behind his commission to do the frescoes and he always felt grateful whenever he saw him, even more so now for his friendly greeting – no small thing to a man tortured by an archbishop and condemned by a pope as being wicked. In the amiable smile of the provost, the past withdrew. It was all behind Filippo now: the summons to return to Florence, the arrest, the trial, the torture, the interview with the archbishop, the long wait to get started on the work since he had returned to Prato.

'Such delays,' said the provost, 'such painful, inexcusable delays. Are the *buonomini* of the Ceppo treating you well? Not too many committee meetings, I trust. And have you been paid? Hmmm?' Inghirami brought his hairless face right up to Filippo's. 'Hmmm?'

Inghirami was, Filippo knew, a friend and confidant of Cosimo de' Medici and in the presence of his goodwill he felt the protective Medici arm about him. 'Yes, they have paid me at last, thank you, Provost,' he said.

'Forgive me for asking, I am sure you must tire of this question, but when will your work be finished?'

Filippo winced. 'You can see how little we've done – just the vault and top tiers. The roof repairs – which I paid for – held everything up for months.'

'Yes, most unfortunate, most unfortunate. Hmmm. Rain started to seep in during the winter.'

'I paid for the repairs but haven't been recompensed yet.'

'That is inexcusable! I will speak to the *buonomini*. When will the window be finished?'

Fra Filippo did not know. The vast window of stained glass that he had designed was being made in a Florentine workshop. He shrugged. 'I'll make enquiries.'

'Any chance for the festival of the Assumption?'

Filippo had no proper sense of time and its measure. In spring, September seemed a long way away. 'It's possible,' he said.

'Wonderful! Assumption it is, then,' said the provost, wandering off down the nave, intent on putting his tired feet up in his library. 'No doubt we shall see you here, ready for work on Monday morning.'

'No doubt, Provost.'

Filippo went up the steps of the choir to the scaffolding that didn't hide the bare walls from view as much as he would have liked. But there was colour aloft. The vaulted ceiling with its four Evangelists was complete, if a little flaky in the corners because of the damp, and the scenes in the left and right lunettes of the top tier were almost done. Fra Diamante sat on the upper platform, swinging his legs, waiting for him. When Filippo arrived at the platform and stood viewing the scene of the birth of Saint Stephen, Fra Diamante rose to his feet.

'The money is in the bank,' said Filippo. 'We can start again.'

'When? Monday?'

'I'd like to get my altarpiece finished first.'

Diamante looked at him guardedly. Knowing his master's inability to complete anything, let alone on time, this sounded dangerous. 'Finished? Don't you mean started?'

'There's plenty for you to be getting on with here. We need to apply pastiglia to the details in the lunettes.'

'I thought I had plenty to do painting the altarpiece.'

'Don't be difficult, Diamante. It's all a juggling act as you will learn.'

'With you as my teacher, no doubt I shall.'

Having instructed Diamante on what to do next, Filippo left to do some shopping. Once outside Santo Stefano, he turned right and went down by the canal past the convent of Santa Margherita to the Piazza Mercatale and the shops of fabric merchants.

✝

When Fra Filippo appeared in the cloisters in the afternoon he was carrying a basket full of off-cuts. Lucrezia threw herself at the basket and started to pull out its contents, naming each type of cloth with delight: *damask! brocatello! bouclé!*

'I do not usually discuss costumes with my model, but since you are an expert, what do you think Saint Margaret should wear?' He laid them out, these scraps of Prato's most expensive fabrics. Lucrezia cooed like a dove and plunged her hands deeper into the basket to pull out taffeta, lampasso and those soft, soft velvets with motifs of lobed leaves, pine-cones and pomegranates.

'Truly,' said Fra Filippo, 'each of these scraps contains more skill and beauty than I have produced in a lifetime, yet the artisans work anonymously at their looms.'

'I think making these stuffs must be reward enough.'

'I doubt whether they do. So what do you suppose our saint will wear?'

'I told you – Syrian wool!'

'There's no such thing. I asked in all the shops. Or if there is such a thing, it's coarse and scratchy and has no sheen. Come, Lucrezia, shall we not robe her in jewelled brocade?'

'She was a shepherd girl – in jewelled brocade? No!'

'This is heaven, remember! I am painting a supernatural scene of the Virgin at her Assumption, and Saint Margaret has to be present because she gave her name to this convent. I think, as an inhabitant of heaven, she would be wearing the finest stuffs imaginable for the occasion – especially for an altarpiece in Prato.'

'Well, I don't agree. Shall we compromise? A plain green velvet, please, like this.'

It was a fine piece she had chosen but completely unadorned, something that Fra Filippo had difficulty in accommodating. But he consoled himself that he had a golden mantle of griccia velvet for Saint Gregory and for Saint Augustine a tiara of precious stones, brocaded velvet and a jewelled mitre with emeralds the size of frogs. For the Archangel Raphael he intended a dark robe of inferriata velvet decorated with golden thistles that would be swathed in a silken mantle of rose madder. Too bad if the sister wanted to be plain. Then he glanced at her sideways, suddenly understanding her caution: if he were to give Saint Margaret Lucrezia's beauty and Prato's finest fabrics, the saint would distract all attention from the Virgin. It was the same mistake he had made with that wench, Dianora, in the Sant' Ambrogio altarpiece. Painting from life could make the heavenly figures seem wan in comparison.

'Very well,' he said, 'we shall put her in dark, plain stuffs.'

'Good!' said Lucrezia.

He fastened a sheet of tinted paper to his desk. It was time to make the full sketch.

'Can we keep these scraps?' she asked.

'Yes, of course. Why?'

'I could make baby's clothes from the longer pieces.'

'Baby? Which baby?' Filippo brushed the paper with a goose feather to smooth it and remove any dust.

'There are always babies needing clothes.'

Filippo smiled at the thought of foundlings and paupers' infants dressed like little kings.

Lucrezia went back to her pose and gazed at the floor. 'Who will sit for the Virgin?' she asked lightly, but failed to mask the keenness of her interest.

'Oh, I have my eye on someone special for that.'

'Who?'

'You.'

'How can I be both Saint Margaret and the Virgin?'

'Because I only need the form for the Virgin, not the likeness.'

He became intent on sharpening his charcoal with a knife.

'You're humming again,' she said.

'Sometimes I whistle.'

She looked up. 'Does that help you concentrate, too?'

'Yes, humming and whistling – both take my mind off distractions.' He threw back his sleeve and made himself ready to draw her image on the peach-coloured paper. Today he was going to capture Saint Margaret in light and dark.

158

'What distracts you?' she asked.

Beautiful young girls. My lascivious impulses. That kind of thing. Beauty, youth, my lust for things I do not have. 'The Devil,' he said, drawing her ears as if he were breathing on them.

'Ah…'

Filippo glanced at her, intrigued by her sigh. 'Does he speak to you, too?'

Lucrezia's gaze slid away from his but her lips were twitching with a smile. He quickly started sketching a new image to the side of the paper.

'All the time,' she said.

'*Davvero?* What does he say?' He became so concentrated on catching that fleeting smile that it was some time before he realized she had not replied. 'Come on, what does he say?'

She looked at the friendly chaplain, old enough to be her father. 'Is this confession?'

'It's an honest conversation between two like souls.'

'He tells me I'm bored.'

Filippo stood back from the desk with a grin. '*Cara mia!* Who would not be, pent up like this? *Poverina!* Of course you're bored. Tell me, what do you miss?'

'Fields, meadows strewn with flowers, streams overhung by cherry trees and the blossom floating on the water, rabbits and deer, making daisy chains with my sister. We spent every summer in our villa on the lower slopes of Fiesole.' Lucrezia lifted her eyes to the square of sky above the cloisters and yawned.

Filippo was startled by her yawning. She was bored now, at this very moment? How was that possible? Subject as he was himself to boredom, particularly in church services and prolonged sermons, he made it his business to be endlessly fascinating to others. It was time for the big one.

He had been avoiding it, but he had run out of stories. She had had his life thus far in a week, at least his life as he was prepared to tell it; it was a very different version to the one he gave in taverns when in need of a drink.

'On my way back from Padua, I went to see the mosaics at Ravenna. Then I came south via the coast but when I was in Ancona I was captured by Barbary pirates.'

Lucrezia turned. Fra Filippo put down his charcoal. He could not work and tell this one simultaneously; despite the number of years between then and now, his hand still shook at the memory.

26

IT HAD TAKEN MANY WEEKS TO REACH THE BARBARY coast because the ship called in at all ports until it was low in the water with the weight of the slaves. Finally it pushed out into to the open sea to make the crossing from Sicily to Barbary. 'At night the sea rippled like silk under the stars,' he told her. In the market of Tunis he had been put on sale with other slaves along with great jars of wine and oil, caches of arms, bales of precious fabrics and cages of hunting birds. He remained unsold until a man came who appraised him differently, unconcerned by his tonsure and lack of muscle. The man was tall, dressed in a white robe and turban and had a noble bearing. 'He didn't press my muscles or check my teeth but looked into my eyes with a most penetrating stare. The whites of his eyes were yellow, the irises black, the pupils a kind of dim blue. Very handsome. I liked the look of him.' He didn't have that mean look of a trader, the kind of selfishness that ploughs a man's face into ridges and furrows. He was upright and he was honest. Fra Filippo said he was sold for ten silver dirhems, the equivalent of four florins. 'You could get two pigs for that!' Fra Filippo braced himself for the usual rejoinder to this, that it was a bargain. But Lucrezia said, 'That's ridiculous!' Fra Filippo's face lit up with a look of surprised gratitude.

Returning to his drawing, he told her of the journey across the desert to the oasis, the chafing of the neck iron (he showed her the scars he still bore), the snorting of camels and their ill humour. He told her of the village at the oasis and his master who was the owner of an estate of date palms. He lived with other slaves in bare accommodation and had done drawings on the walls to cheer the place, for which he had been punished.

She stood in the pose of Saint Margaret listening to his exotic stories for over two hours and wanting to hear more, but the pain she was suffering began to show in her face.

'What is it?' he asked.

'My back. Can I sit down please? I get such backache. It's hauling all those buckets of water up from the well.'

He helped her to a seat just behind him, facing the sloped desk. 'I'm sorry. I had no idea! Has it been torture to pose for me?'

She did not say but looked at the sketch he had been doing. 'You've finished?' she asked, dismayed.

'Not quite. Watch me finish it. You finish a drawing with light.' He brushed away those charcoal lines he did not need, then at a side table he ground up some white lead on a stone slab, mixing it with water. Taking up an egg, he cracked it and mixed it with the pigment on the slab. 'There, liquid light.' He loaded a brush and with deft strokes gave Saint Margaret highlights on her forehead, nose and chin, then he picked out the raised parts of the folds of her mantle and gown. Lucrezia watched herself come to life on the paper.

'What do you think? I have the pose and expression but I think I must have you present when I do the painting itself, to get the flesh tones right.'

Wonder was running in Lucrezia's upturned face like colour in water. Fra Filippo turned round, took her face in his hands and kissed her on the nose. She didn't withdraw in shock or revulsion: her face remained in his hands, eyes closed, radiant. For a fleeting moment he hesitated, as if in battle with himself, but it was only a moment. Then he kissed her on the lips.

Suor Piera awoke with a start, as if an angel had tapped her on the shoulder.

They hastily withdrew from each other. Suor Piera pretended she'd seen nothing.

After the nuns had left and he had put away his equipment, Fra Filippo went to look at the well and then, on the way back to his house, he stopped off at the carpenter's shop to see how the panel for the altarpiece was proceeding. While he was there, he ordered some wooden beams.

✝

The nuns arose in the middle of the night and went silently to the chapel for the Paschal Vigil. Suor Brigida had remained awake all night saying her prayers but the rest had accepted the offer of the abbess that they take a few hours' sleep. When they came into the chapel, they found the abbess and Brigida already there, along with Fra Filippo who was to preside. He solemnly blessed a large wax candle at the altar and, lighting it with a taper carried from the single candle which had been left burning since Tenebrae, he stepped down and processed through the chapel, stopping three times to chant *Lumen Christi*, to which the small congregation replied, *Deo Gratias*. Each nun stepped forward to light a candle from the Paschal candle. Lucrezia approached, wondering if he would know it was her, even though he kept his eyes lowered: a tremble in the candle flame told her that he did. She lit her candle and, shielding its flame with her left hand, joined the small procession making its way round the chapel, dispelling the darkness.

After the procession they settled – the abbess in her mercy had allowed seats – for the Liturgy of the Word: seven readings from the Old Testament and a psalm. On the altar was a small picture showing the Harrowing of Hell. Looking at it, Fra Filippo imagined himself being left behind when Christ released the pious pagans, for surely pious pagans were worthy of salvation when impious Christians were not. His face grew long, his eyes vacant and his readings from the Old Testament mechanical. One of the nuns, the sister of the abbess, began to snore.

✝

Lucrezia, still warmed by the kiss of the afternoon, stared into her candle flame. She thought about the strange people in turbans who lived in Ifriqiya who had treated Fra Filippo as a slave, wondering what they were doing now, so very far away, beyond the sea, beyond the desert, in the oasis at the foot of the western mountains.

She whispered a prayer for all those who were slaves at that moment, good Christians snatched from Italian shores, thrown on to boats and goaded by the whip to heave and push on the oars, crying out under the burning, tearing lash.

She glanced at the little galaxy the sisters were making with their candles in the chapel and watched Fra Filippo reading the story of the parting of the Red Sea, wondering at his misery – he always seemed sad. Surely anyone who had escaped such a terrible ordeal must live the rest of his life happy? She looked fondly at the man she now loved, then she looked at her sister nuns with the same affection. She faltered with the abbess but it only took a little effort to let the love flow even to her. Yes, that was what love was: unlimited.

The darkness paled into light and, as the sun rose up behind the eastern hills, the nuns went out into the cloister and looked up to see clouds in the raw silk sky tinctured pink and orange. They shook hand-bells to greet the dawn of the resurrected day and throughout the city church bells began to ring, crying Alleluia! Lucrezia smiled sympathetically at Brigida, who was shedding copious tears of devotion; she even smiled at Spinetta. Handing out lilies to her sisters, she led them in the procession to Santo Stefano.

27

AS THE SUN, RISING OVER THE MOUNTAINS, BEGAN TO gild the streets, the nuns of Santa Margherita walked up the lane of the dyers singing a psalm. They converged on Santo Stefano with many other similar processions coming from other quarters. Entering in silence they filled the nave facing the trinity of chapels with their slender, pointed arches, two short chapels attending the tall central one: the scene of Calvary portrayed in architecture. The altar before the main chapel was covered with a white frontal. In needlework of supernatural fineness embroidered in silks and golden thread was the image of Christ rising from the tomb. The plate glinted and displays of Easter lilies filled the sacred space with fragrance. To the sound of the heavy bells in the campanile reverberating throughout the city, down the nave came the final procession, headed by the Bishop of Pistoia in mitre and cope followed by clergy and choir, censers swinging, incense billowing, their vestments a display of the finest fabrics and embroideries of Prato. All was music and colour again, except for the unfinished chapel behind the altar.

Walls of plain plaster, some ladders and scaffolding! It really was a disgrace that after four years there was nothing to show but the two lunettes of the top tier and the paintings of evangelists in the vaulting. Filippo, who had accompanied the nuns but now stood with the men in the right aisle, vowed to do better. Yes, this was the year he would do better. He would become the master and not the slave forever batted about by other people's desires and demands. Yes. He would be as tough as Brunelleschi, as impervious as Donatello, as proof against criticism as Ghiberti, and no one would tell him what to do. He squinted to visualise the middle tier showing scenes from the life of Saint Stephen on one wall and Saint John the Baptist on the other. He had designs in mind, now he tried to see them as they would look on the walls and had to make some mental adjustments.

But before long his eyes were drawn from the walls to the nuns in the left aisle. Strange to think that just two weeks before he could not tell one from another in those enveloping habits and veils, whereas now he could recognize Lucrezia immediately. As if attuned to his thoughts, she looked over to him. He winked. She smiled. Both went back to their devotions, or pretence of them. During the Bishop's sermon, Filippo returned to Ifriqiya. He had told Lucrezia more than he had told anyone of his adventures. Usually he spoke only of the horrors of the slave ship, the despair of captivity and the marvel of his eventual escape. He had told no one before of Abu Ali. What was this young woman going to draw out of him? It seemed he needed to tell her the truth. Yes, but not all of it. There was one episode he could never tell her: the one where he had spent a night in his idea of paradise.

✝

Staring blankly at the bishop, Lucrezia sighed inwardly with sorrow for the infidels, that they had no Easter Day and nothing to look at on their walls other than geometric shapes and flowery arabesques. She wondered about infidel women since Filippo had not mentioned any in his account of the village that belonged to his master, Abu Ali ibn Yussef, surrounded by a large estate of date palms and olive groves. She remembered umbrella pines in the woods near her father's country villa and imagined date palms to be the same, only as high as the campanile in Florence, with men crawling up them like ants to pick the dates. She wondered what it would be like to live in a desert village made of mud bricks, slave to a man who, on warm nights perfumed with jasmine, sang plaintive songs to the oud in his courtyard garden of fountains and running streams.

Despite being a slave, Fra Filippo had admired his master, even loved him. He was generous with the poor, patient with his workers and dealt with them justly. Abu Ali was a noble man born of a long line of Sufis, but the straightness of his spine was the result of self-discipline rather than birth.

Lucrezia admired the straightness of the lilies in the tall vase on the altar. Could an infidel be noble while she, a Christian woman of Florence, was not? It seemed inconceivable.

✝

Filippo tried to concentrate on the Mass but the mingled scents of lilies and incense kept wafting him back to Ifriqiya, that and the thought of it being the end of Lent. His stomach rumbled in anticipation of roast meat.

On one of his six-monthly visits to Tunis, Abu Ali had taken Filippo with him. Although he was out of earshot, at the harbour Filippo watched his master purchase wine after a long negotiation with a Florentine merchant, saw money change hands and a terracotta jar being taken to the camels by one of Abu Ali's men. Filippo thought about it all the way back to the mountains, that jar of Italian wine. Was it white or was it red? Red, surely, and Tuscan. Once back at the oasis, he found it difficult to sleep at nights for thought of that wine, wondering why Abu Ali had bought something so expensive and so forbidden, unless as a gift to his favourite slave. Was that it? Of course not. There must be some other reason. It was maddening to know that nectar was so close yet he could not have it. Sometimes he thought of seeking it out when everyone was asleep, but his love and respect for Abu Ali overcame this idea. It was, after all, the period of fasting.

✝

He had learnt about Ramadan from Abu Ali, as an example of abstinence practised by Abu Ali's faith, but it was his fellow slaves who told Filippo that, when the crescent moon next appeared, they would not be eating for a month. Alarmed, Filippo started stealing from the kitchen and, in the dark nights approaching the new moon, he chewed on scraps and leftovers to build himself up for the ordeal to come. He ate the peelings of vegetables and the crumbs of meat and fat left after carving in the belief that he was not going to eat again for forty days. He ate so much he became a bag of wind and the cook threatened to spike him in the belly like a bloated sheep, conveying his meaning through mime.

Although he could speak in Latin with Abu Ali, with the Berbers of the household Filippo was reduced to dumbshow, but they pulled him out with them on the night when the first sliver of the crescent moon appeared. *Ramadan! Ramadan!* they cried, and he could not understand their enthusiasm for the starvation to come.

When he went into the kitchen the next day, he was staggered to see a meal in preparation. Had it all been a joke at his expense? He reached out for some dates and had his hand slapped hard. By nightfall he had worked it out, that the Arabs only fasted during the hours of daylight. How reasonable! He forgot his store of nuts and dates and accepted the challenge of the fast.

When night fell, the family, friends and associates of Abu Ali dined together, then went to prayer at the mosque. Later, just as the staff and slaves settled to eat, Fra Filippo was attacked by a fierce pain in his bowels. He went out of the village into the desert where the silence swallowed the noises he made as he squatted and stretched and did everything he could to rid himself of excruciating wind. Once he was empty, he was very hungry, but when he got back to the house, the kitchen was locked.

He endured the night and following morning with his gurgling stomach but as he helped prepare the meal in the afternoon, his resolution failed, he cleaned a trencher with his tongue and was caught doing so. Abu Ali gave him a lecture on self-restraint, the lesson of Ramadan, but did not punish him, for that was against the spirit of the holy month.

As Ramadan proceeded and Fra Filippo found its rhythm, knowing how much to eat and when, he began to appreciate it. Lent had restrictions so impossible that Filippo had never succeeded in keeping them a week let alone forty days. At night, after the family had eaten, the slaves went to their own table, but Abu Ali had food for Filippo brought to his room so that they could talk while Filippo ate. Abu Ali questioned him long and hard about Christianity, and was gratified to learn that, in Filippo's opinion, Ramadan was better than Lent.

'That is the trouble with Christians,' said Abu Ali, passing him some dates. 'You advocate abstinence from all sensual pleasure, even sex. You embrace poverty! Or you try to. I have never met anyone who succeeded in any of it. With disciplines so difficult, is it any wonder you are all hypocrites? The Prophet set us aims we could achieve and each man is proud to be master of himself. In my faith, each man trains in self-discipline and self-restraint. We have no Church, no pope, only the imams, usually married men, often men of business. An imam is a teacher and he teaches from the Qur'an and from experience. We do not ask the impossible of him. It would be a fool who would suggest to any Moor that he quell the natural impulses of his body, for no Moor would be able to keep to it, just as, I suspect, no Christian can. Eh?' He raised an eyebrow quizzically.

'I keep to it!' Filippo protested. 'I know that some priests, monks and friars break it now and again, but the principle is sound. To become spiritual, we must master our bestial nature.'

'The body is your slave. If you thrash a slave, he will overthrow you. No, you must wash him and cleanse him gently of all impurity.'

'Be that as it may, I have had no difficulty with my bodily impulses.'

'You have lacked opportunity, that is all. Just as a man in prison finds fasting easy, so a man in a monastery brags of his virginity.'

'I have not been in the monastery for more than two years now.'

'So then, women are repelled by you?'

Filippo grew red with fury. He was, in his own opinion, quite handsome. Perhaps his looks were spoiled by the short hair and tonsure, which Abu Ali had allowed him to keep, but he had a robust figure and attractive eyes. What kept him distant from women was his nervousness. The only ones available were prostitutes, and if he satisfied himself there, he was surely bound for hell. He'd had a lifetime of instruction from his own 'imams' on the punishments of the damned.

'There is Divine Love, *ishq-e-haqiqi*, and there is Earthly Love, *ishq-e-majazi*. Two forms of the same love. You cannot deny your body love without denying it to your soul. A man's seed, kept inside himself, sours the spirit,' said Abu Ali. 'It is not natural.'

'The grape on the vine is natural, so is its fermented juice. But you won't drink it – and you say that we Christians have impossible disciplines! Our Lord drank wine. He turned water into wine. I am going mad for the lack of it here. I know you have some in the house. Why? Why did you buy a jar of wine in Tunis when you don't drink it?'

Abu Ali smiled. 'It was a gift from an Italian I trade with. It would be ungracious not to accept. One day I shall find someone to give it to.'

'You find the idea of celibacy strange; I find the idea of not drinking wine even stranger.'

'It is very easy.'

'So is celibacy.'

Abu Ali raised one eyebrow. 'We shall have a trial,' he said, 'to test our powers of self-restraint.'

The following day, he had the sealed jar of wine put in a small room in his house. In another room, he put one of his most nubile female slaves – his favourite when it came to the arts of love. 'So, you think it is harder to resist wine than woman?' he asked.

'I have taken no vows to avoid wine,' said Filippo. 'Therefore it is harder to resist.'

'Very well, I shall sleep in the room with the wine.'

Abu Ali ushered Filippo into a room of cushions and perfume. Filippo entered nervously, wishing he had not been so facetious. The cool evening air and starlight filtered in through the latticed windows upon the curvaceous form of a young Andalusian woman lying propped on one elbow upon the divan. Her breasts billowed

169

in the restraint of her silken bodice, and her hip formed a sinuous line, down to her knee and along to her braceleted ankle. She smelt of oranges, cloves and rosewater, and Filippo, forgetting what the test was about, ran his hand over her body. She caught his fingers and sucked at them with her painted lips. Convinced now that the trial was to see whether he was a natural man, Filippo proved himself several times over, and in each moment of ecstatic release, he understood what Abu Ali had been telling him, for in the dark, scintillating height of that moment was the undeniable, the palpable presence of God. In the morning, when he remembered that it had been a test of willpower, he decided failure was a small price to pay for what he had experienced.

In the neighbouring room, Abu Ali ibn Yussef was at prayer beside a sealed jar of wine.

'That's not fair!' Filippo protested when he walked in. 'If the woman had been sealed in a jar, you would have found me at prayer also.'

'Praying for a knife!'

'No, we must run the trial again, only this time, the wine jar is open.'

'I had a knife.'

'But you couldn't smell the wine! Your senses were not tempted.'

Abu Ali smiled. 'I think my point is proved without further trials. I request your formal surrender.'

Filippo went down on his knees and bowed until his forehead touched the floor. 'I surrender.' The memory of the night was still strong in his blood, and he wanted more nights like it, so much that he would do whatever it took. Tentatively he asked whether he could convert to Islam.

Abu Ali roared with laughter. 'It has all gone to your head. You rose too late to eat. When we have eaten tonight, ask me again.'

As Filippo rose up he became dizzy and stumbled against the jar of wine on its tripod. Both jar and stand moved too easily. Filippo tried to catch the jar but only sent it more quickly to the floor, where it smashed. He stood looking at it stupidly, wondering when the wine would run out.

Abu Ali cleared his throat nervously.

'When did you drink it?' Filippo thundered at his master.

'As soon as we got home I started. It lasted only a month. Do you want more woman? I certainly want more wine.' He took a deep breath and straightened his spine with resolve. 'Here, here is where the work starts. We renounce these temptations now, together, yes?' Filippo nodded and together they formally renewed their vows of abstinence.

Filippo, staring at the ceiling of Santo Stefano, wondered how Abu Ali was faring all these years later. He himself, well, he had failed. Repeatedly. He stood with a fond smile on his face when he should have been making his way to one of the stations to receive the sacrament.

Fra Diamante nudged him sharply with an elbow. 'Wake up, caro mio.'

28

FILIPPO WAS SHARPENING A METAL STYLE, ROTATING IT on a stone, when Lucrezia arrived in the cloister the following afternoon. 'Did you see your wooden beams?' she asked. 'The carpenter delivered them this morning.'

'Yes.'

'What are they for?'

'It's a surprise.'

Lucrezia pouted.

'Don't spoil your face by that expression. Noble ladies do not pout.' Returning to the drawing he had made previously, he began fixing the lines in silverpoint. Truly she pouted like a whore.

'Tell me more about Abu Ali,' Lucrezia said.

'I wanted to do some sketches but Abu Ali said it was forbidden. He said that love of the outward form distracts us from God. In my country, he said, we depict God in abstraction and make no attempt at reality. Master and slave, we met in the courtyard garden each evening to discuss the merits of our respective faiths. Once, having asked him for a translation into Latin of a song he had just sung, I was introduced to a mysticism that is familiar in our own tradition, the rose of the rose garden, the song of songs, the theology of Love. Suddenly I realized that, far from being a false god, "Allah" is just another name for our own God.'

Lucrezia looked bemused. She was quiet for a while, then she whispered, 'They didn't convert you, did they? Are you an infidel?'

Filippo laughed. 'Perhaps I am, at heart. But listen, God is love, as our Lord said, and therefore love is God. The infidels know this and theirs is the religion of the Lover and the Beloved.' He looked at her with liquid eyes, willing her to understand what he was saying and what he meant. She thought she did understand and swiftly lowered her gaze.

'God is love and he who abides in love abides in God,' he said softly.

She picked up a portrait he had sketched of Abu Ali. 'You were never in Barbary. This is not your Moorish master – it's a portrait of Cosimo de' Medici.'

'My, you're contrary!' Filippo snatched the picture and stared at it. Why had he never seen the resemblance between Cosimo and Abu Ali before? Or had Abu Ali taken on the form of Cosimo over the years in his imagination? It had all been so long ago. In truth, the portrait was a composite of the two men he respected above all others. There were touches of Plethon there, too.

'Cosimo,' said Lucrezia, stretching, 'in a jubba or whatever you call it.'

'Djellaba. They do look alike, I agree. I hadn't noticed it before.'

'Ha!'

172

He glanced up at the young woman and began to sketch her on another scrap of paper. *Behold thou art fair my love; behold, thou art fair; thou hast doves' eyes.*

'What is it?' she asked, more softly now.

'Abu Ali taught me that it is wrong to avoid human love in some vain hope of getting closer to God. Celibacy, he said, was the devil's invention to make us think about procreation all the time.'

Lucrezia coloured and Filippo apologized quickly. 'The theology of Love is that we find God in each other, he said, and I believe it's true.' *Thou hast doves' eyes.*

'A painter must have a lively imagination but yours is livelier than most. Barbary pirates indeed!'

'It's true!' Filippo rose and went to peer at the lowered face of Suor Piera. Finding her sound asleep, and the convent quiet apart from various snorings, he undid his rope girdle, turned his back and pulled his tunic over his head to show Lucrezia the whip marks. 'That's what the captain of the slave ship did to me.'

'When did this happen?'

'Twenty years ago.'

He felt her fingertips on his wounded back, as if she were searching for imperfections in the gesso ground of a panel. 'Brother,' she whispered, 'these scars and weals are recent.'

The tolling of the convent bell allowed him to evade further questions. He dressed hurriedly. It would be just his luck to be caught naked with a nun and for everyone to jump to the wrong conclusion. It was a repeating theme of his life that he was only ever accused of things he had not done, and never found out in the things he had done. Except that one time, which had landed him on the rack.

As he returned to his house, he felt as if he had had a drink of sherbet. He began to wonder whether he had caught her or she him. And did it matter? Did anything matter compared with that tingling virility, that sappy aliveness in his stiff old bones? *Stay me with flagons, comfort me with apples, for I am sick with love.*

29

IN HIS WORKSHOP, HE BEGAN ON THE COMPOSITION, drawing a square and its diagonals. The Virgin would be in the centre at the top and he decided to enclose her with the mandorla, the almond shape of two overlapping circles, which was traditionally the radiant body of holy figures. Although he had used Lucrezia for the pose, he would paint the Virgin's face without reference to any living model. Enthroned, she would hold out her girdle of green wool to the raised hands of Saint Thomas. Those two part-circles forming the mandorla: in the right circle he outlined Augustine, Raphael and Tobias; in the left, Margaret, Gregory, Thomas, and the kneeling abbess. The composition became a pleasing pyramid with a symmetry that was yet fluid and full of interest. For the background, some rocks and pine trees; for the foreground, a plant-filled meadow. He sat back, pleased with himself and his design, master now of an art that had eluded him until his time in Ifriqiya.

✝

Abu Ali had observed Filippo closely and said he found him slovenly in his personal habits and greedy at table. He wanted to know how, in Christianity, it was possible for blatant sinners to wear the robes of holy men. 'Putting a decorated cover over a cesspit doesn't mask the smell.' Fra Filippo did not know what to say. 'We do not have holy men as you do,' Abu Ali continued, 'and thus we do not have hypocrites. I am a farmer. My spiritual teacher works in the library of the Great Mosque in Tunis and I see him twice a year. We are ordinary men who seek to purify the inner self from filth.'

Fra Filippo thought Abu Ali proud to the point of arrogance. 'It is for God to make us perfect,' he said. 'All we can do is to confess and pray for the remission of our sins. God smiles on humility.'

'Ah, humility – the highest of the virtues, so difficult to acquire. It is not a matter of convincing others of our humility but of realizing ourselves that we are capable of nothing, that we have as much power as blades of grass.'

Nights under the date palms and in the scented, spicy air; nights under the velvet cloak of the sky, its brooch of the moon and the pendant diamond of Venus; nights that seduced reason and undermined conviction. It did not take many such nights for Abu Ali to persuade Fra Filippo of the truth of Sufi wisdom. In return, Fra Filippo tried to persuade Abu Ali of the sacredness of representational art.

'I know God,' he said, 'when I watch my brush at work on a panel or a wall.'

'That is hubris. What do you know of geometry? Not merchant's geometry or the gauging of barrels; I am speaking of the kind that reflects the natural laws of a harmonious universe.'

Fra Filippo stared at his master through narrowed eyes, his interest hooked like a fish. All the famous artificers – Brunelleschi, Donatello, Ghiberti – had learnt their geometry from a master called Antonio Manetti. Filippo had taught himself and had not got very far. Yet geometry to a painter was as important as colour.

Abu Ali unlocked a chest, took out a long pair of dividers beautifully carved in wood and drew a circle in the sand in front of their feet. 'How many similar circles fit round the circumference of one circle?'

'Doesn't that depend on the size of the circumference?'

'It does not! The answer is *always* six, if you use the same radius. So how do we divide a circle into six equal parts?'

Filippo had that jarring, chewing-on-gristle sensation he used to get as a boy during lessons.

'Easy,' said Abu Ali. 'Don't change the span of your dividers, and start anywhere on the circumference. Off you go. Draw a flower.'

A flower? Like a boy, Filippo yawned and sniffed but when he got six circles, which created flower petals, he experienced the delight of symmetry and law. Thus began his instruction in the sacred art of which Abu Ali claimed to be not a master but a perennial student. 'You will learn things here that you will never be able to put into words,' he said.

Abu Ali taught the friar the secrets of geometry and how to draw even the most complex patterns with a pair of dividers and a straight edge, without need of measurement. Fra Filippo learnt how, after dividing a circle into six, he could construct hexagons and pentagrams, and how to make their edges curved. Abu Ali took him on a geometric tour of his house, showing him the various constructions behind the decorative tiling of floors and walls, and how patterns repeated in latticework. He took him to the mosque to see even more elaborate constructions.

One evening, when drawing alone in the sand, Filippo divided a circle into sixteen and, just for his own amusement, joined all the intersections, creating a web of lines. Perhaps it was a trick of the light or a passing angel, but suddenly he saw something within the design – the ghost of an image that, when he rubbed his eyes and looked again, he could no longer see. But it had been a house. A house in true perspective. It was like one of those dreams from which you wake knowing that you understand everything, but the very awakening is the death of that understanding that can never be reclaimed. Fra Filippo erased the design and started again. *You see,* he told himself, *you are always so quick to look for results, so slow to look for causes.* He smiled to hear himself speak thus to himself, as if part of him had become Abu Ali. *You begin with the point, the source of all, then you draw an horizon line. That is the beginning of a circle: a dot and a line. A dot and a line. Now place your compass on the point and draw.* The other point of the dividers made a satisfying swoosh through the sand as it scored its circle. *And there we have it.* Fra Filippo stared at his circle divided in two by the horizon. The horizon. The point. *All things come from the point. And return to it. Ah!* Quickly he was dividing the circle into sixteen again, but this time he did not join all the intersections to one another. This time he joined the intersections to the point. Then he had rays. Then he had parallel lines joining at infinity. Then he had the secret of perspective that Brunelleschi had demonstrated but not revealed, that Brunelleschi had left each artist to discover for himself. Fra Filippo found it in the sand of the desert. *Ah ha!* he cried to the mountains. *Ah ha!* the mountains replied. *Ah ha!*

The pity of it was that he could not show it to Abu Ali without receiving a lecture on the evils of representation. Perhaps if he demonstrated it as an optical trick? He did so and Abu Ali was impressed. He looked up from the sand to the buildings around him. 'So they do,' he muttered to himself, 'so they do. Parallel lines appear to converge in the distance. And you discovered this trick in my fourfold geometry? That is wonderful.' Abu Ali gave him a sidelong glance. 'But,' he said, so suddenly that it made Filippo jump, 'do not be tempted to play with this trick. It's the devil's.'

Filippo laughed. 'You say that so often, how Christians have lost the way by learning how to depict nature.'

'There is only one Creator. You should not compete with God.'

'I don't! I think of myself as His instrument.' Filippo settled down cross-legged to have an evening of debate with his master. Abu Ali sat beside him and tried once more to convince this so-called holy man that, in painting the world, he would lose touch with heaven. Filippo replied with a very well rehearsed argument in favour of representation, of how important it is not to see heaven as elsewhere but in the eyes of the one looking at you. 'The kingdom of heaven is within, according to Jesus the Prophet.' But as he spoke, he had a very vivid memory of the Masaccio frescoes and, in a coruscating moment of understanding, he knew there was nothing truly holy in them. They were clever and they were brilliant but they would never make him think of God. His argument petered out and he fell into deep, reflective silence. The setting sun made indigo and aubergine shadows of date palms over the oasis and he gazed in silence at the beauty.

'There are two minds,' said Abu Ali softly. 'A noisy one, full of chatter, and a silent one. Art should come from silence.'

30

FILIPPO WAS IN THE CONVENT'S CHAPEL, PREPARING FOR the Mass he was to say later, when he heard violent scuffling in the cloister. He went out to find Lucrezia and Spinetta fighting. Without a sound they tore at each other: veils, scapulas and wimples were ripped from heads and nothing was said except the occasional hiss of *Ouch! You harlot!*

'Now,' said Filippo coming between them as chaplain, not painter. 'What is this all about?'

'It's always her!' Spinetta growled. 'Just because I was born second I have to come second in everything! And now look what's happening! You! You should be ashamed. You're a disgrace. Both of you!'

'Suor Spinetta! Retire to your cell and recite the Magnificat ten times without error. If you slip or fumble your words, start again!'

Spinetta struck out and sent a small potted bay tree crashing from its pedestal. But she went to her cell, grumbling all the way.

'She's jealous,' said Lucrezia, fetching a broom and pan. She collected the debris while Filippo rescued the plant. Once they had finished, Lucrezia sat down to put her headwear back on.

'Leave your hair free for now. How do you think Saint Margaret would wear it?'

'Like this,' Lucrezia said, drawing her hair straight back from her forehead. 'Plain, and mostly hidden under a simple linen veil.'

'A gossamer fine linen I would have thought.' He drew from his bag some things he'd won off a merchant in a game of dice; he'd been looking for a long time for an excuse to try them. Silently he covered her hair with a braided headband and a square of linen so fine it was transparent, tucking it artfully into a chaplet of beads – beads, not pearls, if only they'd been pearls! That would have been a game worth winning – and he caught its long ends with a brooch at her breast. Florentine women had turned such headwear into a *fantasia* of opulence and seduction, but his Saint Margaret was to retain her purity and innocence. Over her habit he draped a green velvet mantle. Standing at his sloped desk in the cloisters, he made a study of her profile in colour.

'Where did we get to with Abu Ali?' she asked.

'Sssh. I'm trying to concentrate.'

'He was teaching you geometry.'

'Yes! And then he taught me the secrets of colour.'

✝

Abu Ali sent Filippo to the village apothecary. In a vaulted cellar he was taught how to create pigments other than simple earth colours by a thin, bearded man who had spent a lifetime making solutions and fusions of earth, air, fire and water. The apothecary had once killed an apprentice by failing to seal a retort properly in which he was burning mercury. He had lost a forefinger in another explosion and his eyes were half-blind with cataracts. Vermilion, he told his astonished slave-apprentice in the Berber language that Filippo could barely understand, would be his downfall. He then said something about making mercury sweat, marrying it to sulphur and listening for the din of their love-making, after which vermilion crystals are found in the retort. Filippo learnt more by watching than listening. At the end of the demonstration, the apothecary showed him two dishes of red powder. 'Vermilion and cinnabar. Which is which?'

Filippo studied the two dishes and saw no difference. The apothecary bound the pigments using egg white and water and Filippo painted a piece of paper with both colours. 'They are identical,' he said.

'So why make vermilion if all we need for red is ground cinnabar?'

Filippo could see no reason to go to such trouble, and even kill an apprentice in the process.

'Because the marriage of sulphur and mercury will be in your painting. You won't see it, or taste it, or touch it, but it's there. In your faith, isn't your Lord in a wafer of bread? It's the same thing. Transubstantiation. People will look on your red and will feel an excitation of spirit, an awakening, and will not know why.'

Filippo learnt all he could from the apothecary, put it together with what he had learnt from Abu Ali and gathered to himself the knowledge that would have taken an apprentice years to learn, if he ever did learn, for Filippo suspected that here in Ifriqiya he was being taught forms that Brunelleschi could not guess at, colours that Masaccio had never dreamt of. He had been given the secrets of Colour and Form, secrets that the Arabs expressed with such restraint in the patterned stone of their holy buildings.

He was moved to thank Abu Ali for the teaching he had received.

'You may pass it on to only one man in your lifetime,' said his master. 'You will know him when you meet him.'

Fra Filippo looked at his master askance. There was an implication in this which he had not missed.

Abu Ali nodded, picked up his copy of the Qur'an and began his *sottovoce* chanting of verses.

Filippo was breathing hard at this intimation of what he knew in his bones to be true: that he was not going to be here for the rest of his life. Abu Ali intended to free him; one day he would be going home. Tears were making his eyes swim and he blinked to clear them.

Abu Ali was wearing a linen robe bordered with *tiraz* bands, beautifully embroidered with quotations in Kufic script. Fra Filippo had no wish to learn Arabic. After two years in the village he had enough Berber words to satisfy his needs and learn the art of colour. But the script itself enchanted his eye and, while Abu Ali rocked backwards and forwards, Fra Filippo practised drawing letters. They spelt nothing but gibberish and, once his prayers were over, Abu Ali laughed fondly at his slave.

31

HIS SPINE TENSED WHEN HE HEARD THE CLIPPED STEPS of the abbess approaching through the cloister. He heard her stop, felt her eyes boring into his back.

'Yes, Mother, what is it?' he asked without looking up from the carpenter's donkey where he was sawing one of the wooden beams.

'What are you doing?'

He began to breathe again. 'This?' he said, stepping back from the A-frame he was making. 'It's something for the well. When we put a rope through here, the contraption takes the strain and we can raise a bucket much more easily. I thought it up. Clever, isn't it?'

'Who do you think you are? Brunelleschi? We have no need for such a thing.'

'Every day Suor Lucrezia has to pull up a dozen or more buckets of water from the well. She has a long back. It's agony for her.'

The abbess came close, peered into his face. 'I hope you're not growing too attached to that young woman. You have no idea. She's in that laundry for a reason, you know. How does the painting proceed?'

'Slowly, I'm sorry to say.'

'Shouldn't you be at Santo Stefano? Provost Inghirami is anxious that you spend all your time at the walls now that Easter is past. I hear you've made a new agreement with the Ceppo. I'm giving you one more day with Lucrezia. *And* I want my nuns confessed before the next showing of the Holy Girdle.'

He straightened up to confront her. 'Do you want your altarpiece or not? If you do, then I need a model who can stand for an hour without crumpling in pain, which is why I am making this hoist. And if you do want your altarpiece, and if you want it to be innovative, then I must paint from life. Not draw. Paint. I want a permanent place to work here so I can call on Lucrezia to join me at any hour of my choice. That way and that way alone may I keep all of you wolves satisfied.'

The abbess stood in shock.

Filippo smiled suddenly and touched the cheek of this *donnona* who was five years his junior and acted like his grandmother. 'Please?'

The abbess brushed him off like a fly.

✝

The sketches he was doing were superfluous. If he was here in the cloister with Lucrezia, for the last time together alone (apart from the dozing chaperone), it had nothing to do with the altarpiece. He barely made a pretence of work.

'How did you escape Barbary?' she asked. 'I must know!'

'I didn't escape,' he admitted for the first time. 'I was given my freedom by the good man who was my master. Where did we leave off?'

'It was Ramadan.'

'Ah yes! Well, Ramadan lasts a month and ends with the festival of Eid ul-Fitr, the night the sky opens and all the Arabs stay up in the hope of meeting God.'

✝

The master and his family went to the mosque leaving Filippo alone. He went out into the garden tiled in marble with fountains playing over long channels of water that reflected the starry sky. He gazed at the stars in the pools and channels then threw his head back and stared at the sky. Suddenly, involuntarily, he began to turn as the Sufi dancers did, slowly at first, then faster, his arms outstretched, turning and turning without growing giddy. The sky did not open, but his heart did, and he saw himself as a man covered by sheaths like the layers of an onion, each one, an identity: Man, Italian, Florentine, Friar, Christian, Filippo, Sinner, Painter. As he turned, the sheaths grew transparent and vanished until only *he* was there, turning under the sky in the Moorish garden. And then images arose: Masaccio, Giotto, Brunelleschi, Ghiberti, Donatello. Images of domes, doors and monumental figures, of saints, of Christ and his Mother. Images dearer to him than any identity. He stopped turning and subsided by a pool. He played his fingers through the water, making the stars swim. Everything about Islam appealed to him, except two things. He would have to give up wine and painting figures.

Abu Ali woke him gently at dawn with a salver of flat bread. 'You should eat,' he said.

'I have been reflecting on everything you've shown me, Master, and I have realized that I am a Christian as much as I am a man. A hypocrite, too, perhaps, but so be it. There is nothing about me to recommend me to God. But when I am painting, I am not myself, I am greater than myself. Calligraphy and geometry would never satisfy me. All that control and restraint! You say we Christians set impossible disciplines, but nothing would be as impossible to me as to live and not paint as I paint, in conversation with God, advancing, going beyond what I think I can do and what my patrons expect me to do, edging ever forwards into the unknown territory of the imagination and spirit.'

'The Festival of Eid,' said Abu Ali, 'is a time to give to our fellow men and to God. Fra Filippo Lippi, I give you the freedom to be a hypocrite in your own country.'

32

SHE WRITHED SLEEPLESSLY ON HER COT. SHE HAD LIED TO Fra Filippo. She would tell him in confession. Yes, she would tell him. He deserved nothing less. It was not the death of her father that had brought her to this convent. No, it had been that night, and the day after that night, when her brother had discovered what had happened in the night and had summoned the physician.

She had been made to lie down and to raise her knees while the old physician with garlic on his breath pushed her legs apart as if dismembering a chicken. She screamed. Someone slapped a towel over her mouth. Servants held her down. She felt his fingers exploring her. She raised her head as much as she could and looked at him with a wild-eyed fury that terrified all in the room, including herself. Her blood boiled with a surging, incandescent rage. The cold, slanted eyes of the physician gazed right back at her as he withdrew his hand from between her legs, wiped them on a rag and pronounced her a whore, he who had sired bastards on his slaves as everyone knew.

Then Spinetta, who had been forced to watch all this, was commanded to lie down on the bed, except that she fainted, which made the job easier. She too, the physician declared, was a whore.

I am Lucrezia, she thought, twisting on her cot. *Lucrezia – with a name like mine, I should have killed myself, but I didn't. Because I was not raped. I was seduced and betrayed, yes, but I was not raped. Oh, Filippo…* She could not bear the idea of never being touched again except by the rough wool of the habit against her skin. She could not bear the idea of never having a child.

Now sometimes she awoke in the middle of the night, and her body moved as if to find the hand that would touch it, that would bring it back to life. *I have offended God, but He was never so cruel as to consign me to this living death.*

184

Once, not long after they had arrived and had begun work in the laundry – *to purify your souls*, the abbess had said – Spinetta had tried to talk. At first Lucrezia would not listen, but Spinetta begged to be heard.

'You are going to tell me he forced himself on you.'

'It's true. He did. Why would I sleep with any man and lose my virginity? Why would I sleep with your betrothed? But he had the eyes of a deer and seemed innocent of sin, no matter what he did, and he bribed our nurse to let him in. He lay in my bed.'

Lucrezia sat with her hands over her ears. Spinetta pulled them away. 'He kissed me all over my body, so softly, pleading with me to love him, saying that you were cold and denied him. He was like a little boy.'

Tears rolled down Lucrezia's cheeks. 'Don't. Don't.'

'Listen to me, Lucrezia. He was the thief in the night. He lied. He betrayed both of us. Don't let him kill our love for each other. It's difficult enough to bear without your anger on top of it. Please, Lucrezia, forgive me.'

Lucrezia had clasped her sister to her. She tried to forgive. They both tried. God in his wisdom had prevented their marrying. Now they were here, not as punishment, but as refuge. Thus Lucrezia told herself. But sometimes one sister would spring on the other in a wild rage that could not be stopped and since Fra Filippo had arrived, they had barely spoken to each other.

Despair welled up inside her like blood from an internal wound.

33

THE SCAFFOLDING ROSE ONLY TO THE MIDDLE TIER. TO reach the lunettes they had to use ladders and both friars went up to the vaulted ceiling of the chapel feeling unsteady after a night spent in the tavern of the dyers.

'I've done the pastiglia.' Fra Diamante pointed to the black blobs of wax on halos and the borders of gowns. Fra Filippo was more interested in admiring the perspective he had achieved in this scene, the interiors and exteriors sitting comfortably and correctly in space. 'I just need some gold leaf,' Diamante said.

'And I have to go and buy it, do I? On behalf of those who haven't reimbursed me for the roof repairs yet? Forget it! We'll make the gold ourselves.'

Fra Diamante gazed at his master with huge eyes.

'I can do it!' said Filippo. 'D'you think I can't?'

What had the pope meant when he said that Filippo was 'the perpetrator of many wicked crimes'? What crimes? Alchemy and magic? Fra Diamante decided not to argue with his master.

They descended to the scaffolding and checked the plaster of the middle tiers. The fresco season had begun a month ago and Filippo felt anxious to get on with things. He remembered feeling this same sense of excited anticipation the previous year, but then he'd been hauled off to Florence, put on trial and tortured. And after that he hadn't felt much like painting. He'd lost a year and a month.

Between them they unrolled the cartoon that Fra Diamante had brought to the church. They fastened it to the middle tier of the northern wall. Diamante had spent all of yesterday pricking holes along the lines of the figures, giving himself a stiff neck in the process.

'A wonderful composition,' he said, 'but an odd one.'

'In what way odd?'

'Saint Stephen is disputing with the Sanhedrin, but these men are not a group and they are not Jews. Each of them – well, we'll call them Pharisees, but this is a Christian prelate, a Christian lawyer, a merchant of Prato, surely, and this black-capped friar with the round eyes, round face and protruding ears – who could he be?'

Fra Filippo grinned. 'Looks familiar, doesn't he?'

'And this fine fellow with his beautiful profile.' Fra Diamante ran his finger down his pudgy nose and over a chin that merged seamlessly into his fleshy neck.

'He also looks familiar,' said Filippo, 'although with him I've improved on nature a little.'

Fra Diamante sniffed. 'And the grinning chamberlain sharing jokes and gossip with fellows at the window – I'm sure I've seen him before.'

'The procurator at the convent.'

'Yes, I have seen him before. Just the other night I saw him leaving the convent at midnight, and what was he doing there at that hour? So *we* are the Pharisees, the hypocrites.'

'That's the point I'd like to make. What is odd about that?'

'Nothing odd – it's novel. What is odd is the composition. It shows disparate individuals. It's a disunity. Each man is lost in a world of his own. This lawyer fellow even seems to be praying, but he has his eyes averted from the saint, as they all do.'

'Eyes and ears. No one is listening. That's our condition, isn't it? *Ye stiffnecked and uncircumcised in heart and ears, ye do always resist the Holy Ghost.* That's what I'm trying to show, and from what you say I've been successful. It's provoked you at least into thought and reflection.'

Fra Diamante stood back, rubbing his neck and looking at the cartoon now pinned up on the wall. 'It's a masterpiece, caro mio,' he sighed. 'No one has done anything like this before. Anyone else would have painted the usual static group of Jews around the saint, but not you! You've not only given them outward movement, you've given them inner life. I'm only surprised they're not breathing.'

'I could feast on your praise but time is short. Let's get on with the pouncing.'

A call came from below. 'Fra Filippo? The abbess wants to see you.'

'Tell her I'm busy.'

'She said I'd find you here making a drawing of the Holy Girdle for her painting.'

Fra Filippo looked down on the upturned face of the garden boy from the convent. 'Tell her I've done that and that I'll call in this evening.'

'She said it's urgent and I mustn't return without you.'

Fra Filippo's face creased up in pain and frustration. 'God,' he implored, 'what is it You want of me that I must be so often interrupted?'

'Patience,' muttered Fra Diamante on God's behalf.

'Will you be all right doing all the pouncing yourself?' Filippo asked.

'Of course.' Diamante wore that expression that was so familiar to Filippo, a face that said, 'of course I'll do the work – don't I always?' Long-suffering but not irritably so, Diamante was a diamond indeed. It was only to be regretted that his talent did not match the quality of his nature.

✝

When Filippo returned an hour later, he was flushed with anger after an argument he'd had with the abbess, that he should be summonsed for something so trivial as a young nun with delayed menstruation, even if it was the fourth month running – and no, he had not been up to his 'old tricks', certainly not, how dare she? When she peered at him askance, he had reminded her stiffly that he had not visited the convent before March.

'Which nun?' Diamante asked, cleaning the tools on the table.

'You haven't – you didn't – have you?'

'How dare you suggest it!'

'It's Suor Brigida. No one would want her, not even you. And certainly not the Holy Ghost.'

'Not when Suor Simonna is near by, no.'

Filippo laughed. 'Why choose a dried currant when you can have a fresh pear?'

'A pear near ripening: crunchy now but get her warm and she'll turn all sweet and juicy.' Diamante smacked his lips.

Filippo looked sideways at his Carmelite brother. 'How do you know that?'

'By the genius of Imagination only, believe me. How are you getting on with that distaff of a girl? You know, the pole lathe?'

Filippo did not answer. He did not wish Lucrezia to feature in such a conversation. She was his, alone, for his private adoration, for that was what he had come to, unable now to think of anything but Lucrezia, dreaming of her at night, looking out for her in the day, waiting impatiently for their next meeting. That he had left his work to go and see the abbess was not because he was afraid of the abbess but because of the possibility of seeing Lucrezia. He hadn't seen her. His skin had prickled with her proximity, but he did not know where she was and had stood listening to the woes of Suor Brigida with only half an ear.

'You're not listening!' the abbess had said, pinching his arm hard.

He missed her so much... What thoughts! He brushed them aside and went up the scaffolding to see how his assistant had fared with the middle tier. He peeled off one of the cartoons to see his designs now transferred to the wall in dots of powdered charcoal.

'I'll do the outline tomorrow,' said Diamante.

'I want you to do the pastiglia in the lunettes tomorrow, then we can be done with the top tier and take the ladders away.'

'Can you really make gold?'

'Come back to my house. We'll do it tonight.'

While walking the short distance to his house at the corner of the piazza, Fra Filippo rehearsed the recipe aloud. 'Take sal ammoniac, tin, sulphur, mercury in equal parts, but a pinch less of mercury. Put into a retort of glass and melt it all on the fire. The sulphur and mercury will thrash in their death throes, but then gold will appear.'

189

Fra Diamante began to tremble as if he were walking beside a muttering heretic, right across the sacred piazza.

'All painters are alchemists,' said Filippo.

'Painters make pigments, not gold. Oh, God!'

'We shall wait until the city sleeps then do our operation by the light of the fire itself. Angels will attend us. All will be well by morning.'

'Oh, God!' Diamante wished he were walking in the opposite direction, towards the Carmelite monastery where he lived in Prato.

When they came to the house, however, Filippo did not stop but walked on beside the canal until he came to the workshop of a cloth gilder, where he went in and did a quick deal with the man, coming out again a few moments later with a small bag of aurum mosaicum. 'It occurred to me that for a few soldi I could spend the night in my bed rather than sweating over an alchemical operation,' he said, waving the bag under his assistant's nose. 'The gold of the mosaic workers will do for us. People exclaim when they walk into San Marco's in Venice, for it seems to be all gold, but it's just coloured glass. What is good for San Marco's is surely good enough for Santo Stefano.'

'One day my heart will stop because of you. I'm going home.'

'Nearly all gold is fake,' Filippo said to Diamante's retreating back. 'Cloth of gold? It's just yellow tin.'

'You,' Diamante turned, wagging his finger at his master, 'only you could turn gold into base metal.'

'Nonsense,' said Filippo. 'Anyone can do that. And most of them do.' Laughing, he entered his house, his home. A few minutes later, he came out again and went to the tavern. A man needs company as well as a home, especially when he has a joke to relate. Poor Diamante – so gullible! Filippo got him every time. Chuckling happily, he went in and was met by a roar of greeting from his friends. One, a dyer called Il Mulo, held up a dice shaker and rattled its contents invitingly.

190

34

LATE ONE NIGHT FILIPPO AND DIAMANTE PUT THE PLASTER on the wall for a *giornata* – an area which could be finished in a day – which was to be one of the Pharisees. They returned at dawn and found it just right, resisting the pressure of a thumb but still feeling damp. Filippo sighed with contentment. While he selected his brushes, Diamante mixed some powdered ochre with clear water and dried egg yolk. He handed the master the porringer of colour. Fra Filippo dipped the brush, as sacred a moment as any other in this church – how long had it been since the last time? – and, as if administering the sacrament, applied the colour to the gown of the hypocritical Carmelite playing the part of one of the Sanhedrin. The wall took the colour in the way that satisfied the painter in the depths of his soul. Not too much, not too little – just right. He began to paint quickly. Every minute the plaster was drying and they only had an hour or two left. His stomach rumbled but he ignored it. Eating could come later.

'Fra Filippo!'

'Go away!' he responded without looking down.

'Fra Filippo!'

'Caro mio,' said Fra Diamante in his ear. 'It's the archpriest, Carlo.'

Fra Filippo looked down, frowning, to see the dark, handsome face of Cosimo de' Medici's bastard son smiling up at him. Those pale blue eyes, that skin the colour of burnt sienna and his black, Circassian hair: Filippo could never resist him. Carlo, he suspected, had been instrumental in his return to Prato despite the spell in gaol. 'My friend! How good to see you! How long have you been back from Rome?'

'Just a day. Are you well, Filippo? I heard they were rough with you. No ill after-effects I hope?'

'I've survived.'

'Can you come down for a moment?'

'The wall is lapping paint like a thirsty cat.'

'Then I'll say no more but see you later.'

'He's not a Pharisee,' said Fra Filippo, returning to his work. 'God be praised for Cosimo and his sons. But sometimes I wish there were a door on this chapel that I could close.'

For the next few hours, however, they worked without further interruption. The wall was no longer thirsty but was beginning to take the pigment as if satiated, lazily and increasingly resistant. Still, the *giornata* was done and Fra Filippo could put the final detail on the dry wall later. Meanwhile he needed to get some food in his belly and perhaps catch up on lost sleep with an hour's nap.

✠

Fra Filippo's house looked across the narrow canal to the Piazza della Pieve and the comings and goings of priests, friars, occasionally the Bishop of Pistoia, and daily the aged provost marching about as upright as a forty-year-old. Church, cloisters, square were the empire of the provost, the bald-faced, hook-nosed Gemignano Inghirami. His house snuggled against the mother church and his library opened on to the inner cloister. At an age when other men had to be helped from chair to bed and from bed to chair, Inghirami went about his duties with a combination of rigour and cheerfulness. But when he reached his chair in the library at the end of the day, and sat before his current reading propped on his desk, then he put up his swollen feet and sighed with contentment.

While Inghirami dozed in his ancient house of fine marble, Fra Filippo took his naps in his more modest house of brick and albarese stone. Although it looked on to the ecclesiastical precinct it was set apart by the canal. Filippo liked it that way: to be simultaneously a part of something and separate from it. The city was networked with canals that had been diverted from the River Bisenzio to provide running streams for the needs of the wool workers, and power for the many mills. The canal in front of his house, with its fast-running green water, separated Fra Filippo from the sacred heart of Prato and he was glad of it, glad that it was easier for him to walk into the district of the weavers and dyers than it was to reach the church, for he felt more at home with those colourful men who earned their living doing physical work. Easier for him to walk to the tavern.

Fra Diamante lived with the Carmelites near the castle but only ever went there to sleep. Each day he was in Filippo's house, painting in the workshop, keeping the house clean and tidy, cooking at the hearth or taking a nap on a truckle bed. They walked there together, over the little bridge. The main door, made of oak and set in an arch, opened on to the workshop dominated by the square panel of the convent's altarpiece. Diamante's sections were almost done, but the figures of Saint Margaret and the abbess remained in outline, as did the costumes of other figures. Filippo led Diamante to a large, woven basket filled with fabrics and took some pieces out. 'I thought griccia velvet for Saint Gregory. It looks like shiny gold, doesn't it? And I love these long, curved branches of lobed leaves. A griccia velvet mantle edged with a border of pearls over a fine linen gown. Do you remember that painting by Van Eyck we saw in Florence? All those pearls and gems? So Gregory will have a gem-encrusted triple tiara, and gloves of the softest kid. What do you think?'

Fra Diamante nodded thoughtfully, running the piece of weightless velvet over his hands.

'And then this,' Filippo took from the basket a length of brocaded velvet. 'I don't begin to understand how they make this, but I thought it would look well on Saint Augustine. He was a bishop after all. And so his mitre will have emeralds as big as frogs, and a ruby brooch to hold the mantle together at his breast. What do you think?'

'Who will lend you emeralds so big for models?'

'There's always glass. By the way, what do you think of my ultramarine work?'

'It's very fine – a handsome sky matching the gowns of Saint Margaret and Saint Thomas.'

'It's azurite.'

'*What?*'

Fra Filippo smiled and raised his eyebrows. 'Do you think she'll know the difference, the old sow? She's not going to pay me, you know. I feel it in my bones. So I'm not spending any more on pigments than I have to. I'm not a fool.'

'You're always accusing the apothecaries of cheating you.'

'Who do you think I learnt my tricks from? So what have we left to do apart from the costumes? The angel Raphael and Tobias, Saint Thomas, the abbess and Saint Margaret. Shouldn't take too long. Trouble is, I want to paint the last two as I have sketched them, from life. Would I get my models to come here? I doubt it. So we need to arrange to have the panel and my easel delivered to the convent. See to it, will you?'

✝

Having eaten, Filippo laid on his bed to sleep but found himself restless, turning this way and that, his blood infected by a twitchiness only one thing could cure. After a few minutes he rose up, padded out of his room and down the stairs in bare feet, so as not to disturb Diamante with the sound of his sandals slapping on the tiled floors. He put his sandals on at the door and went out. The afternoon was hot for April and the Piazza della Pieve was deserted. He could hear snores coming out of the many open windows as he followed the canal down to Santa Margherita's and let himself in at the gate. Yes, there were many snores here, too, as he had hoped and expected. He went to the laundry but found it at rest. A bucket hung from the A-frame he had made at the well. Was it his imagination or was that bucket smiling and happy?

He went into the cloister just to walk past her cell and jumped violently when he saw her sitting there, at the place where he had done his sketches, her hands folded in her lap, her eyes closed. She looked as if she were posing for him.

'Lucrezia?'

Now she jumped violently and clutched her heart, but her frown melted quickly into a look of relief. 'You've come! I've been waiting for days!'

'I told you the work was finished.'

'I miss you. I miss your stories so much. Thank you for the contraption.'

He took her hand in his, gazed on it in wonder, that it sat there as if it belonged there. No flinching, no trembling, no withdrawal. His Lucrezia. 'Would you like to take a walk?'

She looked at him hungrily. Apart from festival processions, she had not been outside the convent since she had arrived. 'Where to?'

'I'd like to show you the frescoes we've finished before we take the ladders down.'

He led her to the convent's chapel where a door gave on to the piazza – so much easier than going through the cumbersome gate with its grilles and locks. They turned into the lane leading up to Santo Stefano: a nun with her chaplain going to church – who would remark on that?

As they crossed the canal by the bridge, Filippo flung out an arm saying, 'That's my house' as they passed it. Lucrezia nearly walked backwards into the canal, fascinated to see where the chaplain lived, how many floors the house had, its corner position on the street. He caught her arm to prevent her from tumbling into the water. 'You'd come out as green as parsley,' he said, 'and try explaining that to Her Holiness.'

At the church, he took her up to the middle tier and from there pointed to the almost-completed lunettes above. She pulled her gown up through her girdle to free her legs as if she were in the laundry and went up the ladder. He watched her calves and ankles as she mounted the rungs. Her skin was creamy, her legs slender – fine columns hewn by a master. When she reached the lunette of the birth of Saint Stephen, Lucrezia did not gasp in awe as he had expected but viewed the complementary scenes of the

birth of Saint Stephen and, over on the facing wall, the birth of
Saint John, with a studied expression that began to border on a
frown. 'I prefer that one,' she said, pointing to the birth of Saint
John on the far side of the chapel. 'I don't like this one.' She
wrinkled her nose at the birth of Saint Stephen.

Fra Filippo was about to say, 'Oh, Diamante did that,' but
found the lie lodged in his throat. Diamante had painted both of
them, apart from the beautiful servant entering the room, bearing
a tray on her head in the style of Donatello. 'What's wrong with
it?' he asked, mortified. He had been pleased with the design
solutions he had found to overcome the difficulties presented by
the shape of the lunette. And the dramatic addition of a dark angel
substituting a changeling for the baby – an apocryphal story
Archpriest Carlo had told him – that must surely elevate this birth
scene above all others. It must then be the pastiglia ornamentation
that she objected to, still at the gesso stage and yet to be burnished
with his fake gold.

'The bed fills the room,' Lucrezia complained. 'How could
you change its linen? What would the poor servant girl do to
make it? Would she have to lift the mattress while she was
kneeling on it?'

Filippo was astonished at what Lucrezia saw – no dark angels
or the beautiful servant, not the perfect perspective or the
resolution of the baby Stephen being handed to a bishop to be
looked after. No. She saw a bed that made life difficult for a
non-existent servant.

'There's a space on the far side, between the bed and the wall.'

'I can't see it.'

'Of course not – it's hidden by the bed.' His mood now
souring, he told her to come down the ladder before she hurt
herself. In silence they descended to the floor of the church and
he escorted her out of the south door and back to the convent
with no further conversation other than his remarks on the
general level of intelligence of the people of Prato.

'I'm a Florentine,' said Lucrezia stiffly.

Filippo prided himself on his skill in the art of love but he seemed curiously unable to get free of his annoyance. Such an opportunity wasted! He should be coaxing her into an alleyway and kissing her on the lips, not stumping along beside her unable to speak. He glanced at her but she quickly turned her head. Had he seen a tear on her cheek? He should reach out to her, speak her name, end the evil spell she'd put them under, but he could not. He ushered her into the convent and then went back home, in such a foul, black mood that Diamante fled as soon as he saw him.

When Filippo returned to Santo Stefano in the evening to continue work, he put a ladder from the platform up to the top tier, hung some lamps and, painting on dry plaster, added the figure of a servant girl behind the bed with an armful of sheets. He repainted the wall, moving it slightly to the right to create a gap at the end of the bed and, for good measure, put an open door behind the servant to show how she'd got there.

'That should satisfy your need for logic, *ma donnina*,' he muttered.

35

ALL THE NUNS WERE IN THE LITTLE CHAPEL WITH THE abbess, her sister, the smiling procurator and the local priest. Filippo had hoped and expected the dignitaries of Santo Stefano to attend, but they had not come; nevertheless, with a flourish he pulled on the cord and the drape slithered from the altarpiece like a silken chemise dropping to the floor. He was gratified to hear gasps. Yes, that was what he liked to hear, a good intake of breath. He turned to gaze on his audience.

The nuns had never seen anything like this before, the richness of colour, the liveliness of form, the immediacy of it, as if these figures were with them here in the chapel.

'Holy Mother of God!' said Suor Brigida crossing herself.

The procurator glanced at her coldly then returned to comparing the figure of Saint Margaret with that of Suor Lucrezia. He turned to Filippo, smiled at him broadly and gave him a conspiratorial wink.

Filippo stood back and viewed the panel critically. In painting the saint and the donor from life, he had thrown the other figures into a kind of shadow. The Virgin was in a mandorla of heavenly radiance, attended by angels above and saints below, all in fine brocades and encrustations of jewels, yet the eye of the viewer slipped sideways to the plainly-dressed young woman on the left whose hand rested on the head of a midget abbess.

'What an abomination!' the abbess suddenly burst out. 'It's a travesty, a shocking travesty, It's a portrait of Suor Lucrezia attended by various saints! How magnanimous of her to lay her hand on my head in that patronising fashion! And why am I so *small?*'

'That's traditional with donor figures,' Filippo countered. He stressed the word 'donor', wondering how he could broach the subject of the fee. He was worried that the abbess was about to proclaim the contract void on the grounds of 'dissatisfaction' or, worse, broken by his neglect of the clause 'by his hand only'. He had his argument prepared for that one, that as his assistant, Fra Diamante was his 'hand'. He spoke glowingly of the harmony of colour and how the panel lit up the chapel 'like a ring of emeralds and garnets'.

'Nmph.'

'The materials were very costly.'

'They've all been paid for, and the receipt was witnessed by two living people. That ultramarine blue cost a fortune!'

'About the fee, Mother.'

She turned on him, her eyes hostile as if he had sullied the sanctity of the place by mentioning money. 'What fee?'

'The fee for my efforts and time.'

'You are the chaplain here. You receive a living – for what? What do you do other than paint? Therefore is it not reasonable to suppose that your painting comes without charge to our community? Surely Fra Giovanni at San Marco charged nothing for decorating the friars' cells?'

'Are you saying you will pay me nothing?' Fra Filippo cried.

'I am saying that this abomination will not be displayed here in the chapel. Have it removed to my study.'

'Nothing at all?'

'You were sent to me to practise your vows: chastity, obedience and *poverty*.'

✝

Fra Filippo went home with all hope reduced to a ball of tar, the black bile he suffered from continually. The world and its preference for some over others would wear him out. He was tired of being humiliated each time he asked for his fee; he was tired of being compared to the late Fra Giovanni, who had *never* stooped to ask for a fee. For Fra Giovanni, painting had been prayer, and it should be the same for Fra Filippo. How he abased himself, they seemed to say, by asking for gold!

The shops were opening for the evening, flies buzzed round carcasses hanging outside the butcher's, snuffling dogs got under his feet. The many canals were a flowing stink through Prato. Wasps followed him – he was a honeypot to wasps and mosquitoes – and he made his way beating the air around his head, muttering and swearing. He had ten soldi in his purse. Ten soldi! – and he the highest 'paid' painter in Tuscany!

Wool carders and dyers were returning to their workshops after resting for the afternoon, the din of their clogs smacking on the cobbles and echoing off the close walls. Everyone greeted one another, and many greeted him. '*Buona sera*, Fra Pippo!' Those who knew him from nights spent in the tavern gave exaggerated bows of deference to his habit. 'Will we see you at "vespers"?'

'No, not this evening.'

The sound of drumming assaulted his ears. The youth of the parish of Santo Stefano were practising for the coming festival at the beginning of May. The Taverna dei Tintori was open, its door under the vine arbour invitingly ajar. Fra Filippo took a deep breath and walked past. He couldn't afford 'vespers' and did not want to start a new debt with the taverner.

'Pippo, my darling!'

He looked up to see the taverner's wife, leaning from an upper window and smiling down on him with more than an air of invitation.

'No, Rosaria,' he said, 'not today.' He sighed and walked on, remembering what the archbishop had told him when he was released from gaol. 'All I have to do is keep saying no. That is the secret of abstinence.'

'Fra Pippo!' said his friend Dubbo, on his way to the dye vats that were set up permanently in the piazza at the side of the church. 'Will I see you at the tavern later?'

'No,' he said.

'Then you had better come now,' said Dubbo, veering from his work. He took Fra Filippo by the arm and guided him back to the Taverna dei Tintori. The friar put up no resistance. If ever he needed a drink, it was now, and the arrival of Dubbo was clearly a sign from God.

At this hour the tavern was quiet, with but few customers there, carders and dyers who had ignored the evening bell and were in no hurry to return to work. Nearly a hundred years had passed since the great rebellion of the wool carders, which had taken power from the guilds for about three years, but the memory of that power of their great grandfathers still flowed in their veins, and these men were not easy, pliable workers but ones who could frighten their masters, the wool merchants, into lenience if not submission. They did the work they were paid to do, but in their own time, and were answerable to no bells. They smiled at Fra Filippo and made room for him at their table.

He was such a rich fund of stories that he rarely had to pay for his own drink. On this evening, Dubbo did the honours.

'Limp as my prick,' said Fra Filippo, dandling his purse lightly in his hands.

'Rosaria will see to that,' said a dyer called Il Mulo. If ever there was trouble in the ward, il Mulo was either behind it or dealing with it, the unofficial *capo* of the district. His hands were permanently stained blue with woad. 'How's your stomach? It looks like you're back to full girth.'

The men in the tavern, having heard all the details of Fra Filippo's torture, several times, were concerned about his welfare. That he had been so severely punished for such a mild crime, if any crime had been committed, had been added to their collection of the injustices of the *popolo grasso* – the fat people, the magnates. Crimes against property always warranted greater retribution than crimes against persons. True, a prostitute might be birched naked through the streets, and a heretic burned in the main piazza, but no one complained about such great entertainment as that; but murderers and rapists too often got off with a light sentence while the prisons were crammed with debtors.

Having assured his friends that he was fully recovered, Filippo started to tell them how he had been cheated by Abbess Bartolommea.

'That *befana!*' growled Il Mulo. 'She comes here with her Florentine airs and graces and sets up a convent to put us all to shame.'

'I heard she wants to shed light on our shadows,' said Dubbo. 'What shadows?'

'It takes light to create shadows,' Fra Filippo offered wisely, draining his cup and holding it out for a refill. 'No light, no shadows.' He was beginning to feel better. The more his friends complained on his behalf, the better he felt. That he was not alone in hating the abbess was enough to cheer him. He told them how she grew mysteriously fat while her nuns only ever grew thin, how she snored when she retired to her cell for 'prayer and contemplation'. He gave them everything they needed to set off rumours all over town of the great hypocrite at Santa Margherita's. 'The altarpiece includes her ugly portrait as patron. What patronage? I told her at the beginning she couldn't afford me, but she said the convent has become wealthy through industry. Oh, she's paid for the materials, and the frame. The apothecary gets paid for the pigments, the frame-maker, the carpenter who cut the panel. But the painter? Not a denaro.'

Rosaria came into the room with a dish of candied plums and made a play of dropping a fruit into the mouth of each man. Fra Filippo caught her and put her astride his lap facing him.

'His purse needs your attention, Rosaria,' said Dubbo.

'Ah, my Pippolino,' said the buxom wife of the taverner, deputed by her husband to keep the customers happy. 'Are you having a difficult day?'

He stared into those twin mounds of comfort swelling over a bodice, the laces of which were tied in a bow. He had only to pull one thread to release those pent-up lovelies. Instead he sank his face into her cleavage and inhaled the scent of rosewater.

Rosaria moved slowly up and down, mystified by the absence of his usual response. Then, realising that her breasts were becoming wet with his silent tears, she held his head. 'What is it, my darling?'

'I'm old,' he muttered into her flesh. 'Rosaria, I'm an old man.'

'No you're not,' she assured him. 'You're an old fool.'

Vengefully Filippo pulled on both threads of the bow. Cupping her breasts with both hands, he growled into them and rubbed them with the bristle of his chin.

'That's enough, Rosaria!' called her husband. 'Fra Filippo Lippi – be ashamed of yourself!'

Amid the laughter, men began to rise from their benches to return to work. Even woolworkers and dyers had something of a conscience and one by one each man left to make his tardy and wine-fuelled way back to his frames or vats, promising the others that justice would be done. 'Let the priests take the Mass – we have God in our hearts and don't need hypocrites.' *We are the people of God,* they sang, a refrain from the great rebellion. *We are the people of God,* sang Fra Filippo as he wove his way back home.

✝

'Nothing?' cried Fra Diamante when he heard about the reception of the painting. 'But you promised me half!'

'Half of nothing? How could I be so mean? Dear boy, have all of it. No, I insist, all of it.'

'You're so generous.'

'Do we have any wine?'

'A jar and a half.'

'Would you like to join me on a journey to paradise?'

'I'll get there before you.' Diamante fetched the opened jar and, a while later, the full one.

As the wine began to swim in his blood and his head to sag, Fra Filippo dwelt on Fra Giovanni. Any criticism he made of the late friar-painter of San Marco burned in his gullet like stomach acid, for at heart he had loved the man as he had loved his paintings, their simplicity, their sweetness.

'Have I ever told you about the time when I worked with Fra Giovanni?'

'Um, yes, I believe you have.'

'It was 1439, during the Great Council.'

A short while later, Fra Diamante was aroused from his stupor by a name. 'What did you say?'

'I said that Plethon was a magus.'

'Who's Plethon?'

'Have you been asleep? Plethon. He was here during the Great Council – had a forked and plaited beard. Obviously a magus. Archpriest Carlo told me recently that, when Plethon went back to Greece, he gave up any vestige of Christianity and founded a mystery school.'

'What's a mystery school?'

'It's a school where, in answer to any question from a pupil, the tutor shrugs and says, "I don't know. It's a mystery".' Both friars found this uproariously funny.

'No, no, no,' said Diamante at last. 'It's a school of secrets.'

'What does it teach?'

'That's a secret!' Again the Carmelites squealed with laughter.

'No, seriously, no,' said Filippo, wiping his eyes. 'Listen. Carlo told me that Plethon was the last of the Magi. That's what he said. The last of the eastern Magi. And Cosimo is the first of the western.'

'*What?*'

'That's what he said. "Plethon was a magus, and so is my father." I remember – I remember back then in the thirties, all that was going on in Florence. The new dome, the sculptures, the bronze doors. And then the Great Council. I remember hearing that Cosimo had discovered a text of the complete works of Plato in Greek. I wonder what happened after that? That was years ago. Cosimo said he was going to refound the Platonic Academy. Has he done it?'

'Do you think he has?'

'Carlo told me that Plethon died a few years ago. So it's all up to Cosimo now, to continue the line of the Magi. But I've heard nothing.'

Diamante re-filled their cups.

'I met him once, you know, Plethon. Coming out of Cosimo's own cell at San Marco. I was with the archbishop. Well, Little Anthony as he was at the time. Do you know, I think they were founding a mystery school right there and then. We could hear them chanting in Greek.'

'Could you?' Diamante's eyelids were drooping again. He dozed only for a moment but in that moment Filippo went off at a tangent.

'Trouble is,' he said, slapping the table, 'people preferred Fra Giovanni.'

'People are blind,' said Diamante, propping up his head and wondering how much he had missed.

'D'you think so? Fra Giovanni had a holiness that I lack.'

'No denying that, caro mio. Just thank God that Fra Giovanni died young.'

'I loved him as I would love myself if only I were more lovable,' Filippo whimpered.

'Now what are you talking about, caro mio?'

'I don't mean to be a bad man. I'm just weak.' Here Filippo went face down on the table, his arms splayed out in front of him, a prostration that was also resignation. 'And I don't know how to be strong,' he continued, muffled. 'The archbishop tells me that all it takes is an effort of will.' He drew himself up. 'All I have to do is say no.' He watched Diamante refilling his cup yet again and pushed his own forward.

'God bless tomorrow!' Diamante raised his cup. 'May it never come!'

'*Carpe diem!*' Filippo raised his cup, drained it and collapsed face down on the table, not to speak or rise again for the rest of that night. Instead he dreamt of being in bed with Saint Margaret, her long creamy legs up around his neck.

36

FIVE TIMES A YEAR THERE WAS A PUBLIC 'SHOWING' OF the Holy Girdle. A week before calendimaggio, all the nuns came one-by-one to make confession.

The box against the wall of the convent chapel was small and confined, with a crucifix hanging above the chaplain's chair and that odour of sanctity that is always someone else's – the lingering, heavy scent of a passing saint. Originally the convent had been founded as a hospital. Were previous chaplains more pious, devoted men? He doubted it, but they were probably better at appearing so. Fra Filippo sat back and stretched out his legs. With luck, he could get through five nuns in less than an hour and be off to his dinner or a game of dice with Diamante. There was no point in thinking about painting on a day as disrupted as this one. He wondered whether there was someone he could hire to do the duties of the chaplain?

The first of the nuns entered the booth with her veiled head hanging low. He was sure it was Brigida, the way her hands were linked under her swollen belly. 'Father, I have sinned.' she said.

Yes, good, at last. 'Confess your sins to me, my daughter.'

'I didn't say my prayers last night.'

Oh God... 'That's hardly a sin.'

'Or the night before.'

He'd have known it was Brigida even if he couldn't see her shape. Always that tang of garlic on her breath and the greyness to her tone that inspired misery in those around her.

'Well, then, a small sin of omission.'

'It is desire, Father.'

'Is it.' He could not be bothered to inflect the question but let it fall out of his mouth as a statement. He always tired so quickly of those who strove to be bad.

'I prefer the comfort of my bed to prayer.'

'Who doesn't?' thought Fra Filippo but decided not to stoke this particular fire. Zealotry was best left to smoulder. 'Forty-two Hail Marys,' he said. 'On your knees without a cushion.'

'Forty-two?' Suor Brigida was astonished. She left the confessional with a clatter and went to find the abbess to complain. *Forty-two Hail Marys! In my condition!*

'It's what she wanted,' Fra Filippo protested when confronted by a furious abbess. 'She wants to suffer. She loves to suffer. Have you not noticed how she thrills to stories of martyrdom? No story so grisly that she doesn't greet it with shining eyes. She is a sick woman, in my view – forty-two Hail Marys may prove something of a cure. I hope you didn't relieve her of the penance?'

'As it happens, I did.'

'Forty-two Hail Marys, on her knees on the hard floor before she goes to bed!'

'Brother Filippo, there is something you should know. Suor Brigida is with child.'

'Well, obviously, but whose? If only she would confess to that, we could make some progress in spirit.'

'I have examined her many times and her story never falters: she woke late one night in December to find light all around her and the Angel Gabriel hovering in the air.'

Fra Filippo bellowed with laughter. 'Suor Brigida is carrying the New Messiah? Forgive me, Mother, I have work to attend to.' He went back into the confessional box where, in her soft, pillowy voice, Suor Piera confessed to missing her children. 'I have not let them go, Frate. Have not surrendered them, nor my life, to the Lord.'

'What happened to your children?'

Suor Piera looked surprised. No one had asked her that before and she had never spoken of it to anyone. 'When my husband died, God rest his dear soul, I had to return to my family but they would not take the children. I had four. Two were taken in by cousins, but the youngest two –' her voice snagged in her throat. 'Aged five and three. Just three. To the foundling hospital.' Her voice was trembling.

Fra Filippo swallowed hard, remembering his aunt's cold face when she abandoned him and his brother in the Carmine for the same reasons. Perhaps, just perhaps, she had not felt as cold as she had looked. 'Weep, my sister. Every tear waters the ground of love. When you weep the hand of the Virgin is laid upon your head. How can it be otherwise?'

The church resounded to Suor Piera's wailing and she had to be helped back to her cell in the cloisters.

The abbess returned to see what the noise was and found Fra Filippo pacing the chapel, his face cupped in his hands and weeping himself. She demanded an explanation for these fountains of emotion suddenly gushing in her convent and wanted to know why Piera had been given no penance. 'God is love,' he said softly, wiping his eyes, 'not a schoolmaster looking for any excuse to whack your legs with a stick. Sometimes the sin is punishment enough.' He went back inside the confessional.

The next to enter was Spinetta.

'Forgive me, Father, for I have sinned.'

'What is the nature of your sin?'

'Ingratitude. I am not thankful enough that I've been brought here for my salvation. I think of the convent not as a refuge but as a prison.'

Filippo was puzzled. 'What do you mean, salvation?'

'It was my choice, my actions that ruined our lives. I could have been thrown into the streets, but I was sent here.'

'What actions?'

Spinetta brought her face close to the grille. 'You don't know? I can't tell you if she hasn't. It has to come from her. Please, give me penance for ingratitude.'

'Tell me who fathered the child on Suor Brigida and there will be no further penance.'

'It was the procurator. He gave her a kind of herb that made her ecstatic – she only saw light, not the man. Are you sure about the penance?'

'Certain. Go in peace.'

Spinetta rose and left. Filippo stared through the grille to the empty space that, so far as he was concerned, should be filled by that stupidly grinning procurator, not these young women who had to go through hours of reflection to find something to confess to. He blinked. The space had been filled by Lucrezia.

'Forgive me, Father. I have sinned.'

'What is the nature of your sin?'

Her slender, white fingers appeared through the grille and curled to grip the iron.

'Hatred.'

'Of whom?'

'Of almost all I know.'

'Even your sister?'

'Especially my sister. Sometimes I think I even hate God. Nothing is fair in this world. I am punished for the actions of my sister and my betrothed. You know, don't you? She told you.'

'No she didn't, but I'm beginning to realize you haven't been telling me the whole truth. Too many mouths to feed.'

'My brother discovered I had had – conjugal relations – with my betrothed. And my sister – she had slept with him, too, on the same night. Antonio had my lover murdered and sent us here for our salvation. If by "salvation" he meant an early death then his plan is almost complete.'

'Lucrezia, you're hating now, aren't you? I can feel it. Do you hate me?'

Her breathing became short and laboured. 'Of course I hate you. You are one of my gaolers after all. I am a Magdalene and, now that you know, you despise me for it.'

'Do I?'

'All men do.'

'If I do, then I'm a hypocrite.' Filippo brought his mouth to those slender fingers gripping the iron grille and kissed them.

'What is my penance, Father?' she asked, quickly withdrawing her hands.

'I'm going to be harsh, Sister, but for good reason. Ten Hail Marys every hour on the hour, and you must recite them with full attention.'

Lucrezia made a sharp intake of breath. 'Harsh indeed.'

'I'm going to speak to the abbess to have you released from the laundry, you and Spinetta. I'll tell the abbess that purity of the right kind is best effected through prayer. Ten Hail Marys, every hour on the hour.'

Realizing how light the penance was compared to laundry duty, Lucrezia now regarded him with watery eyes.

'That's for you and Spinetta to recite together, and tell Spinetta that if she's not grateful, I'll make it twenty Hail Marys.'

37

FOUR SHOWINGS OF THE HOLY GIRDLE COINCIDED WITH
a major feast: the Birth of Mary in September, Christmas, Easter,
the Assumption of Mary in August. The May showing, however,
did not correspond to the liturgical calendar. It was held as if
to remind those engaged in unholy and lustful pursuits of the
ever-present love of Our Lady. For on calendimaggio the youth
threw off their Christian trappings and raced about the woods and
meadows like stags and boars on heat.

Fra Filippo said it was all nonsense and continued painting the
chapel of Santo Stefano where he was beginning to feel more
settled in the work. Diamante was doing the mountains of the
wilderness in the Life of Saint John while Filippo continued
painting the scene of Stephen and the Pharisees. They worked in
silence, ignoring the men beginning to gather below to take the
holy relic from its chapel. The Bishop of Pistoia was not expected
on this occasion, but the provost and the archpriest were in full
ceremonial vestments, attended by canons and deacons. Fra
Filippo looked down from the scaffolding and suddenly his
interest was aroused. He went down to speak to them as an excuse
to see close up the chasubles they were wearing with their super-
naturally fine embroideries of gold, copper and silver threads.
Archpriest Carlo threw out his arms for the painter to admire the
embroidery back and front.

'Miraculous work, no?'

'Miraculous,' said Filippo, peering closely at stitches so tiny
they brought tears to his eyes, such was the skill and humility of
the needleworkers.

Carlo took him by the arm, led him aside and looked him
straight in the eye with that disconcertingly blue stare. 'My brother
Giovanni wishes me to speak to you about the commission for an
altarpiece for Naples. He is anxious for you to begin.'

'But I am so busy here!'

'I've spoken to the Ceppo and they have agreed to give you a year off.'

Filippo was torn between delight at the idea of working in Florence and annoyance that his life was being arranged behind his back. He stood there mouthing.

Carlo squeezed his arm. 'The price of genius is fame. You must learn to live with its demands, my friend.'

'What is the commission? Giovanni said very little in his letter.'

'It's an altarpiece intended as a gift for the King of Naples, to express our gratitude for his support which allowed us to form an alliance with Milan and Venice. I can see by your eyes glazing over that this means nothing to you but I tell you it affects you personally. There have been so many small wars in our lives that we've learnt to take them for granted but now we can travel the length of the country in peace. It is the masterstroke of my father whose dream is of a united Italy. It required endless negotiations and gifts, as you can imagine. He did that all at his own expense, for he holds no office in Florence, as you know. And now, at further personal expense, he wishes to thank the King with this gift, which he wants to be painted by no one other than you.'

Within a minute Fra Filippo had learnt that he was a genius, famous and the favourite painter of the Medici. He was suddenly eager to begin work on their altarpiece.

'A year off, then, starting now, and you will be working in Florence.'

Fra Filippo looked up at the walls. Fame and fortune were in the balance against a quiet, steady life and being near the woman he loved. 'Carlo, do you think Giovanni would allow me to start at Michaelmas? I could get the middle tier finished this summer.'

Now Carlo was equally torn, for Santo Stefano was his church and he was as keen as the provost to see the chapel paintings completed. 'I'll speak to my brother. Are you coming outside for the showing?' he asked, wedging his biretta down on his head of springy hair.

'Not today.'

'Fra Filippo Lippi, do you not believe that we have the Girdle of the Virgin herself?'

Filippo looked into Carlo's azure eyes, saw the humour there and smiled. 'Of course I do,' he said. 'I'm just not one for crowds.'

'You want to see it close to and in private, is that it?' Carlo turned to Provost Inghirami. 'Fra Filippo will attend us in the Chapel of the Holy Relic.'

'Careful,' said Inghirami cheerfully to the painter. 'If you touch that Girdle you will be turned to a pillar of salt.'

'I'll keep well back.' Filippo followed them to the chapel where the bronze gates now stood open. He went in and tried to concentrate on the great reliquary, but his eyes were drawn to the Gaddi paintings. Those blue, blue, ultramarine skies… He snatched his attention back. The reliquary was open and the provost was lifting out the girdle of green wool as if it were the baby Jesus from his cradle. Just a green woollen belt. The provost, followed by priests and two incense-swinging deacons, went towards the door and stair that led to the secret passage within the wall. It ran across the front of the church, above the main door, and ended at the outside pulpit – all part of the stage-managed drama to be enacted. Filippo was looking towards the stair. So was the provost. One of the ends of the Holy Girdle, draped over the provost's hands and borne ceremoniously aloft, lightly brushed the friar's face. Filippo jumped as if stung or burned and clapped his hand to his cheek.

'Are you all right?' Carlo asked.

Filippo was shaken. 'Well, I seem not to have turned to a pillar of salt,' he was able to say before fleeing the chapel.

'What is it, caro mio?' Diamante asked when Filippo appeared back on the scaffolding. 'You look like a man who has seen an angel.'

'Nonsense,' said Filippo Lippi.

He tried to work but felt listless. In truth he wanted only to think on her and to sigh like a boy for his first love. He had barely seen her since the altarpiece was completed – once or twice, that was all. These rare sightings acted like a morsel of food to a starving man, serving only to prolong the agony of his death. He wanted her as he had had her, to himself in the afternoons, talking to her – so freely, so sweetly. Now she was gone, back into the weeds of a nun and the anonymity of communal life.

He went to the convent daily, an attentive, dutiful chaplain with whom no one could find fault, but most days he did not see her. Still, it was enough to be close, to have a chance of a sighting, even if he did have to go home or back to Santo Stefano crippled by disappointment. Twice he saw her in the laundry: both times she saw him first and, ashamed by her confession, closed the door before he could enter.

Suddenly trumpets blared from the pulpit outside: the Holy Girdle was now being held aloft before the Pratese.

'Everyone will be out there,' said Diamante, resentfully, hunched over his work on the wall.

Fra Filippo turned and looked at his assistant's back. Then he threw down his brush, hurtled down the ladder and ran from the church through the south door. The ritual of the showing was always repeated three times: he had heard the trumpets twice and they were sounding for the third time as he came out into the L-shaped piazza, packed with local people. Up in the pulpit, which grew out of the south-west corner like a martin's nest, two deacons were purifying the space by swinging their smoking, pungent censers, then the provost stepped forward, holding the relic aloft for the third and last time.

Diamante was right, everyone was there, including the friars of several orders and the nuns of all the convents. He found the Santa Margherita nuns close to his house, like nervous moorhens paddling to keep their place in the stream.

The abbess, though buffeted by the crowd, held her ground looking radiant, her inner fires stoked by the showing of the Holy Girdle. She was holding her hands aloft as if the belt was draped over them.

'Imagine it, slung over the pregnant hips of Our Lady! Just the sight of it erases all tiredness and doubt. How fortunate we are, my sisters, to be living so close to such a magnificent relic as this. God bless Prato!'

Fra Filippo approached and bade her good day. He glanced across the group of wimpled faces until his eyes were arrested by Lucrezia's. He took a deep breath and began a banal conversation with the abbess, about what a fine day it was, and yes, how fortunate for youth to have such boundless energy that must, of course, be harnessed for God's work. He had his own hands clasped behind his back. Suddenly he felt Lucrezia's hand snuggling into his. She must have moved to stand close behind him. Tears welled in his eyes and ran down his cheeks.

'What's the matter?' the abbess demanded.

'Just slightly overcome by the occasion,' gulped Filippo. To wipe his eyes he must disengage his hands so he let the tears flow. At last the abbess broke the spell by turning abruptly and ushering her nuns homewards. As Lucrezia's hand slipped from his, Filippo reached for his sleeve, wiped his face, blew into it and made for the privacy of his own house.

The following day a message came from Carlo de' Medici saying that he was to present himself in Florence by Ascension Day.

38

DELAYED BY HAVING TO PRODUCE A QUANTITY OF designs for Diamante to work from, Filippo made the short journey to the city at Pentecost, riding on a hired mule. No matter how often he saw the skyline of Florence from the Prato road, the immense structure of Brunelleschi's dome – terracotta tiles ribbed with white stone, an octagon resolving into a sphere – filled him with civic pride, as it was meant to. Within the city walls, and approaching the cathedral, Fra Filippo made the sign of the cross over his breast, to protect his soul should the dome choose this moment to collapse. It had stood now for twenty years, but still the fear and expectation would not evaporate. At the Baptistry, he paused to gaze upon Ghiberti's great bronze doors and their panels of scenes from the Old Testament done in exquisite relief and true perspective: anyone who said that Ghiberti had outdone the ancients was surely right.

Like Fra Giovanni, Ghiberti had died the previous year; like Fra Giovanni, he had completed his life's work before he did so. The perfect death – the perfect life – the perfect man. Fra Filippo pulled a face, knowing his own life and work would never be so neat. He would die violently, murdered probably, or a victim of plague, his work half-finished.

He made his way up the Via Larga past San Lorenzo, now rebuilt to Brunelleschi's plans. He had gone to see it on a previous visit and had been repelled by its austerity, so now he passed it without a glance, his attention taken instead by Cosimo's new house on the corner. Here he paused to appreciate a style of architecture more to his taste. The great rusticated stones of the ground floor made the place look like a fortress, but the masonry of the second floor consisted of trimmed blocks separated by deep grooves. The third floor was of fine, dressed stone, topped by a projecting cornice. He knew the way Cosimo thought – always symbolically – and read the message of the stone with ease, of the ascension of man from rude bestiality to the fineness of the cultivated life. It did not escape him that the bestial level, which had an open loggia on the corner, was given over to the banking business, the source of Cosimo's fortune.

Men said that Cosimo's lavish patronage of religious houses was designed to keep his account with God in balance; that may be true, Filippo thought, but no one, not even the archbishop or Pope Eugenius, had required Cosimo to rebuild San Marco *before* building a house for himself. Cosimo was the kind of man who clears a debt before incurring a new one.

The Palazzo de' Medici was complete externally but building work continued on the inside. Filippo stood in the courtyard, waiting for Cosimo's son, Giovanni, and watching in concern as a seven-year-old boy hoisted his little brother from the ground to the first storey in a builder's bucket.

'Ah, Filippo!' said the broad-faced, broad-chested Giovanni, coming out of a room off the courtyard, his arms spread wide in greeting.

'Is that child all right?'

Giovanni looked up at the gallery. 'Lorenzo!' he bellowed at his nephew, so loud that the boy started and nearly let go of the rope and bucket. 'Where is your tutor? Let Giuliano down now, gently! Does your father know what you are doing?' He turned back to the friar with a shrug. 'My brother, Piero, is ill and his sons run wild. Come, let me give you a tour of the house.' He led the way up the stairs to the first floor, its grand sala and suites of chambers. Recently appointed director of the bank, he was dressed soberly in a dark, pleated tunic that reached down to his knees and was girded by a supple leather belt. The only thing about him that betrayed his wealth was the heavy belt buckle of pure gold.

As he showed Filippo the bare rooms, Giovanni told him that the altarpiece they were commissioning was in the service of diplomacy. 'We need to keep the King of Naples sweet and fond of Florence.'

'I've only recently agreed with the Ceppo that I will finish the fresco cycle at Santo Stefano within two years.'

Giovanni shrugged. 'Carlo can get that extended if needs be. The altarpiece takes precedence and should not delay you over-long. We want a triptych – Virgin and Child in the central panel, of course, flanked by Saints Michael and Anthony. Where are we now, Pentecost? Perhaps if you could bring me some trial designs before we leave for our country villa in July.'

Filippo wondered whether to discuss the possibility of not starting until Michaelmas but two months was generous for designs and he decided that he could do them without interrupting his work on the frescoes. If there was any conflict, let the brothers work it out between them.

One large room they came to was being strangely partitioned. 'The chapel,' Giovanni explained. 'A room within a room, in the heart of the house. Has to be this way, according to my father. It muffles all external sound.' He gazed at the friar, to see if his meaning had been comprehended. It had not.

'Muffles?'

'We live on a busy, noisy street: hawkers, house builders, road menders, carters, young men shouting and brawling, drunks, beggars, church bells, heralds, criers. How can you concentrate on your prayers? The lighting will also be dim – no windows to speak of. Everything is designed to make you withdraw into yourself and to concentrate. Isolation from sense perception: my father said that's what the Egyptians did in their initiation ceremonies.'

'Yes, I see.'

'No, you don't, and neither do I.' Giovanni opened the door and peered in.

'Ah, we have it to ourselves. The masons doing the floor aren't here. There is no sense deprivation when they're at work, believe me.' He ushered Filippo inside. The inner room was very dark; of the two small ocular windows, one looked out to a shady courtyard, the other into the outer, embracing room. By the light from the door he could see that the floor was merely plaster inscribed with complex geometric patterns but, before he could study it further, Giovanni closed the door.

Suddenly all sound, of which Filippo had barely been aware, was reduced to near silence and the loudest thing was the life pulse in his own ears.

In the poor light, Giovanni was reduced to a grey form without colour. 'Now do you understand?' he boomed, making Filippo jump. 'Complete isolation of the senses except for the words of Scripture. This is how Cosimo wants it. But it is a family chapel with a family function and so we cannot let him have his way. It will be decorated.'

217

The word 'decorated' always had an effect on Filippo, like female scent or the taste of sugar. 'Decorated?' He all but smacked his lips.

Giovanni's ghostly arm swept through space to indicate the entire chapel. 'Frescoes on all walls – there are six walls in here because of the recessed chancel – a coffered ceiling, floor of inlaid stone – porphyry and serpentine. And many, many sconces for candles and torches to illuminate it all.' Giovanni opened the door again so that they didn't have to be mole-blind any longer. The sound of one neighbour shouting at another, calling him a toad-faced lecher and spawn of Satan, flew in with other aural furies of city life, the wheels of passing carts screeching, an overloaded donkey braying, along with all the hammering and tapping and gossip that was the city's chatter.

With enough light now to see by, the two men trod carefully on the duckboards the masons had laid across their plastered floor. Filippo looked down on a design for inlaid stone and marble such as they had in the grandest churches and sank to his knees to see it better. The pattern began with a huge circle at its centre.

'It will be porphyry,' Giovanni said. 'The men are at the quarry – I remember now. Lots of fuss and bother about getting the stones cut exactly to size.'

'As is necessary,' said Filippo, 'if you want a perfect floor with no joins showing.'

'No joins at all.'

Porphyry: the imperial purple stone. Emperors of Byzantium stood upon such discs and Filippo wondered at Medici pretensions. He felt a moment of compassion for whoever was cutting it, for porphyry is hard.

'We've imported great blocks of it from Egypt,' said Giovanni. 'My father dreams of being a pharaoh.'

Filippo was counting the small circles around the circumference of the larger circle. Fourteen. Why fourteen? Despite his familiarity with geometry, he couldn't immediately think how to do the construction.

'Why fourteen?' he asked.

Giovanni shrugged. 'Ask Cosimo. He's the master of symbols. As I say, the walls are to be painted,' he said, nodding at the unpolished plaster. 'How long are you going to take at Santo Stefano?'

Filippo's fingers itched at the sight of those bare walls. He inhaled loudly. 'It's a big project. I've agreed two years, but that's now only after I've finished your altarpiece.'

'You must learn to speed up,' said Giovanni. Commanding in his air and posture, he led the way out of the chapel and to his own suite of rooms. These, too, were in the process of being decorated but his studiolo was almost complete and inhabitable. Already a cabinet had been installed displaying his collection of coins, cameos and small bronze sculptures. A lute was propped artlessly against a chair, a large manuscript of music open on an intricately carved lectern, as if the musician had been here but a moment ago but had been called away. Giovanni looked at his lute with some longing.

Fra Filippo gazed up at a deeply coffered ceiling in glazed terracotta by Luca della Robbia. As always, della Robbia's work brought a lump to his throat: such sweetness – the same quality as Fra Giovanni had, only in clay. He sighed.

'Beautiful, isn't it?'

'Very, very beautiful. How can you concentrate on your studies? I'd want to lie on the floor all day, staring up at the ceiling.'

'Sometimes I do,' said Giovanni, seating himself at a table. 'Now, the Naples commission, let's discuss the detail.' Filippo sat opposite and did some quick, brief sketches to make sure they were agreed on the general outline of the design. They discussed colours and the surface decoration involving much silver and gold. They agreed on the shape and size of the frame.

'It needs to be lavish. Spare nothing in its decoration and ornamentation. It's why we have chosen you for the task, Filippo – no one else has the skill and talent for surface detail that you do.

It's almost two years since the king signed the Peace of Lodi. We don't want to delay any longer in thanking him with this gift.'

'Where is your father?' Filippo asked as he rolled up the drawings at the end. 'I'd like to see him.'

'He's not well, my friend.'

Filippo blanched. 'Nothing too serious I hope.' The world without Cosimo would be insufferable.

'He's in agony with gout. He has to be carried everywhere these days.'

Filippo blinked rapidly – that fine, strong, energetic man, reduced to being carried in a chair? He sighed. 'I will pray for him.' Filippo was shocked when Giovanni laughed at this.

'Sorry, my friend,' said Giovanni clapping him on the shoulder. 'But if you think your prayers will help, then yes, do.'

Filippo understood this to reflect badly on himself. 'I'll need some money in advance for the materials. Fourteen florins will be sufficient for now.'

Giovanni, who had been leading him to the door, spun round. 'Do you have to be so squalid? Why do all conversations with you end with a bill? I keep telling myself you're a painter of genius but in truth you are just an amoral, greedy friar with gambling debts!'

Filippo reeled backwards but Giovanni walked off, intent on the next appointment of his busy day.

'See Martelli in the bank,' he called back over his shoulder.

'Such an ill temper!' Fra Filippo muttered as he went down the stairs. 'I mean, what's fourteen florins to the Medici? Laughable.' He went to the bank on the ground floor of the palazzo where he told Ser Lapo Martelli that Giovanni had said to come and ask for twenty florins. Martelli counted them out and Filippo filled his purse.

39

Duomo where he could seek solace from friends and oblivion in the wine butt. 'Giovanni de' Medici has such an ill temper!' he told Andrea del Castagno, who had once been his pupil. 'You say some little thing and, *bang!* As if you've stepped in a trap. I have too much work, that's the nub of it. Everyone thinks they have priority over me. Frate do this, frate, do that. I get no time to myself.'

'You need an assistant,' said Castagno, who was not in the mood for a self-pitying Lippi.

'You were a good assistant. Why did you leave me?'

'You made it impossible for me to stay, that's why. You were always disappearing and leaving me to do all the work. Look, there's Domenico over there by the door. Ask him. He usually knows where to find an apprentice.'

Fra Filippo made his way across the tavern, past tables loud with inebriated artisans, to Domenico Veneziano. 'Will you come and join us?'

'Not if you're sitting with Andrea del Castagno, no, I won't.'

'Now then, now then, goodwill to all men. I need an assistant, Domenico. Can you lend me someone?'

A man sitting close by raised his head.

Domenico said he could not lend Filippo anyone. 'I'm far too busy.' This was the favourite claim of every painter when speaking to a rival. 'Haven't you got an assistant already? Where's Diamante?'

'At Prato, working on our cycle in the main chapel of Santo Stefano,' replied Filippo.

'You're still working on that?'

'I'd have finished by now but for "quick" commissions – mostly altarpieces, and now a triptych for the King of Naples.'

Domenico couldn't beat that with any boast of his own and subsided in defeat. Filippo made to leave – he'd forgotten how unpleasant the company of fellow painters could be – but then the man at the table nearby introduced himself. 'Antonio dei Filipepi, goldsmith. Let me buy you a drink.' He beckoned to the wench at the bar. 'I have a young brother, aged thirteen, who was going to join me and become my partner, but I've been ruined by the price of gold and my business has collapsed. He has remarkable talent in drawing and would make an excellent apprentice, but I'm not sure we could afford the indenture.'

'Let me meet him anyway.' Filippo, who had not enjoyed an apprenticeship himself, was keen to give to another what he had never had. What if this boy was, like him, born to paint but was prevented by circumstances? 'Yes, let me meet him.'

Antonio dei Filipepi took him to a tannery at the Santa Trinità bridge and introduced him to his father, Mariano, who was writing in his ledger. A repulsive stench oozed from the room behind him, under a door kept firmly closed though to no avail. The nearest Filippo had ever been to a tannery before was adding his contribution to the process by using the piss pots on nearby street corners. Although he loved leather as well as the next man, he considered tanning an occupation beneath human dignity.

'Father,' Antonio said, 'Fra Filippo may be persuaded to take our Alessandro as an apprentice.'

Mariano dei Filipepi looked up from his ledger. He had that beaten look of one on a rung of humanity only slightly above that of beggars and scavengers. 'All I want for my sons,' he told Filippo, 'is for them to better themselves. My eldest is a notary. Antonio was a goldsmith until a turn of Fortuna's wheel pitched him off. Now he has to join me here and scrape hides for a living. Our Alessandro – I'll be honest, Fra Filippo. He did not do so well at school. Every animal has just enough brains, as they say, to preserve its own hide, and it's true of every creature on God's earth, except my youngest. You put him in a vat with his own brains and he'd turn into gloop.'

'He was bored,' Antonio said quickly. 'He wasn't stupid, he was too intelligent.'

Mariano shrugged. 'I don't think it's intelligent to skip school. Anyway, whatever the truth, Frate, I have to tell you he played truant.'

'Father!' Antonio objected. 'He played truant so that he could spend time drawing!'

'He was expelled three times.'

'Dear me, my father, your talent is not in selling!'

'This is a holy man and you should always speak the truth to a holy man.'

Filippo laughed. 'Bring him out and let me determine his nature.'

Mariano opened the offending door a crack and called for his youngest son to come from the workshop. Fra Filippo reeled from what smelt like decaying horse carcasses and clamped his sleeve over his nose.

✝

Alessandro dei Filipepi was in a dream so deep it had become a trance. He was kneading scraped skins by treading them in a vat of dog and pigeon dung. Whenever he felt bad, he thanked God he was not Boffo the cretin who had to stir the skins soaking in a vat of animal brains. Boffo's own brains were so addled that he found everything funny and laughed all day long.

For Alessandro, closely supervised these days by his father, the only way to escape the horror of dead animal and warm dung squidging through his toes was to dream. When his father called his name, he was paying court to a woman whose remarkable beauty was ethereal, her skin as pale and veined as alabaster, and slowly, slowly disrobing her to study her form. He sketched her in his mind's eye, the shape of her arms and shoulders, the curve of her neck, the gentle swell of stomach and breasts.

That his imagination was anatomically correct came largely from the time he spent spying on his sisters and peeping through windows of bathhouses.

223

'Alessandro!'

Awakening with reluctance, he climbed out of the vat and into a small bowl of water where he washed his feet before padding out of the workshop into the front office. He found his father and brother standing with a Carmelite friar.

His first thought was that they were arranging for him to enter the Order. Tall, gangly and with a look of stupidity, he glanced at his father in alarm.

'This is Fra Filippo Lippi,' said Mariano.

Alessandro's eyes, fluid with changing emotion, now gazed in near rapture at the man who, since the death of Fra Giovanni, had become in his opinion the greatest living painter. And if that wasn't enough to interest him...

'Was it you who was in gaol last year?' he asked breathlessly. 'They tore you apart on the rack!'

The father clipped the son round the ear but asked if it were true.

'I was the victim of an injustice!' Filippo said.

'But you *are* the painter who did the work at San Marco?' asked Mariano.

'No, that was Fra Giovanni.' Filippo began to wonder whether he was wasting his time.

'Father,' said Antonio, 'Fra Filippo is doing the main chapel at Santo Stefano in Prato, and has lately been commissioned to paint an altarpiece for the King of Naples.' He turned to Alessandro. 'He is looking for an apprentice.'

Now Alessandro stood speechless.

'If you can prove your skills,' said Fra Filippo. 'Do you have anything to show me?'

Alessandro opened a cupboard and took out a folder full of pen and ink drawings: heads, hands, plants, birds and copies of paintings to be seen around the city. Filippo looked at them briefly, for it took but a glance to recognise the boy's native talent. Assenting with a nod, he handed the drawings back. *Giotto's goat,* he thought, *definitely Giotto's goat.* 'Why do you want to be a painter?' he asked. 'The apprenticeship is long and has no reward other than what you learn from me.'

In a series of jerky movements suggesting the dance of St Vitus, Alessandro shrugged, stroked his throat and tapped himself on the chest. Filippo interpreted this to mean: it's in my heart but I haven't the words for it.

Filippo did not need a skilled assistant. The Naples commission was too important for him to delegate and he intended to do it all himself. All he needed was a lad quick and ready to learn who would mix the colours and stand by with the bowls of pigment and not moan, groan, pick his nose and complain of boredom. There was something about this boy, some indefinable thing. He would not be one of those leeches who fastened on the master, sucking out the blood of his skills for his own, later use. Why was Alessandro Filipepi reminding him of Abu Ali? There was something to him, some honesty and integrity, some quality that, Filippo had to admit, he lacked himself. Alessandro was neither a leech nor a fawner. No, he liked this boy. He nodded. 'I'll have a contract drawn up for a seven-year apprenticeship.'

Now words of gratitude were spilling jumbled from the boy's mouth. Fra Filippo coughed in sudden embarrassment and turned away. Alessandro's appreciation was making him uncomfortable. 'Come along,' he said sharply to his new apprentice. 'Work to do and a living to earn.'

40

WHEN THEY WERE BACK IN PRATO, FILIPPO BEGAN Alessandro's apprenticeship with lessons in colour-mixing and geometry. He had Diamante teach him how to lay a gesso ground, putting layer upon layer of plaster upon a panel and polishing it until it was as smooth as a river pebble. While Alessandro did all these tedious and wearying chores without complaint, putting all the energy of his young body into the task, Filippo went to find a frame-maker capable of doing arches and pinnacles worthy of a French cathedral. The taste of Naples was 'courtly', Giovanni de' Medici had said, which meant – to Florentines – about thirty years behind the times. At last he found a good man near Santo Stefano and spent days with him, working on drawings that were exactly to scale.

He showed Alessandro what there was to see of any artistic merit in Prato, including the Gaddi frescoes in the chapel of the Holy Girdle and the pulpit where the showings took place. Designed by Michelozzo, the pulpit, drum-shaped and with a lead-covered canopy, grew out of Santo Stefano's façade like a mushroom from the bark of a tree. On the drum were marble reliefs by Donatello of little *putti* laughing and dancing hand in hand.

Alessandro gazed up at the sculptures in awe. 'Donatello can do anything,' he said, 'old men, young men, women, babies – anything. I suppose you know him well.'

'No,' said Filippo. 'I regret that we never met.'

'Never met? Is he dead?'

'I believe so. Either that or he's in exile. I haven't seen him for years.'

'I thought you said you'd never met.'

'Well, you can see someone without meeting him. Donatello is – was – a famous sight around Florence, always in his working clothes with his dusty cap askew on his head, talking to important men as if he were their equal. But I haven't seen him for years. Must be in heaven, God rest his soul.'

'You'd have thought we'd have heard.'

'Not in Prato.'

'But I've only just arrived in Prato.'

'You must have been asleep that day.'

✛

Work on the walls of Santo Stefano proceeded slowly with Fra Filippo spending too much time working on his designs for the Naples altarpiece. He intended to take them to Florence at Saint John's tide but as midsummer approached the air became stifling and people found it difficult to breathe.

The first report of plague came from the Piazza Mercatale. By the second day, twelve people were dead. Filippo went to the convent to see whether the nuns were safe. To his consternation he found that the abbess was re-converting the place to a hospital to take in the sick.

He remonstrated with her but found himself on shaky moral grounds, for how could he be so low as to suggest the convent should not do its utmost to help the sick? He went to elicit the support of the provost. Gemignano Inghirami went at once to the convent and persuaded the abbess that her nuns had not been put in her care to be sacrificed to her ideas of doing good. The theological points of his argument were superb, as slippery and lively as a fresh catch of fish. When the abbess tried to withstand the provost's rhetoric, he assumed his authority. 'Do as I say, woman!'

Filippo saw Lucrezia passing through the cloisters. He gazed at her as if to say, 'I have saved you today, and I will protect you every day that I live.' She did not spare him a glance.

By the end of the week the plague had spread across the city and reports from beyond told of it raging through Tuscany. Filippo and his team worked at the walls and when not working they went home. All visits to the tavern or other crowded places were stopped. Alessandro, who was living in Filippo's house, had met plague before in his young life but somehow in Prato he felt more confined and afraid. Filippo did his best to keep the boy hopeful by pouring knowledge into him.

It had been in a half-dream, between sleeping and waking, that Filippo had found himself back at the oasis and his master saying, 'Pass it all to one man – you will know him when you meet him'. And he did know him. Something in the lad, some quick, intelligent thing, called out to Filippo. Far from using Alessandro as an extra pair of hands to do menial labour, he tutored him, divulging his knowledge and keeping nothing back. No secrets, not from Alessandro dei Filipepi.

So, as people died in their dozens, as bodies were piled into carts by the Misericordia, as newly-made orphans wailed from hunger in the streets, as maddened widows beat on the doors of the church for sanctuary from this stalking death, Filippo Lippi taught his apprentice everything he knew, every arcane secret learnt either in Florence or Barbary, about perspective, about the alchemical creation of pigments, about colour mixing – how to make gesso smooth, how to cure mistakes, how to make ultramarine blue from lapis lazuli.

He had Alessandro grind the stone from the land west of paradise in a big bronze mortar. The boy pounded it for a day, the workshop ringing to the sound of his labours. By the end of the day he was groaning from the pain of his efforts, but he did not stop until the job was done. On the next day Filippo had Alessandro work up the powder on a porphyry slab, making it ever finer, sieving it then pounding it again until it reached the ultimate fineness. He lifted the boy's chin to look into his eyes.

'Tired yet?'

Tears spilled from those blue eyes that could not look at him.

'Do you want to give up?'

'No!'

'Well done,' he said, releasing him. 'Listen, Alessandro. Preachers, priests and archbishops will tell you that, to be happy, your life must be disciplined. You tell them about discipline. Because you know it now, what a painter must sacrifice. Those ascetics have no idea what discipline is.'

Fra Diamante, at work on a panel, chuckled.

Filippo showed Alessandro how to mix the powdered lapis lazuli with a melted mixture of pine resin, gum mastic and wax, kneading it into a ball with oiled hands.

'Be careful. That piece of lapis cost me the price of a small house.'

Alessandro blanched. 'And you trusted me with it?'

'Should I not have?'

Alessandro shook his head. 'No. Please. I will never let you down.'

Fra Filippo reached out and patted the boy's hand. 'If I am pouring everything into you as if there is no tomorrow, it is because there may be no tomorrow. If we survive this, I'll tell you everything again, more slowly. Meanwhile, keep kneading.'

'For how long?'

'Three days,' said Fra Filippo, washing his hands.

Alessandro's knees began to shake.

Fra Diamante chuckled again. 'Don't listen to him, Alessandro. It's not all the time but on and off,' he said. 'Three days, on and off.'

On the third day, a parcel came from Florence with a letter for Alessandro from his eldest brother, the notary, telling him that their father had died in the plague and that one of the last things he had done before falling ill was to make Alessandro a pair of leather boots, 'because whatever you may think, he loved you and was proud of you.'

Fra Filippo would not allow Alessandro to touch the boots until two weeks and all risk of infection had passed. After that, despite the soft-leather boots looking home-made and crumpling round his ankles, Alessandro would wear nothing else upon his feet, no matter how hot the day.

✝

Thunderstorms came upon them at the end of July. Hail lashed the survivors of the plague, and people took to lashing themselves to be rid of sin. Great crackings in the sky, followed by fiery streaks of lightning fizzing and stabbing the earth, came daily off the mountains. The river Bisenzio overflowed its banks and all the canals flooded the city. Up on the scaffolding in Santo

Stefano, the two friars and their apprentice looked down on the tiled floor of the nave that lay under a foot of water. Every few minutes Fra Filippo checked the vaulting, praying, always praying, that the roof repairs would withstand the thunderous downpours of rain. The stained-glass window was not yet installed and its space was filled with stretched oilskin; badly fitted, it offered little defence against the weather. The friars got wet in their work, but they worried more about their plaster than about themselves.

A week or so later, a wind came from the mouth of hell. It roared and moaned round Santo Stefano. People trying to cross the piazza had to lean head-first into it while their clothes flew out horizontally behind them. Hats were lost, never to be seen again. The wind subsided but then picked up, even stronger this time, and those mad enough to be outside spoke of an 'eye' staring down on the city. Filippo, never fond of wind, paced in agitation. A letter had come from Giovanni de' Medici asking when he might expect to see Filippo's detailed designs for the altarpiece, but Filippo put the letter down and forgot it.

Day after day, week after week, throughout that pestilential summer, he had spent in fear of bad news from the convent. He went there whenever he could, made what surreptitious inquiries he could, but the nuns were so preoccupied with Suor Brigida coming to term that they didn't have time for him. Lucrezia, he heard, was leading a campaign to keep the baby in the convent when it was born and not allow it to be sent to the foundling hospital. 'That sounds reasonable to me,' he said.

'Reasonable?' the abbess cried. 'What do you know about reason? We cannot have our reputation sullied this way. The child will go!'

At the Assumption showing of the Holy Girdle the loyal provost, despite his age and infirmity, despite the plague and rain, or perhaps because of them, went to the pulpit with the precious relic protected by a case. There were no processions that day, no glad crowds filling the L-shaped piazza, just a few stragglers wrapped in oilskins against the beating rain. The provost held the relic aloft to the sky, to show God that faith held true if only in the few. Fra Filippo was leaning out of his window, watching from his house, when someone knocked on his door below.

'Fra Filippo!'

He looked down on a message boy.

'The Ceppo asks you to present yourself at the Palazzo Datini!'

Filippo went as bidden to be told that, because of the failure of the harvest, there were no funds to pay him for at least a year. And then there was the delayed request that Giovanni de' Medici had made via his brother, Carlo, for the city to release Lippi for a year. Perhaps now was the time to grant it.

Filippo walked out through the studded door. He went out into the wind and rain and struggled home, growling aloud all the way. These men stopped and started him with no thought to his well-being. Yes, he had the Naples commission, but that was not the point. He raged like the weather for days until suddenly the wind dropped and a late summer blushed on the hills above the town.

41

THE FESTIVAL OF THE NATIVITY OF MARY COINCIDED WITH the annual wool fair in September. Thousands of pilgrims and merchants crowded into the city and God and Mammon mingled in the squares. On this most lucrative festival of the year, every able household rented rooms to guests. In the convent, Abbess Bartolommea busied herself freeing five cells by turning the refectory into a makeshift dormitory that her nuns would share. There was another cloister with cells long out of use, but really she didn't have time for renovation, only for thorough cleaning.

Simple dusting would not be sufficient for her guest, a silk merchant of Florence and his family. She had accommodated him before, several years ago when his first wife still lived, and she knew him as a man with a deep desire to balance body and spirit, drawn as much to Prato by the Holy Girdle as by the fair in the Piazza Mercatale.

Matteo Peruzzi was of high standing in the Arte di Calimala, the major guild of Florence, of a distinguished, noble family, and one might have imagined more salubrious accommodation for him, but the abbess understood why he chose to stay in a convent, that he preferred cleanliness over comfort and needed to balance his ledgers with God. During the day he would be out, striking deals that would leave the seller peeled to the bone, and then return in time for holy office and prayers.

Each cell had to be thoroughly scrubbed and the walls lime-washed. The abbess always intended to begin this work in July but somehow it never happened until the enervating summer had passed. This summer in particular, with its freakish weather, had not been conducive to housework. So at the beginning of September, besides their usual duties, the five nuns cleaned their cells, took out rugs to beat them, dusted all surfaces, polished all metal and lime-washed the walls. Food was bought and stored in the larder, food to be prepared for the guests to come. The nuns ate their usual poor fare whilst plucking pigeon and gutting carp to serve to others.

When the Peruzzi family arrived the day before the festival, Lucrezia was in the laundry. Ser Matteo's voice boomed through the cloisters as he allocated cells to his wife, her mother, the nurse of his two-year old son and the wet nurse of his infant son. Lucrezia came out wiping her hands on her apron and watched as the two nurses and the children moved into her cell while the merchant's young wife moved into Spinetta's. She recognised Ser Matteo as an old acquaintance of her father's, but he did not recognise her. Treating her as a mere servant to his needs, he asked for beds to be rearranged, hangings to be installed and a bowl of fruit to be brought for his wife, who was, he said with some pride, with child.

The young woman, the same age as Lucrezia, was swathed in a mantle of the finest wool over a gamurra of fluted silk that looked like samite. Lucrezia knew the fabric, well known and much loved for its evasion of the sumptuary laws; fake sumptuousness almost as expensive as the real thing. Lucrezia listened to the rustle and brush of her as she settled herself into Spinetta's cell and went in to help disrobe her of her mantle. Over the young woman's shoulders lay an embroidered partlet so fine it was almost transparent. Unable to resist the urge to run it through her fingers, Lucrezia withdrew from the cell saying, if there was anything else Madonna required, she was only to ask. A pain had started in the middle of her, a fierce hunger.

The abbess was bustling about the cloister, trailing the merchant like a duck a drake as he visited his wife and then his mother, and called in to see his sons with nurse and wet nurse. All doors were open as the family went in and out of each cell, reconnecting to each other in this strange separation. The abbess bustled, suggesting additional comforts and elbowing aside any nuns in her way.

Lucrezia felt a deep and sudden need to be in the laundry where she was free. Free? Yes, free. Free to throw things around, cry, blaspheme, sulk. Having performed her small act of hospitality, she was gone. She slapped at her washing with the wooden beater for the rest of the morning, and with Spinetta wrung the linen like the necks of chickens.

At the midday meal, the merchant's wife appeared in the refectory dressed more demurely, if no less richly, in moiré silk. Over her beautifully dressed hair she wore a little cap of sheer linen tied under her chin. She glanced up at Lucrezia with kind eyes but Lucrezia remained sullen, putting down a dish of cold meats as if feeding pigs. The young wife flinched under her sour gaze. Lucrezia tried to do better, tried to remember all that her faith had taught her, but that hole of hunger was beginning to yawn.

After the meal, she took a plate of food to the wet nurse who had remained in her cell. She knocked on what was her own door and went in.

'Ah, thank you, Sister,' said the woman, holding out the baby for Lucrezia to take. 'Can you look after him while I eat? He will not sleep in his cradle today but must be always held in living arms.'

Lucrezia, startled, took the baby. He barely stirred in the transition and settled himself at once against her own breast. She stroked his soft head, his fine, dark hair that was silky and sparse. He was so new, so beautiful, so innocent. And now the hole became a chasm and she falling into it, overwhelmed by the vacancy in her life and the anguish of longing for what she could never have. Jesus dolls were no compensation for this! Love of the Lord was no compensation for this! This, this is what she had been born for, to be a mother. Like the Virgin herself. She swayed under the power of the thought and the nurse, thinking she was about to faint, jumped up and took the baby back.

'Sit! Sit down!'

Lucrezia refused, said she was fine and left to hurry back to the laundry.

Passing the cellar door, she paused to wipe away the wretched tears that burned her eyes. She tried the handle but it was locked. Brigida was down there, alone in the dark on a cold, damp truckle bed, close to term and locked up to prevent the convent's reputation being ruined. Breathing heavily, Lucrezia wanted to rattle on the door until the lock gave but she knew it never would. The abbess was insistent that the baby was going to be sent to the foundling hospital at birth and Brigida, convinced that they were making her abandon the new Messiah, was half-maddened by it. She had to be locked up, the abbess said, for her own good.

'Spinetta!' Lucrezia said to her sister, who she found folding clothes. 'Where are there nuns in the bible?'

Spinetta shrugged and splayed her hands. 'How should I know? They must be there somewhere. I haven't read it, have you?'

'But we hear the stories all the time, and there are no nuns! And no monks! And no friars! So why are we here?'

'Well, I suppose there's something we don't understand, something in the history of the first Christians, the martyrs and all that. Wasn't it St Anthony?'

'To hell with the saints and martyrs!

'Lucrezia!'

'Brigida was put in the cellar yesterday.'

'I know. I'm supposed to be looking after her.' Spinetta held up the cellar key which she'd hung from her girdle. Lucrezia eyed it keenly.

'What is Christian about walling up a nun just because she's pregnant?'

'She's not walled up! It's only while the guests are here.'

'To protect our reputation. For our reputation, she is imprisoned in a cold, dark cellar, and she so close to her term. Are you looking after her well?'

'I took her some food but the abbess said I wasn't to linger, only to take her food and empty her bucket.' Spinetta's voice began to shake. 'Lucrezia, it breaks my heart.'

Lucrezia embraced her sister, and in that embrace, Spinetta began to sob. 'I can't bear it. I can't bear another moment of it,' she said, muffled. 'Your coldness, my guilt, nothing helps, no amount of prayer or confession. For as long as you don't forgive me, I suffer.'

Lucrezia said nothing but stared into space as she stroked her sister, aye, stroked her, as she had once stroked her as an infant, but now that baby sister was clothed in rough wool which reddened her skin. 'I will make it all better, I promise,' she whispered.

Returning to her work, she emptied out a basket of dried washing and started to fold it. Among the chemises and bed linen was a dear and familiar mantle that, from her frequent attention, was nearly white again – as white as she would ever get it. Why did all whites turn yellow? Putting it to her nose she smelt fresh air. She smoothed it out and folded it tenderly. She intended it to be a message, although she was not quite sure what the message was: she wanted him to see the delicate pink flower of the soapwort that she hid in the folds of the habit and to understand that he was to come at once. That was all. Just come and calm her down from these rioting emotions that were bound to keep her awake all night, writhing with envy and despair on a hard table in the refectory.

She made a pile of the friars' washing, not only Filippo's but Diamante's, too, for somehow it had become accepted that she be the laundress for both of them despite Fra Diamante having no role in the convent. Recently she had even taken on the long hose and big shirts of the new apprentice. She thought it was only fitting that all the assistants of the painter of Santo Stefano were clean.

'Clean clothes – pure hearts!' the abbess said, breezing into the laundry, as if reading her thoughts. Lucrezia stiffened, expecting trouble, but the abbess approved of what she saw. 'Who knows the effect of your work? Those two friars, neither worthy of the name – what happens to them each time they put their clean clothes on? They are reminded, child, reminded of purity. But bring your work to a close now – the bell for prayers will ring shortly.'

Lucrezia sent the garden boy off with the bundle of clothes to the chaplain's house.

✝

After prayers, the guests went out to visit the market. Lucrezia began a new load of washing, trying to get into a rhythm but it was impossible. Her arms felt weak, her neck ached, her back grumbled. How is it, she wondered, that clean clothes don't purify the heart of the cleaner? *Mine is getting inky. Black pitch, that's what I've got. A shrivelled little heart leaking black pitch.* She went to the well to draw up water and, as ever, thanked Fra Filippo for the hoisting frame as she turned the handle to bring up the bucket. Suddenly Spinetta ran into the little courtyard.

'Brigida!' she said. 'I just went down to see her. I think the baby's coming! We can't leave her like that. It's not right!'

Lucrezia wedged the handle, left the bucket hanging and went at once with her sister to the cellar. Spinetta put the heavy iron key in the lock, turned it and pushed open the door. Down there, amongst the smells of damp oak barrels, lying shrouded by the dark, the emaciated young nun was suffering her first contractions. She was weeping from fear of spiders and the dark, of being forgotten, or walled-up alive, of having to give birth on her own and making no sound, as the abbess had insisted. No sound at all, not while the convent had guests. The only light they had came in wanly through the door they'd left open at the top of the steps.

'Brigida, Brigida my love,' said Lucrezia, 'we've come to help if we can.'

Brigida just stared at them, her face screwed up with pain and misery.

'She's so cold,' Spinetta told Lucrezia, taking hold of Brigida's hand. 'It's not right. What can we do?'

'We have to get her out of here.'

'How? And where to?'

'I'll think of something,' said Lucrezia. Her first thought was of Filippo but she quailed. What she was contemplating was bad and she had no wish to drag him into her mire, although she knew, with a quiet, soft certainty, that he would help.

She bent over the sick nun and kissed her on the forehead. That warm, pungent smell of the unwashed came from her damp skin and hair. 'Brigida,' she whispered. 'We'll get you out of here. Somehow. I promise.'

Back at the laundry, Spinetta returned to her work but at once cried out, a sound to freeze blood and send the soul in search of God. She collapsed over the linen she was wringing out. 'I can't do this any more,' she howled. 'What difference is there between us and slaves? Have we got to do this until we die? Why? Was our sin so bad?'

237

Lucrezia took hold of her sister and hugged her. Spinetta was right: they couldn't do it any more, but what was the alternative? If they escaped the convent, it would be to a life as vagabonds or street women. A sense of injustice rose from the depth of Lucrezia's being and choked her. This was not the life her father had intended for his two beautiful daughters. She should be a young wife dressed in silks with two sons and another on its way. She folded her arms round her sister and promised her something would be done.

'But what?' Spinetta asked.

'Let me think. I'll think of something.'

At dusk she went to the convent roof to collect the tablecloths she had hung there earlier in the loggia. She tried to think of ways of escape but could think of nothing that did not lead to prostitution, poverty and an early death. Down on the Piazza Mercatale, on a stage like a raft amid the sea of stalls, a band of travelling musicians was gathering a crowd. She felt hot and wiped her face with a forearm, trying to quell her resentment of the young wife, her anger at what was happening to Brigida, her sense of impotence.

On bagpipes, shawms and tamburelli the musicians began playing a saltarello. It was her favourite dance as a child. Kept outside of the sala during banquets Ser Francesco Buti held for business friends and trading contacts, she and Spinetta had played five stones in the loggia while their elders trod the floor sedately, but whenever a saltarello was played, they got up and skipped around. They knew the steps to all the dances, but the saltarello was their favourite.

She began to move to the music, tight and tense at first but soon the beat of the tamburelli and the whine of the pipes seduced her, stroked her. There was no one here, after all, none to see her. As the harvest moon began to rise above the mountains, she took off her veil and the hairy habit and stepped free in her chemise.

✝

At dusk, Fra Filippo went to the Taverna dei Tintori. The evening was warm and he felt like drinking with friends. The moon had not yet risen and the dice were already in play but Fra Filippo sat on a barrel outside the tavern, preferring to study and admire the young women passing by. 'Study,' he called it, this need for his eyes to caress the female form. Dice lost their appeal when women were around. The city was beginning to fill with people coming out of workshop and hostelry to amble through the streets, going from square to square to take in a dozen entertainments: sacred plays, acrobatics, flag-throwing, musicians, singers, poets stirring up a riot with their imitations of the *popolo grasso*, the fat rich. Fra Filippo was happy to sit where he was, to rest after a good day's work, to gossip and to study. He had a notebook on his lap to justify himself, in which now and again he did a rapid sketch of a leg, a hand, a grimace. He never drew the women: he preferred just to rest his eyes on them and make mental notes.

'Full moon tonight,' said il Mulo, leaning against the door jamb. 'Is it?'

'Harvest moon, large and red. It's always special, when the moon coincides with a showing. I think so, anyway. Significant.'

'You're an astrologer now?'

Il Mulo crossed himself and denied it. 'It's just that some moments are potent, don't you think? I think so.'

As yet the moon was still behind the mountains. Filippo, suddenly impatient to see it, went inside the tavern and up to the roof.

It was a pleasant roof, unlike his own, its small seating area garlanded with vines which grew in large urns. He stood there alone, looking out over the city and its walls to the mountains and the halo of light beginning to swell above them. There were raucous music coming from the Piazza Mercatale and, as the moon rose at last, he saw a woman – a nymph – dancing alone on a roof by the piazza, caught in the moon's pulsing, growing orb like a flying swan, her slender shape, her loose hair and waving arms somehow ancient beyond ancient. He stood entranced until

the thought dawned – like a smack between the eyes – that he
knew which roof that was and who it was dancing upon it.

✝

Taking up a length of linen, she draped it over her hands like the
Holy Girdle and offered it to the moon, now huge and red above
the mountains. Turning in time to the music she skipped on every
third beat, turning and hopping, her chemise flying free of her
legs. Barefoot she danced on the roof of the convent. She bent
her head and her hair fell in a curtain, she lifted her head and
tendrils stuck to her face; she turned and her hair whipped round
behind her.

He came like the shadow of a man, a man-shape darker
than the night, his own arms raised, his fingers clicking to the
increasing tempo of the music. Shouts were coming up from
below as weavers and dyers, carders and millers jumped to the
triple beat, holding hands and dancing in circles. He embraced her
without touching her, moving around her his arms outstretched
and waving to the music; he was a buck to her hind, a billy to her
nanny, both predatory and protective. She could smell wine on
his breath and it was natural, the smell of a man. His eyes swam
with adoration. He adored her. Yes. That was what she could see:
his adoration.

The music from below grew faster and changed tempo. More
tamburelli joined in, along with naker drums. The rhythm was
now throbbing in the square like blood in a fevered body as
the saltarello became the tarantella. The cloth workers gave
themselves up to the moon, as their ancestors had done before
anyone had thought of Christianity, the wine-red moon now full
above the mountains. Lucrezia was turning with her eyes closed,
a smile on her lips, dancing for herself alone.

They could have danced until they dropped like sacrificial
victims but the trance was broken when the convent bell
began urgently to ring. Lucrezia stopped, panting for breath and
blinking.

Below the abbess was marching out into the square towards the musicians and dancers brandishing a broom, shouting that this was no way to celebrate the Nativity of Our Lady!

Lucrezia moved close to Filippo, her skin glistening with sweat, her chemise sticking to her. She met and held his gaze. 'So, you got my flower?'

'What flower?'

'Please,' she said, 'oh please, I beg you' – and here she fell to her knees – 'you must help us.' And here she became incoherent, all her desires tumbling out of her in a speech that did not draw breath. Brigida, Spinetta, justice, cruelty, imprisonment, walled up alive.

'Lucrezia,' he said, pulling her to her feet, 'I am your slave. Whatever you need, just ask and I will do it. But first put this on,' he said, picking up her habit, 'or you will catch a chill.'

'A chill?' she laughed harshly. 'Come with me to the cellar and see Brigida.'

He followed her down the stairs, through the now sleeping convent to the cellar door. It stood ajar and the spluttering light of a candle showed in the darkness below. They went down and found Spinetta sharing Brigida's fouled pallet, embracing the nun who was too cold to sleep.

Filippo looked at the scene before him and knew hell as a reality.

'Piera came to see her,' Spinetta told them. 'She said the baby will be born tomorrow.'

✝

As the moon, now yellow, arced across the sky, getting ever smaller and more distant, Fra Filippo thrashed and rolled in his bed, unable to sleep. Sleep? Why should he sleep? Not when he had such images in his mind, of the nun in her chemise in her trance of desire, her skin glistening, her mouth upturned at the corners, possessed as she was by the god. God? Yes. She Ariadne, deserted by Theseus, and he Bacchus, come to rescue her. He was the god who possessed her. So he imagined himself, young and

241

lithe, holding at bay a truer image of himself as a goatish old Silenus with a pot belly and hairy buttocks.

What was in her look? Truly, what was in it? Come on now, Filippo Lippi, be honest with yourself for once. She's a frosty wench to be sure, always moaning and complaining, but last night on the roof, when she saw me, what was in her eye? Was it desire? Truly? No, very well, I admit it wasn't exactly desire, no, not the kind I feel for her. But it was licence. Yes. She was allowing me to desire her. Yes. That is what it was.

And he turned in his bed and went over the images again; with each repeat of the dream, he further erased the image of Brigida that kept arising like a vengeful wraith to spoil everything, a memento mori, the skeleton in the Dance of Death. The worm in the apple. He need not dwell on her. He had settled everything. He had returned to the tavern from the convent and had settled everything. He awoke suddenly and sat bolt upright, sweat beading his face. Jesus! What had he settled? What had he got himself into now? No, no, let's not spoil everything and make ourselves sleepless. Forget it. Leave it for tomorrow to sort out. He laid down again, muttering, 'Now, where were we?' After a little while he could hear the saltarello again and began dancing across the roof on cloven feet to meet his nymph.

If only it were a matter of honest-to-goodness lust. He knew all about that. How to feel it, deal with it, be done with it. Like hunger. You're hungry, you eat. You don't worry how the food feels about it. But this wasn't pure lust, no, not pure. It was sullied by compassion. Somehow it would be easier to be wholly bad rather than half-good. Suddenly he remembered her falling to her knees and begging something of him. What? What did she say? It was about Brigida, surely. But no, don't let's dwell on that. He rolled over. 'Now, where were we?'

He caught up with sleep in the morning. While the city began to thrum in the fever of the festival, he slept through it all with a smile on his face.

✝

Lucrezia hurried to the kitchen where Suor Piera was doling out roasted figs on to a large pottery dish and Suor Simonna was drizzling honey and crushed nuts on top. She took up the dish to take to the guests. Steeling herself, she went into the vaulted refectory and under the poor and peeling fresco of the Last Supper, put her dish down on the table covered with fresh linen, noting with annoyance a wine stain under the glass of Ser Matteo and splatters of goose fat from the plate of his mother. Another load of tablecloths to do.

The young wife's eyes followed her, a gaze mixed with curiosity and distrust. Lucrezia concentrated; in her mind, she danced under the full moon again, with him circling her, his arms raised and waving like water reeds in time to the music. That ancient, healing music; the music which had disrobed her of all that was false and left her cleansed and naked beneath the moon. She had no need to consider herself an object of pity, or a lesser mortal or, worst of all, simply invisible. She straightened. *I, I am adored by Fra Filippo Lippi. You may wear beautiful clothes every day, but I shall wear them in perpetuity, immortalised by my artist lover.* Raising her eyes, she glanced at this woman who was causing envy to run like poison in her veins and graced her with a warm smile, sudden and fleeting like winter sunshine.

Ser Matteo's wife responded. 'You look very tired,' she said.

It has been a long morning.'

'Have you eaten?'

'Not yet.'

'And where did you sleep?'

'Here, on this table.'

The young woman coughed suddenly, embarrassed. 'Your sacrifice is very great,' she said. 'I wish I could be like you, full of grace and purity.'

Lucrezia drew a deep breath and returned to the kitchen.

42

HE AWOKE TO THE NOISE BUILDING ON THE PIAZZA, the shouts of stewards organizing people, the shouts of those resisting, the laughter and squeals of children, the deafening thunder of what sounded like huge planks of wood being dropped from the sky on to the paved square. He stared at the brick vaulting of his ceiling. It was one of those mornings when he woke up still drunk but also suffering a hangover, a hot and cold kind of morning, full of excitement and dread. Had he promised Lucrezia something? What was it? Could he keep it?

He got up, staggered into his habit and went downstairs to his workshop. When the world became this oppressive, his only escape was work.

At midday he went with Diamante and Alessandro to his own roof garden, a flat area with a few dead plants in pots, to look down on the piazza while they ate cold pigeon and boiled eggs. Drumbeats were reverberating down the narrow streets and alleyways, the rhythms of one approaching procession clashing with the rhythms of another, and the closer the processions got to the centre, the worse the cacophony. Not just the wards of Prato were represented, but neighbouring cities also: Florence, Pistoia, Lucca all had their processions, in their city colours, each attempting to have banners taller than the others in cloths more colourful, more precious. This was the culmination of the religious calendar for all woolworkers and cloth merchants in Tuscany. Time to show off.

The din reached a crescendo as all the processions converged on the square. They did not enter but paused in the lanes and alleys to outplay everyone else with their drums. Alessandro's agitation, which had been increasing all afternoon, now broke its bounds; he pleaded to be allowed some time off. He could not be a distant observer to all this pageantry – he had to be down there, in the middle of it all. Filippo, who had merely been testing his endurance, sent the lad off with his good blessing.

The town magistrates and the bishop were seated outside Santo Stefano, waiting to receive each procession in turn. With a great rapping on the drums of Prato, the Gonfaloniere walked solemnly forward in all his finery and directed the processions one by one into the piazza.

This was Fra Filippo's favourite part: each procession moving forward and joining the rhythms of the dancing, music and flag-throwing going on outside Santo Stefano, all dissonance resolving into civic harmony. He watched half bewitched by the goings-on below, half in a dream about Lucrezia. He searched the crowds for the nuns of Santa Margherita but saw no sign of them, although he did see Alessandro watching enraptured a ring of young girls dancing.

'Aren't you attending at the Chapel of the Holy Girdle?' Diamante asked. 'Shouldn't you put on a fresh habit?'

Filippo, who had forgotten he'd been invited to Santo Stefano, followed his assistant down to his chamber where Diamante went through the stack of washed clothes delivered the day before and pulled out a fresh black habit and white mantle. As he shook out the habit, a small flower floated to the rushed floor. 'Soapwort,' he said, picking the tiny thing up. 'How...?'

As the events of the previous day fell into place in his mind, Filippo was having trouble breathing.

'What is it, caro mio?'

'There's something I need to tell you my friend, my dear friend. I don't think it will happen, but it might, so just in case...'

He told his assistant what he had promised Lucrezia, that he was going to help her escape Santa Margarita. Diamante stood there gulping air like a landed fish.

'And her sister, too.'

'Caro mio...'

'Oh, and Brigida. We cannot leave Brigida. If we only take one, it must be Brigida.'

'Brigida?'

'She's been locked in the cellar and left to give birth alone.'

'Madonna! That's not right!'

'And so,' Filippo finished, 'as soon as we see the nuns in the square, we must go to the convent.'

'Fra Filippo Lippi, I am your assistant, your devoted assistant, but it was never in my contract to aid and abet you in abduction.'

'Abduction? Brigida is being held against her will. We are freeing her, Diamante. We are doing God's work and saving a life. Two lives, perhaps.'

They went to a window with a view over the piazza. Shortly after the first bell rang to announce the showing in an hour, the abbess appeared at the head of her nuns coming up the lane of the dyers. The friars made for the stairs and ran down them. They arrived at the door as the abbess marched past, her nose raised and her hooded eyes unseeing. She passed and Fra Filippo was left staring at the small procession of nuns in her wake.

'Here we are,' said Lucrezia simply.

Hardly knowing what he was doing, for he had no clear memory of this part of the plan, if indeed any plan had been made, he opened the door to his house and ushered the nuns in. 'There's a garden on the roof. It won't give you much of a view, but you'll be out of the crush. We'll be back very soon.'

Lucrezia handed him the large iron key to the cellar. 'Did you speak to them at the tavern?'

'It's all settled.' He closed the door behind the nuns and started off down the lane with Diamante. 'Come – we only have minutes to act!' Filippo hurried down the lane against the stream of people coming up it to the piazza. It was happening, as if the Fates had decreed it, and nothing now could alter his destiny. It was now, the moment was now, when he, Bacchus, had snatched his Ariadne from this foul world and placed her as a constellation of stars in the heavens.

What are you talking about now, caro mio? he wondered as he broke into a run.

'What I do for you! What I do for you!' Diamante complained from behind, finding it hard to keep up.

'Not me, blunderhead, but for God and Natural Justice!'

'You have a high view of yourself suddenly.'

Filippo stopped at the convent's gate. 'You'll think differently in a moment. Go to the tavern and fetch Rosaria. She'll be expecting you.'

He let himself in with his own key then went to the cellar with the key Lucrezia had given him. Opening the door he jumped back, repulsed by the stench. For a moment he thought Brigida must have died but then he heard her moan and call on Holy Mary for help.

He went down the stone steps which seemed to be slippery with his own sweat. How could that be? Even the walls felt as clammy as his face and by the time he reached the makeshift bed amongst the barrels he himself was calling on Holy Mary.

'My dear, my child,' he said to Brigida. 'Help is coming.'

'The baby!' Brigida moaned again, the sound rising like a gale in a broken barn.

'We must prepare you for your travail... prepare you in case... you understand ... prepare your soul to meet God.' His eyes growing accustomed to the dim light of one squat candle, he could see the horror in Brigida's eyes.

'I don't want to die! Please don't let me die!'

Instinctively he wanted to comfort her with assurances, but he had his job as chaplain to do and he had to offer extreme unction as a precaution, although he had none of the materials to do it. 'Is there any oil here?' he asked. Yes, tall clay jars of it, local olive oil stored in the cellar, but Brigida pointed a wavering finger to a small dish on the floor beside the bed.

'Lucrezia gave me a massage.'

Filippo took the oil, blessed it and anointed her, praying that the Lord might pardon her sins.

Brigida howled like an exorcised devil, really frightening Fra Filippo, but she was only responding to a new contraction.

'You must go,' she said, struggling for breath. 'You can't stay.'

'I can't leave you!'

'You must, you must! It's not right!'

'I'll stay until Rosaria arrives. She'll be here soon.'

The contractions were coming every few minutes. As Brigida let out another howl, Fra Filippo began to pray. What was keeping Rosaria? It was true, what Brigida said: he could not stay. It was wrong, so wrong for a man to be present during a birth. He couldn't even think what the punishment would be – burning at the stake, probably. But his innate faith, which ran through his being like fine golden wire, told him to set aside his personal concerns and to help the poor woman who was now writhing and twisting as if in her death throes. He called on the Virgin and Saint Margaret, 'Come, come to your poor servant! Help me to help her!'

At once he felt that warmth he had felt when touching the Holy Girdle. 'Holy Mother, help me!' he prayed again, and the answer surged in him, a wave of confidence.

He clutched Brigida's hand, telling her to be strong and have faith. 'Faith, Brigida! Who knows it better than you?'

'*Blood of Christ!*' she screamed. '*Merda!*'

Filippo was shocked. This feeble, bird-like little nun was shouting like a whipped captive on a slave ship.

'*Cazzo! CAZZO!*' She tried to sit up and when she couldn't she pulled up her habit and drew up her knees.

Filippo had a full view of the bulging hole between her thin legs. He clamped his eyes shut but that warmth of divine presence soothed him. Was she here? Was the Holy Mother really here? And Saint Margaret? Oddly, in his imagination neither looked as he had painted them. He could barely see faces at all: they were sound made visible, a touch on his skin, an exhalation of prayer. 'What do I do?' he whispered.

Slowly, solemnly, he followed the instructions spoken in his mind. *Prop her up with cushions, bring her legs over the side of the bed, encourage her to bear down, tell her all will be well.*

Brigida's cheeks blew out, her eyes bulged, she wept for shame and pain and shouted one last blasphemy at God – *Dio merda!* – as the baby's head emerged. Her voice thundered in the vaulting and bounced off hocks of ham, rounds of cheese, wine barrels and oil jars. Fra Filippo fell to his knees before her. Everything in him was shrinking away from what he had to do, but it was as if someone else were operating his body, informing his actions; it was as if his hands knew what to do when he did not. He watched in awe as they reached out to support the emerging head with the grace of a saint painted by Fra Giovanni. He didn't know whether he was going to be sick or burst with love.

The slimy, visceral umbilical cord was round the baby's neck. He watched his hands lift it gently over the head. The head turned and at once the shoulders and body appeared in what seemed to be a rush of watery blood.

He heard voices at the top of the steps, exclamations of shock, and Diamante saying, 'This is no way for the new Messiah to be born!'

'Don't come down, Diamante! Go and get some hot water! Have you got Rosaria with you?'

'A little late by the looks of it,' she said, clattering down the steps in her clogs. She leaned over to see what was going on. 'My niece was going to come and help but, when it came to it, I couldn't find her. Gone to the showing, I suppose.'

'How am I doing?' Filippo asked.

'You're doing well. You're both doing well. All three of you are doing well.' She took Filippo's place to assist the delivery, guided the baby out and placed it on the mother's belly, covering them both with a light clean blanket she had brought with her. She listened. There was no sound from the baby, so she picked it up, held it upside down and smacked it. Filippo was shocked by the brutality of it but immediately forgot it when the baby gasped its first breath and wailed. As Rosaria sat on the bed and cradled Brigida who cradled the baby, Filippo made a mental note for a composition of Saint Anne and the Virgin and Child. Brigida was still having contractions but he did not like to ask why. She seemed quiet now, exhausted and relieved.

'Mother Mary and all the Saints and Angels, I thank you,' she muttered, back to her usual mode of speech.

Fra Filippo regarded the women and now-suckling baby in wonder and went to get up off the floor.

'There's more to come,' said Rosaria softly.

'What?'

'The afterbirth. Get a dish to catch it in.'

Filippo had heard of it, but only as the viscid stuff you have to bury. It was a few minutes before it arrived, a few minutes spent on his knees with the smell of blood in his nose. Brigida groaned, pushed and the placenta fell into the dish. Now Filippo felt hot in the head and very sick. Trying to stand, he collapsed like a hayrick.

'Men,' said Rosaria. 'They just can't cope.' She felt the umbilical cord for a pulse and, when she found none, tied it expertly with two laces, took her sharp knife and severed mother from baby.

'My son,' Brigida breathed, holding out her arms to take the baby.

'Your daughter,' Rosaria corrected her.

'I have hot water!' Diamante called from the top of the steps.

Rosaria called back, 'Let's just get her to the tavern before anyone returns! Come down here and get your master back on his feet.'

Diamante came down cautiously, his hood drawn low over his face and his head averted from the women. With his foot he nudged Filippo in the ribs. Filippo stirred, groaned and struggled to his feet. Trying not to look at the afterbirth, now sitting in a dish awaiting its ritual disposal, he asked Rosaria what they were going to do with it. It should be buried, he said; then he grinned. 'Or shall we leave it for the abbess to deal with?'

'Not likely!' she said. 'That's a good supper, that is!'

Within his hood, Diamante turned green.

'It should be buried!' Filippo protested.

'I can see you've never starved.'

'Rosaria! I insist!'

'Or we could sell it to the apothecary. It makes good medicine, afterbirth. You know it won't be cheap looking after these two.'

'Rosaria!'

She looked at him crossly, annoyed that Fra Filippo Lippi of all people should have strong views on such matters. Friars! Hypocrites the lot of them! But she acquiesced and agreed to the burial, putting the bowl of placenta in her basket. They wrapped Brigida and the baby in a blanket then, with Rosaria leading the way and on the look-out, Filippo and Diamante helped the young mother out of the cellar and the convent. Between them they carried mother and child to the Taverna dei Tintori. With all the townsfolk now packing into the main piazza for the showing, the lane of the dyers was deserted and they got to the tavern without being seen. When they arrived, Rosaria took full charge and waved them away.

'You go off now and see the woolly belt,' she said, 'and leave the work of God to me.'

Filippo offered her his purse but she declined it. 'What, you want all the glory of this action? No, leave some charity for us to give.' She shooed the two friars away, telling them to hurry or they'd miss the showing. Filippo suddenly remembered his appointment at the chapel of the Holy Girdle, and the earthly part of him reasoned that it would be a good thing to be seen in public on this day.

'You will bury it, won't you?'

'Of course. Trust me!'

Filippo looked at her guardedly. These peasants, these hill folk come down to live on the plain, you could never trust them. They regressed into paganism as soon as you turned your back.

But he did turn his back and hurried off to Santo Stefano while Diamante remained behind to re-fortify himself with a jug of wine.

✝

Filippo found the great men of the town gathered around the bronze gates of the Chapel of the Holy Girdle – the Inghirami, Datini, Cicognini and Giuntalodi – all in their best brocades and silks, the product of the looms that had made them rich. They rustled and swished in their importance, and were treated as the most honoured guests by the bishop, provost and archpriest of a church grateful for – and dependent upon – their benefactions.

If only you knew, thought Filippo moving amongst them with a smile, *that I have just abducted five nuns.* The abbess herself was amongst the select company, tossing her head and blinking incredulously.

'Is all well, Mother?' Filippo asked.

She peered at him, her eyes large with disbelief. 'I have lost my nuns! They were behind me when we set out, but not when we arrived. It's all so crowded out there. They must have become detached somehow.'

'You will find them again,' he said, squeezing her arm. 'The nuns are missing,' he turned to tell the archpriest, Carlo de' Medici.

'I'd promised them, you see,' said the abbess, shouldering Fra Filippo out of the way. She was not going to let that ill-bred friar stand between her and a Medici. 'I told them if they stayed in the convent at prayer all day, I would bring them here this evening so they could see the Girdle, perhaps even touch it. You'd given your permission, if you remember, Your Reverence.'

Carlo nodded. 'I had indeed. And now they are lost you say?'

'They're out there somewhere. Anyone would be lost in that mass of people,' said Filippo.

'Go to the pulpit and see whether you can see them,' Carlo ordered him.

Filippo pulled a sulky face – the Holy Girdle was about to be brought out from its case – he might miss the opportunity to touch it – he needed all the divine help he could get – but he went nonetheless, to strengthen his alibi. He went up the stairs and through the passage behind the façade to the pulpit. Naturally, movement in the pulpit caught the attention of the straining crowd below and he became far more public a figure than he had intended as he made a pretence of looking for the nuns. Trumpeters came into the pulpit as if he were not there and blew their fanfares to heaven; he glanced towards his house where, on the roof, he could discern some wimpled heads. With a smile, he turned back into the passage and met the Holy Girdle being borne toward him, draped over the hands of the Bishop of Pistoia.

'Filippo, touch it,' said Carlo de' Medici.

Filippo reached out and laid his hand on the camel-hair belt, softer than he had supposed, and, as back in May, he jumped as if bee-stung. Was this sharp sensation the fire of divine remonstrance? Had his sins called it forth? Or was it the fire of mercy, signifying that the Virgin approved his action? He did not know, could not say, could only flatten himself against the wall as the bishop, provost and archpriest made their way to the pulpit for the showing. Loud cries and cheers came from the crowd, followed by deafening clangs of the bell in the campanile.

When he came down the stairs and into the chapel, he found the abbess waiting for him, clutching her hands anxiously. 'It was impossible to see,' he told her. 'It's an ocean of bodies out there. I'm sure you'll find them waiting for you back at the convent. Did you touch the Holy Girdle?'

The abbess nodded with tears in her eyes.

'What is it?'

'I didn't feel anything,' she said, holding her face.

'What did you expect to feel?'

'The last time it was as if I touched the Virgin herself – I felt purified. This time, nothing.' She wept helplessly into her hands. Filippo decided to leave. He went out to struggle through the crowd straining towards the pulpit and echoing the bishop's prayer with their responses, to cross the piazza to his house – where he found four nuns in the kitchen making supper, with the boy Alessandro chopping vegetables for them.

He peered at his apprentice.

'I found them here,' Alessandro explained. 'They said you'd let them in.'

'You can't stay,' Filippo said weakly to the nuns. 'Not all of you.'

'And we cannot go back,' said Suor Piera, radiant, her mouth full of apple. 'She had us on our knees all day. If we complain, we are told to look to her as an example, and often it's true, she does have more devotion and more stamina than the rest of us. But we're too tired to care any more. We are being sacrificed on the altar of her pride, because all she wants to do is to impress the bishop, the provost and the rest of them, especially the Archbishop of Florence, who she thinks is a saint! She wants her convent to be famous and wealthy. *Very* wealthy. And it is our suffering that will gain these things for her.'

'How very perceptive of you.'

Suora Piera smiled. 'I have much time for contemplation and even she can't oversee what it is I contemplate.'

'And what do you contemplate?'

'Motives.' She gazed penetratingly at Filippo and led him out of earshot of the rest. 'Simonna and I have relatives we can return to, here in the city, and tomorrow we shall be gone. But who will look after Lucrezia and Spinetta? When it comes to motives, Frate, I can see yours as clear as your face.'

Filippo coloured vermilion. 'What do you mean?'

'They are better motives than you may think,' said Suor Piera kindly. 'You're in love with her, aren't you? And is that any different from the procurator fathering a child on Brigida? Yes, it is. It is as different as it can be, the difference between the sacred and the profane. My faith, I confess to you, my confessor, is in tatters – the warps hang torn from the loom and cannot be restored. For the rest of my life I shall give the semblance of piety, nothing more. For I cannot believe in this church that promotes suffering for the many and privilege for the few.'

✝

Over supper, Filippo established that what Piera had said was true: she and Simonna had somewhere to go but Lucrezia and Spinetta did not. 'You cannot stay here,' he said. 'Not for long. Look – just across the canal, Santo Stefano, the house of the provost, the cloisters. Ha! Everyone will know.'

'Who will know? We'll never go out.'

'Who will know? Why, every weaver and dyer in this ward and his wife. It's easier to catch water in a sieve than keep a secret round here.'

Lucrezia shrugged. 'Let them know. They love you.'

'What do you mean? Who says so?'

'Those who come to our church. They're always asking after Fra Pippo and saying how kind you are to them, how you lend them money with no hope of return, how you buy physics for them and pay for doctors.'

Fra Diamante, rising to leave, looked at his master with a frown. 'Is that where all the money goes?'

Filippo bade his assistant good night and asked him whether, on this night, he would take Alessandro with him to the Carmine. Now Fra Diamante had a face like an alabaster lantern, all illuminated by a candle within. 'Oh ho!' he said, leading Alessandro away for his moral safekeeping.

'Alessandro!' Filippo called after them. 'Not a word about this to anyone. Under the terms of our contract, you are sworn to silence and secrecy at all times.'

Alessandro smiled at Diamante. 'I have a very long contract.'

'You'll find it gets longer every day.'

'It's in your contract, too, Diamante!'

'Of course, caro mio. We bid you good night, emphasising, perhaps unnecessarily, the use of the word *good*.'

Lucrezia drew close to Filippo. 'Your neighbours love you as we love you,' she told him. 'And they know what the abbess is like. We fall upon your charity. The people will understand.'

'Lucrezia,' he whispered, the scent of her tickling his nose. 'We must be chaste.'

'Of course! Now where shall we be sleeping?'

43

FRA FILIPPO AWOKE WITH A START AS THE SUN SHONE on his eyes. His room faced south: it was late in the morning. He looked at Lucrezia beside him, her fine, wheaten hair in a frothy tangle on the pillow. He began to tease out the knots. In answer to his many dreams of anticipation, she had not lain like a board, nor resisted, nor shouted in pain. She had met him more than half-way with a lust that was as startling as it was arousing, her coltish legs wrapped around his waist, pulling him into her even as he tried to withdraw. Every prostitute in Prato had something to learn from this young nun. Who was, now, one of their number. How could it be otherwise? Feeling bilious at the thought, he arose. He found the three other nuns sitting in a row on the bench in the parlour, hands in laps, silent. He stared at them, they at him.

Arriving for the day's work, Fra Diamante walked in with Alessandro.

'You may wish to find work elsewhere,' said Fra Filippo, 'for I am damned.'

'Far from it,' said Diamante, taking some figs from a bowl and peeling one. 'We've just come via the tavern. Brigida and her daughter are doing well, thanks to you. Caro mio, have no fears about the wrath of God.'

'Just the wrath of men.'

'Ah, well, yes.'

'Any news from the convent?'

'Only that the abbess and her sister did the work of five to provide dinner for the guests, who left early this morning. Whether they believed her story that her nuns were all abducted during the festival, we shall never know. It must have been queer there last night.'

Filippo asked his assistant to visit the relatives of Piera and Simonna and make all the necessary arrangements for them to go to their houses under cover of darkness during the night to come. 'After that, could you convert your room into something more comfortable for Lucrezia and Spinetta? Buy new sheets, bolsters, coverlet – whatever they need. As for your own accommodation, buy a new bed.'

'I'll not be staying here overnight again.'

'Diamante! Are you becoming prudish?'

'I've been thinking about my being a Carmelite and what it means, long before all this blew up. I've come to the conclusion that I need to try harder with the discipline. That no one else follows it is not a licence for me to do as I like; no, discipline must be self-discipline.'

'Well, I hope you are able to help me finish the walls before you achieve sainthood.'

'I would be helping you with them today if I weren't aiding and abetting you in kidnap.'

✝

Fra Filippo spent the day at the walls with Alessandro. Now and then he stood back from his painting to give a high-pitched laugh that ended in a whimper. He would now be living in perpetual expectation of a hand falling on his shoulder, the heavy hand, strengthened by a leather wristband, of the gaoler. He painted the hair of Saint Stephen and found himself in tears, not the pious tears of Fra Giovanni, but the tears of a sinner very afraid of the jaws of hell. 'It was wonderful, it was beautiful, but never again,' he promised himself. 'I can smell the fumes of the pit.'

That evening he returned home to find a supper waiting for him as good as anything he'd ever eaten. The whole family – for it seemed like a family – gathered at the table to eat well for the first time in years, with food cooked in their own hearth rather than at a market stall. The nuns took the wine that Fra Diamante offered without any persuasion and their smiling faces shone pink in the candlelight. Fra Filippo sat at the head of the table like a satisfied king. What could be wrong in this? Nothing in the eyes of God, surely, although everything in the eyes of the righteous. He glanced at Alessandro, thinking the boy's laughter at one of Diamante's jokes was high and shrill as if he were trying too hard to be non-judgemental. He resolved to speak to him when he could, to explain everything, to justify his actions morally. Suddenly wine spurted down his nose, which he had to blow into his sleeve.

'Nothing, nothing!' he said in answer to Lucrezia's concern. 'Just the devil smacking me on the back. Jolly fellow. Likes a laugh.'

Men from the families of Simonna and Piera arrived after dark to escort their cousins to their house. All the nuns clung to each other, aware now of impending loneliness. 'Dear God,' said Piera, stricken, 'am I going to miss the cloister?' She looked accusingly at Filippo, as if he had dragged her from a happy life.

'We'll find you a better cloister in due course,' he promised. Later, after Diamante had gone home to the Carmine, he and Alessandro sat in embarrassed silence with Lucrezia and Spinetta. Alessandro, he had decided, must get used to the new arrangement and he had not asked him to go to the Carmelite house on this night.

'Well,' said Filippo, striking the table with his palms. 'Time for bed – and you two,' he said to the sisters, 'can share Diamante's as last night, only now with some lovely soft sheets.' Lucrezia and Spinetta retired, leaving Alessandro by his pallet in the kitchen.

'Alessandro,' Filippo began. The boy turned, his eyes half-closed in weariness. 'No, you're tired. I'll speak to you in the morning. I want to assure you that I planned none of this. As with everything else in my life, it happened to me. Do you understand?'

Alessandro nodded. Before he climbed into his pallet, he knelt beside it to pray. Filippo cleared his throat and went to his room, resolved to be good. For the boy's sake. He was his master, after all, and a master's responsibility is that of a father's.

An hour later, when Lucrezia slipped in beside him, Filippo held out his arms to her. His resolution? – well, he would renew it on the morrow. For now, why fight?

44

ALESSANDRO'S UNWAVERING INTEREST IN EVERYTHING the painter did reminded Filippo of himself at that age. He also had a precision of attention that Fra Filippo soon began to miss if ever he sent the lad out on an errand. It was difficult to believe that this studious, attentive boy had been expelled from school three times.

With the godforsaken summer behind them, Filippo began to enlarge on his instruction of the apprentice and to initiate him into the secrets of geometry. Having shown him the figures of the composition for the Naples altarpiece, the triangles and circles that would become its hidden essence and matrix of creation, he began to draw the sinuous lines that were suggested by the geometry and not dictated by it. At one point he gave the boy the chalk, put his hand over Alessandro's and drew, so Alessandro could feel the sensuous pleasure of the line – a skill that could not be taught. 'It will come in time with practice,' Filippo said. He took Alessandro's hand up, down and around the form of St Michael, allowing him to experience the firmness of a master's hand, who could draw lines with confidence, with a flourish, indeed. 'Doesn't it feel good?' Filippo asked. 'It's like peeling the chemise off your mistress.'

Alessandro snatched his hand away.

'Oh, don't look so offended. Doesn't it say in our contract that the apprentice is to make no judgement of the master nor find fault with him?'

'Does it?'

'I'm sure it does. You're growing up, Alessandro, and are about to join the man's world. You'll have to get used to the smutty thoughts of painters. And their dubious actions.'

'But you are a friar!'

'The kind of friar that Boccaccio mocked in his tales, the kind that merciless Dante consigned to his circles of hell. The kind that people either scorn, denounce as wicked or find uproariously funny. That's me.' He continued to draw lines, his mind only half on what he was saying. Alessandro watched the miracle of the armoured archangel appearing on the tinted paper and scratched his neck as if to rid himself of the itch of what his master had said.

Filippo glanced at him. There was something of the pious in the lad. Nothing overt, just a maidenly blink of the eye at some of Fra Filippo's bawdier jokes, a moment of shock at some of his remarks, like this one about the chemise. 'I have a nun in my bed at night. I was imprisoned and tortured last year by the archbishop for falsifying a contract. According to the pope, I am a contumacious liar and the perpetrator of many wicked crimes. So you see there is no hope for me. I am damned.'

Alessandro looked so upset at this confession that Filippo was forced to retract it. 'He's only a pope and not God. He can say what he likes about me – I don't have to believe it, and neither do you. So, I am not a model friar, but my sins are small compared with those of others. Indeed it's only because I am a friar that they're considered sins at all.'

Alessandro's screwed up his face in the effort to understand this sophisticated theology.

'I mean, no one else is chastised for eating his fill, but everyone seems to think that a monk or friar should be half-starved. It seems more reasonable to me to eat when there's food available in readiness for those times when it is not. You've never known hunger, have you? That's why you're big and lean. I starved as a child and I have never fasted since. Why impose on yourself that which Fortuna is only too ready to lay upon you? If there's food around then thank the Lord and eat it, that's my philosophy. Then there are the more serious sins of the flesh. Any man who has a varied diet of women is considered accomplished and fortunate – unless he's a friar. I'm supposed to be celibate.'

Alessandro was colouring to a rich shade of madder.

'Can you compel men to be virtuous? Yes, but only by fear. They tell me that if I'm not celibate then I'll have my balls chewed off by a four-headed dog at the gates of hell. It's just to frighten me, you see, but I'm not that gullible. I say, let those be chaste who want to be chaste. But for those of us dumped in monasteries just because our relatives didn't want us, I think it's asking a great deal – don't you? Frankly, it's asking too much. I was always a lusty lad, Alessandro, the same as you, only you blush like a girl and look offended.'

'Fornication is wrong!'

'Who says so?'

'Everyone! All our elders and betters. The Holy Book.'

'We were brought up by bitter old priests and nuns. If they couldn't stop us fornicating, they could at least make us feel guilty about it.'

Alessandro had his hands clamped over his ears. Fra Filippo prised them off. 'I've seen your drawings.'

'No!' cried the boy. 'They're private! Have you been prying?'

'I'm your master – I wanted to see your studies. Woah! Very interesting studies of the female form. All from the imagination?'

Alessandro was now near fainting from shame.

261

'It's keeping it private that creates sin, boy. Get it all out in the air, that's what I say. There's nothing about you that's not normal, healthy and common to us all. Nothing. So, you're a failed Christian. Who isn't? You should have heard what my Moorish master had to say about that. No, the only thing that makes my sins of interest to others is that I'm a friar.'

'You don't have to stay a friar, do you? Surely your friend Cosimo can get your vows annulled?'

'Annulled? I'm not giving up being a friar just because I find it difficult!'

Give up being a friar? He would have to pay taxes; he would have to play his part in government and get caught up in the squabbles of minor committees. He would have to be seen in church on Sundays. And he would have to dress in colours, make daily choices in his apparel, record all his income and expenditures and be careful not to spill things on himself or dribble. The wonder of the habit was that he had nothing to consider in the matter of costume. He could arise in the morning and be dressed in one Hail Mary. If he were a layman, they would probably make him Gonfalonier and he would have to lace himself up in civic finery, bear the city flag on important occasions, and pretend that he cared about Prato. To give up the cloth would be to give up a life lived according to his own wishes: how many men could boast that? Not even Cosimo de' Medici.

'You don't understand,' he told Alessandro. 'It's complicated.'

He went back to giving the design his full attention. His innovations he thought to save for the surface detail, as Giovanni de' Medici had remarked upon. He would dazzle the viewer with gilding and gold leaf, with glazed metal, with jewels painted so realistically you would reach out to pick them off. He described what he was doing to the boy, how one seeks to show the structure of the body through the folds of cloth. He took a length of very fine wool he had bought from a haberdasher's as a present for Lucrezia, tied it round Alessandro's waist with a single loop bow and draped the length of it over the wrist of his right arm.

It was, he admitted to himself, done to impress the boy. In a lesson on drapery, he was using the finest fabric and all its tiny pleats to show what, in the hands of a master, could be done with paint. Alessandro soon forgot venial sin in the wonder of the sinuous line.

45

WHEN A FEW DAYS LATER FILIPPO WAS SUMMONED TO SEE the abbess, he found her alone in the convent with her sister, Jacopa. She had licked the wound of the missing nuns raw. They must have been abducted and could not possibly have run away. Could they? And what had happened to Brigida? Had it been planned? By whom? For how long? Filippo wasn't sure whether she had summoned him to interrogate him or was so reduced that, for once, she sought his advice.

He stood before her nervously, listening to her tumbling questions. *Does the provost know? Will I be dismissed? We did our best to cover up but rumour is running everywhere. Who planned it? Somebody did! I daren't go out.*

He imprinted every flicker of the abbess's distress on his memory so he could tell Lucrezia about it later, how she blinked rapidly, how her voice kept rising, how she had to keep clearing her throat.

'If as you say they've been abducted by some unknown person, then it must be reported to the authorities.' To prove his innocence, he offered to go and do it himself, straightaway.

'No!' she said fiercely. Then again, 'No!', this time quieter. 'The authorities already know, surely. Archpriest Carlo was there when they failed to arrive at the chapel.'

'He will have presumed that they turned up later. You must make an official report.'

'Oh, Fra Filippo, how will it reflect on me?'

'Their abduction?'

'What if they weren't abducted. What if they left of their own accord?'

'How would that be possible? Why should they want to?' He chewed his lip to kill a smile. He tried to say, 'Where would they go?' but knew he couldn't get the phrase out and keep his face straight.

'Perhaps it was because of Brigida.' The abbess looked momentarily haunted as she thought of the nun locked in the cellar, then she shook her head. 'I've done everything by the rules of Saint Benedict. I've done my best for them. This is a good house, not a fallen place of sin like some. Haven't you seen me chase off young bucks from my does with a broom? This is a good house. Why should they want to leave of their own accord?'

'Sometimes,' said Fra Filippo gently, 'discipline can seem harsh.'

'Oh! The discipline I've put them under is nothing to that which I suffered. The young these days have no stamina, no will, no real vocation. Was I too harsh? I never meant to be harsh. You read of abstinence and spiritual effort in the lives of the saints: should we not seek to emulate them? What is the alternative? A life of soft luxury lived in dedication to God? Piff! I was training them in service and self-sacrifice. What is the duty of a nun, if not to be mother to all? These young things are so selfish. They think only of themselves. Spoiled as children, they come here and act as if they're in prison. What am I supposed to do? How may one instil a love of God that doesn't arise naturally? Don't tell me by kindness – that's just more spoiling.' She glared at him suddenly. 'Do you know where they are?'

Fra Filippo took a step backwards. 'Me? Why should I know?'

'You've lost your pretty Lucrezia.'

'I'm sad if that is true, but I've hardly seen her since your altarpiece was completed.'

The abbess peered at him doubtfully before resuming her tone of appeal. 'What am I to do? I can't make inquiries around the city without letting it be known they are gone.'

'Those who come to the chapel will realize it soon enough, if they haven't already.'

'I'm closing the convent and chapel, saying there is sickness here.'

'You can't do that forever.'

'Oh, they'll be back soon, surely! What can they do on their own? Where would they go? Someone must be harbouring them, but who?'

Fra Filippo twitched and slapped his arm. 'Mosquito,' he muttered. He prepared to leave, promising to make discreet inquiries.

'No enquiry can be discreet enough! Just investigate it, Brother. Keep your ears open, and your eyes. They are in the city somewhere.'

Fra Filippo went home in a cheerful mood. The family could continue as it was for the indefinite future.

✝

The whispers were going round the district by the end of the week. Everyone had known about the nun's disappearance since the festival, not least because Ser Matteo Peruzzi had told his Pratese friends before he left for Florence. But no one thought much of it until a dyer's wife had seen a young woman looking out of one of Fra Filippo's windows; then there was that new bed delivered to the friar's house; and it was generally agreed that even Fra Filippo could not eat all the food that Fra Diamante was bringing back from market. The convent of Santa Margherita had suddenly and mysteriously closed and had an X painted on its main door. And so suppositions were made which, for once, were accurate: the missing nuns were in the chaplain's house.

Old men who gathered on benches under the vine arbour covering the door of the Taverna dei Tintori discussed the matter heatedly, that Fra Filippo had abducted nuns – one, two, three, all of them – who knows? Il Mulo joined them, throwing his legs up on the table, each foot pushing the clog off the other. He clasped his blue hands behind his head and stretched.

'Have you heard?' asked his father.

Il Mulo laughed. 'I've heard. Good for Brother Pippo!'

It's terrible – it's disgusting – it's a scandal on our ward – he must be birched naked, and the whores with him – we've heard what goes on at the convent. So the men complained, brows knitted and mouths down-turned with furious disapproval.

'You sound like a lot of old women,' said il Mulo. 'What did Jesus say about the first to cast a stone?'

'Let him be without sin,' said his father.

'Well, you stone-throwers, heed the word of the Lord.'

Il Mulo's father shook his finger at his son. 'No blasphemy from you!'

Il Mulo put his legs back down on the ground, sat up straight and faced his father and friends. 'You sons of rebels, listen to yourselves and be ashamed! We know what that abbess is like, how she is blind to the likes of us, thinks we are the maggots of Satan. The only men she notices are those who might donate to her convent. We don't count. Well, I can be just as dismissive. Those girls were treated like slaves. I'm not going to be the one to tell anyone outside this ward where they are. And if I catch anyone betraying Fra Pippo...' He ran his finger across his throat.

'How can he call himself a friar?' his uncle dared to protest.

'Have you seen what's going up on the walls at Santo Stefano?' il Mulo asked. 'Have you seen it? You look at that and tell me Fra Pippo's a sinner. He is bringing glory to this city to match the Holy Girdle itself.' He put his legs back on the table. 'And I'm not going to be the one to betray him. Anyone that does,' – he put an imaginary noose round his neck and jerked it tight – 'must answer to il Mulo.' The capo of the ward had spoken.

The sound of a baby crying came from an upper window.

'What's that?' he asked.

'Rosaria found a baby abandoned, floating down the canal in a basket.'

'What's his name, Moses?'

'It's a girl. She's taken her in and called her Mary.'

Il Mulo nodded and smiled, pleased. He looked for virtue in his family and neighbours. Vice lived on the far side of the canal, in the palaces, the grand houses and the holy church.

✝

By the following day, no one was making any mention, not even to each other, of what was happening in Fra Pippo's house. That was his business, not theirs. Il Mulo had stirred their pride. One old woman even called at the house to see if 'the young ladies' required anything. Lucrezia answered the door and told the woman sweetly how kind she was and no, they needed nothing.

'Very sweet girls,' the old woman reported to her neighbours.

'You can't stay here,' Filippo told Lucrezia at least once a day but, as the days passed, all ideas of where else they might go became exhausted. He asked Diamante to buy some material for Lucrezia and her sister to make simple gowns and chemises. If the nuns were in his house to stay, there was only one solution: he himself must go. Yes, to make his life right he must step out of it. Thus he thought at night, staring into the shadows of the bed's hangings. He would go to Florence and concentrate on the Naples altarpiece. That was what he should be doing, after all, in this year when he had been released from the frescoes. Now that the fresco season was coming to its end, he felt more able to leave them to concentrate on the altarpiece. All signs pointed to 'Go!' He rubbed his cheek against Lucrezia's sleeping head. What, and abandon her, his beauty? No, he couldn't do that.

✝

As winter came upon them he still had not decided. Why make a journey to Florence when the rain was lashing down and the road churned to mud? Why do that when he had his Lucrezia to snuggle up with? It was what an ascetic would do, and no one could accuse him of asceticism. No, he shuttered the windows, lit the fires and lived as a husband for five months. He continued work on the designs for the Naples altarpiece he was supposed to have delivered back in July and did odd jobs around the city, decorating the vaulted chamber of one rich man with a pretentious fleur-de-lis design, painting a banner for the Gonfalonier, designing a tomb for the provost who was convinced that the coming year would be his last. The poor, sweet provost who was not even aware that any nuns were missing. Filippo thought he could make things right with God by not charging the provost for the design, but reason got the better of him: he had a family to look after.

He received letters from Giovanni de' Medici, about one a month, and he replied dutifully, writing letters illustrated with designs which were quite difficult to make out, small and sketchy as they were.

At the end of February, windows were opened again and neighbours became reacquainted with one another. Now it was time to leave. As the weather warmed, the walls of the chapel called to him but he could not heed them. He was running out of excuses for delay – he must go to Florence. Before he could do so, however, a party of armed men arrived to 'collect and escort' him on the orders of the Medici, 'to discuss,' they said, 'a very overdue commission'. When Giovanni de' Medici had said that he wanted to see the sketches in July, he had meant 1456, not 1457.

'A moment, spare me a moment at least to put my affairs in order!' Filippo cried.

The captain of the guard assented.

Filippo took his assistant aside. 'Diamante – look after them.'

'What? No! My reputation!'

'Blame me for everything,' said Filippo generously. 'Everyone will believe you. Tell them the truth.'

Florence
1457

46

THE SCENT OF FRESH PLASTER AND SAWN WOOD IN THE
new Medici palace tickled Filippo's nose as he was taken up
a grand stone staircase, accompanied by Alessandro carrying a
roll of sketches for the Naples altarpiece. The place was looking
more like the palace of a king than the house of a merchant and
Filippo wanted to linger at every turn to take it all in – the pillars
and carved friezes of the courtyard, the statues on landings, the
glimpses through doorways of marble tables, but he was led
smartly to Giovanni de' Medici's chamber.

'Sketches? Is that as far as you've got?' Giovanni thundered.
'I was expecting to see these last year!'

'There was plague, Giovanni, and tempests. I've commissioned
the frame. Other than that, I've been busy!'

'Were you not told to stop work on the frescoes for a year?
I was rather expecting that in a year –'

'Family matters and suchlike.'

Giovanni's low eyebrows dipped threateningly. 'Has anyone
found those missing nuns yet?'

Filippo wanted to shout, *How do you know about the missing
nuns?* but realized it must have been Carlo; Carlo had found out
somehow. Alessandro was intently studying the scuffs on the
leather boots his father had made for him.

'Let me see these sketches,' said Giovanni, taking Filippo off
the hook and throwing him back in the river.

Filippo unrolled them and showed Giovanni the Saint Michael
and the Saint Anthony Abbot of the two wings, told him the
colours he had chosen and about the surface decoration involving
much silver and gold. 'As for the frame, it's going to be as lavish
and elaborate as you wished.'

He nodded, approving the designs for the wings. 'And the central panel?'

'Here – a Virgin and Child, as we discussed.' He unrolled the sketch.

'Enthroned? I don't remember agreeing to that. You were going to try several designs for me.'

Not knowing what to say, Fra Filippo took off his cap, scratched his head and put his cap back on. It was true, that had been said, but then he had been so pleased with his Virgin enthroned he could only suppose that Giovanni, being a man of developed taste, would agree.

'It's now three years since the King of Naples signed the Peace of Lodi and we can't go on waiting for you, Filippo Lippi, do you understand?'

'I need more money.'

Giovanni's eyes blazed. Alessandro began to tremble so much he had to sit down.

'I have nieces,' protested Filippo. 'Yes, my sister died and I am responsible for her daughters.'

'First I've heard of it. How old are they?'

'Young, and no hope of marriage, not without dowries.' Filippo went to the window to avoid Giovanni's violent gaze.

'See Martelli in the bank. He'll advance you the money.'

'Good, then if that is all, I shall be getting back to my workshop.'

'Oh no, we want you where we can see you. A room has been made available in our old house next door.'

✝

Hearing that Fra Filippo was in the palazzo, Cosimo had himself carried to Giovanni's chamber. His arrival startled the two men who, between them, had created a miasma. Seeing Filippo's shock at his altered appearance, Cosimo glared at him, daring him to overlook the real Cosimo in this body of an invalid crippled by gout.

'I want to see several sketches for the central panel by the end of next week,' Giovanni said sharply to the friar before bowing to his father and leaving the room.

'Cosimo...' said Filippo.

'Who is this?'

'Alessandro di Filipepi, my apprentice.'

Cosimo assessed the boy with an investor's eye and approved of what he saw. 'How old are you?' he asked him.

'Just fourteen.' Alessandro looked both awestruck and trapped.

'Are you still able to play as a child?'

Alessandro stared at him, speechless.

'My grandsons are creating havoc in the garden. Lorenzo is eight and Giuliano is four. Could you direct their play and bring order, do you think?'

Alessandro with his large limbs stood looking gawky and unable to direct anything.

'Be a horse or something – they'd like that. I'm afraid they don't get such games from their father and grandfather any more. Go on, boy, do as you are told. I want to talk to your master alone.' The two men watched Alessandro leave, his ill-shod feet slapping on the new floor.

'The last of the brown feathers,' said Cosimo enigmatically.

'Eh?'

'Cygnet to swan – end of the phase.'

'I hope so.' Fra Filippo looked momentarily concerned, then gave him an affectionate smile.

'He seems an improvement on Diamante, at least,' said Cosimo. 'How is our diamond? Still without lustre?'

'He will always be dull.'

Cosimo picked up the sketch for the central panel. 'As will be anyone complacent about his abilities. Who told you to do a Virgin and Child enthroned for King Alfonso?'

'Giovanni. Well, to be accurate, he said, "A Virgin and Child, of course."'

'Of course.' Cosimo leant forward to peer at the drawing. He wore the red lucco and red cap of a citizen, but on an ageing form. His skin was shrinking, making the bones of his skull protrude, his nose large, his temples bulge.

'You don't like it either?' Filippo asked nervously.

'Is there anything as dull as the predictable? Filippo, if we give you a free hand, for the love of God, use it.'

Fra Filippo's breath became rapid as he realized his error. 'I'll start again.'

'And what will you do?'

'What do you suggest?'

'Ah, another shortcut? No, Filippo, no. It's time to listen to your heart. What are you now? Fifty?'

'Fifty-one.'

'And I am nearly seventy. We have no time to waste.'

'Precisely!' said Fra Filippo. 'So let's get the work done quickly.'

'That is not what I meant. Headlong rush in work is wasting time. Think of the cross. There's the horizontal bar, and then there's the vertical. With what time you have left, plunge deep. Tell me what's there.'

Fra Filippo swallowed and seemed reluctant to speak.

'Come on, tell me what you love.'

'Painting. The feel of the brush on plaster. The resolutions that come, as if by grace, when I'm confronted by problems.'

'How lofty! If you'd have asked me thàt question, I would have said my grandsons. Come on, Filippo, tell me what – who – you love.'

And then it spilled from Fra Filippo, what filled his heart, the light, airy beauty of his Lucrezia. Cosimo listened to it all without comment; he did not blink when he learnt that Lucrezia was a professed nun; he did not blink when he learnt that she was living in Filippo's house. But suddenly he roared with laughter. 'I'd heard they were missing. It's the Mystery of Prato. All of them at your house?'

274

'No!'

'You haven't got them all?'

'No! But they did all run away from the convent, and for the same reason: maltreatment! No, the others have been taken in by their relatives – I made sure they were all safe. I have only Lucrezia and her sister Spinetta, who have been rejected by their family.'

'Ha! Oh, is there anyone else in the world with as much talent as you for getting into trouble?'

'No one,' said Filippo mournfully.

Cosimo's laughter bubbled up again. 'If we didn't have hell to consider, I would rejoice in your adventures.'

'Please don't mention hell.'

'At your age, Filippo, you should have it at the forefront of your mind. Papal Indulgences are for the gullible, and in my time I've been gullible to the tune of tens of thousands of florins. Penance is for the faithful, but you are a doubter like me. We think, What if it doesn't work? What if remorse does not expunge sin? What did Our Lord say? – Go, and sin no more. I don't know about you, but each time I go to confession it's for the same thing as the last time. "Take me as I am, Lord!" – that's what we're saying, "take me as I am – a miserable, repentant sinner. I can't do anything about my behaviour except feel remorse so I fall upon Your mercy to take me as I am." Would you take anyone into your house on that basis? I wouldn't. We must atone. We must work to perfect ourselves.'

Fra Filippo's eyes narrowed. 'Isn't that heresy?'

'Off your high horse, old man. We're alone here. Let's speak of things as we find them. There is something about you I don't understand. Under all the dross that is Filippo Lippi, when he finally gets down to work, there is grace. Quite astonishing grace. Where does it come from? Tell me about the grace.'

'When I sit down to paint I find I have a headache suddenly, or I need to piss, or I hear the handbell of the baker in the street below. If I don't know what to do next, I can't sit in front of my easel in patience but must run to the tavern and seek oblivion in the butt. I make it hard for myself and that's why I take so long with everything. But every now and then, the storm subsides and I'm working. I need peace, long hours of peace, to work properly, and I never get them – always being distracted by this and that.'

'Yes, yes, but tell me about the grace. Where does it come from? Can you summon it?'

Filippo laughed. 'How I wish I could! No, grace comes from and by grace.'

'So it is divine.'

'Yes, it is divine.'

'You are a vessel of divine grace.'

Cosimo had been reading Ficino's first translations of Plato and was becoming familiar with Platonic thought. He smiled with deep satisfaction to know that he had just caught Lippi with Socratic reasoning. The friar was looking startled.

'Not how you think of yourself, is it?'

'I am a wicked, contumacious liar.'

Cosimo sniffed loudly, deriding the opinion of the pope. 'So what is causing all this delay on our altarpiece?'

Tears welled in the friar's eyes. 'I believe I'm not capable of it.'

Cosimo leant forwards and stared at him. 'Tell me that again?'

Filippo smiled wanly.

'So what stands between you and divine grace,' said Cosimo, 'is an erroneous idea about yourself. Give it up, Filippo, that's all you have to do. All your thoughts and prayers must be directed to that. If your painting requires little effort, it's because your talent comes from God. I want you to go to the room we have prepared for you next door, and I want you to sit there in silent and peaceful contemplation until the image – the true image – for the central panel arises. Do you understand?'

Filippo looked at him with glowing eyes and nodded.

'Come and see me when you've produced something. I want you to come and see me at every stage. We shall complete this commission together.'

✢

When Fra Filippo left the palazzo, he went to the small, enclosed garden but it was empty except for workmen laying a cobbled path. He eventually found his apprentice with Cosimo's grandsons in the office off the courtyard where a painting by Paolo Uccello, originally in the old house, had recently been installed. The two boys were staring up at the vast scene of the Battle of San Romano, a decisive battle, Lorenzo explained importantly, in the war against Lucca of 1432. The victorious condottiere, Niccolò da Tolentino, dominated the painting, sitting astride a white horse which, with its bared teeth and flaring nostrils, looked as if it had been whittled by a woodworker for a four-year-old.

Oblivious of his master's presence, Alessandro gave Cosimo's grandsons a discourse on the art of perspective. Without regard to their age and intellectual ability, he quoted Alberti word for word: 'Having placed the centre point, you draw straight lines from it to each of the divisions on the base line. These lines show how successive transverse quantities visually change to an almost infinite distance.'

Giuliano turned to the friar in the doorway; Fra Filippo pulled a face and rolled his eyes. The child's trill of laughter made Alessandro turn. He blushed to see his master. 'Please correct me if I have it wrong.'

'No, no, carry on,' Filippo assured him. 'You're doing well.'

'Look at the spears on the ground,' Alessandro continued. 'Horizontally they are parallel to the picture plane, but the orthogonals – the ones at right angles – seem to converge at a distant point.'

Lorenzo, who was short-sighted, went up close to the painting, his mouth open in wonder.

'That's how perspective is done,' said Alessandro.

'All an illusion of course,' said Fra Filippo gazing at the central panel. 'The illusion of reality.'

'Even Tolentino's velvet mazzocchi is painted in perspective,' said Alessandro.

There was, Filippo had to admit, something awe-inspiring about a soldier in battle wearing a vast cushion on his head. 'I think the boys have had enough of vanishing points for one day. It's time to go.'

'No!' whined Lorenzo, taking hold of Alessandro as if he possessed him.

'Your grandfather wants you, Lorenzo,' said Fra Filippo.

47

THE ROOM THEY HAD BEEN GIVEN IN THE OLD HOUSE was on the second floor and faced the street. The walls were painted with geometric designs and the colours were darker where hangings had once been. It was but a small antechamber. Someone as lowly as a friar-painter could not be allowed to stay in a main chamber even if there were several completely empty. There was a bed in one corner – the posts remained although the curtains had been removed – a small table, a ewer and a basin. Near the hearth there was a pallet for Alessandro.

He always travelled with basic equipment and he had his small easel and boxes of brushes and pigments brought to the room, sending to Prato meanwhile for a long list of other items he required from his workshop, including all the panels for the altarpiece which had been prepared ready for painting. Giving it to Alessandro to organise, he settled himself at once, for Cosimo's words had inspired him. He wanted to work. There was no reason why he should not have a design for the central panel that very evening.

He did as instructed and sat quietly in silence, waiting for the image.

It did not come.

It still had not come when his things arrived from Prato two days later. He busied himself setting up his workshop in the old Medici house, overseeing the delivery of the panels, bellowing at the men lifting them to take great care. He went to help them prop them up against one wall in the chamber, the central panel flanked by two wings, all soft, powdery white, waiting for their images. The approved designs were tacked to the wings, leaving the central panel blank. Filippo sat on his stool, stared at the white square and prayed for grace to come to him. He felt a sudden desire to go to the tavern.

He jumped to his feet. 'I shall be out for a few hours,' he told Alessandro. 'You are free to amuse yourself. Go and visit your family.'

'Master?'

'What is it?'

'You told me to stop you if you said you were going out.'

'Did I?'

'I think you saw this coming.'

Filippo crossed to the windows and threw them open to air the room. A chill blast entered which made Alessandro hug himself. Filippo leaned out to look down on bankers and merchants haggling in the Via Larga. 'Bring my stool, boy. Those vultures... this is a very good place to piss on their heads.'

Alessandro laughed and refused. 'Do you know yet, what the image will be?'

'Come, pray with me.'

Filippo knelt at a prie-deux and made space for his apprentice, but as both of them could not fit on one cushion Alessandro knelt on the floor. He looked askance at his master. It was not like Filippo to pray at any time of day – certainly not just before starting work, when he was usually busy sucking the loose hairs out of brushes or humming to himself as he chose pigments. After a few minutes, no longer, Filippo was back on his feet again, muttering, 'Pah! Nothing!' He went to his easel and knelt before that. This time he prayed aloud, asking God to inspire him with an image. A moment later, he was sketching on paper with chalk the Virgin and Child, not enthroned. She was simply standing, holding the child in her arms.

'Yes, that's good, good,' he said a few hours later. Giving thanks to God, he went to find Cosimo and hurried through the corridors joining the two houses. He had never worked like this before and was pleased with the results. This must be how Fra Giovanni had worked. Why had it taken him so long to wake up? Yes, it was a fine image and, with this trick learnt, he need never delay or stall again. From now on his life would be one long flow of work, a growing river of beauty.

He found Cosimo in his chamber, reading with a young man.

'Go, Marsilio,' Cosimo said as Filippo entered. 'We shall continue our discussion later.' He beckoned Filippo to him.

This was Filippo's first sight of Ficino. He whose reputation as a scholar was mighty turned out to be in his twenties and very short. As they passed each other, Ficino smiled and struck the friar as being kind and genuine. With a large book under his arm, strong, golden hair, bright eyes and his shortness, he seemed like a divinity who had just delivered a message to Cosimo and was now on his way back to the angelic realm.

'Show me,' Cosimo said, reaching out to take the drawing from the friar and unravel it. His hands seemed huge and the knuckles and joints deformed, but Filippo gave him the roll rather than insult him by doing it for him.

Cosimo unrolled the paper, clutching it on both sides to peer at the design. Filippo watched Cosimo's face with great expectancy, an expectancy that, with passing time and no exclamation of joy from Cosimo, faded into disappointment.

'No,' said Cosimo at last, letting the design spring back into a roll. He handed it to Filippo like a baton. 'Dull and lifeless.'

'But how can that be?' Filippo exclaimed, for he had convinced himself it was the work of God.

Cosimo shrugged. 'Start again.'

✝

Filippo set to work painting the wing panels of Saint Michael and Saint Anthony Abbot, as if this peripheral commitment would somehow help him with the blankness at the heart of the piece. Leaving Alessandro to paint the sky, he turned to sketching a Nativity, using an antique ruin instead of a stable as the setting, an excellent idea that had come out of nowhere which, he thought, would be more to the Medici's taste.

'No,' said Cosimo. 'Start again.'

The next day, while Alessandro painted the wall, Fra Filippo did the Assumption of Mary, where the dying Virgin was held by her son.

'What rubbish!' said Cosimo. 'Leave that sort of thing to the Greeks.'

Day after day, while Alessandro worked methodically with a fine brush, laying down stroke after stroke of colour, Filippo writhed and groaned, dragging ideas out of himself like sausages. Day after day, for an entire week, he met Cosimo in the evening only to have the day's work dismissed as rubbish.

On the last day, he went to Cosimo, held up a sketch and, before showing it to his patron, ripped it in pieces which showered on the floor. 'Why bother to show you,' he said angrily. 'You'll only be rude.'

'What was on it?' Cosimo demanded. He clicked his fingers to summon a servant and had the man pick up the pieces. 'They are blank, both sides,' said the servant.

'I am empty!' cried Filippo. 'I have no more ideas!'

'At last!' said Cosimo. 'The truth!'

In a storm of ill temper, Fra Filippo strode away, telling Cosimo to dismiss Alessandro, for he would no longer require any assistance.

48

'NO! ALESSANDRO CRIED, WHEN FILIPPO TOLD HIM himself that he was dismissed. 'No!'

'I have no need of you, boy. I will not be completing the altarpiece for the Medici. I'm going back to Prato. Or perhaps even Barbary. Yes, I should like to go to Barbary.'

Alessandro followed his master disconsolately as Filippo stumped across the city to the Carmine although, when he got there, he was too angry to go in and veered off in another direction. Alessandro would follow Filippo Lippi to Barbary if he had to. He was not going to go back home to scrape the bristle from pigskin for a living, up to his ankles in squidgy hides soaking in pigeon dung. He followed his master round the city, in and out of taverns, waiting for him outside a brothel, or while he placed –and lost – a bet on a donkey race. Alessandro always remained, he thought, out of sight but at one point, along the Arno, Fra Filippo suddenly lifted his arm and pointed to the tannery at the Santa Trinità bridge.

Alessandro coloured to realize that Filippo had been aware of him all along.

'No!' he shouted at his master's back, 'I'm staying with you!' He followed him to the old Medici house and saw a servant hand Filippo a letter as he entered.

'It's from Diamante,' Filippo said angrily as Alessandro came in. 'He says he desperately needs money to keep the household fed.'

Alessandro stared at his master with puppy-dog eyes as Filippo swore, cursed, kicked out at the wall and yelled at the pain.

'It was a mistake,' the friar puffed, rubbing his toes. 'I shouldn't have taken you on. I don't need any help – not now. I'm going back to Prato, alone.'

Alessandro fell to his knees in front of Filippo, too bereft for words. He was beyond protest. He knelt there, hugging himself, swaying back and forth. Fra Filippo watched him for a while then he went to lie down on his bed; within the minute, he was snoring, great sail-fillers that would bear his galley over the sea of dreams.

Alessandro busied himself tidying up and washing the equipment to show that he was indispensable but when Filippo arose an hour later he failed to notice. 'I'm going out,' he said. 'I shall return soon.'

Alessandro gazed at the retreating friar, wondering when he would see him again; Filippo returned shortly afterwards. 'I've been to see Domenico Veneziano. He's busy and could do with some help – it's only temporary – you're still contracted to me. But it will be a wonderful opportunity for you. Domenico trained with Gentile da Fabriano and has worked with Pisanello and Piero della Francesca. A little over-fond of pink, in my opinion, but you needn't let that influence you.'

Alessandro glanced at the Saint Michael panel and the pink wall that dominated the background of the painting.

'I'm giving you what I never had myself – training in the great stream of tradition. You will become part of that stream. I – I am an isolated pond. I don't want your reputation to be sullied by mine. I want the best start for you. Don't look at me with those big eyes! Alessandro, pack your things and I'll take you to Domenico. He's a good man, a very good man. You will work with him until I return to Florence – in happier circumstances, I hope. For this commission needs to be finished and, once Cosimo comes to his senses and realizes he is not my judge on earth, I'll be back to complete it.'

✢

Given that all the painters of the city had known Donatello, that they had all worked at some time or other with Lorenzo Ghiberti on the bronze doors of the Baptistry, and that most of them had learnt the art of perspective direct from Brunelleschi himself, was this not a race of heroes? Any pain at being left behind by his master was diluted by Alessandro's eagerness to absorb everything going on around him. The workshop of Domenico Veneziano was large and lively, with several assistants working simultaneously on different altarpieces, all under the supervision of Veneziano, a broad-faced man with fair skin and blue eyes who seemed keener to know what Alessandro had learnt from Lippi than to teach the boy anything himself.

'According to Alberti,' he said, 'a painter must exercise self-restraint. I've never seen Lippi exercise any. So how come he is favoured by Cosimo?'

Alessandro was at a loss: he knew nothing of any theories of painting other than what his master had taught him. He tugged at his sleeves: each day they seemed to be shrinking, his hands to be poking out ever larger and more disproportionate to his trunk. His big toes had punched holes in his homemade boots. Despite his height, breadth and gauche angularity, his fellow apprentices took to calling him Little Barrel, given that he was the brother of the rotund notary known as Big Barrel. He had expected the painters to be diligent and clever, always studying, examining, thinking, enquiring – like Fra Filippo. As they were all members of the Guild of Saint Luke, he expected them to be on committees and always looking out for one another. He expected them to meet in local taverns after work and get gloriously drunk. All of these expectations they fulfilled. What he did not expect, however, was a war of bitter invectives that had been longer and more drawn-out than the siege of Troy.

Snips of paper passed daily among rival workshops, telling the recipient that he had reversed the revival in the arts. 'Truly your figures look like the walking dead.' 'We didn't invent perspective for your soldiers to die neatly on orthogonals.' 'You say you've painted shadow to show form but to my eye it's just a nasty blotch.' 'I can understand two of your sources of light – one material and one divine – in your altarpiece, but which is that illuminating the mangy cat under the table?' Hefty men, some of them bearded, most of them unwashed, of at least two-score years, were known to sit crushed in front of their work, unable to lift their shoulders for days. Reading Alberti's book for himself, Alessandro discovered that Apelles, the famous painter of ancient Greece, used to hide behind his work to hear what others truly thought of it. Not a painter in Florence had that kind of confidence.

When Domenico got a verse from Andrea del Castagno about pink being the flesh-tone of pigs he already had a verse of his own waiting to go out and sent Alessandro with it.

'Don't linger while he reads. Andrea usually responds to criticism by punching the messenger in the teeth. So give him the note then run for it!'

Andrea del Castagno was working at the Duomo. With black hair singed by the sun and eyes hard and dark like raisins, he had been born of Tuscan soil. 'Son of a mountain peasant!', according to Domenico. There was even a resinous afternote to the scent of his sweat: his was the colour and smell of the pine-forest. 'The black pine-forest where the sun never shines,' said Domenico. 'How can he be blamed for having no sense of colour? What does he know of red other than blood and flame?'

Castagno was working on a portrait of Niccolò da Tolentino, the great condottiere, in a monochrome to resemble a marble equestrian sculpture upon a marble sarcophagus. It was a companion piece to match Uccello's painted monument to Sir John Hawkwood, another condottiere who had saved Florence from destruction in war. Alessandro stared up at it. Tolentino was the same figure in the same ridiculous hat that Uccello had painted in his battle scene for Cosimo, and on the same nursery horse – all big teeth and flaring nostrils – but the difference in line was stark. Where Uccello's was static, Castagno's was lively, the horse's tail and the captain's cloak blown into movement.

'Are you looking for me?' asked Castagno from his ladder. 'Haven't seen you before. Which workshop are you from?'

'Temporarily, Domenico's.'

'Temporarily, eh?' Castagno came down the ladder and wiped his hands on a rag.

'I'm Alessandro, Fra Lippi's apprentice.'

'Yes? Fortunate boy! I was with Filippo myself when I was your age, but not for long. He soon found a reason for getting rid of me.' Castagno, not noticing how crestfallen Alessandro had suddenly become, took the paper and unfolded it. 'Have you read it?'

'No.'

'Liar.' Castagno opened up the day's message and found it was all but the same as yesterday's.

'Don't tell me,' grumbled his chief assistant, Antonio Pollaiuolo, 'we're so inept at producing flesh, we've been reduced to depicting stone.'

'Correct!' Castagno tore up the paper, rolled it in a ball and stuffed it into Alessandro's mouth. He went back up the ladder to his simulation of marble.

Alessandro pulled the paper out. 'Any return message?'

Castagno thought about it. 'For your penance, young Alessandro, you're to return to Domenico's shop by way of San Miniato. Do you know San Miniato?'

Alessandro's eyes widened at the thought of the church alone on a high hill overlooking the city. As diversions went, that was a long one and the day was hot.

'You're to make a pilgrimage there on your knees.'

'I'm only the messenger,' Alessandro breathed.

'And you'll be the only beneficiary of this spiritual exercise. When you arrive at the church, ask to see the Assumption. And when Domenico wants to know where you've been all day, say you've been studying with Andrea del Castagno.'

It would not have occurred to Alessandro to ignore the instruction. He crossed the Arno at the old bridge and, finding the path of many steps cut into the hillside, he began a long and arduous pilgrimage to the top. Almost two hours later he was standing before the old church, bent double, panting with thirst, rubbing his knees and trying not to weep from pain and self-pity. A monk of the place came out to give him water from the fountain.

'Andrea del Castagno sent me to see the Assumption.'

'Is it to happen here, today?' the monk asked.

'His painting of it,' said Alessandro bitterly.

'Oh, that's at San Miniato.'

'This *is* San Miniato.' Alessandro's chin was beginning to tremble.

'San Miniato al Monte. You want San Miniato Between-the-Towers, down in the city. The Assumption, you say? Yes, well, seems you've made one and got it wrong.'

Alessandro jumped back down the hillside, striding down the broad steps, back over the bridge to find the other church dedicated to San Miniato. He had it in mind that, when at last he stood before the Assumption, he would scratch at it with his nails and get what paint off he could by gouging. But when he did stand before it, he saw two things simultaneously: a wild storm of clashing colour and *that* face. He stared through the flames of scarlet and crimson to the face, the upturned face of the Virgin, now an old woman and wimpled liked a nun, her face upturned to heaven, upturned in the most perfect exercise of foreshortening that Alessandro had ever seen, so perfect that the picture was lifted out of tradition and made timeless.

Why had Castagno sent him here and by such a painful route? To teach him humility, perhaps, or to exact revenge for the message. But Alessandro knew what he was looking at: a moment in Castagno's own career which had been so sublime that, ever since, he had been unsettled by no one's criticism. In this face of the Virgin, Castagno must have surprised himself, must have gone beyond his own ·sense of expectation and limit. Now, whenever he got a barb from Domenico Veneziano, or from anyone, he would only have to close his eyes to see Mary looking at heaven.

Alessandro returned to Domenico's workshop where saints stood full-face on the picture plane as if Masaccio had never been. He listened to the talk around him as he swept the floor.

'Define a dog.' 'Small animal, domesticated, four legs, two pointed ears, a snout, a tail.' 'Define a cat.' 'Well, the same.' 'Not the snout, though.' 'No, not the snout.'

The men enjoyed philosophical discussion as they worked, testing their understanding of the world. 'So what is the difference between a dog and a cat? How do we show it?' 'It's the shape, isn't it? The shape of the head and the back. You would know the difference just in silhouette.' 'Ask Alberti – he'll know.'

Having finished sweeping, Alessandro sat darning the holes in the knees of his hose with nothing to do but listen. Everyone could tell the difference but they couldn't define it, which made it a problem with words, not with knowledge. A cat walked past and rubbed herself against his long legs. 'It's just your is-ness,' Alessandro whispered. 'You're a cat at your core.' The cat purred and pushed against his hand, raising her front paws, head back, eyes closed in pleasure. Alessandro smiled.

'But what is a cat geometrically? A cylinder for body, cone for head, two cones for ears.' 'Truncated cylinder and cone for head.' 'Are you sure?' 'If you define a dog geometrically, it comes out the same.'

Alessandro scribbled his fingers under the cat's chin, felt the hollow of the bones there, knew the miracle of fur, blew gently on the cat's nose.

'What's this?' 'It's a man with his hands raised in the air, his eyes wide, his mouth open.' 'Yes, but what am I portraying with this gesture?' 'Your surprise.' 'My surprise at what?' 'Don't know.' 'Your stupidity!'

Alessandro yawned. There was too much talk in this workshop where everyone was too busy to teach him anything.

'Little Barrel! Botticello! Make yourself useful and go and buy some bread and eggs.'

49

IT WAS SAINT JOHN'S DAY BEFORE FILIPPO RETURNED TO Prato. Spring had become midsummer and he had nothing to show for it. Had he been in Prato all those months he would surely have finished the frescoes by now. He didn't stop at the church on his way across the piazza to his house, not wishing to be delayed by Diamante and his long list of complaints, for his loins were stirring with anticipation of seeing Lucrezia. Half way across, he was intercepted by a servant of the provost, sent out to call him into the provost's house. The servant led him to the small, vaulted library.

'Is it true?' Inghirami demanded, still standing by the window through which he had seen Fra Filippo pass by.

'Is what true?'

'That you have the nuns of Santa Margherita in your house.'

'No, that's not true. Ha! What a thought!'

Precious books were piled on shelves – the lives of saints, the writings of the early fathers, Dante's poetry: scripture and devotional works that served to prick the friar's conscience with a thousand tiny pins. The provost was studying him under heavily-lidded eyes. There was not a single hair on him, no beard, no eyebrows, nothing but big, sleepy eyes in a pink, featureless face. Filippo wished there was something reprehensible about Provost Inghirami so he could lie freely and with some pleasure, but there was nothing. He liked and admired the man.

'I'm lying,' he said, subsiding. 'Forgive me.'

Carlo de' Medici, the archpriest, entered. 'You called for me, Provost?' His tall, slender frame was dressed in a rose-pink robe and cap. *Those colours shouldn't work together,* Filippo gazed at Carlo's blue eyes, brown skin, black shiny hair and costume dyed in madder. *But they do. On him, anything would look handsome.*

'Oh, you've just missed being stunned to hear this wretch confess to lying. He does have the nuns!'

'Just two.'

'Just two! What are we going to do with him?'

Carlo sat down with a thump. 'You do have them? You've had them all this time?'

'Don't give me that expression of innocence, Carlo!' Filippo exploded. 'If your father knows, it's because you told him!'

Carlo smiled to himself, crossed his legs and smoothed out the creases in his robe.

'And how did the provost learn of it if not from you?' Filippo continued.

Provost Inghirami flinched.

Carlo, still smiling, looked up at Filippo through narrowed eyes. 'If you are trying to deflect the guilt on to us...'

The provost raised his hands to keep the peace. 'The action is done. All we can be concerned with is how to make good and save appearances. Yes, Carlo knew and told me, and we have discussed it at length. We've decided that there is only one course of action, and that is for us to arrange to have your vows annulled.'

'Vows annulled? No, never!' Filippo broke out in a sweat.

'Everything that needs to be arranged can be arranged,' Carlo continued affably. 'Look at me, holding high office when I am the bastard son of Cosimo de' Medici and his slave my mother.'

'The power of a name! You keep a concubine yourself but no one is suggesting you give up your living and marry her. If you were called Lippi, however, it would be different. I am not going to annul my vows. I may break them – I may break them daily – but I will never give them up.'

With that, Filippo left the provost's house and went to his own, all fire gone from his earlier anticipation. He was not going to stop being a Carmelite friar. Never! It would be easier to stop being Filippo Lippi. Meanwhile he needed to be on his best behaviour.

✠

Lucrezia watched him come in. Four months she had been dreaming of this moment, of throwing herself into his arms and being carried to their bed, but seeing the foul mood he was in she withdrew into her chamber and stayed there for the rest of the day, expecting him to visit her, to call her out, but he did not. She spent the night with Spinetta as usual.

When she asked her sister what had happened over supper, Spinetta said that Filippo had said prayers, that his piety was exemplary, that you'd think he'd renewed his vows.

Lucrezia turned her face to the wall. He didn't love her any more. It was that simple. He must have found a new lover in Florence. She wept into her bolster. The only thought which gave her any relief was that, however miserable she might feel, she was happier here than in the convent.

✝

Over the following week Filippo resisted sleeping with Lucrezia. He resisted her miserable weeping, and did not go to comfort her; he resisted her more cheerful teasing and coaxing, where she sat on his lap and stroked his cheek; but the days grew hotter, each one hotter than the one before, and he could no longer resist when, taking a rest in the afternoon, Lucrezia appeared in a chemise and linen cap in his chamber, climbed into his bed and nestled up against him.

He ran his hand the length of her form, over her shoulder, down to her waist, to her hip, to her thigh. When he reached her knee, he eased her legs apart. Time for that neat little cap to come off and her hair to spill.

He knew the technique of withdrawal, and so did she. She clamped his legs with her thighs and would not let him go. She licked his neck, fiddled with his ears, did everything she could to make him lose control. With a great cry he succumbed. He groaned, he moaned, he shuddered from top to toe and fell on top of her. 'I'm so sorry,' he said. Lucrezia looked up at the

291

ceiling and smiled. 'That's all right, my darling,' she said, stroking the back of his head until he fell asleep.

To enter sleep, he had to go through a mouth of fire, into the pit. His recurring nightmare of being tortured by the archbishop had stopped when Lucrezia had entered his life. Now it came back in an altered form: it was Cosimo who was pulling his innards out on a winch. He was left with an empty cavity, like one of the carcasses he used to see in his father's butcher's shop: all bloody ribcage and no organs. He could put his hands inside himself and feel his bones. He awoke screaming.

Lucrezia sat up, gathering the sheet over her nakedness. 'What is it?'

The door opened and Diamante looked in, full of concern. 'Caro mio? Is it the dream again?'

Filippo lay staring at the ceiling with round eyes, his breath rasping in his throat. 'Yes, the dream.'

'Wake up then and be free of it, for you have a visitor.'

Filippo sat up, startled and nervous. 'Who?'

'A most beautiful boy. At least, he was until recently. Now Goliath seems to be bursting out of David.'

'What?'

'Walked all the way from Florence, so he says.'

'Alessandro?' Fra Filippo swung his legs out of bed. 'Where is he now?' he asked, hurriedly dressing.

'Spinetta is making a big fuss of him.'

Pushing Diamante's helping hands away and tying his girdle himself, Filippo went down to the kitchen where he found Alessandro eating heartily of everything Spinetta could find to put on his plate. His face expressed nothing but satisfaction: a journey successfully completed, a stomach now filling. He didn't interrupt his eating with any speech. He blinked slowly. Through his eyes and only by his eyes, Alessandro smiled. He swallowed then refilled his mouth. It was only twelve miles from Florence but the walk had given him a roaring appetite and he could not spare a moment to smile with his mouth. His eyes creased at the corners.

292

Filippo studied Alessandro's face and saw only good things written there: relief to have arrived, pleasure to find the two nuns still *a casa*. No criticism. No moral outrage. None of the things that had concerned him about his apprentice. 'Why have you left Domenico without my permission?'

Alessandro concentrated on peeling his boiled eggs.

'Well?'

'Andrea del Castagno – did he study with you once?'

'For a short time, yes.'

'Why short?'

Filippo shrugged. 'Fiery, vain young man as I remember – got on my nerves, probably.'

'Do I get on your nerves?'

'No. Why?'

'Everyone says you get rid of apprentices very quickly.'

'Do I?'

'That's what I heard. They told me I'd been dumped on Domenico Veneziano like an orphan.'

Fra Filippo shook him amiably by the shoulder. 'Eat up, boy. You're putting on a spurt of growth, I see. So what did you learn in Domenico's workshop?'

'Not much of use, although I do understand the difference now between extrinsic and median rays and I know what a reflection is.'

'Oh, you do, do you? What is it?'

'It is where the extrinsic rays bend.'

'It is, is it?'

'Yes. As when a man walks through a meadow in the sun, his face appears greenish.'

'So, if I were to paint a young man or a maiden in a meadow, I must paint their faces green? Would that make them seem more realistic? How would the viewer be able to tell the difference between reflection and a slightly poisonous lunch? How could we say that this figure is not on the point of vomiting, having eaten the wrong kind of mushrooms? Never take any theory to the

293

point of absurdity.' Filippo hit Alessandro on the crown with a spoon. 'Observe nature – use your noddle. That's my theory of painting.'

Alessandro grinned, glad to be back with his master – the one painter he knew with true grace.

'I'm glad you've come back,' said Filippo, as if it had been his own decision. 'Tomorrow we'll be finishing Stephen and the Sanhedrin. I've started work on the design for the Feast of Herod. This is going to be the best scene yet.'

50

ALESSANDRO RAN INTO THE WORKSHOP. 'THERE ARE Medici riders on their way – just arrived in Prato – come to get you!'

Filippo sighed, sat back and looked mournfully at the panel he was working on. His tongue clicked against his palate and he rose reluctantly. 'Pack my bag, will you? And I shall want all my pigments and brushes in the chest.'

Alessandro looked at him wordlessly although his large eyes were filled with the question, 'Am I coming with you?' Filippo ignored him and went to say goodbye to Lucrezia.

When the horsemen arrived, clip-clopping smartly over the piazza, Fra Filippo went out and was startled to see that they were armed. The horses were snorting from wide nostrils that could have been painted by Uccello. 'Is there a war on?'

'Fra Filippo, we have come to collect and escort you back to Florence on the orders of Giovanni de' Medici.'

The neighbours, drawn from their homes and workshops, presumed the friar was under arrest for his misdemeanours and started making a racket, but Filippo put his hands up to still them. 'This is simply for my protection on the road. Somewhat overdone, I know. The Medici require me to do some work for them, that is all. But pray for me, nonetheless, good neighbours!'

Inside the house, and keeping out of sight, Lucrezia and Spinetta looked stricken but Fra Diamante assured them there was nothing to worry about. 'It's all show. Once it wasn't, I know, but this time it is, I'm certain of it. They're just trying to frighten him.'

Everyone went back to their various duties except Alessandro, who put on his tired boots and set off for the city. Unable to keep up with the riders, he trailed on the Florence road and it was a day later that he found his master in the Medici house, miserably sketching a Virgin and Child. 'Cosimo and the family have gone to Careggi for the summer,' Filippo told him. 'So there is no one here to tell me what I should or should not do. I'll do a Nativity, I think. A few rocks to indicate the stable, some angels, the Virgin and Child. I've been told I must write to Giovanni de' Medici and give him an absolute and final date for completion, which I think should be in a week or so, but let's play it safe and give it three. So the whole thing is to be finished by Saint Bartholomew's day. And I need to ask him for more money. I've spent thirty of my own florins on materials. I'll have to speak to him.'

Alessandro gazed at the hunched and dejected man and did not know what to say.

'You walked?' Fra Filippo asked the boy. 'It's hot, eh? You must be exhausted. Go and rest, Alessandro, go and rest. I'll not need your help with sketching. I can do this alone.'

As the sun rose over the city the next morning, Alessandro left his pallet and went to the easel to study the finished sketch of the Madonna on her knees, her hands together in prayer over the kicking baby, with St Joseph and some shepherds looking on and some angels flying in from the top corners. Filippo opened one eye, groaned and and rolled over, pulling the sheet over his head.

'What's the matter?' Alessandro asked. 'This is beautiful!'

'Those angels look like gulls,' his master replied, muffled. 'If Cosimo were here, what do you think he would say about it?

He'd say I'm being lazy, that it's jaded and tired and I should start again.'

'But he's not here! Let's paint it. Let's start today.'

'He IS here!' shouted Filippo, bringing his fist down on the bed. 'That's the trouble. I'll never be satisfied again with anything I produce. What time is it? It's already getting hot. Let's get painting. I don't want to spend the summer in Florence. I want to go home!'

But it got hot quickly on that day and even before they had begun to transfer the design to the prepared panel, Fra Filippo declared it was far too hot to work and that they would start again at midnight, working by candlelight. At midnight, however, he was back in his bed.

The heat sapped their energy and stewed their blood. Fra Filippo spent the next morning on the local piazza with his feet in the fountain, fanning himself with a rejected sketch of the Virgin and Child. With a faraway look in his eye he watched the young women of the neighbourhood pass by, the line of the spine, the sway of the hip. It was so hot that he was only mildly interested in their beauty. One turned and raised an eyebrow at him. 'It's too hot,' he muttered. After an hour or so, he went for a rest. Perhaps he should go back to Prato. The Medici agents would not miss him for at least a week, but then they would send those apocalyptic horsemen again to 'collect and escort' him, a Medici euphemism for bending a man to their will. No. Best that he complete the work then legitimately be gone. He scratched himself as if he'd been bitten. Complete the work. His stomach tightened. To complete anything required making final decisions. And commit himself was something Fra Filippo Lippi could not do. Too final by far.

✝

A month later, on Saint Bartholomew's day, Lapo di Martelli, agent of Giovanni de' Medici – himself still summering in his villa on Fiesole – came to the workshop to see how matters proceeded. He found the frame had been delivered from Prato and that the two panels, one of Saint Anthony Abbot and one of Saint Michael, had been fixed into it. The frame itself required painting and gilding while the central panel was still on the painter's easel and in the earliest stages of design.

'You said you would be finished by today. You've hardly begun.'

'Hardly begun! I've lived with this commission for two years! It's all there – just requires the colour. A day or so, no longer.'

'I can spare a day or so.'

'What do you mean?' asked the friar, alarmed.

'I can sit with you for a day or so until the picture is completed. It sometimes helps to have company.'

Although he was boiling inside and out, Filippo shrugged. 'Sit there if you like. You will find the seat hard, the air hot and the company dull, but be my guest.' He turned to his work, making tiny brush strokes in egg tempera, head to head with Alessandro at the panel. Alessandro's work may only have been to hold the porringer of pigment but Fra Filippo found the boy's rapt attention acted as a magnifying lens. If both stared where the brush was laying colour on the gesso ground, then the work was all very clear and lucid.

Martelli had only ever seen fresco painters at work. He had no idea what a miniature activity tempera painting on panel was. He couldn't see what they were doing from where he sat and, as the day's heat began to build, so he began to nod. When he awoke an hour or so later, they had made no noticeable progress. He went away to write a report to Giovanni de' Medici.

The next day he returned, and the next. Giovanni de' Medici had stipulated a final date of the end of the month – no more, not an hour, not a minute more. On the thirtieth of August, when most of the central panel was completed, but the pinnacles of the frame were yet to be gilded, and Fra Filippo was not happy with the three angels in his nativity scene and wanted to rework them a little, Martelli said that the painter must work all night. 'And I shall sit with you.'

He went away to tell his wife where he was going to be, and to collect from her a herbal preparation for stomach cramps, for he was becoming nervous on Fra Filippo's behalf. When he got back to the workshop, he found it abandoned.

✝

The friar-painter and his apprentice arrived in Prato early in the morning. Filippo found Lucrezia and Spinetta sitting together in quiet conversation at the well, their heads bowed and touching, Lucrezia fiddling with the fabric of her gown as she spoke to her sister. Since they had been living in his house, the tension between the two had dissolved and they were as close as sisters should be.

'Oh, Filippo!' Lucrezia said as he walked into the courtyard. 'We weren't expecting you until the festival.'

'I finished the commission early. Is there anything to eat?' He had been made thoughtful by what he had seen – the pair of them at the well, their talk quieter than the chatter of the birds. It was so peaceful, private, sweet: the enclosed world of the female. The hortus conclusus. He felt left out. But he also felt oddly privileged, like an elder who had seen Susannah bathing and had not been put to death in yet another triumph of Virtue. He followed her inside. The house was cool, swept and freshly strewn with fragrant rushes and herbs. A breeze off the mountains played through the rooms, moving hangings and a mobile that Spinetta had made of twigs and bird feathers. Filippo sighed. They would come for him soon enough and probably before the festival in September. For now he must just rest his head in the lap of his wife and wonder what it was he had seen at the well.

As she stroked his face he fell instantly asleep, to dream of the Virgin Mary kneeling in a flowery glade with the Christ Child in

298

her lap. No Joseph. No shepherds. No angels. Just the Virgin and Child. Of course...

✝

When he awoke Lucrezia told him that she had had no issue of blood for nearly two months. He gazed up at her with round, unblinking eyes. 'No,' he whispered. He struggled on to his elbows. The last time he had been upright on his feet, he had been a free and single man – a celibate friar, indeed. Now the world had tipped on its axis and he was sliding off it. 'No!'

'I think you will make a wonderful father,' said Lucrezia dreamily.

'No!'

'A much better father than brother!' She laughed merrily at her own joke.

He almost wished he were back in Florence and melting like a tub of lard. He broke his fast with cheese and fruit and cried while he ate, at the mess he had made of things. But gradually a new idea emerged like a chick from an egg, the idea of being a father. He became oddly affected. This was the real miracle – not a few daubs of paint on a panel giving the illusion of life – this was life, created by a man and a woman. From Lucrezia's womb would spring a babe. He realized then what he had seen at the well: a woman content; a woman expectant; a woman fulfilled.

51

AN ADORATION. A NEW IMAGE WHICH, SO FAR AS HE KNEW, had not been done before. The Virgin would be kneeling over the Child. They would not be in a stable but in a flowery meadow. There would be saints present, in contemplation, but it would be a very unified scene both in composition and colour, in which the central subject was the relationship of mother to child. This was right. He knew it. He did not have to consult Cosimo about it. He decided to return to Florence straight away. As he and Alessandro left Prato by the Lily gate, however, they met the Medici soldiers come to collect him. Fra Filippo was given a horse but, as usual, Alessandro was left to trot behind the party on his own legs.

Fra Filippo was taken to the new palazzo where he was bundled upstairs to the chapel like a common criminal. There he was thrown in and the door closed behind him. It took a good while for his eyes to adjust to the gloom. By the light of a single candle burning on the altar, he could see the sheen of the polished stone floor and the golden highlights of the coffered ceiling. Filippo waited with some dread for the arrival either of Cosimo – the familiar sound of panting, both of the servants and of the one they carried – or Giovanni. He had his excuses and promises already well-rehearsed. He'd had to go back to Prato for domestic reasons; he'd had a vision; the panel would be reworked but finished this very week – that kind of thing. It wouldn't take long to win Cosimo round, although his son could be more intractable. Someone in the shadows cleared his throat. Filippo jumped. There was someone there already! Now that his eyes were adjusting ... he discerned the outline of a small, seated figure, the diminutive figure of Little Anthony, dressed simply as a Dominican friar despite being the archbishop of Florence.

'Your Grace! I didn't see you,' Filippo said, even as he quailed. It was Filippo's habit to dress up stories in glorious raiment and he could not always remember himself what the truth was. But he knew that, when he told others he had been tried and tortured by the archbishop, what he meant was the archbishop's court. Antonino had been his judge but not his executioner. Nevertheless Filippo blamed the archbishop for the punishment, just as he credited Cosimo with his release: on no evidence whatsoever other than sound supposition. What *had* happened was that after his release he had had a conversation with the archbishop about the condition of his soul, much the same as when they had been two friars sitting together on a bench at San Marco. But with the title had come authority and Antonino no longer suggested cures; as archbishop, he insisted on them. Perhaps that had been the real torture.

'What's this I hear about the nuns of Santa Margherita?' Antonino demanded. The soft voice of Fra Giovanni's most trusted friend had become harsh with office.

'The nuns? They've gone missing,' said Filippo cautiously.

'The abbess thinks you have them.'

'Me? Five nuns? How would I hide five nuns? And what would I want with them in the first place?'

'The abbess says you've turned your house into a bordello visited by every dyer, weaver and wool-carder in your district. Her girls, she says, are pleasuring the perverted desires of the vilest churls.'

Filippo tried not to smile. 'I can imagine her saying that.'

'Is it true?'

'Of course it's not true!' cried Filippo, with the full force of his innocence. But the archbishop was canny and knew this slippery friar too well. A master of dialectic, he went for the kill.

'So what is true?'

'It is not a bordello.'

'What is true?'

'They are not prostitutes.'

'What is true?'

'Two of them are living with me.'

'In what kind of arrangement?'

'As a wife and sister-in-law.'

The archbishop inhaled loudly and breathed out through his nose. His tongue tutted against his palate.

'Bad, eh?' said Filippo with a grin. He'd expected to win the archbishop over with his honesty, but Antonino had heard more than he could bear.

'How dare you! How dare you insult God in this manner, after all He has given you! Do you suppose laws only apply to others? What kind of life would this be if we all followed our desires as you do?'

'I am weak,' mumbled Fra Filippo, 'and I don't know how to be strong.'

'By the power of your own God-given will! After all the years you've lived comfortably in the embrace of the Church, surely you've learnt that? – that free will is what God has given us. Now what about your concubine? Have you no thought about her at all? You are content, are you, for her life to be ruined because of your action, your momentary pleasure?'

Filippo fell to his knees. 'There is to be a child,' he confessed.

'A sweet babe to spend its life being castigated as a bastard!'

I didn't make the law, Filippo wanted to shout. I only broke it! 'I'm ready to accept any penance,' he said, head bowed.

'Penance! You sin, you repent, you carry on as usual. Well, I am here to tell you that that cycle is now broken. There will be no penance.'

Fra Filippo blanched. 'There must be…' he whispered.

'I shall be speaking to your prior and advising him not to punish you.'

Fra Filippo wrung his hands. 'You must punish me!'

'What, so that you may blame me and the Church for all that you suffer? No. This time it's between you and God. You work out your own punishment and apply it to yourself. It is time for you to take some responsibility, Brother. Get up.'

Filippo rose and, seating himself as the archbishop indicated, found himself in the penetrating beam of the old man's bright gaze. As the archbishop's body grew ever bonier under the years of his asceticism, so that he was now all but skeletal, the youthful and intelligent lustre of his eyes remained undimmed. They were windows on a soul of increasing purity. Already, just two years after his death, Fra Giovanni was being referred to as blessed, 'the angelic brother'. Antonino was surely going to be beatified himself in due course, when that brittle frame finally crumbled and his soul flew to heaven. What a privilege then, for Fra Filippo to be in private conversation, yet again, with a saint. Alas, he did not think so, and shifted uncomfortably on his chair. 'After it is born, perhaps the child should be given to an orphanage. I will pay for its keep.'

'That's one solution,' said the archbishop, easing his stiff joints.

Filippo stared at the porphyry and serpentine beneath his feet, wondering at the sheen and the invisibility of the joins as stone met stone in the floor's elaborate patterns. If only an axe would come down and sever his neck. But blood on this floor, and a rolling head: that would be a foul stain on such beauty.

'Cosimo has formally requested my permission for you to be released from your vows, and the nun likewise, to which I have consented. Both of us have written to the pope in the expectation that he will look on our request favourably. If a man, put in an order at a tender age, fails to grow into his vocation, he becomes a blot upon Holy Mother Church. It is best that he becomes a layman.'

Filippo felt giddy. He was a bad friar and would be the first to admit it, but the idea of not being a friar at all was a kind of death, or at least an exile. It was unimaginable. What would he be then? – just a painter who had not served a proper apprenticeship, out in the marketplace vying for work with every other painter in the city. As a friar-painter he had a reputation and a standing. As mere Filippo Lippi, he did not. And everyone would laugh at him.

'I cannot,' he whispered. 'Please, let me try to improve.'

'But what shall we do with Lucrezia Buti?'

'I agree she should be released from her vows. Let her raise the child. I will look after her.'

'A friar and his concubine?'

'It's not without precedent. Even popes…'

'Enough! Enough of your profanity and selfishness. If you refuse this help we have offered you, I want all the nuns to be returned to the convent, wherever they are. The child can be put in an orphanage, as you suggest. Make yourself right with God, Brother, make yourself right. The only happy heart is a pure one. Do not sully your colours – remember?'

Filippo nodded. It seemed to be the only solution. The interview was clearly at an end – the usual end, wherein Filippo felt chastised but not humbled. All he had to do was to keep his eyes lowered, keep nodding and sidle away, then he could give vent to his fury alone somewhere, telling a deaf world all about its hypocrises and injustices and how he was never understood. So he rather took himself by surprise when he suddenly began unrolling his sketch to show it to the archbishop. And if that was not in itself an unusual act of humility, there was more to follow, for he asked the archbishop's advice. 'The image just came to me, apparently out of nowhere,' he said, holding the altar candle over it. 'I wasn't even looking for it at the time – I believed I had finished the design for the Naples panel. Well, more or less finished. A few bits left to do. And then this image came to me, and I drew it. So far as I know, it has no precedent. Do you know of a precedent? If there is no precedent, then I would like your blessing upon it, for it is no small thing to add something new to the great and holy tradition.'

The archbishop walked with him out of the chapel to the nearest window so that he could see the drawing properly. He examined it, looking for the sin of pride, vainglory, some display of prowess or independent thinking: anything by which to condemn it. But what he saw was innocence and devotion. Tears came to his eyes. 'You are a mystery to me, Fra Filippo Lippi, a mystery.'

'There's no precedent?'

'Only in the writings of Saint Bernadette, who had a vision of the Virgin in just this pose and location. I presume you've read Saint Bernadette?'

Fra Filippo smiled. 'Me? Read the works of the saints?'

'If you have, I'd be surprised. If you haven't, and this vision has come to you independently, then I am astonished. This,' he said, 'is a portrait of the adoration of the Child in the garden of the soul.'

52

AS THE WEATHER WAS NOT BLISTERINGLY HOT AND THERE was no epidemic of plague that year, the Medici returned early to the city from their summer retreats. Cosimo was sitting at a table with the gardener in the new garden, looking at plans he had drawn himself with a clawed, arthritic hand, a symmetrical layout of pathways with a central fountain, of beds and statues, some antique, some newly created. 'In monastic gardens,' he was saying, 'they always plant a mustard seed at the centre, symbolising the Kingdom of God, but we shall have a fountain to symbolise Christ as living water.' He looked up as his daughter-in-law entered the garden, pulling Alessandro by the ear.

'I found this misshapen tramp taking a prurient interest in the new statue.'

'It's Lippi's boy. Let him go.' Cosimo beckoned Alessandro to him, who came rubbing his ear. 'What do you think of the statue?'

The boy looked from one to the other.

'Well, what do you think?' Cosimo asked again.

'It's, um, uncomfortable.'

Cosimo watched the colour rising up the boy's neck from his shirt and could imagine what had been going on. It wasn't so long since he had been that age. No doubt the pertly-breasted Judith wielding a scimitar over the broken-necked Holofernes had stirred his loins and he had been enjoying a delicious flow of heat round his body when Monna Lucrezia had caught him suddenly by the ear. *Prurient interest.* Well, at least the boy now knew what 'prurient' meant.

Alessandro, nearly dying of shame, asked the name of the sculptor in a voice that squeaked and growled like a broken sackbut.

'Donatello. Perhaps not the happiest of subjects for a private garden, though.'

'You do not mean to say!' cried Monna Lucrezia. 'You intend to install it here?'

'I thought it could serve as the central fountain.'

'What, with blood running out of it? It's a terrible thing, Cosimo, terrible. Please don't spoil your garden with it!'

Cosimo smiled at Alessandro. 'Women never understand symbolism.'

'Symbolism?' yelped Monna Lucrezia. 'Judith saved her people by presenting her loveliness to the Assyrian general –'

'Seducing him.'

Lucrezia cleared her throat. 'Then decapitating him while he was drunk. What does that symbolise? The triumph of humility over pride.'

'Virtue over tyranny.'

'Fine. But does it have to be in my garden? Of course I understand symbolism – who does not? Virtue over tyranny? What will the servants make of that?'

'You're right! Pride – that's what Holofernes represents. Judith, the triumph of humility. I think of you as my Judith, ever present to curb my excesses.'

Monna Lucrezia was tall and of a figure surprisingly fine for a woman who had had five children. She ate with a moderation that Cosimo wished he could emulate. That he was thin he allowed others to believe to be the result of abstinence, whereas he had always been thin, no matter what he ate. Unlike his younger son,

Giovanni, who as he aged was beginning to inflate like a sheep with wind.

'Should I put an inscription on the plinth? Just in case anyone mistakes it for the triumph of servants over masters, or worse, women over men. Some quotation saying how Pride is overcome by Humility. I'm sure I read something relevant in Antonino's writings.'

'That should clear up any ambiguity,' she agreed reluctantly.

'But what do you think of the statue?'

'Ugly, like so many things by your precious Donatello. There's much violence in that man's work. What did you tell me once, that every painter paints himself? Well, if it's also true of sculptors, then Donatello is a tortured soul.'

'Few understand him,' said Cosimo petulantly, hurt that his favourite daughter-in-law did not share his love for his favourite sculptor. 'What is it, boy?' he asked, noticing Alessandro mouthing like a landed fish.

'You said "is". Donatello is alive?'

'Of course!'

'But… but… Fra Filippo…!'

'What is it? Spit it out.'

'I thought that Donatello had died some time ago. Whenever I asked about him, Fra Filippo shrugged and said, "he's not with us anymore".'

'Well, he did work for some years in Rome, then in Padua. Perhaps that's what he meant. But no, our Donatello is old, of course, but very much alive and still working in his shop behind the Duomo.'

More gasping from the boy, then, 'I would love to,' he began but stopped himself.

'What is it, Alessandro?' Cosimo asked again.

'Perhaps, one day I shall be a grandfather myself.'

'And blessed by God if that is so.'

'I'll want to tell my grandchildren about the famous men I've met.'

Cosimo puffed up and made ready to say something self-deprecating.

'Such as Donatello.'

Cosimo peered at him, trying to fathom the implication of what he was saying. Surely no apprentice of Fra Filippo needed an introduction to Donatello. He frowned, trying to remember whether he had ever seen the friar and the sculptor together. 'Are you telling me that Fra Filippo does not know Donatello himself? That's impossible!'

'He's never mentioned him as a friend, only as someone whose death has ensured his immortal fame.'

'How strange.' Cosimo exchanged a puzzled glance with his daughter-in-law. 'Pride, you see. First of the vices and source of all the rest. Artisans and artificers – is there anyone like them for pride?'

'Bankers,' said Monna Lucrezia.

Cosimo smiled and told Alessandro to go upstairs and have his secretary write a message to Donatello.

'What should it say?'

'Whatever you wish.'

Alessandro ran up the shallow stairs on his long legs.

'So, Fra Filippo has returned?' said Monna Lucrezia, sitting beside her father-in-law on the stone bench.

'He's in the chapel now with the archbishop.'

'The archbishop is in our house?' Monna Lucrezia leaned forward teasingly. 'I thought you had banished him because he makes you feel tetchy.'

Cosimo glowered. 'The man has no respect for his betters. If anyone else spoke to me the way he does… But he needed to see Filippo and knew he would never get him to go to the archipiscopal palace.'

'Of course he wouldn't. He remembers the last time.'

'Except you.' Cosimo regarded her from under his lowered brow. His servants kept him informed of Monna Lucrezia's frequent excursions, always to see a holy man or a site of sanctity.

'The archbishop is a wise counsellor and there is no need to fear him,' she said.

Cosimo garrumphed. 'Have you forgotten that he burned a heretic, right where Ghiberti's sublime bronze doors now stand? Forgive me if I tremble when I hear his name.'

'Is Fra Filippo in trouble again?'

'Other than being scandalously late with the altarpiece do you mean? I tell you, King Alfonso will be dead of extreme old age before that picture arrives in Naples. Yes, Filippo's in more trouble. He has no sense of probity or limit. He has talent, yes, but it's fine wine in a rotten barrel. He is contumacious. He has unchecked, rampant appetites. If he sees something he must have, have it he does.'

'Unlike your good self,' Monna Lucrezia pinched Cosimo's cheek.

'I will not have that, not even from you! What do you mean?'

'I was thinking of a rare collection of armour and gems, a new palazzo, a sumptuously decorated chapel, a garden-to-be.'

'Unchecked appetite, eh?' asked Cosimo morosely.

'It's not unique to the friar, that's all.'

'What is unique to this friar is that he has abducted and seduced a nun.'

Monna Lucrezia gravely demanded the full story. As she listened, her frown deepened. 'That's appalling! Send him from this house at once!'

'Don't be so hasty. The archbishop is finding out the full story. We've only heard the gossip and rumour. I feel bad for relaying it to the archbishop, but clearly Filippo needs to be released from his vows and I'll need the archbishop's aid to secure that from the pope.'

The autumn sun was warm and Cosimo's eye went to the cobbled paths now outlining the shape of the garden. 'It was Alberti's suggestion, to use the quincunx – four roundels round a fifth – as the basis of the design. I'm going to make the circles with box and laurel, and plant within them dwarf palms surrounded by oranges and roses, irises, lilies and pinks.'

'I can see it!' she said, her eyes closed. 'I can smell it! I can hear the breeze playing with leaf and water.'

'Each flower will have its meaning and refer to the Trinity or the Virgin.'

'The qualities of God's goodness laid out in beds, displayed by nature herself. I wish others knew you as I do,' she said softly. 'They think of you as the all-powerful citizen, the most astute banker, the richest man in the world. Their ideas about you create a gulf they cannot then cross, and you are left lonely and isolated by the immensity of your fortune. I wish they knew you as I do, a dear old man who keeps his humour despite being in great pain, who loves flowers and would make a posy of the qualities of God. You are an artist yourself – look at your architecture and your gardens! Tell me, do you ever envy the painters and sculptors?'

'Envy them? Envy is a weed that chokes the garden of the soul.'

'Enough of the archbishop's aphorisms.'

'It's *my* aphorism. Envy is a plant that should never be watered, it should be left to die of drought. But men water it, this worst of all weeds: envy.' Cosimo stared opaquely into space, trying to evade her question by becoming reflective.

'Tell me the truth.'

'Envy the painters? I do, I suppose, regret that I am not one of them. I would love to spend my days in creative work. It looks so peaceful and relaxing, while my business creates a multitude of things to think about, consider and decide upon, often with lives depending on my decision. That's why I used to retreat to my cell at San Marco. As Little Anthony says, one should have a closet in one's heart where one may retreat from the world. But sometimes a physical closet helps. What do you think of the chapel? Now that I can't get anywhere without being carried, that is to be my closet.'

310

'It's very beautiful in proportion, and the floor is exquisite. But the walls – are you sure Benozzo will be the right painter for them?'

'The walls are nothing. Frescoes? Just cheap tapestries intended for adornment. I've reserved Filippo for the devotional image, the altarpiece.'

'Strange choice, given the rottenness of the barrel.'

'But, ah, it is the finest wine. Of all the painters alive, Filippo is the one with the potential to reach out and touch God.'

Lucrezia nodded in agreement.

'Benozzo can't start for two years but then, he assures me, he'll work fast. I trust him utterly.' Cosimo was quiet for a moment, then said, 'Why do I feel disappointed when a painter delivers on time? It's perverse. But I feel as if art is reduced to a mere business transaction.'

Elbows on the arms of his chair and shoulders hunched, he stared out at piles of rubble from the building work. 'Yes, lilies and roses, oranges and palms, and a sweet plashing fountain in the centre. Perhaps not the Judith since it upsets you so. Do I wish I were an artist? Why should I, when I am one? An artist is not someone with technical skills in wood, stone or paint – that's an artisan. An artist is a man of *ingegno*.'

'What does that mean?'

'The power of the human intellect and spirit by which man discovers for himself what he has not learnt from others. Yes, that's it. Finding the answer within yourself. It's there in Fra Filippo, you know, oh yes, behind all that fat. He's just too lazy to look for it. Where are your sons, Lucrezia? Where are my boys?'

'Studying with Marsilio Ficino.'

'Isn't Giuliano too young for philosophy?'

'Ficino is teaching Lorenzo Latin and Greek, as you arranged. Since Giuliano insists on being wherever Lorenzo is and will not be parted from him, he shall have to be precocious in his studies.'

'I'm sorry to keep Ficino from his work translating Plato but, really, where could I find a better tutor for my boys? Just think, they will grow to read Plato in the original.'

'I'm beginning to suspect that you're procrastinating, that you'll do anything to avoid founding the Platonic Academy, as you vowed to do.'

Cosimo looked winded. 'That's ridiculous!' He flinched as the archbishop came into the garden.

'Well, my old friend,' said Antonino, sitting on a chair facing Cosimo to tell him what had transpired, and his decision to give Filippo no penance. 'The shock will do him good.'

'But what of the nun?' Monna Lucrezia asked.

'She must return to the convent. I'll be writing to the provost in Prato. And the child will go to an orphanage.'

'What child?'

'The nun is pregnant,' said Antonino.

Cosimo threw back his head and laughed.

'So, the friar is to go unpunished,' snapped Monna Lucrezia. 'And the young woman?'

'She too will not be punished.'

'You don't think having your child wrested from you at birth is a punishment?'

'Daughter,' Cosimo warned. 'Do not speak to His Grace that way.'

Monna Lucrezia turned on him. 'Unpunished! I'll tell you what unpunished means. It means to sire a child on your slave, to raise the boy in your family and shower him with ecclesiastical preferments until he rises to be archpriest of Santo Stefano in Prato. And – any day now – provost, no doubt!'

'Daughter, you are going too far!'

Monna Lucrezia sprang to her feet. Unable to say anything good, she decided to say nothing at all and left the garden.

'Cosimo, my friend, I would like your advice,' said the archbishop, deflecting the old man's attention to himself. 'This sordid affair is not an isolated case. Sin and licentiousness are common amongst both clergy and friars. Take gambling for instance. Just last week I came across some louts playing dice in the loggia of Buondelmonte and, spurred by who knows what divine impulse, I overthrew the tables.'

Cosimo laughed. 'Yes, I heard about that. You had them all on their knees weeping in repentance.'

'At least two of them were priests! If the clergy are corrupt, how can I get my message to the people? Cosimo, we need a law which bans priests from gaming.'

Fra Filippo entered the garden looking for Alessandro.

'What do you think, Filippo?' Cosimo asked. 'Do we need a law to stop the clergy gambling?'

'Not as much as we need a law to stop them using loaded dice.'

Cosimo roared with laughter; Filippo smiled, pleased with himself; Antonino gazed on them both with contempt and rose to leave.

'I wanted to ask you about Judith and Holofernes,' Cosimo protested.

'Another time,' said Antonino, passing the statue with a glance of disapproval on his way to the courtyard. Filippo watched him mount his mule, a sweet-faced beast whose trappings and their golden bosses were the only sign of the rider's status. How he would have liked to have sat and conversed with these two men but no, his arrival had merely hastened Antonino's departure. Archbishops may sit in conversation with bankers, but not with painters. Confessions and inquisitions only. 'Was it something I said?' he asked.

'Men have no adequate defence against your undiluted honesty. But I, as you know, have the skin of a turtle. Come and sit with me. Dare I ask how the altarpiece for Naples is progressing?'

'Cosimo, I have it at last – the image for the central panel!'

'What?' Cosimo's practice of the virtue of patience came to a jarring halt. 'I thought the central panel was nearly finished!'

'I'd like to start again, with your approval of course. Look!' Filippo unrolled the sketch. 'I call it the Virgin in Adoration.'

Cosimo studied it for some time. 'Does it have any precedent?' he asked at last, once his annoyance had subsided enough for his interest to come to the fore.

'None. Even the archbishop can't think of one, except a vision had by Saint Bernadette. He's given it his approval.'

Cosimo stared at the design, at the young Virgin on her knees in a woodland clearing, her hands together in prayer over the child that lay upon the flowery grass. It was new, it was innovative, it was strikingly beautiful. Touching God.

Cosimo was so quiet that Filippo checked to see whether he were still breathing. 'Do you like it, then?' he whispered.

'Yes, yes, do this for Naples, and do it quickly. Then, when you're finished, do it again for me. This will be the altarpiece in my chapel. Where will you work, here or in Prato?'

'I'd like to go home but can't keep transporting the panels back and forth, so I'll do it here, I suppose, and will be finished soon, I promise. How long would I have for the altarpiece in your chapel?'

'A year, no more.' Cosimo looked up as Alessandro came into the garden and, while Filippo was intent on rolling up his sketch, took from him a slip of paper, folded and sealed.

'On your way to the tavern,' said Cosimo, giving Fra Filippo the note, 'would you deliver this message to Donatello?'

'Donatello? Is he back in Florence? Alessandro can take it.'

'I want you to deliver it in person.'

'Do you not have servants?'

'Humour me. Think of it as a penance.'

Fra Filippo coloured, knowing he had been discussed by Cosimo and the archbishop.

53

WITH A NERVOUS AND EXCITED ALESSANDRO AT HIS HEEL, Fra Filippo went round the back of the Duomo to Donatello's workshop, where they found the old man hunched over his work, chiselling a block of poplar wood. The sculptor had his back to the door: all that the two painters saw on entry was the tortured face of the Magdalene staring over the sculptor's shoulder. Filippo recoiled at the image, so haggard and emaciated, her form withered and skeletal, her eyes mere hollows in her skull, her hair wild and unkempt – a Magdalene starving the sin out of herself.

'What do you want?' Donatello asked without looking up as he hammered at his gouge.

'Cosimo sends you a message.' Fra Filippo put the piece of paper on the sculptor's bench.

'Fine. It's delivered now, so go.'

Fra Filippo quivered with outrage, to be dismissed like this. Alessandro stepped forward. 'Cosimo said to get your reply,' he lied.

Secretly, Filippo had spent his life in awe and admiration of Donatello, had studied all his works and derived inspiration from them. So now, now that he had finally dared to approach the great man, he felt as if Love itself were spitting in his face. Although words burned in him to be spoken about the Magdalene, he said nothing. He would be damned if he would say anything. Nothing would persuade him to praise this vain man who treated his work as if it was all that the world contained. Imagine! Imagine living such a blinkered, selfish life as never to be troubled by distractions. Fine. It's delivered now, so go. The great Donatello, single-minded and of one purpose. Meh! Filippo wanted to kick the stool from under him.

'Read it,' said Alessandro, waving the fold of paper under Donatello's nose. He had laboured long on its wording.

Donatello sniffed, took the paper and broke the seal. As he turned on his stool to face them, both painters took a step backwards in shock: the Magdalene was a self-portrait. Donatello's face had sagged into hollows like melting snow. His two remaining teeth were separated by a large gap. His eyes were sunken and dim. 'Pride,' he read, bringing the paper close to his face, 'is the worst of sins. Do not die before you have spoken to this man.'

He grinned suddenly. 'My friend Cosimo,' he said, 'always oblique. Which of us is he referring to?' Donatello leaned forwards to peer at the friar. 'Fra Filippo, I have waited years for you to come and see me.'

Bastard! You bastard! Filippo thought. *Why should I come and see you?* 'Well, you know how it is. Always busy.'

'What do you think of her?' Donatello asked, indicating the Magdalene behind him.

'The truth?'

'The truth.'

'She lacks all grace and beauty.'

'According to Archbishop Antonino, the Magdalene was dishonest in body and soul. As Saint Augustine said, "Oh body, mass of corruption, what have I to do with thee?" Don't you feel like that, Filippo, the older you get? I can smell my own corruption and decay.' He breathed into Filippo's face. 'There, get that! Is that not the stench of a rotting body?'

Fra Filippo swayed on his feet. All he could smell was diseased gums and the pong of garlic – both of these strong, but not quite amounting to the stench of decay.

'I'm going to paint the statue, her skin the colour of old leather, and I'll gild her hair. She's lived in the desert, you see, in penance.'

'Where does it say that in the Bible? And where does it say she was a prostitute? She loved Jesus – that is all we know about her. She was the first to see the risen Christ.'

'The archbishop is my authority, for he has read widely, and he tells me she is the patron saint of all penitents.'

Suddenly Donatello was shrinking in Filippo's estimation. What did he know of real emotion, of truth, of love? What did any man vaunted by Alberti in his book know of these things? These men whom all must worship for their excellence – what did they know of any real value?

'Yes, she lived in the desert, perpetually hungry, thirsty, burnt by the sun to expunge her sin.'

'What's the purpose?' Fra Filippo suddenly shouted, making both Donatello and Alessandro jump. 'What is the *purpose?* Is life to be lived in self-immolation, starvation, to crawl in deserts crying out for mercy from the Lord? What for? This is madness! To think so badly of your body is madness! If I saw a man whipping a donkey the way an ascetic whips himself I would have to act. This is tyranny, absolute tyranny of the spirit over the body, and why should I have anything to do with tyranny? Beauty! Grace! These are my truths. Starve yourself, Donatello, whip yourself on the back if you enjoy the pain and the flow of your own blood, but don't tell me that this vision of supreme *ugliness* is what God wants of me. I don't believe it!' With that Fra Filippo strode from the workshop, his apprentice clattering against a chair and a trestle in his eagerness to get out.

In the street, Alessandro gazed up at the apse of the cathedral soaring above them, up to the terracotta dome and the blue vault of the sky above, imagining what he would tell his grandchildren should he ever have any. He would have to tell them that which had impressed him most powerfully: the resemblance between the sculptor and the image. With his little midget selves gathered round his knees, he would stand before the Magdalene in the Baptistry and say, 'That is a portrait of the sculptor, Donatello. Oh, his hair was not so long and he was not dressed in ragged skins, but the face was just the same.' And the little mites would be horrified by this vision of remorse in old age. At which Alessandro would raise his finger and give them a lecture on the wisdom of overcoming sin in one's youth. 'Pull out the weeds when they are young!'

He smiled suddenly at Fra Filippo, who'd become distracted by a beautiful young woman bending over a well. If what Cosimo had said were true, that every painter paints himself, then Fra Filippo and his sweet Adoration had, Alessandro believed, every reason to feel great joy.

Filippo sculpted the shape of the woman's backside in the air and kissed it. Coming back to the moment, he led Alessandro away from Donatello's door. 'Poor wretch!' he said. 'What a poor, sad old wretch. God, what sins lie on his conscience? May I never grow so old or regretful. Now, as I remember,' he said, steering Alessandro suddenly to the right, 'round the next corner is the best bakery in Florence. You look to me like a boy in need of buns.'

✝

By the time they completed the Naples altarpiece and returned to Prato it was February. They found Lucrezia and Spinetta with Diamante, toasting themselves by the hearth, making baby clothes out of luxurious scraps of fabric that had provided inspiration for the costumes of bishops, saints and archangels.

'Oh, you've come!' Lucrezia cried softly. 'I've been praying for you to come.' She reached out her hand to Filippo who took it and kissed it. He sat beside her, while Alessandro sat beside Spinetta, smiling and dumb. The family reunited. Painters and nuns. Why did something so odd feel so natural? Filippo ran his hand over Lucrezia's swelling form. She cooed; he cooed. The others laughed at them.

'Have you found a midwife?' Filippo asked Diamante.

'It's too risky. The secret will get out of the ward. Suor Piera says she will do it. She's had three children herself and knows what to do.'

Lucrezia, already paler than marble, began to sweat from fear.

Fra Filippo stroked her back. 'Two months to go. Are you scared?'

'I have an angel with me all the time, telling me everything will be all right.' Lucrezia's eyes took on a faraway, wistful look.

As Filippo gazed at her beauty, knowledge came to him like a butterfly to a flower: these men of the church – he couldn't trust them. Even when they weren't hypocrites they were misguided or arrogant and had, so far as he could tell, no greater access to the truth than he had himself. And, at some point, one of them had decided that denial of all bodily pleasures – the way of the hermit – was to be recommended to all, and failure in it was to be met by punishment. Filippo was not a man who could formulate his thoughts easily, but he got that far, to an intuitive understanding that the Church stood on a shaky foundation. And these men who set up the construction of what is right also set up that of what is wrong. So, by not being abstemious, Filippo was sinful. What in his love for Lucrezia could be wrong? Yet wrong it was, and she was a Magdalene. As soon as she stepped outside the protective circle he had drawn around her with Medici help, she would be a whore. And what was the fate of whores in Prato? To be whipped naked through the streets. Tortured. Burnt alive.

Thus he was thinking when Lucrezia stood, stretched, yawned and said she was going to bed. Spinetta retired with her. Filippo continued staring into the fire. Alessandro was trying to stay awake but as soon as the ladies had left the settle he stretched out and was asleep.

'Well,' said Diamante. 'Time for me to be retiring to my monastery and my cell.'

'It's not right, is it?' Filippo said. 'I've made my beloved Lucrezia a woman of sin. No, it's not right. Diamante, you must marry us.'

'What? A friar and a nun? How is that possible?'

'It's just words – anyone can say them – but it would make it right with God. And that's all I'm concerned about.'

'Well, I think you should be a little more concerned with the laws of men, caro mio. God is all-forgiving but the archbishop is a roaster.'

319

'He's offered to have our vows annulled but I've refused. Please, I beg you, marry us, then she at least will be right with God and man.'

'And you?'

Fra Filippo scratched the floor with the toe of his sandal. 'I'll take my chances that our God is merciful. All-forgiving.'

'Just don't die suddenly,' Diamante advised him. 'If anyone will need the last rites, it will be you.'

✜

The abbess commanded her chaplain to see her. She steeled herself for the interview, telling herself, 'I am right, I am right, I am wholly in the right.' But when he arrived there was a trembling in her bosom and a quivering in her jaw.

'I have heard,' she said, trying to keep the quiver out of her voice. 'I am the last to know, but now I have heard. You have my nuns.'

'Only two of them.'

'*Only* two?'

'The rest have returned to their families.'

'I want them all back at once, do you hear?'

'I will speak to Archpriest Carlo de' Medici about it.'

Her nostrils flared. 'And I shall speak to the arch*bishop!*'

'You already have, but he's powerless. He has no jurisdiction here. Here we come under the archpriest, the provost and the Bishop of Pistoia.'

'All Medici men.' The fight was going out of her. She had right on her side but they had money on theirs. The Medici controlled everything, even the morality of the town. This friar was their creature. What could she do to fight such abomination? What could she do?

'I hear,' she said, 'that Suor Lucrezia is with child. Never harbour a thought of having it baptized here. Over that much I have control.'

✜

Two days later, Filippo knelt in his panelled chamber beside Lucrezia, whom he had dressed in fine fabrics and fake pearls, while Diamante spoke the words of betrothal and marriage. Filippo had presumed it was but a formality to make everyone feel better – a legitimization, that was all. But as he knelt there he felt the same sensation as when he had touched the Holy Girdle. Touched by power. In that moment and for that moment the sin dropped off him like dirt that is ingrained until soaked in a solution of lye. It dropped away and left him there, pink and vulnerable, newly-born. His breathing quickened, for he was in the presence of the Divine. He looked sideways at his wife. Her eyes were lowered. She was so beautiful in profile. And she was his flesh, his blood, his soul. She was the best of him, made external, for him to dwell on in awe. He'd heard it so often, that the woman is the soul of the man, but when he looked at *this* woman, he saw – if it were true – that his soul was profoundly beautiful, and before he could do or say anything about it, he was howling in a potent mixture of joy and grief. His new wife took him in her arms where he cried like a baby.

After a few minutes, when he found his voice again, he said, stuttering, 'I never meant to be like this. It is not who I am.'

The Adoration
1458

54

SHE WAS BEING EATEN ALIVE: DEVILS HAD HER ON A spit and were turning her over molten, sulphurous fires. Her flesh was dripping off like hot wax but there was always more, always more. They were tearing at the lips of her womanhood, pulling her in half, in quarters. And was this not her just deserts? She, Eve, mother of all pain. This would last forever. Even death would be no respite, for she was already dead. Dead and in hell, suffering unendurable agony for eternity. It was her just reward. Eating the apple was not the crime – the crime was making Adam eat it. She had sinned. She had listened to the serpent and had sinned against God. For what? The serpent had offered her happiness and freedom, and she could not resist. And now the tongs pulled at her fingernails and tongue, and the hot knife seared away her breasts.

As the images changed from Judgement Day to martyrdom, her screaming subsided into intermittent moaning and in the midst of her agony she found a pause, a new idea. What if she endured all this for the love of God and His saints? What if she forgot Eve and threw herself instead on the mercy of Mary? Or Saint Margaret, patron saint of childbirth? She was a nun of Saint Margaret, after all, a nun of Saint Margaret. In Filippo's painting, she was Saint Margaret. Her breath began to steady. The terrible, impossible pain came again, but this time she transcended it, kept her mind fixed on an image of Saint Margaret that was an image of herself, painted by her husband.

'Push!' cried Suor Piera, and she pushed. The pain flowed out of her and carried with it the baby.

She was fainting backwards from the birthing stool, into the arms of Spinetta who was saying, 'It's over, it's all over, everything is well!' She was aware of fumblings and clippings down below and was beginning to be afraid when came the lusty cry of her baby, a boy according to Suor Piera, chuckling as if she had made him herself.

'Give him to me, blood and all. Bathe him later. Give him to me.' She could not allow a moment's separation. She cradled the warm little thing to her breast. He had strands of black hair plastered to his scalp, and a blood-red face like a pickled walnut. His limbs were pudgy but his little hands were images of perfection, grasping and relaxing, grasping and relaxing, feeling the air of this new world to which he could not immediately open his eyes. He twisted in her embrace and sighed. Lucrezia's heart filled to breaking.

'They will not take you from me,' she whispered into his scalp. 'They will not take you.'

The boy opened his eyes and his mother fell into them as if into the heart of the universe.

'We must bathe him,' Piera said gently.

'I will bathe him,' said Lucrezia. Not for a moment must she be out of touch with this gift from heaven.

✝

Fra Filippo came at once from Santo Stefano in a fit of anger. He had only just started painting the frescoes again – now this. Everything was Lucrezia's fault. She had tempted him and he had, despite all efforts at resistance, fallen. Now he was bound by obligations he did not want, set about by fears for his soul, and afraid. So afraid. His innards jiggled as if seething with maggots. When he arrived at the house, all was quiet. No keening of mourners. He stepped tentatively over the threshold. Then took another step, and another, across the rush-strewn floor. Everything was exquisite: the rushes, the terracotta floor tiles, all unbearable in their reality. Spinetta came to meet him. She was smiling. 'Hello, father!' she said. 'Brother Father.'

'Enough of your jokes, Spinetta. Is she well? Does she live?'

326

'She does.'

Fra Filippo went to enter his chamber but Spinetta stopped him, saying it wasn't right, but Filippo brushed her aside saying he wouldn't see anything he hadn't seen before. What he saw was Lucrezia sitting up in bed, the very image of all the Saint Elizabeths and Marys he had ever painted, although without the veil and the demure look. Her hair was wild, as were her eyes, wild and accusing. She hugged the baby to her. 'You'll not take him.'

'Just for a moment. Let me hold him.' He approached the bed in a room dimmed by curtains and nearly trod on the bowl of placenta.

'Bury that!' he said.

'Of course,' said Piera.

He had to prise the baby from its mother. Lucrezia howled.

'Only for a moment, only for a moment,' he said soothingly. 'He's my son, too.'

He gently opened the shutters. The baby blinked but kept his eyes open to the sun swelling through the open window, watching the linen curtains move in a light breeze. Filippo held up his son and bathed him in the light. The baby stared back at him, mirroring his wonder.

Fra Filippo had never seen anything as beautiful as this, this baby and this howling, angry woman. Forget, he told himself, forget everything taught by the apostles, by the church fathers, by the popes and the preachers. Forget it all. In the face of something this beautiful, how can it be wrong? God. He stripped away from his mind all images of God. Forget it, he thought, it's a mistake. No bearded old man in the sky, ready to send thunderbolts in wrath or beams of beaded light upon the righteous. This is God. Seeing reality aright for once and holding God in his hands, tears trickled down his stubbled cheeks.

'You'll not take him away,' said Lucrezia, her howls having subsided at the vision of Filippo holding his son up to the light.

'No one will take him. I shall never abandon my son.'

Now Lucrezia began to cry again, this time from relief. 'He's called Filippo,' she said. 'Piccolo Filippo. Filippino.'

'Piccolo Pippolino!' said Fra Filippo, giving his son back to her. He sat on the bed. Just for this moment, all was well. Only let the moment last.

Diamante put his head round the door. 'May I see him?' he asked.

'Men are not allowed in!' said Piera.

Diamante ignored her and crossed the room with a radiant smile and a posy of forget-me-nots for the mother. He looked down on the baby. 'Oh, caro mio,' he murmured.

✝

'We have delivered the child, Mother,' Filippo said brightly that April morning to the abbess of Santa Margherita. His mood and manner were intended to disarm her. 'Yes, it's a boy. I have a son.'

'What you have is a bastard born of a whore!'

Fra Filippo jerked backwards as if she had spat in his face. 'He needs to be baptized, Mother. I believe the Church does not object to that.'

'I've told you that I will not permit such a ceremony to be held here in my church. No. A thousand times no! Try Santo Stefano. With a Medici as its archpriest, anything is possible there. But here – here I struggle for purity. At the moment, that means our house is reduced to myself and my sister. So be it. God's way was never easy. But the archbishop has decreed that the nuns are to be returned. When will that be, pray? They will not be punished, Fra Filippo, you can assure them of that. I am not a cruel woman. We shall simply – all of us – renew our vows before the Bishop of Pistoia and continue as before.'

'There is no such thing as an illegitimate child,' said Fra Filippo. 'It's the act of conception that was illegitimate and Lucrezia and I will make our peace with God about that, but I will not have my son punished for my sins.'

'Oh, but even unto the third and fourth generation,' said the abbess. 'Remember, Brother, each time you sin, you blight unborn children.'

Fra Filippo pulled open the string of his purse and emptied the contents on the table between them. 'How much do you think they will charge me at Santo Stefano? Forty, fifty florins? A hundred?'

Abbess Bartolommea's eyes widened at the pile of coins on her table, but she held firm. 'They'll charge you whatever they think they can get. Now get out of here. You besmirch this place, besmirch it! I want nothing more to do with you!'

'That's not your choice,' he reminded her. 'I am the chaplain here until the authorities state otherwise.'

'Do you never have a care for the feelings of others? You have ruined my reputation. All that I have worked for, all that I hold to be good and true, has been turned into a midden by your snout and trotters. No, a thousand times no!' Her bosom was heaving with all that she had yet to express but for which she had no adequate words. 'You've cheated me, you've lied to me, deceived me, made a fool of me. You destroy everything in your path. My poor girls. My poor Lucrezia. Ruined! Baptise the baby? Then what will you do, live in sin and laugh at anyone who objects? We religious, the priests, the clergy, the monks, the friars, the nuns – it is our duty to lead by example. What value do our words have if our actions are not in line? We are hypocrites. If we allow you to get away with this, we are all hypocrites. You are a stinking rotten apple in the barrel and I want you gone!'

Her redness increased, her eyes bulged and she began to choke. She clawed the air. 'Help me!'

Fra Filippo stood staring at her, not knowing whether she was feigning apoplexy or, if she wasn't, not knowing what to do about it. 'Oh, sit down, woman. See where anger gets you.'

But the abbess dropped to her knees, bringing the chair down with a crash. Her sister ran forward to help her, knocking the chaplain out of the way. 'Bartolommea!' she cried. 'Bartolommea!' She looked up at Fra Filippo in horror. 'She's stopped breathing!'

'And not a moment too soon,' thought Fra Filippo. He went to fetch a doctor.

When he returned, they found the abbess sitting up, supported by her sister who was fanning her. Fra Filippo chastised himself for feeling disappointed to see the abbess recovering. That was not a Christian feeling. The doctor sent him to fetch porters from the Misericordia and, within the hour, the abbess was being carried to the hospital on a litter.

✝

It was two weeks before she was back, fully restored. She said she would have recovered faster had she not been put in a room in which a painting by Fra Filippo faced the bed.

Bitter, and grown reclusive, the abbess lived in the convent alone with her sister and waited for the authorities – or God – to act. She was not going to fight for justice and retribution herself, there was no need. She was so clearly in the right that she need do nothing.

Afraid of distressing her sister and causing a relapse, Suor Jacopa neglected to tell her that, in her absence, Fra Filippo had baptized his son in the convent's chapel.

55

FRA FILIPPO LIVED COCOONED IN DOMESTICITY. IF HIS work at Santo Stefano suffered further delay, it was because he spent most mornings drawing portraits of his wife and child. He made dozens of studies, trying to capture Lucrezia's soft look of adoration, Pippolino's sudden smile or moments of intense concentration. If his own wife and son were not just posing for the Virgin and Child but becoming them, no matter – it was only his notebook.

The work became a trinity: mother, child and father drawing them. In that year, Fra Filippo's subtle agitations of soul became quiet as long as he did not think about the future or worry that the Pratese despised him; if he just stayed where he was, mind and body at rest, then he was happy in a way he had never anticipated: settled contentment.

Everyone in the house was in love with that little bundle of burps and smiles, Pippolino. Dark eyes, black hair, he gazed out of his swaddling with such wonder that his father half-expected the boy to wink at his mother or aunt. But that would come later. For now it was Pippolino's business to keep the household in thrall to his tiny majesty.

✝

Filippo stood back to look at the scenes of the middle tier in the chapel of Santo Stefano. His critics – those crows who strolled the nave cawing their opinions – complained that both scenes were too empty of figures. There were too many rocks in the Saint John scene, too much architecture in the Saint Stephen scene. It was true. While Filippo had been dawdling at home, sketching his family, Fra Diamante, working from some unfinished designs, had painted a wilderness of rocks. 'It *is* a wilderness!' Diamante protested, when Fra Filippo mentioned it. 'What do you want? A wilderness without rocks? What does that look like?'

'We need to bring the figures more into the foreground, somehow,' said Filippo, quick to mollify his assistant, 'and send the rocks into the background. I suppose we could hack it all off and start again.'

Fra Diamante found he had to sit down.

Fra Filippo was torn. Part of him was so tired with this project that he just wished to be finished with it. In which case, he would shout down the critics, remind them that it was a scene of Saint John in the *wilderness*, and carry on blithely. Another part of him was eager for any excuse to delay in Prato.

For he dare not finish the work. The last brushstroke would signal the day he must leave forever and seek his fortune elsewhere. Prato was too small to keep him in commissions. He must return to Florence, living from one day to the next, not knowing whether a new commission would ever arrive. Such a life with its uncertain future was best not hampered by a wife and child. Proper painters, those who had served an apprenticeship and founded their own workshops, could be confident of a stream of work that would keep their families housed and fed. Fra Filippo had no such confidence. He had always lived on whim – which he thought of as the will of God – going where fate led him, always surviving but never quite sure that he would. He lived on the edge. That was how he liked it. Being a Carmelite was the only cushion he had: if all failed, he could return to his mother house and be a simple friar. Living as a layman with a family was not an edge, it was a precipice. He would wake each day in a sweat, certain of looming disaster. He would be found out. He would be revealed for what he was: not a proper painter but a fraud who, by luck alone, had so far pleased (most) people with his accidental triumphs. They would throw him out of Florence, saying he was not fit to live in the city of beauty.

No, he must definitely arrange for some cheap labourers to come in and chisel all the plaster off the middle tier. Then they could start again. He glanced down at the bowed, crushed figure of his assistant, sitting in misery with his legs dangling over the platform.

'You're right, Diamante,' he said. 'It's a wilderness. Why fill it with figures? These men who give us the benefit of their knowledge and opinion – they are philistines.'

As Diamante sprang back to life, Fra Filippo stood staring at the north wall and the Mission of Stephen, yet to be completed. He turned to the paint-spattered Bible they kept with their equipment and found what he was looking for in Acts.

'Fra Filippo?' called a voice from the nave. 'You are required in Florence. We have bought a mule for you.'

'I have finished the altarpiece!' he protested.

The Medici servant shrugged and said he knew nothing about any altarpiece, only that Fra Filippo was required at the new palazzo. Immediately.

56

FILIPPO FOUND THE COURTYARD FULL OF FAMILY AND servants mounting horses, preparing to leave the city for the summer. The invalid Piero de' Medici was being lifted, whimpering with pain, into a litter. Cosimo's eldest son, he was all but a recluse because of gout. Filippo had not seen him for many years but he recognised his still-handsome head. The young man who had entertained his father's guests with poetry and song was now grey both in hair and complexion, his eyes screwed up with pain and blind to the world.

The courtyard eddied with two streams: one, the outgoing party, the other, all those trying to enter, calling to secretaries and waving rolls of documents. Filippo and Alessandro made their way in amongst them, supposing them to be clients of the bank, and went up the stairs to the chapel as instructed by a harassed servant. Filippo expected to see Cosimo but the only person awaiting him in the chapel was a woman in prayer. Monna Lucrezia de' Medici was on her knees at the candle-lit altar, saying her prayers aloud, urgent prayers for the family. Filippo and Alessandro stood back respectfully.

'Amen,' said Monna Lucrezia at last.

'Amen,' echoed the friar.

Monna Lucrezia looked round at him. She had eyes with no visible lids until she blinked; eyes embedded in a fold of skin; eyes as fixed as a kestrel's and as all-seeing as an owl's. Filippo felt himself colouring, a tinge of rose suffusing his skin.

He apologised if he had disturbed her. 'I was called here, I thought, to see Cosimo.'

'No, it was me who sent for you. I have a commission on behalf of my husband, Piero.'

'Oh, Madonna, no! I'm so busy at Prato.'

Monna Lucrezia held him in her unflinching gaze. 'Are you so eager to finish at Santo Stefano?'

'Indeed I must, if I am to be paid.'

'I hear you have a son, Fra Filippo.'

The rose tint in his cheeks deepened. He was about to justify himself to this pious lady and declare that, whether or not it was a sin, he had been blessed by God, when Monna Lucrezia continued, 'You must miss him.'

Filippo choked on his reply. 'I've only been here a day but I do,' he managed to say. 'And his mother, who shares her name with you.'

'There is no reason why you should not do my painting in Prato, for it is an altarpiece.'

'Oh,' said Filippo, relieved. 'Is it for this altar, Madonna?'

Monna Lucrezia nodded. 'Yes. Cosimo promised you the work, I believe.' She looked at the bare chapel. 'The walls are to be painted with a procession of the Magi.' She pointed to the wall on the right. 'It will begin here with Caspar, on the wall behind, Balthasar, and over here,' she pointed to the left, 'Melchior.' She watched him carefully. 'We have chosen Benozzo di Lese to do the work.'

Fra Filippo swallowed visibly.

'We could not commission you while you are still so heavily engaged in Prato. But we thought you could do the altarpiece. After all, it will be the place to which the procession leads, so just think of the walls as stage scenery, a backdrop for the divine image.'

'You are very kind, Madonna. There is no need to be so concerned for my feelings or pride. Cosimo said he would like an Adoration.'

334

'Yes, like the one you've done for the King of Naples.'

Filippo relaxed and sighed with pleasure.

'But I want a different setting, something more...' She drummed her fingers lightly on the altar.

'More?'

'I have in mind a landscape that I love well, which I would like as the setting. I shall take you there tomorrow, into the mountains of Camaldoli.'

'That's a day's journey at least!'

'Yes, and we shall stay at the monastery for a day or two, but you can be back in Prato by the end of the week.'

✝

'Composition,' Filippo told Alessandro, back in their workshop in the old house, 'is the first step – the arrangement of figures on the plane. But immediately we are confronted by a problem, for what should the composition be? Commonly painters choose a triangle or pyramid, a pile of figures one atop another, for the pyramid is always a satisfying composition. This altarpiece is to be square and we are to paint an Adoration with five figures. What does that suggest?'

'A pentagon.'

Fra Filippo sketched a pentagon and tried to arrange his figures in its pattern. He began to wish he had had a clear idea of where he was going before he began this lesson for Alessandro. It was all so arbitrary! – he could choose any shape he liked. He had used the pentagon for the Naples picture, but hadn't been satisfied by it.

'It pays to imagine the finished painting in its context,' he said to Alessandro, taking him to the chapel with a board, some charcoal and a pair of compasses. 'It will sit there, on the altar. Does that suggest anything to us?'

Alessandro stared at the bare altar. In the dim room with its bare walls, it was difficult to imagine anything. The floor was beautiful though, with its geometry of inlaid coloured stone.

'Fourteen,' he said, having counted the roses round the central disc. 'Why fourteen?'

'The generations of David,' said Filippo. 'And the seven mornings and evenings of the days of Creation.'

Alessandro looked at him, puzzled. Why go to so much trouble to depict something of such minor symbolic importance?

'Or it could be the Seven Gifts of the Holy Spirit, or the Seven Joys of the Virgin, or the Seven Liberal Arts.'

'It's fourteen, not seven.'

'Days of the week, planets, metals. Who knows? Ask Cosimo. Are there not fourteen beatitudes of Saint Bernard, seven of the body and seven of the soul?'

Alessandro shrugged. 'Is this porphyry?' he asked, pointing to the disc with his toe.

'The hardest of stones and incredibly difficult to work. Cosimo is fond of Saint Bernard,' Filippo continued, 'so how would you divide a circle into fourteen parts?'

'Oh, that's easy. Construct a heptagon then bisect its sides.'

'And how do we construct a heptagon?'

Alessandro's eyes rolled up as he tried to remember the principle.

'Is it easy to draw an accurate heptagon?'

'No, it's difficult.'

'Yet these masons have done it in one of the hardest stones.'

Alessandro's appreciation of the floor deepened.

'It would be good … satisfying…' mused Fra Filippo.

'What?'

'To use a heptagon in the altarpiece and marry its composition to that of the floor.' Excited by the idea, he set his compass to the rough board and drew a circle. Then he reminded Alessandro of the principle of drawing a seven-sided figure in a circle. 'The trouble is,' he said, 'it can come out anywhere. I mean, it's not a symmetrical figure, so there is not necessarily a top or a bottom. Where do we place our heptagon? And how do we indicate it? First things first.' He drew in some saints, and the holy infant on the ground, then the figure of God in the sky, arms outstretched above the descending dove. 'The hands of God will show a side of the figure,' he said, sketching rapidly. 'And now – herself.' He drew in a figure of the Virgin that dominated the composition. Alessandro stood with his mouth open, watching this divine image appearing on the rough board; contained within a square, a circle and a heptagon, a magical vision only the initiated could see.

There came the clumping sound of Cosimo being carried to the chapel, his stick tapping on doorways and his constant shouts of 'Look out!', fearing, always fearing, that someone was going to knock his swollen, sensitive leg against a jamb. The entourage arrived in the chapel.

'Do you know,' he said to Fra Filippo, 'that by the end of this month the Medici will be annihilated and Florence in the hands of our enemies?'

Filippo looked at him aghast.

'It's true! Our rivals are about to attack us. I have the support of the people, oh yes, they sent a deputation of allegiance yesterday. But the big families: they're as treacherous as ever. Close the door – I want to be at peace.' The door was closed and the chair set down.

'Would you like us to leave?' Filippo asked.

'No.' Cosimo leaned forwards, looking at the sketch on the board. 'What are you doing?'

'Trying to find the composition of the altarpiece that your daughter-in-law has commissioned.'

'A heptagon. You've taken that from the floor?'

'Yes, I thought we could marry floor and altar, Earth and Heaven.'

The old man, who all morning had been receiving alarmed deputations from the Palazzo della Signoria, said nothing.

'Well?' said Filippo nervously.

'Why do you always plump for the first thing that occurs to you? It's fine. It's an interesting proposition, but keep looking. Do you know what the Pythagoreans said of the number seven?'

Fra Filippo knew nothing of Pythagoreans whatsoever and was not in the mood to wonder. He loved Cosimo but, oh, how he wished he didn't act like Herod towards his newborn ideas. He was sulking for his heptagon.

'They call it the number of the Virgin, for it is neither begotten nor begets. So the heptagon is a good idea, but I think there is more. I think there is more because as usual you are trapped in the mire of your own thinking and have no idea there's anywhere else to be.'

'Ackh…'

'Clear it all away. Make yourself an empty vessel, then the Lord may make Himself known. Painters are agents of the Creator, you know, but to look at them is to see so many usurpers, each thinking, *believing* himself to be the sole author of his work. Huh!' Cosimo turned his stiff neck until he was looking at the apprentice. 'Are you listening, Alessandro dei Filipepi? Do you understand?'

Alessandro nodded.

'I hope you do, because I can't delay here any longer, much as I'd like to. I have a family to protect and a city to save.' He banged his stick on the floor as if to awaken his servants. 'Take me to the armoury!'

The top floor of the new palazzo had been turned into an arsenal of crossbows, halberds and various other weapons. Alessandro, who had been shown it by young Lorenzo, had presumed it to be a collection of antiquities. On impulse, he ran out after Cosimo to speak to him. A while later, he returned.

Filippo looked steadily at his apprentice, waiting for him to relate what had passed between him and Cosimo.

'The number fourteen,' said Alessandro sheepishly. 'It's the Seven Virtues and the Seven Vices. Cosimo said you know all about them and was surprised you hadn't worked it out for yourself.'

For a moment, Filippo was back in the Scrovegni Chapel in Padua and looking at the Giottos with Cosimo. He grieved that such a fine man had become crippled by age and beset by troubles.

'Is it true?' Alessandro asked. 'Are the Medici in danger?'

Fra Filippo squeezed him reassuringly on the shoulder. 'Power shifts, cities fall, new ones rise – but art remains unaffected. Trust me, it is so. We will paint this picture, and it will survive.'

'Yes,' said Alessandro, 'but what good will it do us if the Medici do not?'

'There's something you don't understand about Cosimo. He's more than human, you know. Did I ever tell you about the Great Council of Florence, when Cosimo was elected Chief Priest of the Platonists in a secret ceremony of initiation?'

'You're lying,' said Alessandro, his eyes popping.

'It's true. I was there. The ceremony was performed by an alchemist called Plethon who had a tall hat and very long beard plaited in three strands.'

'Absolutely lying.'

'And Cosimo was granted immortality by the pagan gods. But, alas, he forgot to ask for health.'

'My father always told me that God strikes liars to the ground and all you find of them is scorch marks in the dirt. It's you – you're the immortal one. Diamante says you made a pact with the devil.'

Fra Filippo chuckled. 'It would be worth making a pact with the devil just to get Cosimo to accept the first thing I show him some time. Now we have to tear this lot up and start again. So, my fine boy, what is our composition of the Adoration going to be?'

57

AT DAWN THE COURTYARD RESOUNDED TO THE CALLS OF servants organising mules and horses for Monna Lucrezia's party. The lady herself was in the gallery of the piano nobile, having urgent words with her father-in-law, insisting he follow her husband Piero to the villa at Careggi. Everyone in the courtyard below could hear them.

'I'm going,' grumbled Cosimo. 'Tomorrow, perhaps.'

'Today, Father, today! I cannot leave you here in danger.'

'Lucrezia, you must do as I say, and I'm telling you to leave now for Camaldoli.'

Despite using a mounting block, Fra Filippo had trouble getting into the saddle and lost all dignity in the effort. Cosimo's grandsons laughed at the puffing friar but then Lorenzo dismounted to help him find his stirrups. Although he was only nine, Lorenzo was already playing the man.

'It's years since I was on a horse,' Fra Filippo complained. 'Apart from when I'm collected by your men, that is, and then they put me on a donkey.' He got his foot into the stirrup and allowed Lorenzo to give him a helpful lift on the other leg.

'She's a steady old mare,' Lorenzo assured him. 'She'll be no trouble.'

With everyone in the saddle, personal servants, secretaries, her children, the boys' tutor, men-at-arms for protection, Monna Lucrezia mounted her favourite brown mare. She frowned on ostentation at the best of times but, when on the way to a hermitage, she forbade it. There was no glitter or sparkle as the Medici party set off along the Via Larga to the Porta Gallo, then took the road to Ponte a Sieve. When they were beyond the city walls and out in the country, Lorenzo impressed everyone with his singing while Fra Filippo trailed at the end of the line, looking about him.

The ground was rising into hills and, beyond Ponte a Sieve, into the mountains. As they progressed ever upwards, he looked down upon valleys, noting the sweep and profiles of hills, the unreflective darkness of pines, the paintbrush tips of cypresses, the colour of the sky, the forms of clouds, the play of light over distance. At the summit of the first ridge of mountains, the cool air cleared his head and he began to feel almost happy.

Alessandro, riding ahead, was amusing Lorenzo and Giuliano by naming colours, saying what pigments he would mix to paint pines, sky and eagles, then testing them to see what they would mix to get a terracotta roof or a stone wall. Filippo noted that his young apprentice seemed to have no sense of inequality. There was nothing in his manner to suggest that he was a humble artisan addressing the sons of the Medici. Nor was he being condescending as he relieved the boys of their ignorance of earth pigments. He was sharing his enthusiasm and Lorenzo in particular appreciated it. Filippo wished he could be so comfortable with his superiors.

By the afternoon, the riders had crossed the ridge and were winding down the mountain into the Casentino valley. Approaching Pratovecchio, they crossed the battleground of Campaldino and Lorenzo gave the party a history lesson. 'The Battle of Campaldino was fought in 1289. How long ago was that?'

His elder sisters, Bianca and Nannina, yawned and rolled their eyes, but his young brother, ever impressed by Lorenzo, chewed on a fingernail as he did the computation. 'One hundred and seventy years?'

'Correct! It was the great battle between the Guelfs of Florence and the Ghibellines of Arezzo.'

While Lorenzo told Giuliano – and anyone else who would listen – about the Guelfs and the Ghibellines and the glorious battles won by Florentines, Filippo wondered how long before they could dismount. He was getting saddle sore.

'Hundreds and thousands died in the Battle of Campaldino. This land is littered with their bones. Look how lush the fields are. Grandfather says that's because of the blood and bones.'

'Who led our forces?' Giuliano asked him.

Lorenzo frowned, unable to remember and annoyed that a gap in his knowledge had been publicly revealed. 'Ask grandfather. He knows the name of every condottiere who has ever fought for Florence in all history.'

'Did we win?'

'Of course! And one of our soldiers was Dante Alighieri, the great poet. He fought right here, where we are. Later, when he had to go into exile for being a White Guelf rather than a Black one, he came back to the Casentino.' Lorenzo pointed south down the valley to the strange, conical hills that featured along its length. 'The hill after next,' said Lorenzo, 'is Poppi. That's where Dante lived in exile, in the castle of the Counts of Guidi.'

'What are White Guelfs and Black Guelfs and which are we?'

'Can we move on?' Bianca asked, kicking her horse without waiting for an answer. Everyone else followed and the party made its way eastwards towards the river.

'This is a blessed valley,' said Monna Lucrezia to Marsilio Ficino, the tutor of her sons riding beside her. 'The holiness of the hermits trickles down in rivulets to join this little river.'

Ficino peered up the mountain to its streams. He had a face inclined to innocence and wonder. At twenty-five, he was only eight years younger than Monna Lucrezia but, because he was peculiarly short, he was used to being treated as a child, even by near contemporaries. Monna Lucrezia turned to her youngest son. 'Do you know what river it is?' she asked him.

Giuliano shook his head. Lorenzo rose up and down in his stirrups several times, impatient to speak.

'Lorenzo?' she sighed.

'It's the Arno!' cried Bianca from the front. Lorenzo, thwarted, stared furiously at his sister.

Giuliano's young face furrowed. How could this be the Arno? It was little more than a stream. Ficino explained to him how mighty rivers begin as trickles in the mountains. He pointed to the far side of the valley and the wooded slopes of the Apennines. 'Here we are approaching the source of that which has made Florence great.'

'The holiness of hermits,' said Monna Lucrezia. Her companions turned to look at her. She nodded. 'It's true: what makes Florence great is the holiness of hermits. The Arno is nothing but a symbol of the divine stream that flows from Camaldoli to our city.'

Coming to the walls of Pratovecchio, the party stopped at last to rest. The boys ran out in the meadows to play at Guelfs and Ghibellines and to look for bones. In fields of ripening wheat they could find none, but they did find a charnel house stuffed with human bones turned up in ploughing and they came back with a smashed skull. Their mother was at the parish church giving audience to the local people who, hearing of her arrival, had hurried to see her. She was their special Mother who could cure all their ills.

'Let me see that,' said Fra Filippo, taking the skull from the boys. The cranium was split but otherwise it was complete.

'He must have been killed by an axe-blow to the head,' said Lorenzo.

Fra Filippo tried to be interested in the skull. Many of his fellow painters paid good money for such things and drew studies of them. In truth, he could not be interested in it and threw it like a ball to Giuliano, telling him to put it back where he had found it and show some respect for the dead. He went inside the church.

The roof of its short nave was supported by massive columns, decorated on the capitals with mythical beasts and foliage. He liked old churches, truth be told, better than the new ones of Brunelleschi, Michelozzo and Alberti. Monna Lucrezia sat in one of the aisles, villagers queuing before her. They reported land-grabs by local lords, an insupportable rise in taxation, the corruption of priests, the withering of the vines, pestilence amongst the mountain people and raids on their livestock. Monna Lucrezia listened and had her secretary note names and grievances. The help they wanted was Cosimo's, but this lady was their intercessor, and each time she came to the Casentino valley, things noticeably improved. They knelt before her, adored her like a saint. La Madonna del Casentino.

343

Fra Filippo watched and listened. He studied Monna Lucrezia's fixed gaze and immobile features and tried to discover how it was that her face said, 'I'm listening.' Rare, that, to listen to another with such undivided attention. It would be enough in itself to repair all injuries. Sometimes, to a cripple or the mother of a stillborn, she touched the bowed head and said, 'You poor suffering thing. I grieve for you.' You could see the recipients quiver. When they arose and came away they looked as if they had received the sacraments.

As the afternoon wore on, she began to tire – something she would never admit. He went to disperse the crowd. 'Enough now,' he said, using his authority as a friar. 'Madonna needs to rest.'

He suggested they take a room in a tavern for her, but she said no, they must ride on. 'Ladies of the Medici do not rest in taverns!' she said sharply, making him wince. 'Besides,' she continued, more gently, 'the longer we stay, the bigger the crowd will get. We'll ride on and rest for the night as arranged at the Castello of the Ubertini in the foothills of the mountains and complete our journey in the morning.'

✝

At the castello, Monna Lucrezia and her party were received royally and invited to a banquet. For the meal the father of the house, Bartolommeo degli Ubertini, had Monna Lucrezia on one side of him and Marsilio Ficino on the other. Throughout the various courses, he asked Ficino searching philosophical questions that the young man parried with enthusiasm, outsmarting Ubertini in complexity and abstraction at every turn.

'How did your interest in Plato begin?' Ubertini asked him.

'In reading the Latins, especially Cicero.' Ficino smiled. 'I collected every quotation from Plato from every Latin source.' He went on to name them all: Macrobius, Apuleius, Boethius, Calcidus. When he passed on to quote from these authors from memory, Fra Filippo retired early saying he had a headache. He beckoned to Alessandro to follow him.

The room they were shown to was, unlike a room in an inn, mercifully free from stinks; indeed, it smelt of lilies. While Alessandro tried to make himself comfortable in a truckle on the floor, Filippo climbed into a bed with a deep mattress and soft pillows. He was to share the bed, obviously, but did not know with whom until Ficino entered about an hour later. By that time the friar was deep in the cleavage of a voluptuous dream but he was a light sleeper and, although Ficino settled beside him as noiselessly as a feather, Filippo awoke. Ficino apologised.

'Not your fault,' mumbled the friar.

'I noticed you ran from the hall as soon as we touched on truth.'

'Truth? Is that what you were talking about? Sorry, my friend, but the conversations of philosophers – I feel as if I'm on a horse without a bridle. I'm not clever, you see.' Filippo rolled over to indicate he'd had enough of talking.

'Philosophy is not for the clever! I understand why you should think so, because it has been so dressed up in fancy words by the universities. But if you read Plato … if you read Socrates in Plato … he speaks to you and me and everyone. Unfortunately it is my task to be able to talk to university men, such as our host, but it is not my desire.'

'What is your desire?'

'To lead a happy life free of trouble.'

Fra Filippo lifted his head. 'That is my desire, also.'

'So you see, philosophy is for everyone.' With that, Ficino put his head on the pillow and was immediately asleep.

Filippo stared into the shadows, wondering why religion could not offer the same thing.

✝

When Filippo awoke in the morning, Ficino was at a table reading from the large book he carried with him everywhere, a copy of Plato's Dialogues in Greek which Cosimo had presented to him. Alessandro was standing looking over the philosopher's shoulder at the Greek text while Ficino translated passages for him.

The sun caught Ficino's curly hair as if it were threaded with filaments of gold. 'Listen to this,' he said to the young apprentice. '*The eternal alone is true, the temporal only seems to be. The soul sleeps in the body and those things that the senses desire or fear are nothing but dreams. Thus all such things are to be regarded with contempt, and to avoid the evils which are plentiful in the world we must flee to the eternal for refuge. For in no other way can evils be avoided.*' He made no hesitation at all as he translated from Greek into Tuscan. 'Plato used to repeat that to himself every day. Imagine – even Plato had difficulty keeping the truth in mind.'

'What d'you mean?' Filippo asked, sitting on the side of the bed as if in shock to find himself awake.

'Our senses lie to us,' said Ficino, turning to him. 'Everything we perceive and believe to be true is a world of dreams.'

'As I told you last night, it all goes over my dim old head.'

'You surprise me,' said Ficino, watching the friar put on his black habit. 'Everything about you surprises me. Sit down. Let me look at you.'

The two men regarded each other wordlessly and at length. Filippo saw a series of planes and crevices, some highlights on the nose and brow, the handsome slope of the eye, the brightness of the pupil, and thought he could do Ficino in three colours: white, touch of sienna, touch of indigo. But that hair – he would need orpiment to catch its likeness.

'By the roundness of your face, I see you are kind,' said Ficino at last. 'Affable, a good friend. Your ears tell me that you cannot abide rules and will adhere to none. Your eyes – melancholy, the kind of melancholy you try to laugh off, the eyes of the man kept at royal courts called the Fool. They speak of deep sadness. Do you suffer from melancholy my good friend?'

'Not knowingly.'

'I do, but only when I'm alone. When I was born Saturn was in the ascendant in Aquarius and nearly square to Mars in Scorpio.'

'Really?' Filippo wondered how long he was going to be kept from his breakfast by this man who did not like to be alone.

'And you? What sign were you born under, and what was the disposition of the heavens at the time?'

'I have no idea.'

'You don't know when you were born?'

'No, not even the month. I was an orphan.'

Ficino studied the friar's face again. 'That makes you sad?'

Filippo shrugged. 'I don't think about it.'

'I have a theory that it is the melancholic man who is capable of profound thought, melancholy that makes the philosopher – and the artist. It tenderizes us, makes us ripe for the marinade. I've seen your work – the work of a man of grace, of a man inspired.'

Fra Filippo laughed sourly as he tied his girdle. 'God does not speak to Fra Filippo, my friend.'

'Perhaps we don't understand what inspiration is.'

'Are you going to tell me it's the Holy Ghost?'

'According to the ancients, it's the Muses, under the guidance of Apollo, Lord of the Sun. They do not, so far as I can tell, whisper only to holy men.'

Fra Filippo sat on the bed again to put on his sandals. 'No? Who do they whisper to then?'

'Anyone who can hear them. Those who will not be satisfied with easy solutions, or with getting a job done for the sake of it, but who will sit late at their work, as patient as a sea angler who waits for the bright fish from the deep.'

Fra Filippo smiled. 'I was about to dismiss the Muses as pagan heresy.'

'Think twice before you do. The Muses do not like to be denounced. That is why they tend to avoid holy men or, should we say more correctly, zealots.'

Filippo raised his eyebrows at this. 'Do the Muses speak to you?'

'I am slow, very slow at my work. Not only have I to master the ancient Greek tongue, I have also to understand exactly what it is that Plato meant by his words. I have to enter his mind.

347

I labour for long hours and sometimes I cry out for help, sometimes I want to give up. But then, often in that hour before dawn when all is still and full of potential, just as the sky lightens, I hear the answer I seek. Sometimes I'm already at my desk, sometimes I awake with the answer from sleep, as if I'd brought back a golden apple from the Hesperides.'

Fra Filippo went thoughtfully towards the chapel of the castello but, halfway down the stairs, he paused, turned and went back to the room. 'Will you be eating after Mass?' he asked Ficino.

'I never eat until noon. Food clogs my brain. Why do you ask?'

'If a man is in control of his appetites, is he able to hear the Muses more clearly?' Filippo asked it lightly, this question that, in many variants of the wording, had dogged him like a horsefly throughout his life.

'The saints would say so.'

'What do you say?'

Ficino graced him with that attention that Monna Lucrezia had bestowed upon her people of the Casentino. 'Of course your body would benefit from the practice of abstinence, your health would improve and you would have more energy. However, what makes you deaf to the Muses is not your body but the condition of your soul. Self-criticism is a poison, self-loathing a sin against God. Be content, Fra Filippo. That you hear the Muses at all marks you out as one of the chosen. Rest with that. Now, go to Mass then break your fast without worrying about it.'

Fra Filippo went quickly back down the stairs, mildly astonished that not only had he been spoken to with such spiritual authority by a man half his age, but that he had listened as if to a saint. A real saint. Not one attended by floating balls of light or who had supernatural roses pouring from his mouth, but a man of knowledge who was part of a tradition that went back to the Magi and beyond. Whatever feeling had been stirred in him all those years ago by that passing glance from fork-bearded Plethon was now stirred again. There was something going on here of which he was not fully aware: Plethon – Cosimo – Ficino – Camaldoli.

Florence: a city with several Greek scholars at its university, and the rise of Platonic thinking. He always claimed this did not interest him, and he shunned philosophy because of its love of abstractions, but Ficino was introducing him to something else: a system of thought that illuminated the soul. Suddenly, as if glimpsing his own reflection as he passed a mirror, he realized that, if he was Cosimo's chosen painter, the reason for it lay in some correspondence between his nature and the nascent Platonic Academy. It was something to do with the marriage of the sacred and the profane, with ideas of holiness being recast in the mould of naturalism. That was the best that his dim old head could come up with, at least before breakfast.

58

AS THE PARTY BEGAN THE ASCENT OF THE MOUNTAIN from the castello of the Ubertini, Fra Filippo rode beside Ficino. Alessandro kept so close that occasionally their stirrups snagged.

'My father wanted me to be a physician like him, and he sent me to the university at Bologna,' Ficino said, 'where I had to study Aristotle and the modern philosophers. When I returned to Florence during a vacation, Cosimo saw how unhappy I was and told my father not to go against my natural disposition. "And what is his natural disposition?" my father demanded. Cosimo told him that he saw in me the one who would translate Plato for him.' Ficino smiled at the landscape. 'Cosimo had already directed my early education – now he took charge of me.'

'Were you there in 1439, when the Great Council was held in Florence, and the city was filled with Greeks?' Filippo asked him.

Ficino laughed. 'I was only six at the time but yes, I was there. I have little memory of it, but what was seeded then was to determine the course of my life. All those bearded scholars in tall hats talking about Aristotle and Plato as if they were old friends. I listened to my father's discussions with Cosimo about the soul. Do not misunderstand me – I'm a devotional man and love the Church of Christ – but knowledge – the ability to question and discuss: this I desired. My father knew his Aristotle, for he had studied medicine. But Plato was new. Enthusiasm hummed in the city and, although I was only six, I was attracted by it, attracted by the idea that not all questions may have been answered by the Master, his disciples and the early fathers, that the inquiry goes on. I loved that: the freedom to think, enquire and ask questions. Although so young, I was on the hook of philosophy and about to be drawn out of the sea. Cosimo never went to university, of course, but he had had a fine education from great scholars in Florence and loved nothing so much as to discuss things with learned men. In the entourage of the Emperor of Constantinople was a strange old man called Gemistos Plethon.'

'Yes, I met him once – that is, I passed him in a corridor. He had green eyes and wore his beard in four plaits.'

'He initiated Cosimo into the Mysteries.'

'He did?' Filippo was momentarily taken aback. He thought he'd made that up to impress apprentices. 'I've never understood what "the Mysteries" are.' A *clack!* caused him to stop and disengage his foot from his Alessandro's. 'Ride behind me, boy, behind me.'

'According to an ancient teaching,' Ficino said, pausing with them, 'which stretches back to the beginning of time, Man bears within himself a spark of the divine. Our Christian faith stresses our worthlessness, but the ancient philosophers speak of our potential for divinity. It's what Alberti calls *virtù*, I believe.'

'Is that what he means by *virtù* – a divine spark? Well, it may be true of some.'

Ficino pointed at Filippo, at a spot between his eyebrows. 'It is certainly true of you.'

Filippo coloured. '*Virtù* as I understand it is excellence, cleverness, being better than anyone else in your chosen field.

350

It is Brunelleschi's dome – still standing against all the odds. It is Ghiberti's doors, which draw men from all over the world to stare at them. It is Donatello's marble reliefs that make stone look as if it is made of flesh. That is *virtù*. It's a top-of-the-class quality.'

'As I understand it, Man has a lower and a higher nature, and his higher nature is his divine part. The Romans had two words for Man: *vir* and *homo*. *Vir* is the higher nature, *homo* the lower.'

'I know nothing of *vir* or *virtù*.'

'Yet your work is infused with it.'

'Well, it is true, I admit, that I am a better painter than I am a man.'

'Only a good man can be a good painter – isn't that what Alberti says?'

'He was wrong. I am living proof of it.'

Ficino smiled. 'What a powerful mixture of vanity and humility you are!'

Filippo reined in to use his whip – lightly but effectively – on his apprentice, whose foot had got into his own stirrup again. 'Ride behind me, I say! The young these days – they just don't know their place!' He turned back to Ficino as they rode on. 'These mysteries that Cosimo learnt from Plethon...'

'He was initiated into the tradition of the Magi, which begins with Zoroaster of Persia, then passes to Hermes Trismegistus of Egypt, Orpheus of Thrace, Pythagoras and Plato of Greece, and so on through a line of masters. The Holy Tradition that flows like a vein of gold through the world's history, and common man knows it not. Cosimo formed a small group to translate Plato into Latin, which produced nothing comprehensible. Then my father spoke to him about me, his wilful and errant son, who wished to be a philosopher rather than a physician. Cosimo called me to see him. By that time, I was eleven and he was in his mid-fifties. You would think that difference in age would create a gulf between us, wouldn't you? But no. With our mutual love of philosophy our conversation was profound, although it

351

was more a question-and-answer dialogue than a conversation. I sat at his feet and asked and listened. Finally he confided in me.'

Fra Filippo's eyes widened. He checked to see that Alessandro was behind and out of earshot, as he was, still smarting from the whip.

'Cosimo told me his secret, that he had been charged by Plethon to re-found the Academy of Plato, but he needed someone prepared to dedicate his life to the translation of Plato's works. More, that man would have to harmonise Platonism with Christianity, to make Plato as acceptable as Aristotle is to Christian theologians. In other words, he was looking for a new Thomas Aquinas. In me, he said, he had found the one he sought. He sent me here, to Camaldoli, to learn Greek.'

Filippo frowned, trying to understand.

Ficino smiled. 'The General of the Order at the time of the Greek Council was Ambrogio Traversari who was the foremost scholar in Greek of the day and had made many translations of Greek fathers such as *The Ladder of Divine Ascent* by Saint John Climacus, early Christian works that were imbued with Platonic thought and which left him with a thirst for Plato. He translated Diogenes Laertius's *Vita Platonis* and presented it to Cosimo, knowing, I think, that the account therein of the founding of the original Academy would lodge in Cosimo like a seed. In the time of Traversari, the Camaldolese houses became meeting places for our urbane scholars, including Cosimo, including Alberti – the wisest of our citizens who wished to learn and debate philosophy. Whenever I come here, to Camaldoli itself, I feel as if I am coming to my true home.'

The track was leading the party into the dark fragrance of a pine wood. '*Nel mezzo del cammin di nostra vita,*' sang out Lorenzo. The boy turned, looked at Fra Filippo and smiled. '*When I had journeyed half of our life's way, I found myself within a shadowed forest, for I had lost the path that does not stray.* Do you not think this is the very forest that Dante found himself in, Fra Filippo?'

'It does look like it, I admit. Are there leopards and lions here?'

'No, but we did see a she-wolf once. And there are wild boar. *I cannot clearly say how I had entered the wood; I was so full of sleep just at the point where I abandoned the true path.*'

Did this prodigious boy have all of Dante's *Inferno* off by heart? Fra Filippo thought he probably did, and wished he did not feel so uncomfortable about it. Then, in the fashion of antiphony, Ficino returned with a verse.

'*But when I'd reached the bottom of a hill, it rose along the boundary of the valley that had harassed my heart with so much fear...*'

'*I looked on high and saw its shoulders clothed already by the rays of that same planet which serves to lead men straight along all roads,*' Lorenzo returned.

Fra Filippo noticed that Alessandro's interest had quickened at the sound of Dante's words echoing in this dense wood through which they travelled, ever upward on a winding road. To be sure, the singing contest brought Dante's words to life, but the discomfort of Filippo's soul did not allow him to enjoy it in the same way as his apprentice was doing.

When Lorenzo's memory faltered at the point where Dante meets the shade of Virgil, he abandoned the poem and took Giuliano off into the trees 'to hunt for leopards'. Monna Lucrezia sent two of the armed guards to follow them and keep them from harm.

'The *Inferno* upsets you,' Ficino observed.

'It's something I prefer not to think about,' said Filippo.

'I find it useful, every now and again, to consider where I am placed in Dante's great scheme.'

'I think the devil will have to tear me in two, for I am destined for both the second and third circles of hell, to lie prone with the lustful, rained on by stinging hail, or with the gluttonous in a storm of shit.'

Ficino winced. 'No one is judged as harshly as by himself.'

'What do you mean?'

'Sometimes it is worth examining the sins you are *not* guilty of. Would you, for instance, betray your city, deny God, ignore a call for alms? No, I thought not. And presumably you do your penances. With a whole heart?'

'At the time of confession, yes, but afterwards – I fail at the next temptation. Where other men have sinew I have soft jelly. I would like to get out of this cycle of sin and repentance, if I could.'

'The virtuous life is your goal?'

'It is, but I'll never achieve it.'

'The desire is what counts, my friend, believe me.'

The boys had rejoined the party as it reached the monastery of Camaldoli. 'Abandon hope all ye who enter here!' cried Lorenzo at its gate. His mother admonished him. 'This sacred place is the very source of hope!'

They were admitted by a white-robed and silent monk. Fra Filippo rode in expecting to find an enclosure of men deluded by the sense of their own piety, who spent their days competing in goodness and lived their lives in pretence of holiness. He had been a friar too long to be anything other than cynical and preferred an honest rogue to a deluded hermit.

The monastery was silent and had a warmth and sweetness to its air that even the cynical friar had to acknowledge. The party dismounted and a smiling monk invited Monna Lucrezia to meet the abbot in his cell. She beckoned to Fra Filippo. 'Look around,' she said. 'You are free to visit anywhere.'

Fra Filippo explored the monastery, found the church, the pharmacy, the hospital and suites of guest rooms.

'I thought there were hermits,' said Alessandro, disappointed.

'Where are the hermits?' Fra Filippo asked a passing monk.

'Secluded in the forest,' was the answer.

Painter and apprentice pulled faces at each other.

'I thought this was secluded.'

'I thought this was a forest.'

Frustrated to find themselves in a hospice, they went to find something to eat. All that they were offered was fresh, brown bread with golden butter and some sweet, yellow wine, but perhaps because of their hunger or the fresh, mountain air, it was the best they had ever tasted. Later, while they stood looking at the arms of the order embedded in a wall, they were joined by a monk. 'Two silver doves drinking from one golden chalice – it signifies the twin disciplines of the order, the monastic and the eremitic. The monks serve the world while the hermits serve God in silence.'

'Where is the hermitage?'

'About an hour's walk farther up the mountain. There is no need to disturb them. Anything you want or need, we can supply. Have you found your room? You will see it is clean and comfortable.'

The Medici, with a great fuss of servants and shifting of furniture, had ensconced themselves. The young members were preparing themselves for a holiday of hunting, fishing and woodcraft. Monna Lucrezia and Ficino were in discussion with the abbot and the Camaldolese scholars, first about the dangerous situation in Florence, but soon about deeper matters of interest to them all. Fra Filippo was left wondering why he had been brought here.

'You need to visit the hermitage,' Monna Lucrezia told him on the following morning as they left the church after Terce.

'It's an hour's walk uphill!'

'I want you to see it, Fra Filippo. I command it.'

'May I take a horse?'

'I would prefer it if you went on your knees, but I am tolerant and gracious: you may walk. Make sure you get there well before midday or there'll be nothing to see. If you leave now, you should arrive in time.'

'In time for what?' grumbled Fra Filippo, setting off into the woods with Alessandro. A cart passed them on the track, filled with tiny trees in pots, miniature pines swaying from the action of the vehicle. Alessandro looked askance at his master, who shrugged and said he had no explanation. On the way up the mountain, they heard the chop of axes among the trees and eventually came across some monks felling pines who were glad to sit down awhile with the travellers and take a rest.

'Are you clearing more land?'

'No, we're making space for what is already here. The forest can choke and die if left to itself. We plant two trees for every one we take, but we plant them elsewhere. You will see the planters farther on.'

Felled trees were being dragged away from the clearing by teams of oxen, and the cries of the drivers echoed through the woods. The forest was still wild – they saw boar and heard wolves in the distance – but it was a wild place tended and cared for. The forest and the monks were curiously unified, a companionship of mutual dependence.

'They all look happy,' Alessandro observed as the two walked on.

'Who? The monks?' Fra Filippo had not noticed and was surprised by the notion of a happy monk. But it was true, the fellers had seemed cheerful.

On the woodland track, they came to the monks who, having taken delivery of the cart, were planting the saplings. After digging a hole, a monk would take up a pot, turn it upside down and tap its base with the handle of his trowel. As the little tree fell out, it dropped between his fingers but his hand caught the root ball. Having shown the technique to Alessandro, they let him plant a tree. He re-filled the hole with friable soil, trod the earth down round the base of the new pine then watered it in. He looked ecstatic, like a man whose wife has given birth to a healthy child.

'Come away,' Fra Filippo said, worried that his apprentice was being seduced by monastic life. He had a deep suspicion of the quiet happiness of these monks: either it was put on for visitors, or it was the result of one of the concoctions of the pharmacy. Happy monks were not natural – of that he was certain. The point about being a monk was self-denial, and that was hardly the root of happiness, now was it? He stumped on, reminding Alessandro that they had to reach the hermitage before midday or there would be nothing to see.

'They all disappear at midday,' he said. 'Vanish like wood sprites.'

At last, when Fra Filippo was beginning to think his heart would burst if he took another step, the red roofs above the stone wall of the hermitage suddenly appeared within an extensive clearing on the mountainside. It was secluded indeed. Met by a monk at the gate, they were admitted with the warning that they were to speak to no one, to disturb no man's peace nor interrupt anyone's work. 'They work until midday,' the monk whispered, 'then retire into their cells for prayer.'

59

WHAT THE MONK CALLED 'CELLS' WERE MORE LIKE hovels, clean and bare, and there were enough of them to make a village. Divided by paved footpaths, each cell and its garden was bounded by a wattle fence. Between Terce and Nones, the hermits gardened. Filippo and Alessandro walked through the 'village', looking now over this fence, now over the next. Although the hermits could eat their produce, some chose to grow only flowers to avoid temptation during fasts. Others grew salads and root vegetables. One or two had nut trees. As the painters walked by, they saw the hermits hoeing, watering or trimming with shears. And, without exception, they were light-hearted and cheerful. Something, some subtle thing in the quality of the place said there was no hypocrisy here. The hermits were gardening, yes, obviously – one man digging up carrots, another sowing a line of peas, another weeding among the onions, not with a hoe but on his knees and with his hands.

'No bread and eggs – I'd die,' Fra Filippo muttered.

'We're not here to consume the earth and its bounty,' said a voice, making him start violently. A hermit had straightened on the far side of his fence. 'Only to tend it and take what we need. And, believe me, you need far less than you think.' The hermit's eye rested momentarily on Fra Filippo's belly.

'I thought you were under a rule of silence?'

'No, there are no rules. No need for rules. We *prefer* silence. But I felt moved to speak, for I see you are a man in deep despair.'

'Oh, am I? I tell you my friend, I would be if I had to spend my day gardening.'

'There is more to the day than that. Seven times in every twenty-four hours we sing the Divine Office. Then we study scripture; then we work. Of all the things I grow here, there is a surplus, which I gather into a basket and leave at the gate to be collected and distributed amongst the poor. I keep a bunch of this and a bulb or root of that, and eat it at the appropriate hour.'

'Live on vegetables? I would explode.'

'You know, if you chew, if you put your full attention on what you are eating and how, there's no wind. Wind comes from gulping.' The monk was gazing on the friar in such a kindly fashion, putting him right without offending him. 'And sometimes,' here he came and leant across the gate conspiratorially, 'sometimes we do have eggs and bread, brought by those who take our vegetables. Cheese, too. Not on Fridays of course. On Fridays we have bread and water only. And we love our fasts so much that we celebrate Lent twice a year, at Christmas as well as Easter.'

Fra Filippo's eyes were screwed up as if he were chopping onions. 'Yet you seem happy.'

'As days pass, we enter the rhythm of work and prayer and any separation between them ceases. I close my eyes to pray and see carrots. I crawl amongst the beans and I remember God. I live in a pen twelve braccia by eight braccia. It is small, as you can see. But it is also vast. I know every inch of its soil and the creatures who live here. I know each plant, raised myself from seed. I know the weather of every moment and what I need to do to help the

358

plants, whether to shelter them or water them. I know the bees who come to take the pollen. I know the birds who wait for me to turn up worms. I know the worms.'

'Verily, another Saint Francis.'

'Happy is the man who is like Saint Francis. Happy am I.'

'According to Archbishop Antonino, the garden is a metaphor for the soul.'

'Brother Antonino lived with us awhile and understands. Yes, it is a metaphor. As your fingers go deep into the soil, feeling for the end of taproot of a horseradish, you know the strength and depth of your own wilfulness. Once I tended a little plant in a pot – pretty thing it was…' the pink-faced hermit smiled at the memory. 'Had tiny little flowers. One day I was weeding it and felt at its centre the nub of something else and I parted my frondy little beauty to see that it had completely enveloped the true plant, which was a cutting of a fruit bush. I had been tending the weed! And that is what the soul is like: there is the true king and there is the usurper, and it takes a wise man to know the difference. Every time I feel sure of myself, I remember my beautiful weed and pull it out again. All the vices are weeds to be pulled: envy, malice, pride, anger – all of them. They grow on their own without help or attention from us. The virtues need to be sown, to be grafted, to be helped in every way to reach fruition…'

Filippo remembered what Ficino had said, about Plato needing to remind himself daily of the truth.

'That is why the garden is a metaphor for the soul. Everything you need to know and to learn for self-understanding and for knowledge of God is here in your plot. When a hermit dies, his plot is left to return to nature. When a new one comes, he has to clear the ground again, because that is how it is. We start by felling the trees of our obvious vices, and we end by delicately pursuing the roots of bindweed. That is our subtlest vice. And now, if you'll excuse me, I'm working on spite.' He turned to a small clump of nettles.

Alessandro's eyes widened. This sweet-faced hermit seemed the least spiteful of men.

'Fetch our notebooks,' said Fra Filippo.

✝

Master and apprentice laboured over studies of hermits and garden plants, of forest clearings and hewn trees, Filippo forever interrupting Alessandro to show him a better way to hold his metal style, how to hatch, how best to show form with line. When the hermitage bell rang at noon for prayers, they ignored it. When it rang again later to call guests to eat – and Alessandro rose to obey – Filippo continued to work. He had only a day here. When Alessandro dithered, wondering whether to stay or go, Filippo waved him away. He wanted to be alone in the gardens.

Something was moving within him, an energy that made him breathless. Not knowing what he was doing, but heeding an inner impulse, he put down his notebook and went to the tree stumps which marked the edge of the clearing. He took up an axe he found lying there, swung it up and brought it down hard into the stump of a pine. It took him over an hour to get the stump up. Where good old monks had pretty purslane to pick at with their fingers, he had tree roots to contend with. At the end he felt both exhausted and purified.

'There you go, Fra Filippo Lippi,' he said, the root ball now upturned towards the sky. 'I am done with you.'

He stood back then and wondered whether it were true. *The desire is enough.* Smiling and light of spirit, he walked into the trees, enjoying the crunch of pine needles, the deep, resinous fragrance, the dash of martens up trunks and across branches. He came to a more natural clearing where the sun penetrated the forest and hit the dusty litter of dead needles. Suddenly Filippo was missing his Lucrezia so much he could see her, sitting there with Filippino thrashing his limbs on the forest floor, gurgling, sucking his thumb, looking up at his father with love. He could see her.

360

As real as the day. And he knew who she was. As impaired sight can sometimes suddenly find focus, so for a moment his two visions became one. What the Muse showed him was his wife as the Virgin. Something he had always known and thought about, but never dared to accept. This would be his Adoration. Could he take the step, risk scandalising everyone, and paint the Virgin with the human face of his wife? No, but he could take a step towards that. The energy that had been surging in him now died back, as a fire new-started settles into a quiet glow that will burn the night through.

✝

A messenger came from the city. Filippo noticed that Monna Lucrezia was shaking as she received the man. 'What news?' she asked.

'All is safe, Madonna. The will of the people prevailed.'

'Grazia Deo! And my father-in-law? He is at Careggi?'

'Not yet, Madonna.'

Monna Lucrezia sniffed in annoyance. 'Will he never do as I tell him?'

The messenger dipped his head and smiled.

60

THE PAINTER AND HIS APPRENTICE CAME TO THE GATES of Prato just as curfew was being called, slipped into the city and took a winding route to Filippo's house to avoid public places. Filippo wanted no one to know he was back, not for a while. At the house, Fra Diamante fell on him, covered his face with exaggerated kisses and demanded more designs for Santo Stefano. 'My work has dried up!'

'Then take a rest, have a week off. It's high summer.'

361

'High summer is when we should be busiest with our frescoes.'

'Only if you are a slave. Go and stay with relatives in the countryside. Have you got any relatives in the countryside?'

Bewildered, Fra Diamante could only shake his head. No, he had not. He looked sideways and bitterly at Alessandro. 'Slave indeed,' he muttered. 'Sometimes I feel like the brother of the prodigal son. The one who does all the work and gets none of that fatted calf.'

Filippo ignored him. 'I need to work on an altarpiece for the Medici. A new commission. Has to be done quickly. I can't let myself be distracted by Santo Stefano.'

Fra Diamante, the blood rising to his face, went to the roof garden to clear his head and think of where he could go for a month.

Filippo jumped when a flowerpot from the roof garden crashed to the ground outside the workshop. 'He needs a week at Camaldoli,' he said to Alessandro.

✝

Filippo found Lucrezia not looking as he had expected to find her. No virginal purity or downcast gaze of devotion; instead a cast of misery was on her face, her hair bedraggled, her eyes hollow. Filippino was bawling.

'Look what he's done!' she said, and lifted the child to reveal her soiled lap.

'Get changed,' said Filippo. 'I'll see to that.'

Lucrezia sighed irritably.

Filippo wanted to tell her that he had had a vision of her and Filippino in a clearing in the eremitical woods, that it had been a sacred revelation and one of the most profound moments in his life, but found he could say nothing. He took the despoiled shift, rolled it up and put it in a bucket in the kitchen. Then he went down to his workshop, lit a few candles and sat with his notebook, trying to recapture what he had seen in the woods, trying to wipe

362

his memory of what he had seen upstairs. The ideal was what he sought: the holy, divine essence of Lucrezia.

A short while later he was distracted by the sound of two voices humming the notes of a slow pavan and went to the kitchen to find Alessandro teaching Spinetta steps he had learnt from Lorenzo de' Medici, who himself had a dancing master. In Alessandro's imagination, the room was full of noble dancers being led through the figures. The gangly youth disappeared in the dance: he flipped his wrist and gesticulated with the grace of a polished knight. At the end he stood flushed, bowing before Spinetta who clapped her hands and called for more. Filippo took up some wooden spoons and began to tap out something livelier on the table. Fra Diamante, drawn down from the roof, joined in by clapping his hands to a complex rhythm. Together the two friars hollered out a bawdy song and Alessandro and Spinetta jumped and skipped like peasants. Lucrezia appeared at the door like a vengeful ghost. 'There is a baby in this house,' she said, 'trying to sleep.'

'What he needs,' said Fra Filippo, catching her by the waist, 'is a happy mother. Come, dance with me, wife.'

✝

In the morning, Diamante left for the abbey of Vallambrosa, saying that the Carmelites were hypocrites in habits and he was going to become a Benedictine. Lucrezia, however, had woken in a better mood and now showed her joy at having Filippo back. 'I've done the laundry,' she said, with no remonstrance against the husband who considered that putting a soiled garment in a bucket was 'seeing to it'.

Filippo adjusted his easel and arranged for his wife to kneel on the floor with her hands held together in prayer. As he sketched for a long hour, he kept her awake and entertained with stories of his time in Florence, of old Cosimo and Monna Lucrezia, of the boys, Lorenzo and Giuliano. After a short rest, he tried placing Filippino on his back before her but the baby thrashed and bawled. Filippino cried even harder when his father picked him up, this man who was a stranger to him; but Filippino was quick to friendship and before long his little squall blew over and the sun came out in his face.

Lucrezia rose, winced and rubbed her knees. She took her son, bounced him in the air and jigged about with him. Now Filippo started sketching again, quickly. How, how, how to get that look of absorption in the mother and the suffusion of happiness in her cheeks? He felt he need never travel again, that all he would ever need was playing out in front of him like light dancing on water. He sat back again and rubbed his chest. 'Oh, it is good to be home.'

But for how long? How long before the Ceppo discovered he was back in Prato and began to hammer at him to finish the walls? How long could he delay his work at Santo Stefano? He had heard speculation about frescoes for the apse in the cathedral of Spoleto. Where was Spoleto? Many miles south and on the far side of the Apennines. A week's journey at least. If the commission came, then he must remove to Spoleto permanently. Taking who with him? An assistant, an apprentice, a son, a wife and her sister? No. People would be scandalised. If he removed to Spoleto, he would be leaving the safety of his ward here in Prato and the support of his neighbours and drinking companions. But if he did not receive the commission – then what? Where must he go to work? Wherever it was, he could not be encumbered by anyone. He must travel alone.

He lived, he often thought, to fulfil the desires of others. Go here, paint this, go there, paint that. Some – like the Medici, or the Ceppo – seemed to think that it was God's Will that their wishes had priority, and complained of his delaying when that delay was caused only by his fulfilling someone else's desire or need. What is *my* desire? he wondered. What is it *I* want? At first he thought the answer must be, 'Sleep late, do nothing, drink, play dice and idle my days away.' That was certainly what everyone else supposed of him. But it was not true. If he were master of his own hours, he would spend them experimenting with form and colour. If he were master of his own projects, he would paint pictures the like of which no one had ever seen or conceived before. Landscapes. Portraits. Studies in colour of small, insignificant things. These were what gave him joy: to paint, to portray the wonders of the mundane, and to find in a flower of the field an image of God. His God. The God he happened to love: the Creator of all things. All he wanted was the kiss of the Muse and the freedom to paint.

That – and this. This domesticity. This wife and child. This exquisite, almost painful feeling of love.

✝

The painting grew from the centre of himself, as if his heart were aligned to that of the Virgin. He painted a dense and extensive wood of dark pines on the rocky side of a mountain, the trees receding nicely into the distance. On a flower-filled clearing of the forest floor, he put the Virgin kneeling, hands touching in prayer, in adoration of her son who lay on the grass, gazing at the viewer.

Filippo had intended that gaze of the baby to be reflective but others said later that the 'adoration' was that of the baby for all humankind. To the left stood John the Baptist in his boyhood, dressed in rough skins and wrapped in a rose-coloured mantle; above him, the figure of St Romauld, who had founded the Camaldolese brotherhood, praying over a small, felled tree.

Around the clearing were many stumps and upturned root-balls, some cut clean through, some torn and frayed. As he painted each one, Fra Filippo visualised one of his sins and tried to cut it down and stump it up. As he worked on his picture, he worked on his own soul. Things would be different now. Camaldoli had given him a taste for purity. God the Father in celestial magnificence opened his arms wide above the Holy Ghost, a dove from which divine light rayed down to the heart of the child in a subtle, spiralling fire.

He wished to break this convention but how else could you portray the Trinity? God incarnate was straightforward, but the Holy Ghost and God the Father: how to portray the invisible? Those rays from heaven – to be gilded with fine gold leaf once he had finished – who had ever seen such a thing in life? A pictorial convention, that was all, but he could think of nothing better. He resolved to discuss it with Cosimo next time they met.

There was still the nagging question of the composition. All his sketches were parts of a whole, but what was the whole, and on what principle should it be organised? His clever heptagon had been dismissed and he went back to the common arrangement of triangles, but dismissed that himself. His fecund imagination presented various ideas but he was haunted by Cosimo's likening his mind to a mire. He dismissed everything he thought of. He went to bed, tossed and turned, grew angry and chewed on his nails. Where was this Creator when you needed him? Finally he swore into the shadows of the bed's hangings and promised himself, as of the morrow, to work with his heptagon, an idea so good it must have come from God, and that was why God had nothing more to say.

But in his sleep he dreamt of climbing date palms. There was something in the fronds of those lofty palms that he needed. When he reached the top and looked down, expecting to see the desert, what he saw was Camaldoli from above – in such clarity that he wondered ever afterwards how the imagination could do that, show a bird's-eye perspective no human eye had ever seen. Beyond Camaldoli was the wooded mountain. Now the perspective grew strange and old-fashioned because. although he was looking down from above, he could clearly see the mouth of a cave, approached by steps hewn in the rock. Then suddenly he was back in the date palm and looking up at the fronds and noticing that they grew from the stem in a spiral, that indeed every step he had taken in his climb had been a step on a spiralling staircase of stubs on the trunk.

'A spiral,' he said to Alessandro the next morning. 'That's the composition. The centre of the picture is the entrance to a cave in the woods and everything in the picture lies on a spiral that begins in the cave.'

'I have never heard of such a thing!'

'I have, amongst the Persians.'

'Are you saying that in the centre of the picture there will be nothing?'

'Nothing. Or everything. Like the centre of a circle. Or a heptagon. It all begins, the Incarnation of our Lord, in a world beyond ours, a world approached in the darkness and silence of the cave. Christ, by this divine miracle, appears in our world and his mother Mary kneels in adoration before him, where he lies on the forest floor.'

Fra Filippo had no intention of finishing the picture quickly: he was enjoying it too much. He fiddled and re-drew, repainted, added details. The prelates of Santo Stefano continued to grumble that the paintings of the middle tier were dull. Carlo de' Medici, away in Rome, was not there to intervene on Filippo's behalf, dear Carlo who would protect him even when he was in the wrong, and he was in the wrong. He was spending too much time at home, not enough in the cathedral, and not only were there too many rocks, they were badly painted. Over the summer, Fra Filippo did what he could *a secco* – painting details on dry frescoes to add more interest. There were too many rocks because Fra Filippo had gone to Florence without leaving Fra Diamante sufficient designs. Diamante was good with rocks. Could fill entire surfaces with them.

'Too many rocks!' said the provost.

'Balance!' Fra Filippo retorted. 'We have all the interest of the top tiers, and wait until you see what we're going to do on the bottom tiers. In between, we have a rest. After all, the Mission of Saint Stephen and the Mission of Saint John are hardly subjects that inspire a wealth of pictorial ideas, are they? No, this is where the eye has a little interlude of peace and calm between the upper

367

and lower scenes. Not that anyone can see these paintings, not from the body of the church. The only thing people will be able to see is the stained-glass window.'

'The stained-glass window is all anyone will be interested in,' said Provost Inghirami. He did not mean to annoy: it was a simple statement of fact.

In a burst of ill temper about the project, Filippo threw down his brush and went down the ladder. 'Finish it yourself!' he snapped and went home.

✝

He went back to his grass blades, petals and the depiction of a stream running through the woods, the stream Monna Lucrezia had mentioned, of the holiness from the mountain running down to the city on the plain. He worked on the blue folds of the Madonna's robe, its highlights of many hues, its shadows; her rose-coloured chemise and dark gown. He barely breathed as he painted the transparent gauze of her veil, through which her sweet ear and neck showed. For a little joke, he decorated the border of her mantle with Kufic script, the words that, although meaning nothing, implicitly said, 'Now do you believe me, you doubters?' In the left- hand corner, he painted an axe buried in a stump, the angle of the handle such that it seemed to have been hurled down by God Himself, but the name he painted on the axe was his own: Frater Philippus, and he added 'P' for *pinxit*, 'painted it'. Although he had signed a previous work, it was not common, though Filippo had heard that they did it in the Netherlands and saw no reason why they should not do it in Italy. This work, this Adoration, this cathartic exorcism of his own soul, he would sign.

Yes, things would be different now.

It required sacrifice, of course: the progress of the soul depends on sacrifice, the willingness to give up everything for God. Throughout the autumn, he grew increasingly solemn and began to look on his son as Abraham looked on Isaac.

61

SOMETIMES THE IDEA OF SACRIFICING HIS SON WAS NOT as abhorrent as it should have been. The infant slept in a cradle in his parents' chamber and, when he woke up crying, sometimes for the fourth time between dusk and dawn, Filippo could happily have put a pillow over his face, if not a knife to his throat. And at such hours he was not overly fond of his wife, either, always rejecting his advances in preference for feeding Filippino. Sometimes, when he was feeling bleak, he suspected that Lucrezia had wanted him only for his seed.

The crying baby wrung the nerves of both parents. The air in the house grew scratchy and it was becoming difficult to work on the Adoration altarpiece. Santo Stefano regained his interest and Filippo turned to designing the scenes for the lower tier. Who knew when he would be summoned back to Florence? He would need to leave as many designs as he could to keep Diamante going. For Diamante had returned from Vallambrosa and, although now a Benedictine, was a still a friar-painter with special responsibility at Prato.

On the left wall, the funeral of Saint Stephen; in the corner, the stoning; on the right wall, the Feast of Herod; in the corner, the beheading. Now here was pictorial matter! Nothing like evil and horror to catch the eye and interest of people and provosts.

He made sketches, life-size drawings, entire cartoons. He was just beginning to feel the benefit of days of uninterrupted work when he was called to attend a meeting with the Ceppo at the Palazzo Datini.

✝

Recently installed in the courtyard was a tabernacle he had painted – one of his better works, although highly gilded, which had not taken him long to do. He went upstairs to the vaulted sala, sat down and began admiring the walls as usual. He would decorate his own chamber like this one day, when he had time.

'Fra Lippi?'

He sat up to face the grey-haired men round the table, the portly and the lean, the merchants, physicians, lawyers and guildsmen, the great and the good of Prato. No one here had a nun for a wife, of that he was certain.

'Are you aware of how much we have spent on your project so far?'

Filippo was not aware.

'Over two thousand florins.'

'As much as that? Are you certain?'

'No painter alive has been paid so much for one project.'

Filippo was doing some rapid calculation. 'I have been working on your walls since 1452 – that's six years. That's about three hundred florins a year to cover my expenses – expenses no other painter alive would consider paying for, such as repairing the choir's roof, hiring the scaffolding planks, that kind of thing; then I had to raise some money myself because you paid me in wool – WOOL! – and I am not a wool merchant. To cover my expenses and the wages of my assistants…'

'Fra Lippi!'

'AND THEN there are the materials. Do you know how much ultramarine costs these days?'

'Of course we know, we understand –'

'Since the fall of Constantinople –'

'We know.'

These heads of families, the Bertelli, Malassei, Pugliesi, Obizi, were beginning to look cowed, but they were determined not to be cowed, not this time.

'We would like you to paint the communal arms above the window once it is installed, and are happy to pay for the gold and the blue – one hundred florins for both.'

'And me? Shall I be paid?'

'You have been paid enough, Fra Lippi.'

The blood was rushing to Filippo's face. He always feared an apoplexy at these moments of incandescent rage: his head would explode from the pressure and blood and brains would spatter all over these fine walls and the oaken table. Or he would be left stiff down one side and speechless and they would have to put him in the hospital for what remained of his shortened life.

Andrea Bertelli leaned forwards. 'Do you think we don't know? Do you think we are ignorant of what goes on at your house? When we commissioned you, it was second choice – you were the next best, that's what Fra Giovanni told us.'

'Really? Is that what he said?'

'In truth you couldn't be more unalike. No, we shall not be paying you any further fee. Consider the work as your penance.'

✤

Alessandro was still at Santo Stefano, grinding pigments for the morrow's work, when Fra Filippo crashed through the door and came hollering down the nave. By his stumbling gait and noise, Alessandro knew he had stopped off at the tavern on his way back from the Ceppo.

'How much ultramarine is left?' Filippo shouted, his voice booming off the vaulting of the nave.

'None. We finished what we had yesterday. I told you.'

Filippo had an increasing tendency to forget anything he was told, which caused Alessandro more irritation than concern. He had been warning him about the shortage of ultramarine for three weeks now, since three weeks was the shortest time it would take to prepare a new batch.

Filippo went through the tools on the table and found a scraper. 'Is there anyone around?'

'No, they've all gone. They left the keys with me.'

'Come,' Filippo led his apprentice to the Chapel of the Holy Girdle and its tall bronze gates. He took the bunch of keys from Alessandro and opened it. He walked around, looking up at the paintings by Agnolo Gaddi, outmoded now, those serene figures on their blue background. 'Here – here – and here,' he pointed to the scenes least visible from outside the gates. 'Start scraping.'

'*What?*'

'We need the blue. We'll replace it once the committee pays us. Once they pay us, we'll put the blue back. But, for now, start scraping. It's a magical, wonderful thing, ultramarine, and one of its glories is that, like gold, it never fades and can be used again and again.'

Alessandro knew enough about the history and traditions of his vocation to know the importance of Gaddi. Besides, he liked him. He did not need anyone else to tell him what a great painter Gaddi had been – he only had to look. And now he was being asked to deface the paintings, strip them of their blue as if he were a Goth or a Vandal. 'I cannot do it!'

'Do it or starve. Do you think it is cheap for me to feed and house you?'

'My father paid you to teach me. You give me nothing. I have no wage. You don't even pay Diamante. You say friars don't need to be paid.'

Filippo had always been kind to Alessandro. Indeed, they had never quarrelled previously, but the more Alessandro argued now, the fiercer Lippi became. 'Do it or starve! I promise you, you'll be out on your ear!'

With tears running down his cheeks that would not be staunched, Alessandro set about scraping the ultramarine off some of the Gaddi scenes, whispering, 'I'm sorry, I'm so sorry,' to the walls as he did so. Behind him, in the glass and silver reliquary set high on the altar, lay the belt of the Holy Virgin. 'Help me,' Alessandro prayed, 'help us all.'

He felt a warmth in the small of his back as if someone's hand was there. His fear subsided and he began to breathe more easily. He could not understand this world which had such a different sense of right and wrong, a difference so stark that he could feel it in his chest. And yet the world preferred shades of grey to black and white.

Black and white. Fra Filippo was walking heavily up the nave in his black Carmelite gown and the white mantle with hood that lay in generous folds across his shoulders. Alessandro was still angry with him; the master should have done this foul deed himself and not have besmirched his apprentice's soul with the sin of theft. Alessandro had learnt from Diamante about the fake gold used in the pastiglia. Once at the Palazzo de' Medici he had asked Marsilio Ficino, in an offhand way, staring at the ceiling as he did so, whether an apprentice is obliged always to do what his master tells him to do, even if he feels it is wrong. Ficino decided on reflection that the duty of the apprentice is to be obedient. 'We never see the results of our good actions,' he said. 'In obeying your master, you may be transforming him and freeing him from future evil. Who knows?'

Alessandro looked at Fra Filippo, who had reached the choir and was gazing at the cartoons for the Feast of Herod fastened to lowest tier of the wall. After all the apparent softening during the stay at Camaldoli, Filippo had returned to his old ways and seemed impervious to reform. Alessandro found his anger draining away. Why fight? He followed his master to the choir and presented him with a bowl of blue flakes. Filippo was staring at the lowest tier on the Saint John wall and its cartoons, humming and smiling to himself as if he were contemplating a vision of supreme beauty.

'What you don't understand, Alessandro,' he said gently, taking the bowl without looking at him, 'is that I must do all I can to finish these walls before I die. If it is taking forever, it is not my fault, you know that. You know about the distractions. What you don't know, because you're too good and can only see the good, what you don't know is the nature of the men I have to parlay with in the Ceppo – those *buonomini* who wear the mask of charity, of good civic behaviour, of moral uprightness, over a heart that is a writhing mess of snakes. They are the Sanhedrin, ready to stone Stephen for his vision of God. You don't see that. Be thankful.'

'As it happens,' said Alessandro softly, 'I do see such things.'

'Then you are a true painter, my boy.'

✢

Work on the frescoes stopped for the winter and Filippo spent the harsh months working on his altarpieces, the Adoration for the Medici and one of the Trinity for nearby Pistoia that had been started three years previously. Of the two, the Trinity was the more overdue and Filippo concentrated on completing it. During Advent, however, an enquiry came from Cosimo: was the Adoration going to be ready for Epiphany as promised? When Filippo failed to reply, a deputation came from Florence, insisting that he accompany them. As ever, he had no say in the matter.

'When will you be back?' Lucrezia asked anxiously, Filippino resting in a sling on her hip.

'I don't know! I am not the master of my own destiny. Cosimo wants his altarpiece finished and when a rich man wants something he tends to get it. Careful, there,' he said to the men carrying the Adoration panel to the cart waiting outside. 'I have to go, my love, but I will not be long in Florence.'

'You always say that but sometimes it's months before you return.'

'I could not stay away so long,' he said, hoping she did not pick up the insincerity in his voice for, in truth, he longed to be sleeping on his own in his bed in the casa de' Medici. Nights of conversation with Cosimo. Fine dining. No baby crying or its mother looking harassed and miserable. 'I'll be back as soon I can,' he told her. He took Diamante aside to tell him he would send back designs to keep him going when the new fresco season started. At the end of a long list of tasks, and with the escort beginning to tug at his reins impatiently, he added as a kind of afterthought the instruction that his assistant should 'look after the women'.

'No!' cried Diamante, but before he could frame his objection, Fra Filippo was drawn away by the Medici men.

The Chapel of the Magi
1459

62

DIAMANTE CAME TO THE HOUSE DAILY AND BROUGHT food and any necessary supplies. There was enough firewood stacked within the hearth, logs that Filippo had himself chopped in the autumn, and the larder was full of grain and cured hams, but fresh things grew increasingly difficult to get as winter wore on. Diamante had to instruct the young women, as he had done the previous winter, in what to eat during the lean times. He gave them recipes for bean soups and onion stews and dumplings. He worried about their vulnerability.

The year before, when Filippo was away in Florence until February, Diamante had taken to visiting the house each evening and making sure it was secure before going back to the Carmine monastery. This year, however, he received a message from his new mother house at Vallombrosa that he was to spend Advent at the abbey. He wrote to Filippo but, flustered by the demand to be elsewhere, flustered that is, by finding himself in an order which imposed the very discipline he thought he craved until it was imposed, left the letter on the table of his cell. 'You have everything you need,' he told Lucrezia and Spinetta. 'Keep the door locked and speak to no one. Filippo will be back soon.'

'What if we need to buy something!' said Lucrezia.

'The larder is fully stocked – you'll have no needs. Filippo will be back before the Feast of the Nativity and I shall be back shortly thereafter.'

✝

The days were cold, dark and mind-numbing. Lucrezia and Spinetta irritated each other until they were spitting like cats. Only Filippino united them, gave them respite from their nerves and helped the hours to pass.

On the top floor of the house Lucrezia opened the window shutters, careful not to dislodge them from their broken hinges. She looked out over the piazza to Santo Stefano, braving the cold for this glimpse of the outside. She longed for winter to pass, to have sudden sight of Filippo making his way back to the house from his work on the chapel, for him to warm her bed. She missed everything about him: his kindness, his attentiveness, his flatulence and the stubble of his chin. He was her husband: in the eyes of God, theirs was a sacred union. She had noticed something about him that others overlooked: that just by his presence he improved the life and lot of those around him. He was the beaten egg that bound the ingredients.

Sitting on the window-seat, she drew up her legs and wrapped her arms around them, hugging herself and wondering. Did she regret leaving the convent? No, she did not. She regretted nothing. She loved her husband and was sorely missing him. She had no need to torture herself with self-doubt. But how long a month was! And would he really be home for the Feast of the Nativity? He might be away longer, you never could tell. For Filippo, life was full of colourful event and distraction; he had no sense of passing time, except that it always passed too quickly. For her, it was like walking through a bog in a nightmare, up to her thighs in mud. A never-ending bog, stretching to infinity. She picked absently at some flaking plaster on the wall by the window and jumped when quite a large piece fell off.

Someone was knocking upon the door below. Lucrezia stood on the seat and looked down to see the dyer they called il Mulo. He waved cheerfully. She knew him; he came often to the house to play chess with Filippo; he was just the distraction she required. She went down to let him in.

✝

After a clumsy pretence at concern for their welfare, il Mulo moved in on his prey. She backed away from those woad-stained hands. Her eyes blazed. He pinned her hard against the wall and

378

put his full and fleshy lips to her neck. She twisted her head away in disgust.

'Come on, my sweet beauty.'

She pushed him violently and held him at arm's length to look him in the eye. 'Do you have a sister?' she asked.

'Yes. Why?'

'How would you feel if any man treated her like this?'

The colour rushed to his face, the shame to his eyes. Thrusting her aside, he blundered out of the house.

✛

For a week the two women lived enclosed in Filippo's house, answering no knock at the door without looking out of the window first. It was always a man; they refused to open the door. The procurator, il Mulo and other cloth-workers, one or two of the Ceppo, priests and friars – all claiming to have their best interests at heart. But then came Rosaria, knocking on the door and calling to them.

Lucrezia opened the door cautiously.

'You cannot live like this,' said the tavern-keeper's wife, walking in and wrinkling her nose at the stale air. 'It's unhealthy. Do you need anything brought in?'

'No, we need nothing. You are very kind.'

'We whores need to stick together,' said Rosaria.

Lucrezia looked offended until she realized that, in the eyes of Prato at least, whore was what she was.

'You cannot live like this,' Rosaria repeated. 'You are like staked goats. Men are prowling about outside and sniffing at your door.'

Lucrezia shuddered.

'In the tavern there is talk of little else but Fra Filippo's abandoned women.'

'We are not abandoned. He has to work. In Florence.'

'I know, I know, but with the scent of women up their noses men will delude themselves about anything. Is there nowhere else you can go?'

'No, nowhere.'

'Not the convent?'

'Believe me, we are safer here. Filippo will be back soon.'

✝

On the eve of the Feast of the Nativity there was another knocking at the door. 'Suor Lucrezia! Suor Spinetta! Open up!'

Lucrezia looked out of the upstairs window and down upon the capped head of the procurator of Santa Margherita, the father of Brigida's child.

'Go away!' she shouted.

He stood back and looked up at her with his disarming smile, the smile which endured no matter what, the smile he graced upon the world until the world submitted to him. 'The abbess has sent me. You are invited to join the convent for the Feast. She says you are not safe here on your own.'

'Go away! We receive no man here!'

'Open up and let me in,' he said, almost laughing now.

But Lucrezia resisted and rained insults down on his guilty head so that all Prato heard of his crimes. The procurator's smile faded like a flower in frost. He thundered on the door and threatened to get the civic guard to break it down.

Then it began, a distant clamour, a beating of sticks on metal and the ululations of women. The procurator looked stricken, frozen in a rictus of anger as, up the lane of the dyers, came the women of the district – weavers, lacemakers and embroiderers – led by Rosaria and banging wooden spoons on copper pans, crying *Lupo! Lupo! Lupo!*

The procurator, spitting at them venomously, yet backed away until he turned to flee in terror.

After the Nativity, which Lucrezia and Spinetta spent alone, Don Diamante returned from his spiritual fast at Vallombrosa. He was surprised when he opened the door to Filippo's house to be received by two harpies. He was feeling guilty about the letter to Filippo he had found where he had left it on the table in his cell at the small Benedictine house he was now living in – slightly guilty, nothing in proportion to the reception he received from Lucrezia and Spinetta who, flailing blindly at him, were blaming him for every ill in the world.

63

'WHY APRIL?' FILIPPO GRUMBLED AS HE DABBED AT THE panel with a rag. 'I mean, what's the significance of April? What does it have to do with the Magi? It's not Epiphany, nor the Nativity. Why consecrate the chapel in April? It's not even Easter – that was last week.'

'There's to be a visit,' said Alessandro, watching his master gilding the fine rays emanating from God in his picture of the Adoration. 'The new pope is coming to Florence.'

'Aeneas Sylvius Piccolomini? Coming here? How is it I don't know that?'

'And Galeazzo Maria Sforza, the son of the Duke of Milan.'

'Coming here?'

'And also Sigismondo Malatesta, the Lord of Rimini.'

'All of them, coming here at the same time? Why doesn't anyone tell me anything?'

'We do, but you forget.'

'I wouldn't forget that! What are those three rogues converging on Florence for? God, what days we live in. A corrupt manipulator for pope, the son of a usurper, a wife-killing lord. And all of them coming here to be received with pomp and ceremony no doubt.'

'There's going to be a joust, wild animal hunts in the streets, a dance, processions, a banquet in Cosimo's house.' Alessandro's eyes filled with dreams of the entertainments to come. He'd heard wild lions were going to be let loose.

'So what are they coming for?'

'The pope is on his way to Mantua, to mount a crusade against the Turks, and Galeazzo Sforza has come to meet him here and escort him the rest of the way. Malatesta is coming to see the pope and get a ruling on a proposed settlement between Rimini and Naples.'

'Sounds like they all want to unite Italy.'

'That's what Ficino says. He says that's what's really going on.'

'A united Italy? Florence, Milan, Venice and Naples are already in alliance; if Rome and Rimini were to join them, that's just about one nation. Yes, I see, that will be Cosimo's intention. I doubt if he's much interested in a crusade.'

'Ficino regards it as folly.'

'Does he indeed?' Filippo sat back and thought about his patron. Cosimo was merely the leading citizen of Florence and held no office. He lived like its lord but he had no real power, other than to make sure that those in government were his supporters. But here he was, privately inviting the pope along with dukes and princes to visit his house. There was to be a banquet, yes, that was what Alessandro had said, and no doubt it would be at the banquet that Cosimo would say to his guests, come and see my chapel. He, after all, was the only man in all Christendom to have a private chapel and that one thing alone would impress his guests more than any jewel or statue he might show off. Yes, he would invite them to his private chapel, perhaps even to Mass. No wonder the old man wanted his altarpiece finished! Why couldn't he have said so? All he had said when Filippo had missed the deadline of Epiphany was, 'Damn and blast you to hell!' He'd said nothing about April. The walls were blank; there was nothing in the chapel to admire but ceiling and floor. Of course he must have his altarpiece!

Here he was, painting the softest, sweetest Virgin and Child he had ever done, and converging on Florence were three of the most powerful, wicked men of Italy to pay homage at the feet of this babe. Always symbolic, Cosimo, always symbolic. Filippo sighed appreciatively. 'Come then, let's get on and get finished. We have to remind some rogues of God.'

'Ficino told me that no man is incapable of change.'

'Ficino tells you quite a lot.'

'I like to spend time with him. He thinks in images. His words paint pictures in my mind.'

Filippo remembered that he wanted to spend more time with the philosopher himself, but there was always something in the way. He took another tissue of gold leaf from his apprentice, laid it on the panel and began to dab it down with the rag. 'I still can't see why this event has been planned for April. I mean, it could be May or the 35th of June for all the significance April has.'

'No. Costello told me that on that date, with the Sun in Taurus, Venus will be conjunct Mercury in the eighth house.'

'Who's Costello?'

'Cosimo's astrologer.'

'Oh.'

'Costello says –'

'Don't listen to the astrologers, boy – you'll burn in hell.'

'That the moon will be in Capricorn trine the Sun,' muttered Alessandro.

'Trine? Jesus, Mary and Joseph.'

'Do you want to know the significance of April or not?'

'Planets are lining up all the time. Presumably with three such busy men, it was the only date that could be arranged.'

'Ficino says,' and here Alessandro came close so that he could whisper into his master's ear, 'that the eighth house is the house of initiation and secret alliances.'

Filippo turned abruptly. 'Ficino said that to a boy of fifteen years? A mere apprentice boy? You've been eavesdropping!'

Alessandro coloured hotly and denied it.

Filippo could play the friar when he needed to and he stared at his apprentice so penetratingly that Alessandro's knees began to knock. 'Lorenzo told me,' the youth confessed at last. 'He was hiding under the table when the astrologers met with his grandfather.'

Although he tried to cover it with a harsh, sarcastic laugh, the disappointment was clear on Filippo's face. He felt left out. Here he was, painting a picture before which the most powerful men in Italy were to kneel in a few weeks' time, which for all he knew may have been intended as a magical talisman, and no one had bothered to inform him about it or tell him why. He was left to discover it himself from his apprentice! His mood grew so foul that he left work for the day.

He walked along beside the Arno, wishing it were the River Bisenzio and that there were mountains on the far bank rather than the squalid district of Santo Spirito. He wondered how everyone was back at home. The day before the Medici riders had come for him, he had been painting in his workshop, dimly aware of scuffling noises on the stairs. A tug on his habit and he had looked down to see Filippino, who had crawled all the way downstairs on his own. Torn between remonstrating with his wife for neglecting the child and sharing the child's joy, he chose the latter and shouted for her to come down and see this miracle for herself. Mother and father sat on the floor with their son while Filippino, gurgling to amuse them and sucking his thumb, stood on his own two feet within the stabilising embrace of his mother's arms. Slowly he detached himself and walked unsteadily to his father. It was only two steps, but they were his first, made in a trailing gown of scarlet brocade edged with a gold border. His parents gazed at him as if he were the only child ever to have walked. Filippino fell back on his bottom and grinned at his father.

'Oh!' said Filippo.

'Oh!' said Filippino, aware of the momentousness of the occasion.

'You're an angel,' said Filippo, reaching out to hold his son's face in his hands.

Now he sat down on the banks of the Arno in utter dejection. He had not intended to stay away from work for long, or to indulge any vice, but such was his mood of separation and melancholy that there was only one cure, and, still struggling inwardly, he got up and made his way to the nearest tavern.

✠

It was on the Feast of Candlemas that Lucrezia, looking out of the window over the piazza, noticed a party of riders accompanying a lady arriving at the house of the archpriest, Carlo de' Medici. She turned to the bed but Spinetta, having been up all night with Filippino, who was teething, was now asleep with her arms around her nephew. Lucrezia did not like to disturb them and turned back to the window. Although they wore no colours and had nothing to distinguish them, she knew instinctively that the riders were Florentines. She watched fascinated as, joined by the archpriest, the head of this small train turned her horse and approached Fra Filippo's house. If Lucrezia thought for a moment that they were not bound for her house, the thought was dispelled when rider and companion looked up and gazed at her, framed as she was by the window.

She went quickly downstairs to open the door before there was any knocking to disturb Spinetta. She found herself face to face with a noblewoman of the Tornabuoni family, the archpriest's sister-in-law, Monna Lucrezia de' Medici.

'May I come in?' Monna Lucrezia asked, making it clear that she wanted to see Lucrezia alone. Archpriest Carlo, looking slightly put out, bowed and left.

Lucrezia's words tripped over each other as she apologised for the state of the house.

'It is difficult to tend to something when you are in misery,' Monna Lucrezia said.

Lucrezia's heart plummeted at the thought that she was about to get a severe lecture about the rewards of immorality. She led her upstairs to the sala and dusted a chair for her. Monna Lucrezia told her not to make a fuss and sat down. They stared at each other in silence for a while then Monna Lucrezia began to speak.

'Fra Filippo has been kept in Florence far longer than he wanted or intended. My father-in-law is a great man, but he is also a greedy man, like any other, and he keeps Fra Filippo like a prisoner, as if locking up genius is going to get a painting out of him. Cosimo knows about you, of course, but he disregards you, as he disregarded his own mistresses in his day, such as Carlo's mother. He is a good man, Cosimo: see how Carlo has prospered. But where is Carlo's mother? Men, my dear, can be blind. I thought I should come myself to see how you are faring.'

Lucrezia stared at the elder woman, in wonder at her kindness.

'I've brought some capon for you, biscuits, marzipan and cheeses. Presumably you are unable to go out?'

'Madonna –'

'I shall be dining with Carlo later and shall tell him to take care of you. You can trust him. Have you been troubled at all?'

'A little, but the tavern keeper's wife has been of great assistance.'

With her hooded, penetrating eyes, Monna Lucrezia gazed at the young woman who shared her name. 'Life would be very much easier in the convent,' she suggested.

'It would not!' Lucrezia spat out, then hastily apologised.

Monna Lucrezia drew the story out of her, of how the abbess had treated the nuns.

'We were punished for being who we were, for past sins, for the sins of our fathers.' Lucrezia was ready to go on at length about the cruelty and injustice she and her sister had suffered but suddenly it seemed peevish of her to rehearse old arguments with this attentive lady. Such attention required the truth. 'I'm a whore, a Magdalene, a fallen woman, and yet here in my house, with my husband, I feel more pure and chaste than I did in the convent. In the convent my heart was of pitch and my thoughts burned like acid. There was no love in me. Here, I know love; I love and I am loved.'

Monna Lucrezia held out her hand to her.

'Tell me then,' Lucrezia continued, grasping it. 'Please tell me. What is virtue? Filippo told me that you are the most virtuous woman he has ever met, so you must know.'

Monna Lucrezia smiled mournfully. 'My husband, Piero, is an invalid. I have to do all his work but he never thanks me, only criticises and finds fault. Whenever I tell him about something beautiful, he looks at me sourly as if I have no idea what pain he is suffering. Sometimes I wish… I wish… Sometimes I say to God, take him, take him now. What virtue is that, to wish your husband dead? You love your Filippo; I have only ever done my duty to my Piero. I love my sons. I love my father-in-law. I love my daughters. My husband I do not love. Where is the virtue in that? Well!' She held up her hand to stop Lucrezia saying anything. 'There is some, even I can see it. All I can tell you, my dear, is that goodness comes from the heart, not from the mind, it has no forethought and no afterthought: it is a simple action done for the sake of another. Goodness is not rightness, it knows and needs no law, it does not follow custom and it pays no heed to what the neighbours say. There is only one witness of the Good and that is God. All this is true within this house. Outside, we have to obey the laws. You would be better off in the convent.'

Madonna Lucrezia had a way of being firm that left no one feeling chastised. Lucrezia smiled at her. 'May I ask, were your husband to die before you returned home, would you mourn him?'

'I would be inconsolable.'

✝

It was three days before Filippo returned to the casa Medici, three days sleeping on floors, three nights lurching through the streets and crooning under balconies, by which time Cosimo was apoplectic. He had been using Lippi as an exercise in the virtue of patience since Epiphany; now, suddenly, he had failed. His stoicism had collapsed into a squirming heap of maggoty anxiety. What would he do if his guests arrived and there was nothing to show them in the chapel?

When he heard that Filippo had at last staggered back into the old house, Cosimo had himself carried to the workroom in his chair, where he found Filippo gilding rays of divine light with the total concentration of a Donatello.

'Where have you been?' Cosimo thundered from his elevated chair carried on the shoulders of servants. Wielding his stick as Jove his thunderbolt, he raged at the painter, called him a pimp, a whoremonger, a scaly-backed insect who thought of no one but himself. 'And you're fat!' Cosimo cried in conclusion, as if this were the worst crime of all. 'Look at you! Was there ever a man less in command of himself than you? You waddle about in the habit of a friar, a disgrace to your order. Eating, sleeping, drinking and screwing – that's all you ever think about. And every now and again, you paint something to pay for it all. Whatever possessed me to commission you? I could have had Veneziano, or del Castagno, or Piero della Francesca, any of a dozen painters as good as you, if not better.'

'So, why didn't you?' shouted Filippo.

Cosimo snorted. The deeper his rage, the greater the pain in his joints and he writhed in his chair. 'Take me away!' he ordered his servants. 'And you – you stay here until you are finished! Alessandro – come with me.'

Alessandro, who had retreated to a corner where he was quivering like a trapped animal, fled out of the door.

Once outside, Cosimo commanded that the door be locked. Alessandro watched the handle rattling and listened to the frantic calls of his master from within.

'You can't – he has a horror of being locked in, since he was in prison. Please, he will go mad!'

'Let him go mad. What do I care, so long as my painting is finished? As soon as it is finished, he can come out. DO YOU HEAR ME?' Cosimo shouted at the door. 'FINISH IT, IF YOU WANT TO EAT!'

'WHERE AM I SUPPOSED TO PISS AND CRAP?' Filippo shouted back.

'See he has everything he needs,' Cosimo snapped at a servant, 'apart from food. Now take me away.'

Cosimo's rope-veined hand, knobbly at the twisted joints, grasped Alessandro's sleeve as they went. 'Come, boy. Come and see my chapel and the designs Benozzo is making for the walls. BENOZZO IS DOING THE WALLS BECAUSE HE IS THE BETTER PAINTER!' he shouted, for Filippo's benefit.

'*Aaaargh!*' cried the friar within.

64

FILIPPO CONTINUED TO RATTLE THE HANDLE IN GROWING desperation but though the door was new, the wood was old, hard and unrelenting. All he had to do to get out was to finish the painting, but somehow this simple truth escaped him. He went to the window and looked down to the street below. '*Aiuto! Aiuto me!* I've been locked in by Cosimo de' Medici!' he cried to anyone who might listen. Invariably shoulders were shrugged and hands raised, as if to say, 'What can I do about it?' Mostly, the passing bankers and merchants just laughed.

It was far too high to jump. Filippo prowled the room snarling like a beast in a menagerie. Bars and locks there might be, but nothing would tame him. He waited behind the door for when the servant came with a chamber-pot but, when the servant did come, that bright young man threw the door back against the wall, pinning the friar and winding him.

'For the sake of God, have mercy! I am a man of the cloth,' cried Filippo.

The servant laughed as he retreated, closed the door and locked it again.

Filippo lifted his gown and, holding it back with his hands on his hips, pissed in the pot and none too accurately. As he pissed, he looked at his bed and got an idea.

He worked diligently until nightfall, tearing the fine linen into strips he could knot together. As soon as it was dark and the city quiet, he tied his makeshift rope to a leg of the bed and fed the length of it out of the window. It had seemed an easy plan but, looking down on his linen rope, and imagining lowering himself to the ground, it all seemed fraught with danger. What if the material slipped through his hands? He drew it back in and put some more knots in it so that he would not rush down its length and scorch the skin off his palms. And then, how to get from the window to the outside wall? He knelt and prayed for angelic help.

Encouraged by this, he made his move, climbed on to the windowsill, turned to face into the room and, not looking down, stooped and groped for his length of linen. Finding it, he gripped it and, with his eyes fixed on the projecting eave of the house, he began to walk down the wall. The 'walk' became a bounce, which was quite enjoyable and, although he landed in the street puffing, sweating and feeling his age, he felt free and not a little exhilarated.

He could not get out of the city with the gates closed for the night, so where to go? The Carmine was out of the question: it would be the first place Cosimo would look. But the district of Santo Spirito – that Filippo knew well, and all its taverns, including one that stayed open after curfew: the Lion Rampant. He went down an alley close to the church of Santo Spirito, found the door he sought and tapped out a secret code of knocks. The door opened a little. Recognised, Fra Filippo was admitted.

In the tavern, lit only by firelight, he saw the scarred and villainous faces that had inhabited this place since he was a youth. Every night these carpenters, joiners and wood-turners drank their wages here – had done so since they were young and would do so until they died. Indeed, to die at table in the Lion Rampant was considered a good death, much to be desired, better by far than plague or pestilence, murder, disease or old age. A man who keeled over in the Lion Rampant would go to hell with a tipsy grin on his face.

These were men of the Santo Spirito quarter. Some of them had never ventured outside of the ward, let alone out of the city. Although they recognised Fra Filippo at once, they did not show it. In leaving the Carmine and Santo Spirito for Somewhere Else he had offended them. This made him, in their judgement, disloyal and self-seeking. These men were dedicated to their evenings in the Lion Rampant spent grumbling about their lot and the boredom of life. Anyone who sought to better himself was a rat and a deserter. So when Fra Filippo entered for the first time in twenty years, he was greeted with beady-eyed silence. To the taverner, however, all customers were welcome. 'Fra Filippo! It's been a long time. What can I get you?'

'I haven't any money. Who will give alms to a friar?'

'I need to make things good with God,' said the taverner, sinking a jug in an open barrel of new wine and bringing it out dripping.

Fra Filippo drank from the jug. 'Oh, God,' he muttered, feeling the rough liquid burning its passage through him. 'Thank you.'

He looked about him. There were men playing dice at the shadowy trestles, others sitting round the fire, some were snoozing, one was picking out a melancholy air on an ill-tuned and ancient lute. No one spared him a glance. It was time for a story.

'I've just escaped from the casa de' Medici,' he told the taverner, loud enough for all to hear. 'I was locked in a room in the old house by Cosimo for no crime at all. He just wanted a painting finished. I'm a painter, as no doubt you'll remember. There was a bed in the room. I ripped up the sheets to make a rope and let myself out of the window.'

Now he had everyone's attention, not least that of a frame-maker who had been a friend at the beginning of Fra Filippo's career. All the cheap panels of the Virgin and Child he had produced for sale in the market when he was a youth had been framed by Stoldo di Simone, but when Filippo's clientele improved, he had taken his custom to the fancy carpenters with workshops along the Arno. Stoldo di Simone had never forgiven him, not so much for having stopped using him as for not being man enough to explain why to his face.

'Come on, Filippo,' he said now. 'There must have been more of a reason than that.'

'None! You know what the Medici are like. Tyrants in all but name. Did you know that the pope is coming to Florence next month just to consecrate their private chapel?' Filippo bit his lip. Sometimes, he thought, one has to exaggerate the truth just to get attention.

The men rustled at the news like a forest catching fire.

'That's ridiculous! Even Cosimo isn't that important,' said a carver.

'We tried to see the Medici off two years ago,' grumbled Stoldo. 'Piero di Ricci – remember him? The poet? – he inspired the contadini to rise up. They were starving, man, starving, and what did the Medici do? Made a fortune out of the rise in grain prices, that's what they did. Usurers the lot of them, *lombardi!* Don't care what pretty name they put to it, commission or compensation or call-it-what-you-will. Usury it is in the eyes of God if not his diabolical Church.'

Fra Filippo was taken aback by Stoldo's vehemence.

'And then that business with the Parlamento last year. Everyone ordered to go unarmed to the Piazza and what happens when we get there? Some notary comes out of the Palazzo della Signoria and mumbles something three times. Well, we all had work to get back to. Of course we agreed. What to, we didn't know. Now we know. A lifetime of being sat on by the Medici. So, Cosimo wants you to finish a painting, eh? But you've escaped. Is he desperate? He sounds desperate.' Stoldo flipped a coin at the taverner and nodded towards the friar's empty jug. 'Why is he desperate?'

'It's an altarpiece for his chapel. He wants it done before the pope comes.'

'How much have you got left to do?'

'It'll take about two weeks probably,' Filippo shrugged. 'But I don't care whether he has it on time or not. I will not be driven! I'm not a pack-horse or a donkey. I'm the best painter in Tuscany and he treats me like an ass.' Fra Filippo eyed Stoldo cautiously, wondering about the man's curiosity and hoping it wasn't leading to an enquiry about who was making the frame. But Stoldo said nothing about frames, only plied Filippo with more wine.

'I haven't eaten,' said Filippo.

'Best not to when you're angry. Loosen up a little and then you can eat.'

Filippo had taken two gulps from the third jug when the room began to swim. He was aware of hitting his chin on the table as he dropped from his stool, of the taste of blood where he bit his tongue. But not much else. Not until early the following day when he awoke in a pigsty and found that, once again, he was locked in.

Meanwhile Stoldo di Simone was negotiating with the Medici bank the price they were willing to pay for information on the friar's whereabouts.

65

AS FILIPPO WAS AWAKENING TO A BREAKFAST OF SWILL, Cosimo was being carried into the empty room to be shown what the servants had found. He looked at the knotted rope of sheets which they had drawn back into the room. He looked at the near-finished painting on the easel. On this his eye stayed for a long while, then he ordered the servants to leave him and lock the door after them.

The servants protested, asked him to repeat the order.

'I said lock the door! Let me be locked in until Fra Filippo is returned!'

Uneasily, the servants did as they were bidden, left the room and locked the door behind them.

Cosimo stared at the painting. His eye now roved, now lingered on the Madonna, on the dark cave in the centre approached by rock-hewn steps, on the dark forest and the many felled trees. He saw himself as just such a tree, cut down because of his pride, and there he was, depicted as a stump, with an axe buried in him. And what was that on the axe? Why, it bore the name of Fra Filippo on its handle. He, Cosimo de' Medici, had been felled by Filippo Lippi of all men!

He smiled wryly. This of course was not the painter's reasoning when he made his picture. The tree stump symbolized the painter, not the patron. And yet his name was on the axe. So what was the painter saying – that he was the cause of his own downfall? No. Cosimo looked again, and now read the axe as the blade of reason, brought down on that sack of animal appetites, the body. Why, Filippo Lippi was turning into a philosopher! He wished Filippo were here, now, to discuss it.

And then his eye went to the Christ Child, the newborn divinity we may discover in the depths of the dark forest of our soul. Just lying there, adored by his mother and two saints. John the Baptist, yes, and who was that monk or friar? Saint Romauld, the founder of the Camaldolese order – for this, he knew, was the forest of Camaldoli and those tree-felling hermits – or was it Saint Bernard of Clairvaux? Saint Bernard's letters were full of axes and fellings. Had Filippo read Saint Bernard? He wished he were here, now, to ask him.

He spent the rest of the day trying to fathom how something so exquisite, so divine, could come from the hand of a man so selfish, so greedy, so lazy and so *fat*. These were two worlds he could not reconcile, the sacred and the profane, both in one man. But then what was he, himself, if not the same? He might have better command of himself, but he was far from innocent. It was Fra Filippo's misfortune that his sins were so visible, whereas Cosimo's were hidden under layers of pretence. Every act of generosity on his part – what was it in truth but his attempt to buy something: love from his fellow men, forgiveness from God. That he did not eat and drink like Fra Filippo was only because it aggravated his gout. It was pain, not self-discipline, that kept him moderate. And as for the sin of lust, he had Carlo and his Circassian handsomeness to remind him of that; and it had hardly been confined to one slave. All the other acts of adultery he had committed had not had issue and remained undiscovered. And yet, after the affair with the slave, he had promised his wife he would always be faithful.

The sloth of the friar – that, too, was his own. Forever busy with his affairs, with making yet more money, fixing the government to avoid taxes, weaving ever-more complicated webs of dependence throughout Italy and beyond so that barely any man of standing could move without his consent – all this activity was a form of sloth for it prevented him fulfilling his promise to Gemistos Plethon to re-found the Platonic Academy. He had been tardy in that matter of the soul, always putting his own safety and security – and wealth – first.

The portrait of the Virgin glowed. He followed her gaze to the Child. Betrayed. He betrayed Christ with his every thought and deed. Bitten by guilt and taut now with contrition, Cosimo wept. Silent tears made their way down the lines and creases of his cheeks. He glanced up again and looked at the painting through a welter of tears so that the Virgin and Child seemed to swim in his consciousness; more, they seemed to live, to live and to breathe. As the figures breathed, so Cosimo's own breath stopped, or at least became very shallow, so that his chest did not move with his breathing. He was hovering at a threshold. On one side mundane life, which he not only believed in but ruled absolutely; on the other, the Kingdom of Heaven, to which he paid lip service. And now, here it was, and he was in it, this numinous reality that is divine. A fat tear rolled slowly down his face, joined another at his chin and fell on his hands, hands that, he suddenly realized, were clasped at his breast. In this attitude of prayer, he rested his eyes on the sweet, unbearably pure Virgin.

This was a work of genius. *Of* genius or *by* genius? Was that fat old reprobate actually responsible for this work, or was he a puppet of angels? If that were the case, what right did he, Cosimo, have to dictate terms of how the painting should be done and by when? He wondered at his own temerity. *Forgive me, Lord,* he prayed.

Although the main figures were painted, there was much background detail yet to be done. Fra Filippo was neat with his equipment. Everything was washed and in its right place, brushes upright in a jug, rags washed and folded, powdered pigments in jars, grinding slabs clean. Filippo had been gilding when he had interrupted him – yes, interrupted – and the only things on the table were a dish of red bole and a dish of yellow bole and some feathery tissues of gold leaf held down by a stone. Cosimo picked up the burnisher and rubbed one of the lines of divine radiance issuing from God the Father. The gold came off. He gasped like a naughty boy and tried to stick it back down with his finger, but only made things worse.

He wanted to *feel* paint. He wanted to mix a pigment, break an egg-yolk into a dish and add powders to make astonishing colours. He wanted to load a brush and feel it move down the smooth gesso surface, the fine plaster taking the colour. But he dared not. No. Everything was all too clean and tidy. Strange, that, in a man like Filippo Lippi. And then, just for a moment, he was in the heart of Filippo Lippi and knew that his skill was his god, to whom he was deeply devoted and for whom he would suffer anything.

At a knock on the door, Cosimo turned and bade whoever it was to enter. When the servants came in with trays bearing food, he sent them away, saying he would not eat until Fra Filippo was found.

'Someone, a frame-maker of Santo Spirito, knows where he is but wants a gold florin for the information,' said his secretary, entering behind the servants.

'One gold florin? Is that all? Well, give it to him.'

'Your son Giovanni has the man in the Bargello and on the rack.'

'We don't do things that way!' Cosimo shouted. 'Give him the florin and be done with it!'

✝

Fra Filippo was released from the pigsty and brought back to the palazzo. Although the friar was the smellier and more begrimed, both men were unwashed and stubbled and regarded each other as if looking in a mirror.

'I apologise,' said Cosimo before Fra Filippo could speak. 'I should not have locked you in. A genius is a celestial form, not a beast of burden.'

'No, I apologise, Cosimo. You have a great event planned for April, and you want your altarpiece finished. That's very understandable. If only you had told – '

'Let's not discuss it any more. Look at us. Two prodigal sons!'

'I've certainly been eating with the swine. I hear you haven't been eating at all. Impressive, as always.'

'You don't understand me. You will never understand me while you persist in seeing me as your superior. See me as your brother and your friend, Filippo. That, by the way,' he said, pointing at the panel and indicating the hidden geometry of the composition, 'is a wonky heptagon.'

'It isn't a heptagon. You rejected that idea, remember? You said it had come to me too easily. It's a spiral.'

'Oh? Explain it to me.'

Filippo showed Cosimo the compositional idea that gave the painting its arrangement and structure, how the cave in the centre was the human heart, how love may spiral outwards and, through the saints, through the Incarnation and the Mother, reach back to where it began, in God.

'This is the greatest painting I've ever looked upon. A work of genius.'

A smile played over Filippo's face. 'You wait until you see it finished.'

'Do I have that long on earth?'

'It'll be done by the end of the month.'

✝

In early April, Cosimo stood in front of the completed altarpiece in silence. Finally he breathed out a word: *Perfect*. Then he added, 'almost'.

66

GALEAZZO MARIA SFORZA ARRIVED IN THE CITY ON A white horse with crimson trappings. Dressed in blue and gold brocade under a tunic of red velvet, this fifteen-year-old boy rode at the head of a great procession of Milanese retainers and soldiers. The Florentines watched in suspicious silence as the riders made their way, first to the Palazzo della Signoria and, later, to the Palazzo de' Medici. The boy's father had wrested control of Milan from the Visconti by none too subtle means and the Sforza had yet to prove themselves to the wary Tuscans. Milanese fanfares masked the silence of the host city.

The blare of trumpets and the clinking of armour drew Fra Filippo and his apprentice to the window of the old house to see what was happening at the new. From the Duomo to the palazzo, the Via Larga was lined with the Company of the Magi, solemn in their white robes and hoods as the gorgeous parade approached to enter through the main gate.

'More than we have on our palette,' Filippo said of the colours. 'So much more. How could we depict that? I've been trying for years to get the dyers of Prato to tell me how they make their dyes. Half the time they say it's a secret; the other half, that it's the same pigments we use. But cloth takes colour so much better than panels or plaster. I could *eat* those colours.'

Alessandro looked down at his own rough tunic of undyed wool. 'Master, as a painter, am I condemned to wear brown all the time?'

Filippo's nose wrinkled. He had spent his life in black and white. 'When you make your fortune you can go about dressed as you wish.'

'Domenico Veneziano, Andrea del Castagno, Piero della Francesca – you only ever see them in drab woollens.'

'Well, they're working all the time.'

'Why does everybody hate Sforza so much?'

'They don't hate him, just despise the baseness of his birth. They prefer to be ruled by men who can trace their family back to great kings or even gods. They say the Sforza took Milan by force, forgetting that the Visconti were originally mercenary soldiers themselves. But when Filippo Maria Visconti died the Visconti had been in power over two hundred years and people's memory grows fuzzy after a couple of generations. They think Visconti was a noble and the natural ruler whereas his son-in-law, Francesco Sforza, was born of a peasant in the woods. It may be true. It was almost certainly true of Visconti in the beginning. Give it time and they will forget about Sforza's origins. Look at that boy down there: every inch the son of a duke, wouldn't you say?'

Alessandro looked down on the boy of his own age who rode a horse as if he had been born a prince: Galeazzo Maria Sforza passed through the gate into the palazzo.

'Cosimo is canny. Cosimo is so canny. He backed Francesco Sforza when he made his bid for Milan. Four years later, and with Sforza's support, Cosimo was the architect of a league that is now keeping all Italy at peace. No one previously had achieved an alliance of three states but the Peace of Lodi established a treaty between Milan, Florence and Naples, and Venice has joined since. It's a wonder of our age. He is so canny.'

With the last of the foot soldiers disappearing into the palazzo, they withdrew their heads with a sigh and returned to work, designing a lunette Cosimo wanted over the door to his apartment.

✝

The following day, the pope arrived in the city and, far from paying the Medici homage, went directly to his lodgings at Santa Maria Novella. Two messages came from him to Cosimo. One said that his only purpose in visiting Florence was to discuss a crusade against the Turks. The other, that he didn't feel he was being received with sufficient pomp and splendour.

The two painters, hearing a tempest in the new palazzo, kept to their quarters in the old house, concentrating as well as they could on their work whilst such a din was going on in the city. They went to the windows again when Sigismondo Pandolfo Malatesta, the Lord of Rimini, arrived at the palazzo in another glorious procession of sparkling, jewel-encrusted costumes and trappings. Considered to be the finest condottiere of Italy, Malatesta's reputation was such that often armies coming out to meet him laid down their weapons without a fight. His conduct *a casa* was little different from that on the battlefield. After the death of two wives in strange circumstances, one after the other, he had recently married his mistress and legitimised the brood of bastards he had had by her.

Malatesta's deportment and striking looks, his long, straight nose and thin-lipped mouth, exquisite in profile, attracted Filippo's gaze. 'I can't imagine him inside the same house as Sforza,' he mused. 'Since the Peace of Lodi, Rimini has been at odds with the rest of the country. I've also heard that the pope condemned Malatesta to hell in a public ceremony before Saint Peter's.' He watched until the last of the procession, with its retainers and mules, dogs and falcons, had disappeared inside the palazzo.

'Is Aeneas Sylvius Piccolomini a good pope?' Alessandro asked.

Filippo looked at his apprentice warily. He himself had grown up at a time when there had been *two* popes, and in the city that supported the one known by the rest of Christendom as the *anti*-pope, John XXIII. It was because of this pope that, as a child, Filippo had heard words such as 'sodomy', 'rape' and 'incest' for the first time. Never forgetting the jarring horror of that waking up to the world-as-it-is, he had sought ever after to protect young boys from the truth, the truth of popes, of cardinals and bishops, of hypocrites. 'It depends what you mean by "good",' he said cautiously.

Alessandro shrugged. 'I've heard bad things about him.'

Filippo realized that Alessandro's childhood would have coincided with the remarkable reign of Nicholas V. But Callistus III, who had succeeded the saintly Nicholas, had been cast in the common mould of popes, and so was this one, Pope Pius II. As Aeneas Sylvius Piccolomini, he had written erotic romances such as *The Tale of Two Lovers*. 'My kind of man,' thought Filippo, 'but not my kind of pope.'

'I certainly don't like what we're hearing about him now, flouncing around like a Caesar.' It was publicly known that the pope had no intention of meeting Cosimo de' Medici. A counter-rumour, issuing from the Medici bank, was that Cosimo was unwell and unable to meet anyone.

'The old man must be in a very spasm of fury,' said Filippo.

'I've heard he's quite sanguine and looking very cheerful.'

'Who says so?'

'Lorenzo.'

'Hmmmph. Yes, I can imagine young Lorenzo coming out with a word like "sanguine".'

The design for a lunette wasn't going well. The stream of inspiration had dried up and he felt desiccated. 'I'm thirsty,' he told Alessandro, 'I'm going out.'

He went to a tavern near the Bargello frequented by stationers. He had developed a morbid fear of drinking with artisans of the lower sort: at least stationers had pretensions. Because they sold materials to lawyers, they comported themselves like lawyers and had temperate evenings in taverns discussing business and politics. One virtue of this was that Filippo never felt like staying overlong, but on this day he stayed well into the night, for the thirst, which was the thirst for inspiration, would not be assuaged, no matter how much he drank. He never understood how one day he could be a genius and the next a fat old friar, but it happened too often.

At the ninth bell he was evicted from the tavern, the last to leave, and he had to hire a lantern-bearer not only to light his way but also to lend him a stable arm. As they came out of the street opposite the new palazzo on the Via Larga, where torches burning in high sconces illuminated the facade and the street below, they saw several men, swathed in capes, being admitted through the low door in the gate. Filippo frowned. They were not robbers, clearly. So who were these night visitors? He crossed to the old house, gained admittance and went up the stairs to his room. By the time he was in bed he'd forgotten the incident.

He awoke before dawn with a feeling he knew something, but the more wakeful he became, the less he knew anything. His head throbbed and for once he thought he would like to go to church. This odd thought he put down to simple procrastination: he would rather pray than stare at blank paper. The Annunciation he was trying to design in a half-moon shape – just the thought of it turned his brain to straw. Yes, the cleansing sound of psalms and prayers at dawn would be most desirable. He opened a window, sending up a flap of pigeons, shuddered in the cold draught and closed it again. The morning was murky and ideas of going to San Lorenzo evaporated.

Since the new Medici house had a private chapel, he thought he might as well use it. No one else would be in it at this hour and he could recite the psalms and prayers himself. He padded through the corridors that joined the two houses and found his way to that windowless chamber in the centre of the new house. It was so early that there were not even servants about.

Although the chapel was not yet consecrated, it already seemed imbued with spiritual presence. In the womb-darkness the light of a single, large altar candle flickered on the gold of the coffered ceiling and the frame of his painting that, itself, glowed from reflected light. The walls, still awaiting their frescoes, were hung with rich tapestries.

Standing before the altarpiece, Filippo began to chant the prayer, *Ad sanctitatis tuae pedes, dulcissima Virgo Maria.* He couldn't help noticing how beautiful his painting was in the mellow, still light of the candle flame.

Remember, most loving Virgin Mary,
never was it heard
that anyone who turned to you for help
was left unaided.

As Cosimo had done, he wondered how he could have produced such a thing. It was always the same: an immense amount of grinding effort, the wheels of invention turning without lubrication, and then at last something emerging to which he could lay no claim.

Inspired by this confidence,
though burdened by my sins,
I run to your protection
for you are my mother.

Was it really like that? Those numinous moments of inspiration – did they really have their source in long hours digging for gold in hard rock? He thought back to Camaldoli. Somehow, just being away from his easel, a long ride through the mountains, the taste of vegetables fresh pulled from the earth, a little bit of woodland clearance and tree-stumping, and there she was, that vision of loveliness, the Virgin in Adoration.

Mother of the Word of God,
do not despise my words of pleading
but be merciful ...

Yes, it was clear now, what he needed was time away to refresh himself.

The door opened and suddenly the chapel was filled with voices, several of them expressing surprise or enquiring, 'Who is that?'

Filippo jumped to his feet in embarrassment. He peered at the men entering, trying to discern faces behind the candles they were carrying. 'I'm sorry,' he began to splutter before quickly pulling himself together. 'I always like to pray before I start a day's work,' he explained.

'Rubbish!' The voice was Cosimo's, as was the following chuckle. 'Well, it can be no accident that you are here, so you might as well stay.'

Filippo stood back as the men entered the chapel. He recognised Cosimo and his sons Giovanni and Piero easily enough, and Lorenzo and little Giuliano. He recognised Sigismondo Malatesta by the beauty of his profile and Galeazzo Maria Sforza by his youth. Others were obviously retainers of these lords. But there was another man, short, elderly, whom Filippo did not recognise. This man stood back whilst everyone else arranged themselves, and then he entered the small sacristy to the right of the altar. Filippo looked about at the rest of the congregation and saw Marsilio Ficino; the golden threads in his hair were catching the candlelight. He squeezed and squirmed through the press of men until he stood by his side.

Ficino looked up at him with bright eyes. 'Good. I hoped you'd been invited.'

'I wasn't invited, not by a mortal man. The Virgin herself drew me here.' Filippo gazed upon his altarpiece and crossed himself.

There was whispering amongst the men while they waited, and an altar boy went about quietly lighting more candles.

'So, master philosopher,' said the friar, 'can you explain to me what is going on?'

'It is time for a change,' Ficino said.

Sensing that was all he was going to get – and who but a philosopher could make such an enigmatic pronouncement? – Filippo went to take a seat by the left wall and towards the back.

It was warm and close but these were clean and perfumed men, the scent of musk and ambergris pleasant. The odour of wealth. The only thing in the room that smelled unpleasant was himself – a pungent mixture of night-sweat, linseed oil and garlic. If only he had known, he would have changed into a fresh habit. In his paint-spattered and oil-dribbled working tunic, he shrank into the shadows at the back.

As a small choir behind the altar began to sing the Kyrie, the door to the sacristy opened. The elderly man who appeared dressed in a cope of cloth-of-gold could only be one person. The rubies, emeralds and gold thread of his triple tiara shone in the candlelight. Standing in front of the altar, Pope Pius II – he who had publicly announced that he had no intention of meeting Cosimo de' Medici – raised his arms to bless the assembly and begin the consecration of the chapel.

Three men stepped forward to kneel on the marble step before the altar: Galeazzo Maria Sforza, Sigismondo Malatesta and old Cosimo himself, who was helped to kneel on a soft cushion. The candle flames danced in a draught, although no door had opened, and particles of light swam in the air as if every mote of dust had become reflective. The source of light was surely the candles, but by some optical trick it seemed to be the ceiling. Fra Filippo looked up. In the shadowy recess of the deep coffering was the IHS symbol in an image of the sun. He became caught by it. As the pope intoned homilies and prayers, the mysterious Christ-light increased as if in a room full of mirrors. Suddenly the pope stopped speaking. Fra Filippo turned and saw him standing there with his mouth open, caught in the space between two words. No one else seemed to notice, except for Malatesta, whose raised face was wet with tears.

Fra Filippo suddenly felt very small, as small and young as the baby on the forest floor of his painting. He felt his mother pick him up and hold him in the light that was beaming down in rays. If Fra Filippo painted divinity that way, as golden rays, it was because it was conventional and he had not yet thought of what else to do, but for a moment, the briefest glance of a moment, he saw those very rays, slender lines of gold, coming from the ceiling to fall on the bowed heads below. He realized that, far from being a pictorial convention, the radiance of God was reality, was what joined heaven to earth, giving life, like rods of gilded rain. The pope had reached his next word, but he seemed a long way away. Filippo was suspended on the threshold between the divine and the mundane and, in that moment, which had a taste of eternity, he knew his own innocence. The light burned up his sins and turned them to ash.

At the end of the Mass the men present seemed unwilling to open their eyes and rise up. A fraternal silence lay on the room, a warm peace. But it was broken, as it had to be, and people began to move towards the door. Most of the congregation were now leaving, including young Lorenzo and his brother. As Lorenzo passed, Filippo caught his eye and, in that gaze, saw that the boy had had a similar experience, some vision of his own.

'This is a magical place,' Filippo said, but his words sounded trite even to himself and Lorenzo just nodded and passed by.

A magical place. The chamber of a magus. Thinking he was alone again in the chapel, Filippo stood in the middle of the disc of porphyry, no longer concerned about the number of circles round its circumference and how it had been done. His mind was quiet. He went down on his knees before his own painting on the altar and prayed in thanksgiving to the God who informed his work. Call it *ingegno*, or inspiration, or what you will. 'And this,' said an angel in his ear, 'is your true essence.'

At least, that is how he thought about it, as an angel, but then he wondered if that subtle voice wasn't his own, the voice of conscience, yes, but his own. And then he felt as two in one, the holy and the profane, all in one. He looked at the axe he had painted, buried in the stump of a fallen tree, and understood its symbolism for the first time. The floor gleamed and glimmered in the candlelight, a geometric labyrinth to the heart. He gazed at his painting, saw its softness and beauty and thought, 'my own'.

The chapel embraced him, closed out the world, its troubles and temptations. The holy of holies, that was what it was, this chapel of the Medici, the chapel of the Magi. And the Incarnate Lord was within Filippo himself, that was what the Platonists had to teach the Christians.

In a banderole on the marble step before the altar an inscription had been engraved and the letters painted red: *The gifts of the Kings, the prayer of the celestial beings, the mind of the Virgin, these are the only things in the chancel. Do not set foot here, O profane crowd.* Fra Filippo stepped over it, approached the altar, leaned forwards and kissed the Virgin.

He stepped back hurriedly as the sacristy door opened. To hide his embarrassment, he ducked down into the shadows. The pope returned to the chapel, accompanied by Giovanni de' Medici, Galeazzo Maria Sforza and Malatesta. Together these men sat down and discussed the peace terms of a treaty that would never be proclaimed – a secret peace, an alliance of all the great states of Italy – made in secret so that no side should ever lose face. Filippo tried to remember what Alessandro had told him, something about some planets being in the house of initiation and secret alliances. So subtle was this negotiation that Filippo fell soundly asleep. Later, when men said that the pope had come to Florence but had never met Cosimo and had left in disgust, he always said, 'I dreamed it was otherwise.'

67

WHILE LIONS ROARED IN THE PIAZZE, WHILE KNIGHTS jousted, while maids danced at the Mercato Nuovo and young men engaged in hunting the deer let loose in the streets of Florence, Filippo returned to work on designing the Annunciation to go over the door to Cosimo's suite of chambers. He worked alone, for his apprentice was drawn to the entertainments as iron to a lodestone. The solutions came easily. He spent entire days sketching and re-sketching the figure of the Angel Gabriel to the merry tinklings and clashes of tambourines and pipes. People passed up and down in the street below like the ebb and flow of the sea.

When Alessandro returned, to tell him breathlessly about the hunt, and how the wild animals were being goaded by a man who walked about in a ball, Filippo had the lad strike poses for him.

'Right knee on the floor, left knee up, now lean forwards as if you were holding out a stem of lilies. What do you mean, walking in a ball?'

'A kind of wickerwork cage, spherical, and as the man walks or runs, the ball runs with him. He was so nimble! And he ran all over the Piazza della Signoria, roaring and spitting at the animals. There are deer, bear, wolves and lions all over the city.'

'What? That doesn't sound too safe.'

'Oh, well, for every animal there are a dozen valiant knights out hunting them. Most people are staying on their balconies. But one child did drop from a washing pole on to a lion. The lion saved him, really, gave him a soft landing, and before the beast could toss the child in the air like a mouse and devour him, it was shot with a dozen arrows.'

Filippo glanced up and noted the exhilaration on Alessandro's face. He tried to catch that look of wonder in his sketch. 'Poor beast,' he muttered.

'They are wild, Master! If we don't kill them, they eat us.'

'Only when goaded.'

That night there was a great banquet in the garden of the Palazzo de' Medici. All day long there had been deliveries to the courtyard of great quantities of food, piles of quail, a cart-load of hogs' heads, another of swans with their broken necks flopping over the sides of the cart, deer and wild pigs caught in the urban hunt. All day the smells of roasting meet wafted throughout both the new and the old houses and made Filippo's stomach rumble as he brought the Angel Gabriel to perfection.

'Are we invited to the feast?' Alessandro asked, his own stomach gurgling.

'Of course not.'

'It's a great pity, after all this, that the pope never came.'

'Isn't it?'

'Apparently Cosimo has been too ill.'

'Yes, apparently so.'

'That must be terrible, to go to all this trouble and expense and then not be able to attend your own banquet.'

'Alessandro,' Filippo took some coins from his purse. 'For God's sake, go and buy us both some roast pigeon from the market. And some marzipan cakes. We'll have our own banquet.'

That night they dined in their room while the lords and their ladies enjoyed a feast in the great sala of the new house. There was the sound of much activity in the street below and guttering lights threw vast shadows about the room. 'So tell me,' said Filippo, 'what is going on?'

Alessandro went to the window. 'They are lighting the street with torches and covering the ground with sand.'

'For what reason?'

'Wait and see,' said Alessandro smugly.

Around midnight, when Filippo's chin was rising and falling on his chest, and his nose was clicking as he breathed in his sleep, trumpets blared. He was up at once and in shock. Alessandro was already at the window. 'Come and see,' he said.

Filippo joined him and leaned out. From the direction of San Marco was coming a procession of boy-soldiery, an *armeggeria*, with drummers setting the pace, ten boys on horseback following and, bringing up the rear, a lord of the same age gloriously arrayed.

Alessandro's friend, Lorenzo, here played the part of a lord of such magnificence that both painters looked down on the scene and hardly breathed. On a white horse decorated with trappings of crimson and gold, Lorenzo sat dressed in cloth-of-gold over crimson hose, with golden spurs and stirrups. On his head was a blue velvet mazzocchio adorned with flakes of silver and three gold feathers standing erect. Straight-backed and regal, this grandson of a banker rode with great dignity, holding a banner showing a falcon caught in a net. Florentines came out on to their balconies in their nightshirts to see this midnight prince.

His lungs now thoroughly starved, Filippo inhaled deeply, remembering the boy Lorenzo in the chapel, just a week earlier, with his transfigured gaze.

'It's a great man,' he said, 'whose inner world is as deep as the outer one is broad.'

✝

Over the following week, on the gesso panel Alessandro had scraped until it looked and felt like ivory, Filippo drew his vanishing point and lines of perspective, then the lines of the loggia on the right, with its central pillar and low parapet, and the lines of the garden walls and its trees on the left. Using a piece of charcoal tied to a stick, and standing back from the panel, with a swirl of confidence Filippo drew the figure of the Virgin, seated, one hand on her lap, the other clutching her cloak to her breast. Even though he kept a feather in the other hand for quick erasure, he barely used it. The lines came of themselves. On the left, the Angel Gabriel kneeling, raising one hand to point at her tentatively. At the centre of the top, the hand of God sending down the Holy Spirit to the Virgin's womb. Even in mere outline, the loveliness of the design was apparent and Cosimo, on a visit to Filippo's room to view it, approved.

Filippo knew what he wanted to do, but still he could not. That would be a step too far, to paint his Lucrezia as the Virgin, even though her identity with that figure was now so bonded in his mind. No, a step too far. Holy figures cannot be real people. But when it came to painting the panel, if he did not paint the likeness of his wife, he painted her inner quality of gentleness and, yes, despite everything, her *purity*. That downward gaze was Lucrezia's as she watched Filippino in his cradle. And the Angel

Gabriel, although a youth in human terms, was yet Filippo's infant son.

Alessandro stood amazed. 'The way he looks at her! The way he looks at her!'

'What do you see?'

The angel was in a garden, the Virgin in a loggia: nature and civilisation separated but united by the heads of the two figures that, at the same level, were both haloed by a disc of gold, not in perspective. (The painting was becoming a hymn in loving memory of his friend, Fra Giovanni.) The angel, whose great wings swept down the curve of the panel, was so awestruck by the woman, he could only look at her with diffidence from under a lowered brow.

Alessandro pulled on his lip. 'Marsilio Ficino says that men are greater than angels in that we have the power to move, to descend to the depths or rise to the height of God himself. This angel knows that. He is cowed by Mary's holiness.'

'I'm glad he knows that because I didn't. Cowed?'

'He's a servant that dare not enter, who waits with the sweetness of humility. That's it, the sweetness of humility. This is the most beautiful Annunciation ever painted.'

Fra Filippo swelled with the praise of his apprentice, although he was disappointed that Alessandro had not interpreted the figure correctly, but then, why should he? He was only fifteen, and no one had ever before depicted the Angel Gabriel as the *soul* of Mary.

'But the hands, they have fingers like sausages.'

Fra Filippo's face puckered. 'What?'

'Hands. You have trouble with hands, Maestro.' Alessandro faltered, regretting what he had said but unable to take it back. 'It's obvious. Er...'

'I was just about to offer you an area to paint yourself but now I've changed my mind.'

'Oh, please!' Alessandro clasped his own hands together in earnest supplication. 'Maestro, I beg you!'

411

'Very well. Which part, hmm? Tree trunks, I think, and the sandy path.'

'Maestro, please, I will do them, but please let me do the flowers. I want to show you what I've learnt from you. I've been drawing from nature. Please.'

Filippo relented and allowed his apprentice to draw the flowers in the grass that the angel knelt upon. He was impressed. They were as good as anything he could do himself. Alessandro was not to be treated as a workhorse like Diamante. Filippo allowed him to paint the single stem of lilies held by the angel, and those in the stone urn on the low wall separating Gabriel from Mary.

Cosimo had left Fra Filippo alone while he painted the lunette. There were no locked doors, no restrictions of any kind. The instructions for the commission had been brief: a scene of the Annunciation to go above the door to his chambers. After the initial approval, Cosimo forbore even visiting the painter in his room, but waited until the panel was in place before he had himself carried to see it. As the workmen laboured to raise the panel, a solemn bell at San Marco began to toll, followed by one at San Lorenzo and then at the campanile of the Duomo, at Santissima Annunziata, at Santa Croce. Half wondering who had died, Filippo was directing the workmen who were securing the lunette above the door when Cosimo arrived in his chair and demanded the panel be brought down. 'I can't see it up there!'

Filippo, standing by as the grumbling workmen brought the heavy panel down again, swallowed nervously, waiting for the old man to shout 'No! No! NO!'

'Bring it here, closer!' Cosimo beckoned with a distorted finger. The panel was brought near so that his old eyes could see it properly. He stared at it for a great deal of time, studying everything, the figures, the background, the details. At last he leaned back and turned to look at the painter. 'The angel – made of the same substance as the Virgin, but living in a different realm.'

Filippo remembered why he loved this man.

Cosimo told the men to put it back up in its place within the lunette arch above the door. 'Have you heard the news?' he asked Filippo. 'The archbishop is dead – have you heard? We've lost him, Filippo, the only man who knew how to make us better.'

Filippo frowned. While what Cosimo said was true, he could not suppress the tide of relief he was feeling. Cosimo, seeing his expression, roared with laughter. 'Let's dance!' he said, and for a moment it seemed possible, that both could lay down the sick weight of the body and dance like angels.

'Look at this miracle!' said Cosimo, pointing to the lunette. 'I want you to do the walls of the chapel! I'll pay off Benozzo – he won't mind. When can you start?'

'I cannot. I must return to Prato to finish at Santo Stefano.'

Cosimo growled, unused to not getting his way. 'I'll make it good with them somehow.'

But it wasn't just duty calling Filippo back to Prato. 'No, I must go,' he said firmly.

'Not before you've done another lunette for me. I have just the door in mind. Come, I'll show you. It won't take you long – you've learnt now, how to paint at a speed most men would consider normal. Come, Filippo, humour me. I haven't long in this world.'

'I should get back to Prato,' said Filippo weakly.

'Carlo will make it well with the Ceppo and the provost.'

And my wife? Filippo wondered.

The following day he began work on a scene of saints.

68

JOHN THE BAPTIST FLANKED BY COSMAS AND DAMIAN and with Saints Francis, Lawrence, Anthony Abbot and Peter Martyr: Filippo arranged the group of saints, not standing woodenly, but sitting in a variety of attitudes and postures on a stone bench in what was the same garden as that of the Annunciation. Nature and civilisation again, harmonised by divinity.

As he painted, he wondered. Cosimo had adopted Saint Cosmas as his own saint for obvious reasons, but why Damian? Cosmas and Damian were brothers, but were they inseparable? He asked Cosimo one evening when he and Benozzo de Lese, at Cosimo's invitation, dined at the villa at Careggi where the Medici family were spending the summer. They dined alone with Cosimo in his chamber overlooking the garden. Benozzo dominated the conversation with his enthusiasm for his project on the chapel walls, speaking at length about the symbolism of the Magi and their importance to the Medici, who were all members of the Company of the Magi. He spoke of his designs for the chancel of the chapel, how he was going to fill it with angels singing *Gloria in excelsis Deo.* When he finally bowed his bald head over his food and ate something, Filippo changed the subject.

'Why Damian?' he asked Cosimo. 'I can understand the significance of all these saints for you, but not Damian, except that he was the brother of Cosmas. In Fra Giovanni's great altarpiece in San Marco, Damian has his back to us. Why is that?'

Cosimo was discomfited. He preferred conversations, especially those at table, always to be about someone or something other than himself. He cleared his throat, hesitant to reply, but then spoke.

'I was born a twin.'

Filippo was embarrassed to have caused Cosimo embarrassment, but Cosimo, having made his mind up to speak, continued more firmly. 'We were baptised Cosimo and Damiano, after the saints, for the saints were doctors, and we were Medici, and we were twins. My father took it as a blessing from heaven. But my brother died in infancy.'

Fra Filippo did not know what to say.

'Do you miss him?' asked Benozzo promptly and easily.

'I so often feel as if I'm only half myself,' Cosimo admitted, and fell into conversation with Benozzo about the soul. Filippo concentrated on his food.

✝

With the family away for the summer, the painters and artisans had the palazzo to themselves. Benozzo worked in the stifling chapel, Filippo in his airy workroom, and they took pains to avoid each other.

Having transferred the design to the panel, Filippo painted the figures of the lunette himself, beginning with John the Baptist, youthful, handsome, only his unruly hair signifying his time in the wilderness.

Alessandro watched with dismay as Filippo painted the saint's raised right hand. He did not dare upset his master again and, besides, it was not his place as an apprentice to criticise him and suggest he could do something better himself. But he could! He could draw hands, he could draw feet. He had studied Fra Giovanni's work at San Marco and he had drawn limbs from life as often as he could. Who was he loyal to, the genius of Filippo Lippi or his own? He took a deep breath. 'Maestro? Could I paint the hands of Saint Damian?'

'Certainly not,' said Filippo, immediately turning to paint them himself.

Alessandro could not bear to see what he was doing. He fell on his knees and pleaded with him. 'Please! Let me do Saint Cosmas! Please!'

Filippo snorted and handed him the brush. 'Go on then, show me how it's done.'

Alessandro got up, loaded the brush with pigment and painted the saint's raised hands, making them fine, delicately boned, the little finger of the right hand slightly crooked, which added an elegance worthy of Fra Giovanni.

Fra Filippo sniffed once or twice. 'Very good,' he said at last, and reluctantly. He allowed his apprentice to paint the hands of

415

Saint Lawrence, also, and took himself off for a walk. Since he had gained his freedom in the casa de' Medici and was not locked up or watched over, he rarely strayed from the house. Having developed a reluctance to visit taverns, he spent most evenings continuing with his work, making sketches by candlelight. Now his short walk was leading him no farther than the chapel in the new palazzo. After the knocks he had received from his apprentice, he needed to make himself feel better about his talents, and a quick look at what Benozzo was painting should do the job nicely. Carpenters, stone carvers and decorators, at work in certain rooms, were filling the palazzo with dust and the smell of new wood.

The chapel was empty. Benozzo and his team, who had to work in the small, square room that was so dark, straining their eyes to paint by the light of flickering lamps, had gone off for one of their frequent breaks. Frequent breaks, yet just two months after they had begun in July, the project was more than half finished. That in itself was a wonder Fra Filippo had not anticipated; that Benozzo could paint at all in such gloom made him grudgingly appreciative. By the light of lamps and candles he studied the great crowd of figures following the magus Caspar, looking for a likeness of himself but finding none; he had been left out of this Medici entourage led by, of all people, Piero de' Medici – the invalid here vaulted to the head of the family – closely followed by Galeazzo Maria Sforza, Sigismondo Malatesta and Archbishop Antonino on his mule with the trappings of golden bosses.

Behind these princes came a host of the Medici family, friends and relations. Benozzo had included his own image, putting himself behind portraits of the boys, Lorenzo and Giuliano, and, in his hubris, beside a portrait of Gemistos Plethon! To Plethon's right was a boy, his eyes upturned, which Filippo presumed to be a portrait of Ficino in his youth. There was much symbolism in this painting, and most of it was lost on Filippo, but to him Benozzo's message was clear with regard to himself: the fellow in the red cap with his name embroidered usefully in gold was saying, 'Here I am in the very heart of the Medici universe.'

He had come here to compare himself to a man of lesser ability and to gloat but, perhaps in some residual power in the chapel, he remembered that envy was a weed he needed to pluck out of the garden of his soul. The portraits, he admitted reluctantly, were excellent, the details of costume, of animals, trappings, foliage – exquisite, if a little over-copious. The joins of the *giornate* were nearly invisible. True, Benozzo had 'borrowed' almost every detail from Gentile da Fabriano, whose *Adoration of the Magi* was in Santa Trinità, and had made some mistakes with scale here and there, but who would not working in such haste and in these conditions?

Filippo turned to the chancel, where scenes of angels had been completed, even to the gilding of their halos. In a room this dark there could not be enough gilding. The angels rained from heaven to an earthly paradise of rose gardens, singing a Gregorian chant, with two conducting angels touching the joints of their hands to give the right sequence of notes. A painting you could hear through the eyes! Now, that was novel.

He noted that Benozzo's halos were all flat-on – he could not do circles in perspective and had no angels in full or three-quarter profile. Filippo's pride in his own accomplishment swelled – why had Benozzo not studied his altarpiece? – but seeing this vice billowing in his soul, he dispelled it. What were halos in perspective but sheer cleverness? Fra Giovanni had been right: halos in perspective implied physical objects rather than divine fire.

Filippo steadied himself to look beyond technical feats to see the beauty, and when he did see it, he was overcome by it. Standing back in the chapel, on the porphyry disc, he viewed his painting of the Adoration against its new setting and, taken with the self-same wave of redemption that had happened at the consecration, he fell to his knees with his head bowed. He resolved to be kinder to Benozzo in word and deed from now on,

417

for were they not brothers-in-art, both recipients of that *ingegno* from on high?

But from this lofty state, Fra Filippo began to plunge. If he could not criticise his rival, well then, he must criticise himself. Coming back to his feet, he turned in the chapel feeling small, insignificant, fat and faulty compared to these sublime figures. The floor of marble, porphyry and serpentine was rich in symbolism of the Trinity. He envied Cosimo his piety and felt its lack in himself. He turned and kept turning, as he once had done under a new moon in an Ifriqiyan garden, for in turning he could spin off the demons that were now tormenting his soul. He would be pure! He would be clean! Unlike the first experience, however, this time he grew giddy, stumbled and fell. He lay on the cold floor looking up at the coffered ceiling, so beautiful. He sighed in wretchedness at his poverty, his hopelessness, his sin. Perhaps this was what chapels were for, to make a man face himself. Tears began to run out of the corners of his eyes and down his temples. He looked again at the wall paintings. Something was missing. He propped himself up on his elbows. Yes, something was definitely missing. Benozzo had trained with Fra Giovanni. He had all the skills and was very clever. But there was no holiness here. The chapel walls dripped symbolism but lacked that numinous something that illuminated his altarpiece, painted in that state of transcendence when Fra Filippo disappeared and was just a brush in the hand of God. Benozzo was only ever Benozzo. And those halos – they glittered in the candlelight like a display of the gold plate of King Croesus.

Filippo sat up. There was a time when he could sit on a floor and hug his knees. Now his belly got in the way. He must diet. Even as he thought this, he was assailed by hunger and desire. There seemed to be no choice: he must go in search of food. Only with some bread, cheese and cold meat inside him, would he feel better. But he remained seated on the floor, weathering the storm, his eyes fixed on the portrait of the Virgin which was a portrait of his wife.

His wife. What sins had he, a friar, committed to satisfy his appetites? His soul was in jeopardy. There was so much wrong that needed to be put right. He sat on the cold stone floor and stared.

✝

When he went back to his room he found Alessandro finishing off a pair of exquisite hands among the saints.

'I think,' Filippo began cautiously. Had to be cautious, because he had never said such a thing to anyone else before. 'I think you have real talent.'

Alessandro, used only to having his confidence destroyed by his master's criticisms, looked at him wide-eyed and suspiciously.

'I think we should make adjustments to the chapel altarpiece.' Fra Filippo was always making improvements to his work, redrawing, repainting, always thinking of better ways to do something, but usually once a piece was framed and installed, that was it, the end. Alessandro followed Fra Filippo to the chapel, bearing the box of paints and brushes. Filippo rearranged the lamps and altar candles. 'Hope it's enough to see by.'

'For what?'

'Do her hands, Sandro. Repaint the Virgin's hands. Here, I'll hold a lamp for you. And when we're done, let's go home to Prato for the Feast of the Assumption. Cosimo is still away and will not miss us.'

69

TEN MONTHS SINCE THEY HAD PARTED, LUCREZIA WAS reunited with Filippo. She looked on him as on a stranger, for she had grown apart in her heart. She relied utterly on Diamante who, for all his faults, had proved trustworthy, tending to all their needs, locking them up at night, leaving his scent around the lair so that no one bothered them.

She was cold when Filippo banged open the door of the house, shouting her name. She did not come from her room.

'Wife? Wife! Where are you? Come and greet your husband, back from the war. Battle-scarred but triumphant. And very rich with spoils. Wife? Lucrezia?'

Slowly she came from her chamber, pasty white and drawn. Filippino was hiding in terror within her skirts and peeping out from the folds at this friar who seemed to possess his mother.

'This complete stranger is your father, Filippino,' Lucrezia said.

'I have presents,' said Filippo lamely.

✝

He went to the showing with Diamante and Alessandro. Two days had passed and he still felt locked out from his wife. Together they went to the piazza that was quickly filling with the pious. The abbess was shouting at the pilgrims crowding the piazza before Santo Stefano, pressing forwards in their eagerness to see the Holy Girdle.

'Have you no respect? Get back! Get back! You vulgar mob! This is the belt of the Holy Virgin herself! Show due reverence!'

Trumpets sounded as the bishop entered the pulpit, and censers swung. Even though there was no space but that occupied by others, the crowd surged forward. The bishop held up his hands to still them so that he might begin prayers and the pilgrims held their hands together in front of their faces but kept one eye open to see the belt as soon as it was displayed. When the provost handed the relic to the bishop, the crowd erupted.

'Holy Mother of God!' cried the abbess among them, her arms held in adoration of the relic. 'We adore you!'

The bishop held it up, draped over his hands, the green woollen girdle that had once encircled the hips of the Virgin Mary. Bells were ringing and choirs singing, on earth as in heaven. Fra Filippo, at the back of the piazza, was imagining the ascension, the circles of the starry heavens, the image of God mitred like a bishop. He was never satisfied with that image and could hear

Cosimo decrying it, but how else could you picture the scene? Disembodied hands were equally unsatisfactory. Perhaps the Moslems were right – any attempt to portray God is a form of blasphemy. As the bell ringing ended with the single tolls of Santo Stefano and the Holy Girdle was taken from view, the crowd began to draw back like the sea and to disperse, some claiming they'd seen the Virgin herself, the lame testing their legs for miracles.

Fra Filippo remained where he was, eyes closed, his brow creased with concentration, wondering what God really looked like. When he came back to himself, there was only a remnant of the crowd left. The rest had followed drummers and pipers to other piazzas for dancing and feasting, but those who remained were gathered at the base of the pulpit, bent over and around something. Porters were running from the hospital with a litter. Fra Filippo ambled over to the church to see who had been trampled and found it was the abbess lying on the ground, twitching and jerking in convulsions, her eyes rolling.

'She couldn't get herself heard,' cried her sister. 'No one listens to her.'

'Do you blame them?' asked Fra Filippo. He leaned over the thrashing abbess.

As her eyes took him in, the abbess's look of pain increased a hundred-fold. She flailed at him.

'Please,' said Suor Jacopa, drawing Filippo away. 'Don't torment her.'

'What was I doing?' Filippo protested.

'Your presence is enough to torture her. Leave us.'

Fra Filippo was about to stump off, mumbling with irritation, when suddenly he was moved to turn and go to the pulpit, where Provost Inghirami was standing, staring down at the scene below as they were trying to lift the heavy abbess on to the stretcher. He was still holding the relic that the bishop had given to him to wrap and put away. 'May I?' Filippo called to him, holding out his arms.

Without a second thought the provost dropped the Holy Girdle. It floated down to Filippo. Stooping, Filippo took one of

421

the abbess's waving hands and folded it over the relic. The abbess became still. Now both hands clutched the belt of green wool to her breast, and her eyes closed with an expression of joy.

No one realized she had died, not for a while. It was Fra Filippo who checked her breathing then prised her hands open to release the relic. Suor Jacopa stared at him, not sure – she would never be sure – whether he had just killed her sister or saved her soul.

✢

When Fra Filippo told his household about the events on the piazza, he was surprised by the varied reactions, ranging from the *good riddance!* spat out by Fra Diamante to copious weeping from Spinetta. Lucrezia said nothing but stared down at Filippino as if there were nothing else in the world she was interested in. Alessandro sat gazing at Spinetta, the tears in his own eyes reflecting those in hers. Alessandro's eyes, always busy studying the play of light on a fingernail or the spirals of his own curling hair, were distracted whenever Spinetta was in the room. He watched her avidly and if Filippo or Diamante suggested that the root of his fascination lay not in drawing, he coloured and denied it. Spinetta was a problem, thought Filippo. She needed to be married. Marriage alone would cure her of her misery, her lassitude, her inability to be interested in anything apart from her nephew. But it was impossible. Ex-nun for sale – slightly spoiled – bargain wife. Alessandro would never forgive him.

✢

At Michaelmas the entire council of the city met to decide what to do about Fra Filippo Lippi and to establish whether he ever intended to finish his work at Santo Stefano. It was, after all, three years since he had promised to complete the cycle in two. A committee was formed to reach a new agreement with the friar. Twenty-five florins would be allocated for the completion of the work and anything else owed to him would be paid in grain.

'*Grain?*'

'And if you do not complete by the stated time, you will be fined.'

'*Fined?*'

'And one more thing, Frate,' said the head of the committee. 'You will stop living in sin. We have been very patient with you, and we've believed everything you've said about Abbess Bartolommea; but the abbess is no longer with us and her sister runs a better house. Lucrezia, Spinetta and the rest must return to the convent.'

With the gradual thawing of Lucrezia, he had learnt what had happened in his absence. He had already resolved that, should he need to leave again, the women must go back to the convent, but only temporarily. 'I don't know anything about the others,' he said.

'You aided their absconding – you must aid their return. Use this coming winter for the profit of your soul.' The man pushed a contract towards the friar, who sat with his hands firmly up his sleeves. 'Frate?'

'You ask too much. My private life is my affair.'

'Sign and complete the work. Don't sign and leave the city tomorrow. Which is it to be?'

'Does Cosimo know about this?'

'Cosimo de' Medici may be the Lord of Florence, or even the Lord of all Christendom. He is not the Lord of Prato. We welcome his suggestions, but in the matter of Santo Stefano it has all gone on far too long. We want the chapel completed. The window is finished and will be installed shortly. We want completion – all scaffolding gone, the floor swept, the church given back to the people again. But those bottom tiers remain to be done. Just bare plaster, after all these years!'

'They won't take long. The designs are finished.'

'How long?'

'End of next summer – it can't be any sooner than that.'

The man leaned across the table. 'Just sign, Filippo. All that will happen is that peace will be restored to your house. You can still see the young women when you're at the convent.'

'And my son?'

'Find a new family for him.'

Filippo took his right hand out of his sleeve and took up the quill being pushed towards him. One little signature – it was not so much – and when did he ever abide by a contract? He scratched his name in a fine Lombardic script with no intention of parting from his wife and son.

✝

During Advent, 1459, the new committee, keen to fulfil their brief to the letter, visited the friar's house to see if he had abided by their agreement regarding the nuns. Placing his finger to his lips to tell them to be quiet, Filippo opened a door to a small chamber in which the *buonomini* caught a glimpse of Lucrezia and Spinetta kneeling in prayer in their habits before a crucifix. The men were impressed.

'But they are not back in the convent yet,' observed one as Filippo closed the door on this tableau of piety.

'Suor Jacopa insists that all the nuns return together at the same time, and I have not found them all yet.'

'How long will it take?'

Filippo shrugged. 'How can I say?'

'There will be no more money from us until they are returned.'

Once the men had gone, Lucrezia and Spinetta erupted from the chamber like furies. They had been warned of this visit, and rehearsed in what to do, but they had not realized the reason behind it all until they'd overheard the conversation between Filippo and the *buonomini*.

'You're sending us back!' Lucrezia wailed.

'No! I'm not! I'll think of a way!'

'There is no way!' Lucrezia fell to her knees and knelt there, swaying and moaning.

Filippo knelt beside her. 'What can we do? What can we do?' He tried to embrace her but she pushed him away violently.

424

'And what will you do with Filippino?' she snarled, as if Filippo and the Ceppo were one in their intention.

'They say he should be given to a new family.'

Lucrezia howled like a dying wolf.

'I think it may be for the best, my darling,' he cried in desperation. 'If we don't comply of our own volition, they will send me away and will force you back into the convent. It's a better place now, believe me, under Suor Jacopa.'

Lucrezia howled. One word came up from the bowels of her. *Filippino!*

70

AS WHEN A SHADY TREE HAS BEEN FELLED AND DORMANT flowers come to life, so did Suor Jacopa blossom in the absence of her sister. Her gentleness was no longer to be mistaken for lack of character. She had reopened the convent, taken in three novice nuns and had been elevated to the role of abbess. Wrapped in his mantle against the winter cold, Fra Filippo went to see her.

'I've agreed that Lucrezia and Spinetta need to return.' He sounded so matter-of-fact, as if he were rearranging the furniture. 'It's not right that they live in my house. Reputations are being sullied.' Where Abbess Bartolommea would have bristled and told him to suffer the consequences of his actions – perhaps now he would learn to think before he acted – Abbess Jacopa welcomed the suggestion. 'I've been praying that this might happen. It's the only happy outcome.'

Fra Filippo lost his business-like air and simply nodded, head down and not meeting her eye. 'Will you take the boy, also? It's not customary, I know, but I could not bear for him to go to a new family or to the foundling hospital, and it would kill his mother to be parted from him. She would lose her wits.'

'It wouldn't be without precedent. He can have eight mothers and be thoroughly spoiled.'

Fra Filippo looked up with hope in his face. 'I wouldn't want that. Let him be useful as soon as he is old enough, and I will pay for his education and keep. At the age of seven or eight I want him back to work with me as my assistant.'

'So young!'

'I'm getting old, Mother, and I have much to impart to him.' Fra Filippo blinked suddenly, remembering that Abu Ali had once told him that he would impart everything to one disciple, whom he would recognise at the time. Without doubt that had proved to be Alessandro. And yet, it was his will and expectation that his son Filippino be raised to be a painter. So he would have to impart everything to him, too. He tried to push to the back of his mind a niggling worry that this was somehow against the subtle teacher-pupil contract he had made with his Moorish master.

'That won't leave much time for his general education,' said Abbess Jacopa.

'Teach him what you can as soon as you can in the letters and numbers.'

'And the faith?'

Fra Filippo caught her fleeting smile and returned it. 'That, too, of course.'

She leaned forward and placed her hand on top of his. 'God judges us by our hearts, not our knowledge of scripture. We'll raise him a good boy.'

Fra Filippo slid to his knees and catching both her hands in his, bowed his head over them. 'Bless me, Mother, for I have sinned.'

'I've met your son.'

'How?'

'This time last year, when you were away in Florence, I called at the house. At first she wouldn't let me in, but once I'd convinced her that I came as a friend, and not as my sister's minion, she opened the door. What a little bundle of good fortune

Filippino is. Adorable! Without your sin, the world would be a poorer place. There, that's a thought, isn't it? Don't tell anyone I said so. And I have to say that I was considerably disturbed by the condition of Lucrezia and Spinetta, who appeared to have been abandoned.'

'No! I couldn't help it. How can I help it? I am forever being pulled hither and thither to do this and that. Mother, believe me, I do the best I can by everybody!' Filippo rocked back and forth on his knees, his large eyes filled with grief. 'If I'm giving them up it's because there's no alternative.'

'Now rise up. What is there to weep over? You're still chaplain here, although we never see you. I hope once our nuns are back, you'll be a daily visitor again.'

Fra Filippo laboured to his feet, caught the abbess by the face and kissed her on the lips. Her cheeks immediately became rosy. 'You're everything an abbess should be,' he said.

'And you're everything a friar should not be. Now then, what about the others? I was told to expect them all to return. Indeed, I can't take Lucrezia and Spinetta unless they all come back together.'

She knew! She and the Ceppo were working together, arranging his life for him behind his back! He left angrily, went home and sent Diamante round the city to find out what had happened to Brigida, Piera and Simonna. To his relief, his assistant reported that each of them was happy to return to the convent. Simonna had been ill-used, treated as a free nurse for her sister's children; Piera was miserable at being cooped up in a house; Brigida had a genuine preference for conventual life rather than be Rosaria's unpaid servant, especially now that Abbess Bartolommea was no longer in charge and she would be able to take her daughter with her: each of the women readily agreed to return. The date set was two days before the Nativity of Our Lord. The last to be told were Lucrezia and Spinetta.

'No!' Lucrezia's knees buckled and she sank to the floor. She clasped Filippino to her. 'No!'

427

'It's my wish and my will and I'll have no arguments. You're all going back.'

Filippino, squirming free, ran in circles, screaming.

'My son!' Lucrezia took the child up again and embraced him fiercely. When Fra Filippo told her she could take Filippino with her to the convent, her wails became hiccoughing sobs and then quietened.

'You'll renew your vows at Christmas and cast off the shame of these past few years,' he said, keeping his distance like a cold and tyrannical husband. When she did not respond with obedience, he dropped the play-acting. 'Lucrezia,' he implored her. 'It's better this way, you know it. I'll be there, too, as chaplain, when I'm not at the walls of Santo Stefano. But I must be at the walls. This project is going on far too long and I need to concentrate. Do you understand, Lucrezia? I don't do this because I no longer love you; I do it because I love you too much. Do you believe me?'

She smiled wanly. 'I never believe anything you say.'

Filippino, who had wriggled free once more from his mother's grasp, now stood holding his nose and refusing to breathe. He collapsed suddenly on the floor. Lucrezia, used to this trick, stooped down and tickled his feet. Filippino kicked back into life, simultaneously laughing and shouting in annoyance.

'Of course I'm not abandoning you,' said Filippo, one eye on his histrionic child who was so utterly distracting. 'Who could do such a thing? This is for the best. It makes everything right.'

'And our marriage. Is that to be dissolved?'

'Lucrezia, that was a private ceremony between us and God. It was never legal. I shall always abide by the vows I made to you, believe me.'

'I never believe you.'

'That,' he said, 'will always pain me.'

'Just as you never believe me,' she continued, her body jiggling with the effort of keeping hold of her writhing son.

'In what respect?'

428

'You're convinced, now that I shall have Filippino with me, that I'll be content to return to Santa Margherita. You're wrong. You have no idea how much I love you.'

'Papà!' Filippino called and, wresting himself free yet again, ran to his father. Neither parent had seen him run before, but the magic of the moment was crushed by the sorrow of parting and of what was being said. Suddenly tears bubbled up and spilled over Filippo's face. 'Without you, I'm nothing. This separation will be the death of me. But what choice do we have? We must trust, just trust in the Madonna. She'll look after us, the Holy Mother.'

✝

Piera, Simonna and Brigida arrived at the house in the morning. Realising that the nuns were about to return to the convent, Alessandro threw his arms round Spinetta's neck. He wept. He howled. He shouted. He clung. He was not embarrassed. Why should he be embarrassed? He was a young Italian in love. This was the stuff of sonnets. Having heard of her impending return to the convent, Spinetta had become frozen. Now she thawed rapidly in Alessandro's embraces and clung to him just as strongly. They had to pull them apart to get Spinetta to leave the house. Alessandro ran after her. He was incoherent in his tears but seemed to be asking her why she couldn't die – it would be so much easier. If she were dead, he could lay on her tomb until he himself died. But locked in a convent? He seemed to think it equivalent to being walled-up alive.

The neighbours came out to see what the fuss was about. At first they bristled, thinking that the authorities were acting. They were about to free the nuns when Fra Filippo raised his arms and called on them to stop: this was a decision, he told them, that his family had made together. The neighbours stood back as the women, dressed in their habits and veils, walked past in a sad, slow procession, leaving Alessandro sobbing in Fra Diamante's arms.

Fra Filippo escorted the women to the convent and held the iron gate open for them. They went in like a small family of ducks, one after the other. Filippino, carried by his mother, was looking over her shoulder at his father. When Filippo shut the gate after the nuns, Filippino's eyes went wide with horror, as if he understood what was happening.

'Papà!' he called. '*Papà!*'

But the gate was between them now and Filippo, who kept a key, turned the lock with a clang. As he walked back up the lane, he heard the sound of his son screaming inside the convent.

✝

Over that winter, Filippo tried to concentrate on his work and busied himself finishing the design for the Feast of Herod with its banqueting hall full of beautifully-dressed diners watching Salome present the dripping head of the Baptist to Herod. The large cartoons were pricked and, in the spring, the design was transferred to the lowest tier of the chapel wall. He made a few changes and additions. To the banqueting hall of King Herod he added the arms of the Ceppo, telling everyone it was the least he could do, he was so grateful to that august and charitable body. Such was the vanity and stupidity of the burghers that they took him at his word and were mightily pleased, even though their arms appeared in the scene where the head of John the Baptist is served on a plate.

Florentine observers seemed more able to decode the painter's intention. When he noticed it, Carlo de' Medici half-choked with laughter and had to hurry to the sacristy.

A Portrait of
the Virgin
1461-67

71

WITH ONLY DIAMANTE AND ALESSANDRO FOR COMPANY, Fra Filippo found his house too big and his days too long. His work began to pall and to hang heavy on him. He fell out of love with the Feast of Herod and returned briefly to Florence to look for diversion.

In the Palazzo de' Medici, he found that the frescoes in the chapel were finished, having been completed by Benozzo in just five months. He turned slowly in the chapel, studying each of the three tremendous walls and then the angel-filled chancel. The three kings, Caspar, Melchior and Balthasar, made a rich and splendid procession round the walls to the altarpiece. 'Everything leads to it,' said Cosimo from his chair. 'The whole procession, winding down from the hills to parade around this room, ends with the adoration of the Christ Child at the altar. Almost perfect, that painting.'

'Why "almost"?'

'You stand on the threshold where two worlds meet, Filippo. You raise your arms and draw down heaven to earth. But the marriage is not yet complete. You stop short. The Virgin is a figure of heaven but, in truth, she was a figure of earth, a mortal woman made divine.'

'I know that, but it would be a step too far.'

'Is it custom that sways you? Makes you afraid of taking the ultimate step?'

'I work from ideals,' said Filippo sharply. 'From archetypes set by tradition.'

'You work from fear. You're bound by it. Oh, people look at you and see a fearless man, one who does not even worry about hell, a man who cheerfully breaks with convention just for the sake of it, who breaks rules, breaks hearts, breaks promises, breaks anything in his way. But this is your limit, Filippo. Are you going to step over it or not?'

'I…' Filippo began, sinking into a chair himself. 'You're right, I fear no man – at least, not now the archbishop is dead, ha! – but I do fear her.' He nodded towards the painting.

'What is there to fear in the Virgin?'

'I mustn't offend her by likening her to a mortal woman.'

Cosimo leaned forward. 'That's superstition. What does Our Lady really mean to you? Tell me the truth.'

'She is where I rest my head at night, in her lap. She is my protectress, who keeps my soul from harm. When I fail, as I do every day, to keep to the commandments, she steps between me and God the Father and pleads on my behalf. I cannot give her a mortal face. How could I do that? But I have come close – closer than any man.'

'I understand that the Carmelites believe that when they die the Holy Mother takes their souls to paradise. Do you believe that?'

'I can only hope, Cosimo. I can only hope.' Filippo gazed at the old man whose head was sunk between his shoulders and whose long nose seemed to reach for the protruding lower lip. Sometimes Cosimo was owl-like, sometimes an eagle, but today he was a sad old vulture, moulting and with no energy for flight. He just sat on his branch and watched. 'What do you believe, Cosimo?' Filippo asked softly.

'Me?' Cosimo's face darkened and then brightened, as if a cloud had passed quickly over the sun. 'Are we alone here?'

'You dismissed the servants a while ago.'

'If I gave you the Christian version, we'd be here for hours, and it would all end in tears. But, since you ask, I believe in neither heaven nor hell but in the goodness of God and his Creation. And, when I die, I shall take on another body, and it will record all my sins. There, have I shocked you?'

Fra Filippo was speechless.

'Let me really shock you. I don't believe in that God of yours,' Cosimo pointed at the painting. 'The one with the long grey beard who lives in the sky. No, I don't believe in him, and it would help you if you threw him out, too.'

Now Filippo was gulping for air. Alone in a small room with a heretic!

'Because, you see, while you believe in him as a *figure*, you're always able to escape his gaze. God is up there, over there and, wherever he is, he is undoubtedly distracted by more important people than a mere friar, and so you commit your sins in private, presuming no one sees. As Boccaccio said, sins hidden are sins half-forgiven. Well, what if that were not the case? What if God were not only omnipotent but omnipresent? Everywhere, in everything. What if all your thoughts and deeds were entirely visible to God? What then?'

Filippo thought he was about to faint. 'You believe that – in the one God everywhere?'

'Utterly and completely.'

'But you're no saint. You still sin. How can you believe in something and act as if you don't?'

Cosimo threw up his hands. 'If only I knew the answer to that one! I don't know! Is it hypocrisy? I asked Ficino about it only recently and he said that creation runs on oppositions. The body is opposed to the soul, the senses to reason, vice is set against virtue and the vices against each other. It's part of the human condition to manifest all these things, and yet it behoves us to seek purification.'

'What does that mean, "purification"? If it means self-denial, I can't see the point. It just makes men miserable and bitter.'

'Purification means a blot-less soul that is a mirror to the divine. It comes from honest practice of the virtues. The effort is all. If we had a choice between an ugly face and a beautiful one, which would we choose?'

'Oh, beautiful, of course!'

435

'Well, so it is with our souls. Through purification we can make the foul fair. Apparently the accumulation of sins takes far, far longer than the remission of them. That may happen in an instant. All that is required is that we should fall down before the Lord.'

'Deathbed renunciation? I live in hope.'

'Don't be cynical! Filippo, take this seriously! Ficino has completed only one of Plato's Dialogues so far, but he has read all of them and tells me what is there. We chose these embodiments. As souls, we can choose how we wish to live our human lives. And, fool that I was, I chose to be the richest man in the world. What a fool! Ficino says I chose it so as to do good, that with my riches I have done great things, not least of which in his view is the bringing back of Plato to the West. He says that my soul saw it all, what the riches could do, and that is why I chose this body, chose to be the son of Giovanni di Bicci de' Medici and become a banker. And yet I'm a Christian still, and sometimes at night I curl up in the agony of contrition, for I have done more harm than good, have ruined men who stood in my way. Where does my wealth come from? Why, from the labour of men who live in poverty. Yes, I have done good things with it, better things perhaps than the labourers would have done, but that doesn't alter the fact that children cry in hunger because of me and my family. I have to believe in Plato if I would sleep at night for, if not, if Dante is right, then my afterlife is an eternal nightmare to be spent upside down in the lowest regions of hell. You may not think so, my friend, but you were the wise man when you came to make your choice, for you chose the simple life dedicated to your talent.'

'Simple?'

'It would have been even simpler if, like Fra Giovanni, you had directed all your love to God. Your love of your own body has complicated things.'

'My body? How could I love this? It's old and unsightly and has become a hindrance.'

'That's just the result of a lifetime's self-indulgence. But you have a chance, you still have a chance. I've none at all. I don't have the years it would take to put everything right. All I can do is to give and to hope.'

'I've always admired your self-control. I've seen you at feasts, making sure everyone is eating well and eating nothing yourself.'

'My doctors forbid me rich food, and my doctors are always at the feasts, or, if they're not, then my wife is, or my daughter-in-law. I am so well guarded. You should see what I eat in secret! But, no matter how much I eat, I can never be fat because guilt consumes me from within.'

'So, are you saying that if I practised temperance I could redeem myself?'

Cosimo laughed – an earthy, Tuscan laugh as deep as it was short. 'What I am saying is that if you learnt to love another more than you love yourself, you would be on your way to loving God. Now, it's your turn. You tell me what I must do to redeem myself.'

'Trust in the mercy of God.'

'How trite! And you think you're not a real friar?'

'I mean it. If I were your omnipresent God, I would have seen you face down in your cell at San Marco, prostrate and in tears. Don't look at yourself through other men's eyes: look at yourself with God's eyes. Perhaps we meet as we pass in opposite directions. For you need to learn to love yourself. Stop worrying about the mistreated slaves and the ruined rivals. If we all chose our embodiments, so did they and, given half the chance, they would have done to you as you have done to them. This thing within me, this talent that is not mine but a gift from God, it would have lain buried but for you. Oh yes! Don't think I don't know, that I haven't detected your hand in every twist in my life, the release from the Carmine, the commission in Padua, maybe even the release from Barbary.'

'Did you really think that Abu Ali Ibn Yussef released you just because it was the Feast of Eid? Ha! No, like all men he had his price and was compliant to our wishes, once we'd tracked you down. He refused to part with you immediately, saying your instruction in wisdom was not yet complete, but said that he would send you back at Eid. Which he did. An honourable man.'

Filippo, who had been joking, was staggered by this revelation but continued: 'My release from prison? My chaplaincy at Santa Margherita's?'

'Yes, all of that.'

'Why the convent? Why put me with enclosed women?'

'Inspired, don't you think? I admit I was wrong in hoping you would learn to be a father to girls rather than their seducer, but, well, at least you fell in love. Why have you sent her back?'

'I made a pact with God.'

'Nonsense. The Ceppo forced you to it. My influence is not as great as you think. I can bend popes to my will but I'm powerless against virtuous men.'

Filippo rubbed his face wearily. 'If God is not a sky-dwelling greybeard, what then is He? What's your picture of God?'

'I have none, for God is not embodied. The image of Christ is as close as we can get, when God was embodied. But you'll find Him in goodness, in truth, in beauty, in love.'

'That's no image at all.'

'So perhaps the Moors have it right.'

'Perhaps they do. So, my Father, what plans do you have for me next?'

'At the cathedral at Spoleto they want the apse decorated with the Life of the Virgin.'

Filippo studied his hands, thinking of Lucrezia and willing himself to rise above desire. 'I had heard whispers of it, and I'm glad. If it takes as long as Santo Stefano, it will see out my days, and how better to spend them than in contemplation of the Virgin?'

'How long will it take you to complete at Prato?'

'Another year or so.'

'Speed up, Filippo.'

'I trust you'll not be locking me in.'

'I've learnt my lesson. By the way, my son Piero wishes to commission a panel.'

'There you go! First it's "speed up" then it's "here's something else to do"! Haven't any of you realized that the cause of my slowness is distraction?'

'Yes, we've all realized that.'

'No, no, not any distraction, but *your* distractions. The man who whips the donkey is the one who has overloaded him.'

Cosimo smiled. He looked around the walls of his chapel. 'It took Benozzo five months to do all this, all these figures. How many years have you been at Prato? Seven? Speeding up is not necessarily going faster, but becoming more efficient. All your second and third thoughts and over-painting (I like the hands, by the way, but don't you dare dabble with another picture of mine once it's finished and delivered). Get to the point and quicker. Your only distraction in the end is your self-doubting. I don't know what you have to do to prove to yourself that you're a real painter but, for the sake of God, just get it proved – the rest of the world needs no such convincing. It's only you who doubts your ability.'

Fra Filippo sat back in shock. He knew Cosimo was shrewd when it came to reading souls, but to be so astute that he could show a man the truth about himself that he himself did not know? He looked round the walls again, at the three Magi and the densely-populated procession.

'I sometimes torture myself wondering what you would have done on these walls,' said Cosimo, ringing a handbell to summon his manservants. 'But you weren't available. Still, I have my culmination point: all these mortal souls progressing to that square of divinity on the altar. Your work, my friend, is a portal into the divine world. Know it. Believe it. And the next step is to bring that divinity into this world. Let not your pictures be windows, but doors.'

'By the way,' he added, as his servants arrived, 'I could make it all right for you very easily, you know. Pope Pius is proving a useful friend. My son, Carlo, has been legitimized, and I could do the same for your Filippino. You only have to say the word. You and Lucrezia, released from your vows.'

It was a generous offer: Filippo laughed out loud. 'You hypocrite!'

'What?' Cosimo demanded angrily.

'After everything you've just said, you're offering to buy me an easier life. Ha! What kind of religion is this, that *deals* with God as if heaven were a bank? Eh? You sit in your chair and spout your wisdom, your proverbs and aphorisms. When asked, you say you believe in goodness and the transmigration of souls. What about the forgiveness of sins? The archbishop said to me, no more penance! That was the wisest thing anyone ever said. Since that moment, I've been responsible for myself and my actions. If I fail, I note it and try to do better. I no longer pay off my debts by clicking beads or saying prayers, for I have no debts, only failures, my failure to be worthy of God. Ficino once told me that to escape the wheel of rebirth we need to live three exemplary lives. Three! So far as I'm concerned, an exemplary life is one lived in poverty, humility and service to others. Fra Giovanni lived one exemplary life; so did Archbishop Antonino. You and I – we have not lived any exemplary lives.'

Cosimo glared at him. Cosimo de' Medici who, for thirty years, had only ever heard words of respect and deference from other mortal creatures, including cardinals, kings and popes. He glared at this unfit friar who dared, *dared*, to speak the truth. He found breathing difficult. He signalled to his servants to lift his chair.

'This chapel you've built is a place of transfiguration,' said Filippo, standing on the porphyry disc, his arms outstretched. 'It would be a shame if you were impervious to that yourself.'

440

Cosimo regarded him in a kind of roaring silence. When the two servants lifted the chair, he told them to carry him to the porphyry disc.

Filippo stepped out of the way as the servants set the chair down on the middle of the floor.

'Now go, all of you. And you, Fra Filippo. Get out!'

✝

Cosimo sat rocking silently back and forth, trying to rise in spirit and transcend the pain that crippled his joints and warped his fingers and toes. He would have given all he possessed for good health. He rocked. He dwelt. He prayed to God, making confession as he so often did of all his sins, requesting forgiveness and relief from pain. What came to the fore of his mind, however, surprised him. Not the finger-pointing hag of redemption, accuser of all his sins presenting visions of his wrongdoing as the cause of his sufferings. No. What he saw in his mind's eye was Philosophy, naked and abused, sitting alone by the side of a filthy road. God required something of him that he found difficult to comprehend. His God, his very Christian God, the Trinity itself, was waiting for him to re-found the Platonic Academy.

'I don't understand,' said Cosimo to God. 'If I have dallied and delayed all these years it's through fear of incurring Your wrath.' His eye fell on Lippi's altarpiece and the gaze of the Virgin upon the Son, God above in his radiance, the Spirit in between. It was a portrait of devotion, a portrait of purity and, for a moment, he realized it was a portrait of *his* devotion and purity. And then he understood in imagery what he could not understand in words. There was no conflict. The love he felt for Plato was the same love he felt for God. Plato was, indeed, his way to God, and he had kept that way barred all these years, distracting himself, procrastinating. How often had he chastised Lippi for not finishing a work when, he, Cosimo, could not even start?

'I am ready,' he whispered.

441

72

SOMETHING NIGGLED IN THE FRIAR'S BREAST. THE FIGURE of Salome dancing kept him occupied all day, wondering what state of undress she could be in, and how to depict seven veils, but then he had to go back to his empty house, to sleep, to wake with that niggling thing, that sense of hopelessness, of lack of purpose, of meaninglessness; that niggling thing which was opening like an ulcer in his soul. It was a familiar sense of emptiness that usually sent him to the larder but he was becoming painfully aware that no physical food ever filled that hole.

He dragged his feet as he walked to Santo Stefano; he shuffled on his way to work. Alessandro, when he walked with him, was always light on his feet, his head turning this way and that as he drank in the details of life around him. Melancholy was not something that afflicted this young man. If anyone asked Filippo what was wrong – which no one did – he would have said he was bored. Life had become predictable and repetitive. He ate, he drank, he slept, he got up and went to work.

Sometimes he visited Santa Margherita's. He liked to stand in the shadows of the doorway and see the nuns without being seen. They had all settled back into anonymity well enough. Dressed alike in their gowns and veils, he had only shape to go on as an identifier. But their anonymity was part of his melancholia, this surrender of a life in devotion to God when the devotion is not real. He would stand in the shadows until she passed and then he would whisper, *Lucrezia*. And she would turn, no longer startled as on the first few occasions; she would turn with a ready smile and hold out her hands to him.

'Where's Filippino?'

Usually she would say he was in the school room or the refectory, but once the little boy had leapt out from the folds of her gown, crying, 'Here I am!' And mother and son had giggled at their naughtiness, that Filippino had been with her most of the day without anyone noticing. Filippo thought his heart would break.

He dragged his feet to Santo Stefano's; he shuffled on his way to work. And then he saw something. He saw a small child hold out its arms to its mother and for some reason he thought of Cosimo. Cosimo whom he had hurt, who hadn't deserved what he'd said, who had been so generous to him all his life long, who had made it possible for him to be a painter, who had made him a better painter than he would have otherwise been, left to himself. He didn't know why the small child's gesture reminded him of Cosimo, but it did, and he knew then what he must do to cure his spirit. He must give Cosimo a gift. The richest man in the world – what did people give rich men as gifts? Filippo had no intention of buying something: that was not what he had in mind. He wanted to give Cosimo a gift of himself. He wanted to give him the painting he had always wanted to do and no one had asked for. It would not be a commission; it would be his gift to Cosimo and, through Cosimo, to God.

He veered away from his path and went to Santa Margherita's to find Abbess Jacopa. 'I need Suor Lucrezia and Filippino to model for me. Would you allow that?'

'Of course, but it must be here in the cloisters.'

But it was no good, working in the cloisters as they had done before. He could not draw Lucrezia in the black, enveloping habit. He needed to see her form. Filippo turned the full force of his charm on the abbess, smiling his boyish smile, cajoling, pleading childishly, telling her that she knew she would give in, so why delay? Eventually Abbess Jacopa agreed and Lucrezia began to make daily visits to the chaplain's house, accompanied by Spinetta and Filippino. Any neighbours they met on the way called out to them affectionately. Of Filippino they made much fuss. He rode on the shoulders of dyers and ate cakes from the baker.

On the first day Lucrezia arrived to find a parcel on the kitchen table that Filippo told her to open. She cut the cords binding it and found inside a linen chemise, a gown of dusky apricot and a robe of blue velvet, all of which he had ordered from the finest haberdashers in Prato using the best, most exquisite fabrics. Lucrezia cooed like a dove as she held them up. Taking off her tunic, she stood naked with her arms in the air so that Filippo could slip the chemise on her. The feel of the soft linen after the coarse habit made her gasp. Her body tensed in pleasure. 'Like a string on a lute tuning itself up,' thought Filippo. He put the brocade underdress on her.

'It's so rich, so soft, so beautifully wrought,' she muttered.

Filippo put the velvet gown on her. Lucrezia sighed. She breathed with her mouth open, that wonderful soft breathing he used to lie in bed listening to, the breathing of a baby. Lucrezia sat down with the grace of a queen and Spinetta plaited her sister's hair with fine lengths of transparent linen.

Filippo wished he knew what he was about to paint. He had spent so much on the costume that he did not have much left for pigments; he could not afford the ultramarines, the gold, the expensive lake – all the colours patrons usually paid for as a separate item. The initial impulse was beginning to wear thin. Was he being a sentimental old fool? He looked at his palette, the colours that were cheap and of which he had a plentiful supply, mostly indigo and sienna. With the addition of white and black, he could make these colours go a long way; they were the colours of rock and sky, of distance, the colours of reality. Right now they were the colours of his soul. Where he skimped on colour, he made up for with dimension and had prepared a panel unusually large.

'What are you doing to her hair?' he asked Spinetta. 'That looks untidy to the point of wantonness.'

Alessandro, who had returned for some advice for the work at Santo Stefano, stood watching wide-eyed as Spinetta pulled back her sister's hair, leaving the brow smooth but making an artful tumble of hair at the crown, threaded through with gauze and pearls.

'This is how they wear their hair now,' she said, without troubling to explain who she was speaking about. In Spinetta's world 'they' were the holders of ultimate authority.

'How do you know how women wear their hair?' Fra Filippo asked, intrigued, imagining Spinetta attending balls and banquets in some kind of disguise.

'Because they come to church!' she replied, as if speaking to an idiot.

'It's true,' Alessandro agreed. 'Some women are shaving their foreheads to get that look of the moon rising, but Lucrezia doesn't have to. And their costume – more chemise than gown.'

'Really?' Fra Filippo was annoyed and bemused in equal measure. How come things were happening in female fashion that he hadn't noticed? 'More chemise than gown?'

'Light, flowing fabrics that move,' Alessandro sighed. 'Flutter. Touching the skin as lightly as a kiss.' He coughed to clear his throat. 'I've been wanting to talk to you about it. Your Feast of Herod – it's full of dowdy old dames.'

Fra Filippo choked and spluttered.

'Salome,' Alessandro continued quickly. 'The dance of the seven veils. We can use this new fashion to suggest it.'

'And what, use the opportunity to make a comment on the morals of young women of our own time? Hmmm. Yes, I approve. More chemise than gown? That's outrageous.'

Everyone present smiled at each other over the head of Fra Filippo bent over his drawing. He glanced up. 'What is it? What do you all find so amusing?'

'You sound like the archbishop,' said Lucrezia.

✝

The re-drawn Salome became a young woman in a gauzy chemise caught at the waist by a ribbon, with the cloth ruched over a band on the hip, from which it flowed and rippled, revealing the form of her thighs. Her feet skipped on the tiled floor that, along with the hall itself, was in perfect perspective. Salome appeared again in the same scene, proffering the Baptist's head to Herod, in a chemise with gorgeous hanging sleeves. Both Salomes had Lucrezia's face. Alessandro, who had painted the entire floor of the scene without once complaining of boredom, asked if he could paint a figure, a guest at Herod's table. Filippo grudgingly agreed. Alessandro began a design for a sleepy-eyed female guest, a portrait of Spinetta.

✝

To paint what he wanted to paint: it was as daunting as freedom is to a man who has been in gaol for most of his life. Filippo stood at the threshold of the imagination and hardly dared to move. Every time an image came to mind, it came from the past, from tradition, from how things had always been done. These he dismissed, even though it meant even longer staring at a blank sheet of paper.

'What is it,' he asked himself, 'that I most want to do? Here I am, near the end of my life, and I have the opportunity to do what I like. So, what is it?' 'Landscapes and portraits' was the answer. He wanted the freedom of the northern painters, and now he had it. At the same time, a gift should be something to please the recipient, not the giver. He wanted to do a picture for Cosimo to contemplate: it seemed natural to do the Virgin and Child. It was, after all, what he did best. But which archetype? Nativity – Adoration – Enthroned: all these he dismissed. He wanted something that was at the same time more simple and more challenging. Cosimo, he knew, loved the sermons of Saint Bernard on the Song of Songs. Filippo's gift would be the Virgin as Bride and the Child as Bridegroom.

He closed his eyes to see the image. He sat with his eyes closed for a long time. He began to sway, drifting in and out of sleep, on the threshold of the imagination. Then he saw a space between the little finger of the Child and the index finger of the Virgin, the space that is the source from which all things flow, the space of the heart. He opened his eyes, took up his compass

446

and drew a circle. Within the circle he drew a pyramid of interlocking shapes of solid geometry. He saw the essence of the form first, the musculature of nature. On this he would build the particular forms of Virgin, Child and two Angels; and he would be even more particular. The Virgin would be a portrait of Lucrezia; the child would be his memory of Filippino as a baby; the foreground angel would be Filippino as he was now, aged four and smiling out at the viewer with that cheeky smile that melted his father's heart.

He looked at Filippino, sitting on the floor with a toy horse, living in a world of his own imagination in which that horse and its rider were annihilating an enemy. Filippino who dabbled his fingers in his father's pots of pigment and then painted his own face; who, in trying to climb on to a table, had knocked over some flowers and broken the vase; who could upturn a plate of food in a tantrum: Filippino the Vile, the Naughty, the Exasperating, who only had to look up at you with that wide-mouthed smile for all your anger to evaporate.

It was the ratio of the mean: as the small is to the large, so is the large to the whole. *As my son is to me, so am I to God the Father.* What if that were true? What if all he had to do for the redemption of sin was to look over his shoulder and grin at God?

Now there's a thought, he muttered to himself as he began to draw. And he realized, suddenly, that if he were to look over his shoulder, his eyes would meet those of Alessandro. 'What, are you still here?'

'I was hoping you hadn't noticed.'

'Be quiet, then, and perhaps I'll forget.'

Alessandro returned to his sketches of Spinetta, whom he had put into the pose of a young woman sitting at table looking dreamy and abstracted, a focal point to bridge the scene on the left, where the head of the decapitated Baptist was being put on a platter, and the right, where it was presented to Herod's mistress, Herodias, mother of Salome. It was a device to liven up the Feast of Herod and unite its two halves that he wished to discuss with Filippo. Every now and then, he looked across to what his master was doing.

Fra Filippo had enclosed his group in the stone embrasure of a window, a window that looked out on an extensive landscape. Alessandro had seen landscapes before, of course, but not like this. He knew landscapes as decorative patterns of hills and trees: here was a landscape conforming to the laws of perspective, a cultivated valley in a mountainous coast, sweeping away to a natural harbour and a walled city in the distance; a river that seemed to get entangled with the Virgin's veil. 'I read some-where,' said Filippo, 'that the source of a river is the ocean. All rivers return to their source. Stop staring, Alessandro. I can't concentrate.'

'Maestro?'

'Yes, yes, I will let you do her hands. It will be your gift to Cosimo.'

'No, Maestro. I mean, thank you, but not that.'

'Then what is it, boy?'

'Why don't you do her in profile?'

The silence between them was profound then a sound came from Filippo like a small pebble falling into a well.

✝

When it came to the painting, Fra Filippo enjoyed the limited palette much more than he had anticipated. Out of just a few pigments he could do flesh tones, hair, rock, sea, sky, trees. Perhaps it was monotonous, perhaps it was strange to have all figures with the same colour hair – which was the colour of their flesh and of the wooden chair the Virgin sat upon. Perhaps that was strange, but Filippo found it pleasing. It was calm, it was restful. This was not a painting to excite the intellect or fire the blood. It was a contemplation in two colours. He had drawn Lucrezia from life; now he painted her from life, making her sit for him, reading the sermons of Saint Bernard. If every painter paints himself, where was Filippo in this picture? He was there in the peace and contentment. Why would he want to be anywhere else doing anything other than this? This was enough: his family in his house posing for his picture for his beloved patron. This was enough.

✝

The painting was completed quickly: from the preparation of the panel to the final touches, a mere two months. At the appropriate time, Filippo called Alessandro to come and paint the hands, and then it was Filippo's turn to sit back, watch and marvel. He thought the positioning was a little awkward, and the flesh tone a shade too dark, but he said nothing. 'Perfect,' he said once Alessandro was done, 'almost.'

The day the picture was finished, Lucrezia folded up the beautiful clothes and made a pile of them.

'Put them on,' said Filippo.

'Why?'

'So that I can take them off again.'

He had restrained himself for two months while Lucrezia posed as the Virgin Mary. Now he was going to have her, but first he would peel her like a fruit. He carried her upstairs.

✝

Later, when they were quiet and resting in each other's arms, Filippo heard love cries coming from the room where Alessandro slept. Well, the boy was seventeen now. It was time. Filippo hoped Don Diamante would not discover how they had spent the afternoon: he had changed since he had become a Benedictine. He was taking it all very seriously. At Santo Stefano, the two painters had agonized for years on what to put in the tall, narrow spaces on either side of the stained-glass window. It had been Diamante's idea to honour the founding saints of their respective orders, Sant' Alberto of the Carmelites and San Giovanni Gualberto of Vallombrosa. He was there now, in the chapel,

449

painting the semblance of statues in niches. Poor, dear Diamante. Filippo hoped he would not be upset.

Lucrezia put her arm around him and snuggled closer. 'What are you thinking about?'

'Diamante. About him becoming Vallombrosan.'

'I heard recently that he ravished the daughter of a wool carder.'

'Is that true? That's outrageous!'

'You can't lie here with me and say that without being a hypocrite.'

'I never ravished you. You flung yourself at me.'

Lucrezia rubbed her nose against Filippo's. 'True,' she confessed. 'I have no regrets. Well, I do have one.'

'Which is?'

'I shouldn't have allowed you to push me back into the convent. Yes, it is better under Abbess Jacopa, of course, and if I were a virgin I'd be content. But in the convent I am a fallen woman, the mother of an illegitimate child, and it's a stain that won't wash off. Here, however, I'm your wife and the mother of our Filippino. Husband, I do not wish to return. Please don't make me.'

'But the Ceppo!'

'Make it right with them.'

Filippo fell back on his pillow and stared thoughtfully at the ceiling. 'There is only one thing that will make it right with them.'

He made arrangements. Within the week he had bought a house in a small hamlet called Coiano, a mile up-river, where Lucrezia and Spinetta were to live with Filippino. When he finished at Santo Stefano, he would remove himself from Prato. For the only thing that would make it right with the Ceppo would be for Lucrezia and Filippo to live apart. But at least she could live as a mother if not a wife.

73

COSIMO WAS DYING. IN HIS CHAMBER IN HIS VILLA AT
Careggi, he lay in bed facing a door open on to an upper loggia.
Although the garden was out of view he could smell the lavender
and listen to the bees droning heavy with pollen. He had designed
three gardens: one in the palazzo in the city; one for San Marco;
one here. He let his imagination roam down the cobbled paths he
had laid to the central fountain, past herbaceous beds, circles and
squares laid out in box containing large terracotta pots of lemons.
He tried to remember the last time he had walked in one, or even
been carried through one, but he could not. So many occasions in
life when he had not realized, 'this is the last time'.

The hollowness of nostalgia began to sap his strength and with
an effort of will he removed himself from memory and began
to walk in the landscape of contemplation, the inner garden of
his soul. For what in the end does death mean as it comes? It's
beyond reason – he saw no need to discuss the whys and where-
fores. Next to the open door was a painting 'in ginger and ink' as
he called it, of the Virgin and Child, 'with a particularly cheeky
angel – surely a portrait of the painter in his childhood.'

With his head propped against his pillows he enjoyed a cooling
draft from the feather fan one of his slaves used to stir the late July
air and stared at the face of the Virgin – such sweetness and
innocence. It was a painting beyond anything he had ever seen, of
a beauty beyond earthly beauty, a gift that had arrived when he
had least expected it. How long was it since he had received a gift
from anyone who wanted nothing in return? All the emeralds and
rubies, the cameos, the agate vases, the silver candelabra – all these
priceless objects he had been given by kings and popes and
emperors wishing to impress him, were as nothing to this simple
panel. In it he saw the marriage of Masaccio and Fra Giovanni, the
two streams of painting, intellectual and divine. Fra Filippo had

outclassed them all in a painting he had done for himself as a gift. It was a painting that said, 'Behold, this is a portrait of my family, and I give it to God.'

Cosimo's rheumy old eyes filled with tears. His son Giovanni had died the previous year. Giovanni, who had been healthy, was survived by the invalid Piero, the invalid Piero who must now assume responsibility for the family and the bank. Cosimo had handed everything over to him, charging his grandson, Lorenzo, to help his father in every way he could. Cosimo must think no more about the bank, about power, about danger and security. He must have faith. Lorenzo would take over one day and Cosimo could leave the continuance of the family in his grandson's capable hands. He must let go his concerns and put everything in the lap of God. It was time for his soul, and the one task he had left to complete.

He had summoned his chosen men and within the hour they arrived at his bedside. Beside his son Piero was Lorenzo, fifteen years old and already, so Cosimo had heard, possessed of a mistress some years his senior. Cosimo would have remonstrated with his grandson and given him an admonitory sermon except that he intuitively felt that Lorenzo's affairs of the heart and his poetry were linked: that, without love, Lorenzo could not write, and Cosimo admired his grandson's writing above all his fledgling skills in diplomacy and statecraft.

'Sing to me,' the old man said, 'one of your sonnets.'

As Lorenzo sang, accompanied on the lute by his younger brother, Giuliano, Marsilio Ficino arrived clutching under his arm like a small harp his book of Plato in Greek that Cosimo had presented to him so many years before. Cosimo raised his hand to him fondly, this man who, after a shaky start, had never wavered from the task given to him, steadfast, loyal, brilliant. It seemed to Cosimo that lights were arranging themselves around his bed.

Leon Battista Alberti, elderly now, but possessed of all his faculties and as handsome as he had been in his youth, with that natural nobility that, as Dante had written, comes to a man by virtue and not by birth. On entering the room, Alberti halted by the painting in ginger and ink and paused to gaze upon it. He began to say something but Cosimo interrupted. 'Look at it in silence,' he admonished him. 'Look and wonder.'

More lights arrived, Cristoforo Landino, Gentile Becchi and others interested in the study of ancient philosophy, many of them students of Plethon during the years he had lectured at the university following the Great Council. Cosimo looked at the gathering lights, the dear faces of friends and relations. He regretted the passing of many, not least his architects, painters and sculptors: Brunelleschi, Ghiberti, Fra Giovanni. Donatello still lived but at the age of eighty he had declined Cosimo's invitation, saying he was too busy with his work and time was running out. But another still lived who was only fifty-eight whom Cosimo could not see amongst the faces.

'Where's Lippi? Did I not invite Fra Filippo?' he asked.

'Yes,' replied his daughter-in-law, Monna Lucrezia, the only woman in the room, 'you did. He's here in the house but won't come to this inauguration. He says he's not worthy and, anyway, philosophy is beyond him.'

'How can it be, if it's not beyond me? Cussed as ever. Very well, let him hide. Marsilio, it's time.'

Ficino stood. His face was lined prematurely, as if he cared more deeply than most about life, but his hair was still golden and fell to his shoulders in generous waves. He called the company together in prayer, a prayer of his own composition addressed to the Good, followed by an invocation to Love that he sang with his pupil, Lorenzo. A silence fell upon the room, as if the gods invoked were indeed present and listening intently. Into this silence fell Ficino's voice as he intoned the names of the teachers of wisdom throughout the ages, followed by a brief history of the institution now being re-founded.

'Just over nine hundred years ago, the Platonic Academy, which had survived for just over nine hundred years, was closed down by the Emperor Justinian. The philosophers fled from Greece and went to Persia, where a school was established that remained until the tenth century, a school that influenced Arab science and philosophy. By our own times, a school of Plato had been re-established in Greece, at Mistra.

'As we all know, Greece was lost to the Turks ten years ago when Constantinople was sacked. Anticipating what was to come, the philosophers had already arranged to pass the teaching to Italy. They came with the emperor and the patriarch when, in 1439, the Great Council was convened.' Ficino lifted a long and graceful hand towards Cosimo.

'With the Council came Plethon,' said Cosimo, his voice catching, 'the last of the academicians, and he told me to re-found the Platonic Academy, here in Florence. We had the books of Plato but we couldn't read them.'

'The matter drifted for twenty years.'

Cosimo tried to slap his hand on the counterpane but it came down weightless. 'It was not the matter that drifted, my dear Marsilio, it was you!'

Ficino kept his composure. He addressed the men around the bed. 'Cosimo often tells me that he knew before I was ten that I would be the man to translate Plato. I went to university but the only philosophy they taught me was Aristotle's. I made a book, a compendium of everything that could be discovered about Plato from Latin sources, and, rather proudly, I presented a copy to him. He read it and told me not to publish anything else until I could read Greek.'

Several of the men in the room, who had themselves enjoyed 'direction' from Cosimo, smiled sympathetically at Ficino. Cosimo did not smile. 'How right I was,' he said. 'You were a lazy young rascal, doing everything you could to avoid your duty. Always indulging your interests, never doing the work. Meh! I sent him to Camaldoli.'

'It is always very difficult when good and wise men advise you. I had Cosimo insisting I should translate Plato; the monks of Camaldoli saying one learns Greek for the sole purpose of reading the New Testament in the original; then Archbishop Antonino commanding me, for the sake of my soul, to study less Plato and more Aquinas. In the end you can only follow your own heart.'

'I didn't know about Antonino,' Cosimo grumbled. 'You should have spoken to me. He was a great man, but misguided, you know.'

At this the company laughed out loud.

'It's true!' Cosimo protested. 'Why do you find that amusing?'

'A saintly archbishop denounced as misguided by a banker,' said Leon Battista Alberti.

'I keep telling you,' Cosimo insisted, 'look beneath the surface! All of you – stop being beguiled by the world of appearances. That way lies deception. Ficino is here, I have put him here, to teach us about reality. That is what this Academy is about. Marsilio, continue. Tell us the history that no one will write.'

'Having mastered Greek, I set about translating Plato but almost at once you called a halt to the work, telling me to translate the Hymns of Orpheus.' Ficino alternated between addressing Cosimo and the company at large. He turned from the bed to say, 'We had discovered, you see, the line of transmission of wisdom from the most ancient times to Plato.' He turned back to Cosimo. 'Once I'd finished the Hymns, you gave me the Sayings of Zoroaster, for Zoroaster, too, was of the line of teachers, and his priests were called *magi*. That ancient teaching passed on to Hermes Trismegistus in ancient Egypt, but his works were lost to us. Having finished the Sayings, I returned to Plato. Almost in that very hour I received a message from you saying that the books of Hermes had just been discovered and were on their way to Florence. You said I was to stop everything until I had translated Hermes. It was wrong of me to say that the matter drifted. It was more that, each time I sat down to concentrate on Plato, you smacked me on the back of the hand with a stick and made me do something else.'

Cosimo harrumphed and nodded, his chin low on his chest. He was silent for a while, then said, 'My good friends, I have something to confess. I was afraid. Afraid of this thing I'd been given to do. It sounds fine amongst us, to re-found the Platonic Academy, but how will it sound to the people and, moreover, how will it sound to men of the disposition of Archbishop Antonino? They would have my guts for lute strings. And so I procrastinated. But then that man,' he pointed a crooked finger at Filippo, who had just slipped in the door, 'that unholy lump of mortal flesh, instructed me to pray in my own chapel, and that is when I received the divine impulse and knew what I should do. Now, this very day, the door of the Academy is open once again, too late for me to read Plato, but not for you my sons and grandchildren, my friends, sons of my friends. Not for you. It stands on the surest foundation we could build. Today is the day. God be praised.'

Filippo had come in late hoping to go unnoticed because he could not imagine why he should be invited to a gathering of the greatest men of the time and place. Was he one of them, one of this intimate circle of the friends of Cosimo, he who was only a painter? He looked about him. His surviving contemporaries, Donatello and Luca della Robbia, were not present.

'Come here, Filippo, come forward,' Cosimo said. He was panting now from the exertion of talking and the breath rattled in his throat. 'When I look upon your picture, I'm ready to leave this world.' Filippo kept his eyes lowered, but Cosimo would not continue until the friar looked up, which eventually he did, and found himself gazing into limitless brown depths. 'I am ready to step into the unknown,' Cosimo told him, 'which, according to Plato, consists of three things only: Truth, Beauty and Goodness. Filippo? Are you listening? Do you hear what I say? Truth, Beauty, Goodness. Do you believe me when I say every painter paints himself? Because in you it's true.' Cosimo fell quiet to steady his breathing. Filippo folded his hands over the old man's and said nothing. 'Why the pearl?' Cosimo wheezed. 'You have that wanton woman of yours as the Virgin, as the Star of the Sea and Port of Our Salvation, with no veil upon her head, just a fashionable piece of frippery topped by a pearl of fabulous size. What's the meaning of it?'

'*Again, the kingdom of heaven is like unto a merchant man, seeking goodly pearls: Who, when he had found one pearl of great price, went and sold all that he had, and bought it,*' said Filippo, quoting Saint Matthew. 'It's your Academy.'

74

A MONTH LATER A HUNDRED WHITE PIGEONS WERE LET fly from Florence. The one that was bound for Prato had the shortest journey. It took off with the rest from the top of a tower in the Santo Spirito district, followed the Arno snaking north-west below and then turned towards the mountains and the small city with its several churches, its tangle of streets and canals, its fullers' mills and weaving shops, and landed in the loft in the bell tower of Santo Stefano. The pigeon-keeper took the message from its leg and conveyed it to the Gonfalonier. The bell of the campanile began to sound at once, followed by those of San Francesco, San Domenico and every church of Prato.

In Florence a man had died who wished to be buried without pomp and ceremony, but the people of his city, and of the cities dependent on Florence, the kings and princes of faraway places who were allies, could not let him go as if he had never been. The bells rang for Cosimo de' Medici along the Arno Valley, throughout Italy, along the entire coast of the Mediterranean – including Barbary – over much of Europe and not a little of the Turkish empire.

In a small house in the little hamlet of Coiano beyond Prato, Fra Filippo was inconsolable. Well, almost. There was one way he could take his mind off his grief. He went to his room and called for Lucrezia. When she got there she found him naked and in bed, requiring consolation. The daughter born to them the following spring should have been called Cosima.

75

THE MULE TRAIN WAS MAKING ITS WAY FROM PRATO TO Spoleto via Florence. Fra Filippo led the way, closely followed by Don Diamante, between them a small donkey carrying nine-year-old Filippino with Alessandro walking at its head. Behind the riders, more mules carrying the equipment of a painter's workshop. He had left behind in his Pratese farmhouse his wife, Lucrezia, her sister, Spinetta, and a two-year old girl they had named Alessandra after her godfather.

At Florence, the quiet party made its way to the workshop of Antonio Pollaiuolo.

'It's all arranged,' Fra Filippo told Alessandro. 'And it cannot be unarranged. You're to work with the Pollaiuoli brothers for a year while you establish your own workshop. No following me to Spoleto to arrive in two weeks, bedraggled and pathetic.'

Now twenty-two years old, Alessandro's childish devotion to his master had disappeared in his eagerness to build his own career. If he looked disappointed, it was at the thought of having to spend a year with the Pollaiuoli. It was unnecessary. He could start a workshop tomorrow and have more clients than he could serve by the end of the week. Fra Filippo reached out and smacked him across the back of the head. 'Pride!' he said. 'I can see your thoughts on your face. One more year, do you hear me? The Pollaiuoli will teach you draughtsmanship – the sure and steady line – the anatomy of bodies – all the things I'm uncertain about and will always be uncertain about. Hands! They can draw hands. And, yes, I know, so can you, but you don't know everything, Sandro. Any man who needs to learn humility is far from having completed his education. Do you hear me?'

Fra Filippo was growing deaf with age and, the deafer he became, the more he was convinced that no one could hear him. Alessandro nodded vehemently, shouting, 'Yes, Filippo. I hear you.'

'And, most important of all, working with the Pollaiuoli will put you in the stream of tradition. You can say that you trained with those who trained with Castagno, who himself trained with Uccello, who trained with Ghiberti, and you will trace your genealogy back to that Adam of art, Masaccio himself.'

'I think men would be much more impressed if I said I had trained with Fra Filippo Lippi, who as a boy watched Masaccio paint.'

'How I shall miss your flattery!'

At the workshop, Fra Filippo did not dismount. 'No long drawn-out goodbyes,' he said. 'Take your things and be off with you. Do well, Alessandro Botticelli, do well.'

Alessandro took a chest and two satchels off one of the mules and put them by the door of the workshop. Then he stood and watched as the mule train moved off. It was the centre of the city and it was only moments and one corner turned before the party was out of sight. The friars did not look back, but the nine-year-old boy turned in his saddle and waved. '*Addio!*'

'*Addio*, Filippino!' called Alessandro.

The city closed behind the party, swallowing it. They were gone. Alessandro felt disembowelled. Then he remembered one of the many instructions Fra Filippo had given him over the past few days. 'Visit Prato often, for the sake of your godchild.' Lucrezia, Spinetta and Alessandra had been left in his care. And in their final conversation alone, Fra Filippo had formally asked Alessandro to become Filippino's master in due course. 'I imparted all my knowledge to you,' he said. 'I would have you impart it to my son.'

459

Alessandro picked up his bags, pushed the workshop door open with his foot and went in. There was work to do and a living to earn. Even as the door closed behind him, however, there arose a powerful desire to escape. He must slip away, somehow, when no one was looking, and spend the day in the city churches; or not arrive tomorrow – send a note about bellyache, headache, strange symptoms possibly of plague.

The men in the shop did not look up from their work, work in which anatomy was all and 'emotion' was grief or pain. These were men who believed in the carcass rather than the soul, who could never see the visions of beauty he, Sandro Botticelli, saw behind his closed eyelids.

'Good morning,' he said to their backs. 'I'm Sandro, from Filippo Lippi's workshop.'

'*Poverino!*' said Antonio Pollaiuolo, 'then you have much to learn.'

'Not half as much as you do,' thought Sandro, putting his bags down and glancing round the workshop to see how many doors there were leading out. But his glance also took in several panels and he noticed that the Pollaiuoli brothers were indeed very good at hands and had as luscious a way of depicting fabrics as Fra Filippo himself. He decided to stay.

Hereafter

FILIPPO STRUGGLED AGAINST FAILING HEALTH TO COMPLETE
the frescoes in the church of the Assumption in Spoleto. In the
lower part of the apse, he had painted the Dormition of the Virgin
– with a portrait of himself amidst the angels at the foot of her
bier – an Annunciation, with feats of perspective to make the eyes
of rival painters water, and a Nativity. In the semi-dome above
the apse he was painting a scene of the Virgin being crowned by
God the Father against a radiant, golden sun around which the
planets and stars orbited in rainbow-coloured bands. It all worked
together in a unity of conception and colour. He was pleased with
it. It was his masterwork. But he thrashed his body like a broken
donkey. 'Get up you fool!' he told himself, when all the aches and
pains, the nausea and weakness, forced him to lie down. 'Get up!
Get up! Get up!'

One day he did not get up. He lay there and wept. He called
for Diamante and told him to send for Lucrezia. 'It's a long way
for her to come, but I need her. Tell her she must come. Give her
this message: *Come from Lebanon, my spouse, come from Lebanon,
come, thou shalt be crowned.*'

☩

She was older, of course, in her thirties and lacking the bloom of
youth, but he did not see reality when he looked at Lucrezia.
He saw an ideal form of her: Lucrezia as she had been, as she
would always be. His Lucrezia. 'Oh!' she said, seeing the change
in him, and ran forward to take his hands.

After a few days of her care, Filippo recovered enough to
paint the portrait of the Virgin being crowned by God as a perfect
likeness of his wife, chatting to Cosimo as he did so as if Cosimo
were there with him. 'Or as if,' said Diamante later, 'he was
already where Cosimo is.'

☩

Lucrezia sat on the bed, stroking her husband's head. His
breathing was becoming increasingly gentle and she was listening

acutely for the last breath. She did not know what life would be like without him, whether Prato would allow her to be a widow or would demand that she return to the convent yet again. She prayed it would not, for she had grown to love her small farmhouse in its orchard at Coiano. It seemed half the hamlet was related to Rosaria, the tavern-keeper's wife, and they kept her like the queen bee.

What she truly wanted was to live at Coiano with Filippo, Spinetta, Alessandra and Filippino, as a family, as they had never lived together; but it was not to be, it was never to be, and as her husband slipped from one world to the next, Lucrezia surrendered her desires and began to accept things as they were, accept and be grateful.

She stopped stroking Filippo's head and gazed at him, her hand raised just above his face as if in benediction. Was he still breathing? Before she could find out, a radiance grew in the room and within her own heart, a soft, swelling acceptance of all things, of the beauty and eternity of all things.

The light took form.

She told no one of what she had seen, only Filippino, and that many years later. 'I saw her with my own eyes, the Virgin, so beautiful in her mantle of ultramarine, her white veil and golden rays all around her head. She looked on me as if she were my mother, or my sister, she looked on me and held out her hands for the soul of my husband. I relinquished him and she carried him like a baby in her arms to heaven.'

'My father is in *heaven?*' Filippino's astonishment amused his mother.

'Of course. He was a Carmelite.'

The two of them, sitting in the orchard at Coiano, laughed merrily at the joke.

'Seriously, Mother, did you see her?' Filippino asked.

Lucrezia nodded. 'Not as I described, with my eyes. I saw her with my heart. His soul is well, my son, believe me. It always was.'

Every painter paints himself.

Cosimo de' Medici

Author's Notes

The story of Fra Filippo Lippi and the nun Lucrezia has captured the poetic imagination since it was first related by Giorgio Vasari in his *Lives of the Painters*. It has become almost archetypal: the story of a lascivious friar who risks hell for the sake of love. This romantic version is so strong it has even affected academic studies of Lippi and questions that should be asked have not been. For instance, Lippi did not abduct Lucrezia, he housed her when she escaped the convent, and she escaped with all five of her sister nuns. What happened to the others? Did Lippi take them all in? And how did Lippi manage to live with Lucrezia for *years* in the close community of gossipy Prato, where whores were birched naked in the streets? These annoying spoilers of a good tale need some scrutiny.

I try to practise something I call 'rational imagination'; that is, I like to imagine what may really have happened. It is all too tempting to put the facts aside when storytelling. I'm not saying it's wrong – some stories have a strong moral or mythic substance that leads to a greater truth. Richard III, for instance, is not fairly portrayed by Shakespeare, but the monster Shakespeare creates is archetypally true: we can find him within each of us. But I do shudder when writers take the easy route for the sake of sensation and greater sales, or when I hear things like 'that's what you get when you knock up a nun' in a song lyric.

There is very little known about Fra Filippo Lippi and what facts there are do not help very much in trying to understand how he managed to live with a nun for several years in Prato. I've done my best to explain it. Nor do they tell us how such a scallywag could paint such divine pictures, but that has formed my theme, that goodness is more than skin-deep and that, in the end, the only accurate judgement of a man is by his fruits. We only have to look at the quality of those who loved him. The unsaintly Filippo Lippi, castigated by fellow citizens, the pope and the archbishop, often in court, once in prison, was loved by Cosimo de' Medici. Perhaps, as a fellow sinner, Cosimo knew better than to react to the scandal. Fra Filippo was adored by his son, Filippino, who persuaded Lorenzo de' Medici to honour him with a tomb at Spoleto. Finally, Filippo was clearly loved and admired by his apprentice, Sandro Botticelli, who would have known him better than anyone.

467

After his father's death, Filippino lived in Prato with his mother, in a house opposite the convent of Santa Margherita. He painted a tabernacle there in honour of his mother when she died in the late 1480s. The place is marked by a plaque. The house was destroyed by Allied bombs in 1944 but the tabernacle has been restored from thousands of fragments.

One cannot help but be more sympathetic to the man on the rack than to the man who put him there, but Archbishop Antonino was indeed made a saint. Fra Giovanni, now known as Fra Angelico, has been beatified and will no doubt become a saint in due course.

Filippo's influence on the next generation of artists was immense; not only Botticelli but also Leonardo da Vinci and Michelangelo – who went to Prato to study the Santo Stefano frescoes – owed him a great deal. While he led the way in the return to naturalism, favoured by those in love with ancient Rome and Greece, he managed to infuse nature with divinity. Perhaps that's how he saw it. If every painter does indeed paint himself, then there was something divine to Filippo Lippi.

What facts there are, I've done my best to adhere to. It is but a legend, repeated by Vasari, that Lippi was captured by Barbary pirates. There *is* a two-year gap in his biography when he was in his thirties so I've made up the story of Abu Ali ibn Yussef to fill that gap. Another flight into the imagination is the scene of the consecration of the chapel. I had completed five drafts before I discovered – in a book I'd had all along (*The Chapel of the Magi in Palazzo Medici* by Franco Cardini) that the pope had *not* met Cosimo on that visit in 1459. That was one of those devastating 'facts' that blow up fiction. But when I spoke to the astrologer Darby Costello, she studied the heavens for the particular day I presumed the consecration to have taken place and said, with great confidence, that what was indicated were 'secret meetings, where no side lost face'. I shall be ever grateful to her for that.

Several years ago, Marella Santa Croce told me that the chapel was, from her own experience, a kind of spiritual incubator, 'a place of transformation'. Ever the sceptic, demanding documentary evidence for everything, I set out to disprove her theory. So far I have failed. There is nothing to say she is right, and nothing to say that she isn't. Cosimo was interested in ancient Egypt but without doubt all the symbolism of the chapel is Christian. But it remains queer that a newly-built palazzo should have a room installed within a room, as if an afterthought, and that the effect is sensory-deprivation; as is thought to have been the case with pyramid initiatory chambers, they give the living a taste of death and invite passage into the divine world.

There are many theories about the significance of the Magi to the Medici in fifteenth-century Florence, but I've chosen to see them not as kings but as wise men, astrologers and scholars who had faith in a star, enough to follow it across a continent. I am certain this was their significance to the Medici who, despite their wealth and political machinations, had a rich spiritual life, especially Cosimo and Lorenzo. I like to think of Lorenzo's experience at the consecration as being the beginning of his life as a poet.

And as if a gift from the angels as a form of 'proof', I discovered something extraordinary in the final months of the project. The consecration of the Medici Chapel would have happened 'around Easter, 1459', the very same date given for the text known as *The Chymical Wedding of Christian Rosenkreuz* (actually published in 1616). Coincidence? Christian numerology features strongly in the Rosicrucian text, especially 7 (the Seven Days of Genesis), 9 and 4. The number 14 in the chapel has yet to be explained to my satisfaction, but it is almost certainly a double 7. Seven is the number of the Virgin.

Whilst studying the chapel walls, I became increasingly troubled by the identification of the old man on the mule in the train of Caspar as 'Cosimo the Elder', for the simple reason that it bears such little resemblance to the known images of Cosimo. It seemed to me that, if three famous, if not wise, men came to visit Cosimo, then riding beside Sigismondo Malatesta and Galeazzo Maria Sforza on the walls would be Pope Pius II. I was heartened to learn that the great authority – and ex-curator – of the chapel, Cristina Acidini Luchinat, shares this doubt when she says that there is 'no certainty to the identification of this figure as Cosimo'. In the very last days of the final edit, however, I re-read Vespasiano da Bisticci's memoir of Antonino and, when I read about his mule 'with golden bosses' on its trappings, I turned hurriedly to the picture, and there they were.

Prato today is completely overshadowed by its neighbour, Florence. Its incredible textile industry is in its death-throes and many of the Pratese are unemployed. If I have any ambitions for this book, one is that it may help, if only a little, in reviving tourism. Although a great sprawling industrial suburb, Prato has a centre that is quiet and full of enormous character. And, of course, those frescoes that took forever to paint are still there. As is the house of Francesco Datini, which was the headquarters of the Ceppo and is now a museum and the house of the state archives.

The conception of this book followed a conversation with two friends, Brian Joseph and Brian Wright, when I had recently finished *The Botticelli Trilogy* and did not know what to do next. Brian Joseph suggested a novel about Cosimo. I didn't like the idea of fictional biography, but then I remembered the tale about the lascivious friar and the runaway nun.

I wrote the book in the closing years of my mother's life, which were painful and exhausting. It was a queer, patchwork thing by the end, and it needed a fresh start. A month after the funeral, my husband, David, and I took off for Prato and found ourselves warmly received by Simona, the patron of the guesthouse, BB Magico, Cristina Cozzi, her historian friend, Simona Biagnone, and the people of Prato in general wherever we met them. Our search for Filippo's house went on for days, with people either shrugging or pointing us in the wrong direction. Instinct was drawing me to one particular area, and it was there that David spotted the plaque, 'Filippo lived here'. This was confirmed when we met Simona, who lived a couple of doors along. She subsequently gave very generously of her time and often put me straight – argued, in fact – via Skype.

I must thank also friends closer to home, who have sustained me over these difficult years with their love and enthusiasm: Darby Costello, Jules Cashford, Julia Cousins and Ruth Dowley. The last three gave very constructive criticism on an early draft which set me on a better path. Marsha Andreola, my teacher in sacred geometry, having spent an afternoon with me, some tracing paper and reproductions of the *Adoration*, saw the spiral when I could only see a heptagon. Dr Emily Pott gave of her inexhaustible knowledge of sacred symbolism. Dr Georgina Hall helped generously with details of obstetrics. Any mistakes or misconceptions in the areas of symbolic composition and representation are, however, entirely my own.

I'm indebted to Susie Geddes for all her painstaking work. She is a very gentle and thorough editor, who made the usually painful process very enjoyable.

I would like to thank Alan and Tina Kypriadis for their generosity and extend my gratitude to all those readers of the Trilogy whose emails of encouragement, coming from the four quarters of the earth, always arrived just when I needed them most. You know who you are. Thank you so much.

Lastly and firstly, David, of course, ever patient and always supportive.

There are plenty of resources on the web for paintings but perhaps the best and most comprehensive is the Web Gallery of Art (www.wga.hu).

The main artists and works featured in the novel are:

Masaccio:
St Peter fresco cycle, Brancacci Chapel in the Carmine, Florence

Ghiberti:
bronze doors, Baptistry, Florence

Donatello:
Mary Magdalene, Bargello, Florence
Pulpit, Santo Stefano, Prato

Domenico Veneziano:
Adoration of the Magi, tondo, Berlin

Andrea del Castagno:
Niccolò da Tolentino, Duomo, Florence
Our Lady of the Assumption with Saints Miniato and Julian, Berlin

Paolo Uccello:
Battle of San Romano, Uffizi, Florence
Sir John Hawkwood, Duomo, Florence.

Brunelleschi:
dome of the cathedral, Florence

Fra Angelico:
Deposition from the Cross, and all works at San Marco, Florence
Adoration of the Magi tondo, Washington

Giotto:
fresco cycle at Scrovegni Chapel, Padua

Benozzo Gozzoli:
the chapel of the Palazzo Medici-Riccardi, Florence

Filippo Lippi:
The Virgin bestowing the Holy Girdle on St Thomas (Madonna della Cintola), Prato
The Adoration (there are three versions; the one that was on the altar of the Medici chapel is now in Berlin)
Adoration of the Magi, tondo, Washington.
Virgin and Child with two angels, Uffizi, Florence
St Stephen and St John fresco cycles, Santo Stefano, Prato
Annunciation (lunette), London
Sts Cosmas and Damian (lunette), London
The life of the Virgin Mary, Spoleto
Two surviving panels of the Naples altarpiece, Sts Michael and Anthony, Cleveland.

Further resources will be given on the page devoted to *A Gift for the Magus* on www.lindaproud.com.

You may also find my occasional blog on writing historical fiction of interest. It's at http://lindaproud.wordpress.com.

Main Sources:

Cristina Acidini Luchinat, *The Chapel of the Magi: Benozzo Gozzoli's Frescoes in the Palazzo Medici-Riccardi*, 1994

Alberti, Leon Battista, *On Painting* (translated Cecil Grayson, 1991)

Eve Borsook, 'Fra Filippo Lippi and the Murals for Prato Cathedral', *Mitteilungen des Kunsthistorischen Institutes in Florenz*, 19, Bd. H. 1 (1975), pp 1–148, XXXII

Alison Brown, 'Cosimo de' Medici's Wit and Wisdom' in Ames-Lewis, Francis, *Cosimo il Vecchio de' Medici, 1389-1464*

Spike Bucklow, *The Alchemy of Paint: Art, Science and Secrets from the Middle Ages*, 2009

Franco Cardini, *The Chapel of the Magi in Palazzo Medici*, 2005

Rab Hatfield, 'Some Unknown Descriptions of the Medici Palace in 1459', *The Art Bulletin*, Vol. 52, No. 3 (Sept. 1970) pp 232–249

Rab Hatfield, 'Cosimo de' Medici and the Chapel of His Palace', in Ames-Lewis, Francis, *Cosimo il Vecchio de' Medici, 1389-1464*

Frederick Hartt, *A History of Italian Renaissance Art*, 1970

Megan Holmes, *Fra Filippo Lippi, The Carmelite Painter*, 1999

Dale Kent, *Cosimo de' Medici and the Florentine Renaissance*, 2000

Ronald Lightbown, *Botticelli*, 1990

Alick M. McLean, *Prato – Architecture, Piety, and Political Identity in a Tuscan City-State*, 2009

Iris Origo, *The Merchant of Prato*, 1979

Jeffrey Ruda, *Fra Filippo Lippi, Life and Work*, 1999

Giorgio Vasari, *The Lives of the Artists* (translated by Julia Conaway Bondanella and Peter Bondanella, 1998)

Vespasiano da Bisticci, *Lives of Illustrious Men of the XVth Century* (translated by William George and Emily Walters and published as 'The Vespasiano Memoirs' 1926)

THE CHRONICLE OF
TOMMASO DE' MAFFEI
IN THREE VOLUMES CALLED
THE BOTTICELLI
TRILOGY

'... the most remarkable work I have ever read,
such encyclopedic knowledge bubbling up effortlessly
to create people, places, situations, dialogue, embellished
with sharply observed vignettes of nature like decorated
capitals in manuscripts.'   Dr Carol Kidwell,
author of *Marullus* and *Pietro Bembo*.

LINDA PROUD

A Tabernacle for the Sun

Linda Proud's novel of the Florentine Renaissance, *A Tabernacle for the Sun*, is a lively novel about philosophy, written in richly beautiful prose peppered with insights.

A boy grows up in the ancient hilltop city of Volterra, one of Florence's subject cities. Uncertain of his parentage, he knows his closest relatives are his Maffei uncle and cousins, whom he "looked in upon … as a leper peeps in through a squint in the church to a congregation which he may never join." His idols are, first, his passionately fair-minded cousin Antonio and, second, the de facto ruler of the Republic of Florence, Lorenzo de' Medici: "Tales of this young man (or glorious knight, in my imagination) came to us with the merchants bringing spices, rich cloth and paper from the distant city on the plain; tales of his wedding and the feast which had lasted a week, of his courage when he had saved his father from an ambush laid by rivals for power, of his generosity, benevolence and love of poetry…. Thus in my fancy Lorenzo de' Medici sometimes approached over the hills, dressed in gold brocade, his white horse draped in crimson, to enter our city, very soon afterwards to notice me and engage me at once as his squire."

Alas, a dispute over the distribution of profits from a mine leads to a Volterran revolt which Florence suppresses with such brutal violence that the boy's hero worship of Lorenzo turns to hatred. Only then, in an ironic and bittersweet form, does his fantasy materialize.

Besides the historic figures already named, those who come memorably to life in this novel include the sweetly philosophical Antonio degli Agli, the Bishop of Volterra; Lorenzo's doomed brother Giuliano; the artist Sandro Botticelli; the extraordinary Florentine beauty Simonetta Vespucci; a teenaged Leonardo da Vinci; and Lorenzo's tutor, the humanist philosopher Marsilio Ficino, who appears in person only briefly but shines like a beacon throughout.

by Margaret Donsbach, www.historicalnovels.info

A novel which affirms the spiritual intellect and the indomitable power of the compassionate imagination ... ranks beside those of Mary Renault and Marguerite Youcenar. Lindsay Clarke.

A great book which I have started to read a second time – to pick up nuggets missed the first time round! Andrew Lawson.

In *A Tabernacle for the Sun* Linda Proud established herself as a historical novelist of genius, a successor to HFM Prescott. Her people are almost unbearably alive. Through their lips we hear the words of neoplatonism, and through their eyes we see the art of the Renaissance, especially that of Botticelli, as it was being painted. Pamela Tudor-Craig, Convivium 4, 2004.

You took me to Florence, you took me to the Renaissance, you took me to the Quattrocento. Lorenzo himself would, I'm sure, have been very pleased to commission such a work. Thank you. Thank you. Thank you. 'A grateful reader' (David Hopkinson).

One is brought through reading a 'historical novel' into a knowledge that transcends history. Jeremy Naydler.

Historical fiction at its best. Historical Novel Society.

A time-travelling trance of inspiration, straight to the heart of the Renaissance. Noel Cobb, Sphinx 3.

LINDA PROUD

Pallas & the Centaur

Set in Lorenzo de' Medici's Florence, *Pallas and the Centaur* is the sequel to Linda Proud's *A Tabernacle for the Sun*. A wider, more complex novel than *Tabernacle*, which was a tale primarily of men and men's doings, *Pallas* opens in the voice of Maria, separated in early childhood from her brother Angelo Poliziano, a poet and protegé of Lorenzo de' Medici. This lively, intelligent young woman is a dissatisfied nun, raised in a convent and yearning for a freer life. Disaster will present her with the opportunity to learn how women live outside its walls.

Lorenzo's conventionally pious wife Clarice actually lives a far more circumscribed life. Barred from her husband's study, from his impassioned philosophical discussions with other men, and from the decisions that lead to his excommunication, Clarice hides beneath her seemingly unruffled exterior a well of fear, grief and resentment. During the war that follows Lorenzo's disputes with the pope, she embarks on a monumental battle of wills with Angelo, deputed as reluctant tutor to Lorenzo's sons in order to nurture them to absorb the rediscovered philosophies of the ancients as he teaches them Greek and Latin.

The name "Savonarola" does not appear—that is for the third novel in the trilogy—but at one level *Pallas* can be read as an extended foreshadowing of the violent orgy of religious fundamentalism that would explode in reaction to the blossoming of Florentine culture under Lorenzo. Other novels set during Savonarola's time present the monk and his followers as inexplicably crazed fanatics. The truth, as usual, is more complex, and while Proud is Lorenzo's partisan, she has sympathy and insight to spare for all sides.

Pallas and the Centaur is best read after *A Tabernacle for the Sun* so the full depth of the characters' griefs, passions and joys can be appreciated. (2004, 491 pages, including a historical note separating fact from fiction).

by Margaret Donsbach, www.historicalnovels.info

A virtue of this book is its understanding of the constrictions of women's roles in the Italy of the period, and the possibility of the transcendence of these which release women's unique qualities, thereby influencing men and history. This is a feature which could be followed up in the marketing : a post-feminist (or pre-feminist) novel which it would equally benefit men and women to read!   Michael Shepherd.

I've read a lot of fiction about the Renaissance; I studied the history at Oxford and am now studying the art at the Courtauld, and Pallas and the Centaur is the novel that has captured Medicean Florence most perfectly. If only there were more writers who could combine Linda's knowledge of the period and her writing style.   Sarah Vowels.

The author's commitment to balance is evident everywhere but most especially in the two narrative voices, one a man's, the other a woman's – a difficult task but stylishly accomplished. In fact, as the story is gradually fused with Botticelli's painting of Pallas and the Centaur, you realize that Proud's resounding conclusion is the 'unity of difference': man with beast, reason with passion, Plato with God, man with woman.
Review in *The Florentine*, 28th June 2007.

Our universities are discussing a 'crisis in the humanities'. Maybe they should shut up shop for six months and read this book. They might learn that one can't teach what one doesn't live, what one hasn't learned, or isn't learning, by heart.   John Moat.

LINDA PROUD

The Rebirth of Venus

The final volume in the Botticelli trilogy, *The Rebirth of Venus,* is the largest and deepest. The Renaissance was far more than art, scientific discovery and religious protest. Behind all these lay the rediscovery of pagan Greek philosophy and a flowering of independent thought the Church could not suppress. Even some clerics embraced the new learning – but it also had powerful enemies. The year 1505 finds Tommaso de' Maffei (a rare fictional character in a novel rich with historical figures) in chilly London, where he has fled after Florence became too hot for safety. His obstinate students exasperate him, and he is still mired in grief years after his wife's death. His beloved philosophy has become a mental exercise, a passionate intellectual escape rather than a guiding light. When Erasmus asks him to set down his memories of Pico della Mirandola, a brilliant but reckless young philosopher who died before reaching his full promise, Tommaso's memory circles back to Florence in 1482. He is in Sandro Botticelli's workshop amid a crowd of friends, patrons and uninvited, rowdy children for the unveiling of a new masterpiece, a nude Venus "rising from the sea and wafting to shore on a shell."

If Botticelli has reached the pinnacle of his greatness, Florence is past hers. Lorenzo de' Medici is plagued by gout. The poor crowd the city while Lorenzo's heir lives in a magnificent new villa ten miles to the north. Savonarola has arrived, a "young Dominican friar, his chin blue with stubble, his eyes black under the cowl, his face overshadowed by a great hooked nose." On first acquaintance, Tommaso finds Savonarola's gentle, enigmatic piety both consoling and unsettling. But the Dominican's rise to power is fueled by more than his gentle sympathy for troubled souls. His preaching can change in an instant from compassion to wild-eyed fury: *"Florence!"* he thunders, *"You will be scourged!"*

Although the reckless, charismatic Pico may be the excuse for the story, it revolves around the mystery of Savonarola: Is he mad, divinely inspired, evil? *The Rebirth of Venus* offers no pat answers. Like the philosophy at its heart, it draws readers into the quest for a deeper, truer wisdom.

by Margaret Donsbach, www.historicalnovels.info

It has already been put to good use, to fend off a bout of midnight depression a few weeks ago when nothing else seemed to help.   J.H.

Having emerged from it I decided to try and animate Lorenzo in my own way - you can see the result on YouTube. Just type in 'The real face of Lorenzo de Medici.'   Leonie Seliger.

The nuanced picture of Savonarola is one of the finest I have seen painted of him - of his complexity, his humility, his simplicity, but also his intolerance and disparagement of beauty, and the resulting lack of freedom which Florence experienced. Raymond Auerbach.

Where scholarship is profound, and intuitive sympathy has brought historical figures to life in such a way that their every act and word rings true, the work is no longer strictly fiction. Linda Proud opens a window on to the Renaissance in all its frequently tempestuous and passionate reality.
Pamela Tudor-Craig, Convivium 4, 2004.

'Like being there' is a cliché often used but very rarely deserved. Linda Proud's ability to succeed in living up to this phrase is almost spooky. This is a special book.'
Jeff Cotton, www.fictionalcities.co.uk.

So full of wisdom and wit, so brimming over with the dance of life...   Jules Cashford.

GODSTOW PRESS

Because philosophy arises from awe, a philosopher is bound in his way to be a lover of myths and poetic fables. Poets and philosophers are alike in being big with wonder. ST THOMAS AQUINAS

THE SONG OF ORPHEUS, the music that charms stones, wild animals and even the King of Hades, is the song of poets who have a sense of the divine at heart. For the forces of greed and evil to succeed, that song must be drowned out by noise.

What is today if not noisy? Not only in our society but within ourselves there is the clamour of many distractions. Just living life we forget ourselves and the song that we heard as children is heard but rarely if at all.

The aim of Godstow Press is to sing the Orphic song, through books of fiction, poetry and non-fiction, as well as through CDs. Besides publishing first editions we shall include on our list works which have been privately produced by writers and musicians who have thought, perhaps, that they sing alone.

Together, artist and audience, we shall form a choir.

Although our books are available through trade, we appreciate the personal contact with our many readers who communicate and order direct – as much a part of the choir as the writers. For information on forthcoming publications and (very) occasional newsletters, please get in touch with us.

Godstow Press
60 Godstow Road
Wolvercote
Oxford
OX2 8NY
UK

www.godstowpress.co.uk
info@godstowpress.co.uk
tel +44 (0)1865 556215